Friends
without
Benefits

By PENNY REID

Caped Publishing

Made in the United States of America

First Edition: February 2014

PRINT EDITION

ISBN-13: 978-0-9892810-2-7
ISBN-10: 0989281027

FOREWARD

I'll keep this brief (which is a rather difficult task for me as my books tend to be in the hundreds of thousands of words).

Two characters in this book are diagnosed with a pediatric rare disease. For the last eight years my (day) job has been focused on biomedical research; specifically, research into the (accurate) diagnosis and treatment of pediatric rare diseases. I felt it appropriate that a percentage of the profits of this book go to pediatric rare diseases foundations which are dedicated to helping the children (and their families) of this underserved and underfunded population. Therefore, at least 10% of the profits from every ebook sold will go to one of these foundations.

Every month for the next year (October 2013 – October 2014) I will be highlighting a different rare disease research foundation on my blog. http://reidromance.blogspot.com/ Proceeds for that month will be sent to the highlighted research foundation.

If you're interested in learning more about rare diseases research and the collaborative efforts currently afoot, here are some great resources:

http://rarediseasesnetwork.epi.usf.edu/ (clinical research network with sites all over the world, studies focused on rare diseases)

http://www.rarediseases.org/

http://rarediseases.info.nih.gov/

If you downloaded this book for free, but really liked it, please consider purchasing a copy for a friend!

See, that wasn't so long/bad.

Sincerely, Penny

DEDICATION

To my new computer: I don't care if it is compudultery, I love you more than my old computer.

To the fans/readers of *Neanderthal Seeks Human*: This book is as much because of you as it is because of my insomnia.

Thank you.

CHAPTER 1

I recognized him instantly even though the last time I had seen him in person he was seventeen, naked, and asleep. I was sixteen, haphazardly dressed, and sneaking out his window.

Niccolò (aka Nico) Manganiello.

Nico.

Freaking Nico Manganiello!

Rooted in place—one hand holding the informed consent forms and patient brochures, the other hand clutching my chest—I could only gape in abject horror, but also in wonder and, much to my infinite frustration, feminine appreciation.

I was entirely unprepared for this.

Everything about this Tuesday had been perfectly normal until now. I arrived to work at 4:30 am for my shift. I argued in the locker room with my nemesis, Dr. Megalomaniac Meg. I planted a lotion-exploding, unopened gag box of latex gloves in Dr. Ken Miles's ER clinic room for my annual April Fool's Day prank. I worked through the backlog of charting I'd left the day before. And, finally, I was paged to the fourth floor clinical research unit to discuss a research study with a family.

Freaking *Niccolò* freaking *Manganiello*.

He was shorter than I expected but taller than I remembered. He looked different in person than he did on TV, and older. On his show, he always towered over his guests, but looking at him now, I guessed his height at about six feet or six feet one.

His hair wasn't brown anymore but had matured into raven black. His face was more angular and strong, as were his shoulders. Even from this distance, I knew his eyes were the same jade green.

Nico was standing in profile, his muscled arms crossed over his chest, leaning against the arm of the couch and speaking in hushed tones to an older woman. I instantly recognized the woman as his mother Rose, who was sitting on the beige sofa, and a little girl–who I did not recognize–was on her lap. The child was clutching a blue blanket.

Blood rushed to and pounded between my ears; it ushered away my ability to hear and replaced it with a steadily increasing rhythm that seemed to chant *oh shit, oh shit, oh shit, oh shit.*

The spike in adrenaline diminished just enough for me to realize that my mouth was agape in dismay, my wide-open eyes were staring in stunned disbelief, and no one was aware that I'd entered the room.

I gulped mostly air and closed my mouth, and then I turned noiselessly to exit unseen and find Megalomaniac Meg. She would be delighted to administer the study's informed consent forms if I told her a hot celebrity was in the room.

I managed two steps before Rose's voice called out to my retreating back. "Oh, nurse—can you help us? We're waiting for Dr. Finney."

I stopped, my shoulders bunched. Before I could nod and grunt then run off in a mad dash, I spotted a very stern-looking Dr. Botstein—my research mentor and somewhat of a stodgeball—rounding the corner of the fourth floor clinical research unit.

My eyes flickered to the object in his fist. He was holding a box of latex gloves, and he was covered in white lotion.

I groaned.

It was the most epic-fail, no-win situation in the history of forever.

My choices were obvious yet odious.

I could step into the hall and meet Dr. Botstein's berating in full view of everyone—and by everyone, I really meant Nico Manganiello—or I could step back into the encounter room and confront the most monumental mistake of my life. Botstein wouldn't interrupt my administration of the consent; as impatient as he was, he would likely get tired of waiting and leave, and I could deal with his berating later.

A confrontation with Dr. Botstein usually wasn't such a big deal, but when I thought of Nico observing it, I was sixteen again.

It was times like these when I wished for invisibility superpowers or a diagnosis of insanity.

Dr. Botstein's weighty scowl-stare was the deciding factor. My gaze dropped to the linoleum at my feet, and I took a reflexive step backward into the room.

"Nurse?" Rose called out behind me.

"Uh...." I tucked a long, loose strand of hair behind my ear and reached for the door. I closed it as though that had been my intention all along. "I'll be right there. Let me just shut this door."

I didn't glance up as it swung shut. I was certain that Dr. Botstein's dark expression remained the same or possibly increased in severity and menace. But I had no time to dwell on his level of enragement. I would feel his wrath later.

The full weight of my decision, to close myself in a clinic room with Nico, landed like an anvil in the pit of my stomach. I gathered a deep, steadying breath and held it in my lungs for a brief moment. I tried to still my shaking hands by tightening them into fists.

He is just a guy...a guy you slept with once...the guy who took your virginity...the guy who tops your list of people you never want to see again.

My frayed nerves took a back seat to my survival instinct, and I mortared a smile on my face before turning. Rose was still sitting on the couch, the small girl on her lap, and I met the older woman's green eyes directly.

"Hi, Rose." I scored myself a point for the steadiness of my voice. The decision to focus solely on Rose was calculated, as was my decision to avoid trying to pronounce her last name. I still couldn't pronounce Manganiello correctly even after going to school with Nico from preschool to high school.

I easily pronounced *trastuzumab* and *hematopoetic* and *tranylcypromine*, but I tripped over Manganiello, and always put the emphasis on the wrong syllable or mixed up the placement of the *g*.

Rose's confusion lasted for a full ten seconds; the fact that I looked quite different from the girl she knew was likely the reason for her prolonged bewilderment. I was still five feet four, but my blonde hair was now long and in a thick braid down my back. I'd also filled out—which was a very good thing because it meant having boobs and hips and a girl shape. I no longer tipped the scale at eighty-nine pounds. My face and features had also filled out. My lips in particular were a source of pride; a previous conquest of mine once referred to them as pouty.

In short, despite the ambiguity of the baggy scrubs and large lab coat I wore, I no longer looked like a twelve-year-old boy.

Finally, her green eyes focused on my blue ones, and confusion gave way to recognition and astonishment. This lasted only a split second then morphed into delighted excitement. "Oh, my God! Oh, my dear Lord, Lizzybella! Oh my goodness, come here and give me a hug!"

My cement smile softened. Rose struggled to stand with the child in her arms. At five feet one, the only two things that were big about Rose were her personality and her expectations for her children—all eight of them.

"Oh, for God's sake—Nico, snap out of it and take Angelica. Help your poor mother."

I noticed in my peripheral vision that Nico turned when I spoke, but now he was standing perfectly still. Since the resolve to keep my attention affixed on Rose held steady, his face was out of focus, and I couldn't read his expression.

I didn't want to read his expression.

Even trapped in a room together, I was avoiding him.

I never avoid anything or anyone anymore. I am proud of my

lack of avoidance. I am many things, but I am *not* a coward.

...unless Nico is involved.

This reminder further aggravated my mood.

He stepped forward wordlessly and took the girl from his mother's arms. I noted as Angelica was passed between Rose and Nico that the child had big green eyes, brown hair, and olive skin. She looked like a Manganiello.

Rose crossed the room with her arms open and wide, and she forcefully embraced me. "Oh, Lizzybella, I didn't even think—when they said Dr. Finney would be coming in, I didn't think it would be you. I should have realized, but I thought you would have changed your name when you got married."

Rose pulled back, her emerald eyes lighting with a familiar hint of mischief. She knew I wasn't married. I noted that for as much as I'd changed, she was basically the same—in looks and in temperament. Her long hair was still black, and her makeup and attire were impeccable and stylish. Despite the fact that her family owned and operated the best Italian restaurant in our hometown, her figure was svelte and lissome. She was beautiful.

I gave her a closed mouth smile and prepared to answer her unasked question. "I'm not married, Rose." Another thing that hadn't changed about her—she was still foxy like a fox.

Her eyebrows jumped. "Ooh! Well..." Rose paused, looked over her shoulder—presumably at her son—then back to me. Her eyes traveled up my form, no doubt absorbing the baggy scrubs, the oversized lab coat, the long length of blonde hair in a haphazard braid, no makeup, no nail polish, and no fancy accoutrements.

I'd been on the receiving end of Rose Manganiello's scrutiny before. It never seemed to get easier.

She pressed a purple painted fingertip to her chin and her head lolled to the right; she gazed at me through narrowed eyes. "Well, you know—I just assumed you must be married now, at your age.

But your father should have told me that you were here. The last time I spoke to him was ages ago. He said you were a doctor in Chicago, but ever since he started dating that girl, he never comes to the restaurant...."

"Ma...." Nico's voice was low and rumbly with warning. I couldn't help—despite everything—that their interaction made me smile. My insides still felt full of lead, but now it was slightly warmed lead.

"Well, she *is* a girl. She's what—thirty?" Rose reached for one of my hands and held it between her own, patting the knuckles. "How are you doing with all of this?"

I tried to flatten my smile. "Well, first of all, she's forty-three, so she's only ten years younger than my father. And, it's none of my business."

"Oh, Lizzy, you're his daughter."

"But even if it were my business, I'm really good with it. If she makes him happy, and she seems to, then I'm happy for him." And I was. My father's relationship with Jeanette Wiggins, bakery owner in our hometown and all-around nice lady, didn't bother me.

It didn't bother me because his relationship with Jeanette was irrelevant. I knew my father would only ever truly love my mother. My mom was his first and only love; if he wanted to have some fun, then who was I to judge? I was guilty of the same type of behavior.

However, I understood Rose's apparent dislike of Jeannette. Rose and my mom had been best friends. My mother died from breast cancer when I was nine, and I think Rose took the loss almost as hard as my father and I did.

But the real reason Rose didn't like Jeannette was because she had the audacity to make and sell cannoli at her bakery downtown, and hers were better than the cannoli made at Manganiello's Italian Restaurant.

"You're a saint." Rose's smile was sweet. "And you've grown

up and become a beautiful doctor," she added, her hands cupping my cheeks, "a profession any mother could be proud of."

Nico's sigh was audible.

"Ma...."

"It's nice to see you too, Rose."

Surprising myself, I meant it. Just her presence reminded me of home: family dinners at Manganiello's with my mother and father kissing under the mistletoe that hung from an archway in the main dining room year-round.

Her hands dropped from my face and reclaimed my hand. Rose's smile widened; again, I was reminded of a fox.

"And Nico? Is it nice to see Nico too?"

Without meaning to, my eyes—the traitors!—flickered to where he stood and met his gaze for the first time since I'd entered the room.

A sharp stab of pain pierced my chest, passed through my body, and jarred my teeth. It felt like a stake to the heart, or a branding iron inserted into my aortic valve. I held my breath.

His wide eyes were haunted by a lingering emotion I couldn't quite place—something like wistful nostalgia or reluctant admiration—as well as a shadow of surprise. He was obviously trying to school his expression, although with little success, and this made him look somehow severe. Mussed black hair and likely twenty-four hours since his last shave added to the harshness of his appearance; but neither, I noted with annoyance, detracted from his good looks.

It was decidedly not the laissez faire attitude or the roguish, cheerful face he wore on his show, nor the unrepentantly flirtatious and unscrupulous face that smiled back at his fans from publicity photos.

He was Nico in person. But he was *the Face* on TV.

The last time I had seen Nico was on the TV in the doctor's lounge two weeks ago.

A group of male surgeons had gathered around the TV set. They were watching a busty blonde and a sylph-like redhead Jell-O wrestle a bare-chested Nico on his Comedy Central show *Talking with the Face*.

He'd been dubbed "the Face" because he used to be a male model in New York before it was discovered that he actually had a brain and a personality. Never mind the fact that both his brain and personality were used for evil. For that matter, so was his face. I had firsthand, secondhand, and thirdhand knowledge of how he used his face for evil.

Even though I avoided his show, I'd purposefully purchased and watched his standup comedy special, and of course I'd come face-to-*the Face* with advertisements for his show plastered on billboards and on the Internet. Regardless, I wasn't prepared for an in-person encounter. In person, he was real and present in a way that he wasn't in a still-life picture or a video clip.

The fact that his mother was in the room, openly inspecting us as we reacted to each other, only served to crank up the awkward dial, but even if we'd been alone, I wouldn't have known what to say to him.

I could have tried, *Hi—about deserting you after your best friend died, that was really shitty of me. Also, about disappearing that morning after I handed you my V-card and never returning your calls or reading your letters—that was also shitty of me. In my defense, I'm pretty sure that one time we slept together meant more to me than it did to you as I was a grieving teenager who was frightened by my feelings for you and you've always had girls tripping over their panties in pursuit. I'm fairly certain that night for you was mostly pity sex. Furthermore, I'm sure you didn't even notice my absence what with all the poontang you must've been getting in New York as a male underwear model. Since you basically made my adolescent years hell, let's just call it even-steven.*

I swallowed memories down, down, down along with all the recriminations that surfaced immediately afterward. I wasn't at all proud of how I'd behaved, but it was a very long time ago. I'd just turned sixteen and he'd just turned seventeen. We were kids. He may have been my first, but I most definitely had not been his.

I knew that if he were still upset with me it probably had less to with my abandoning him after sex and more to do with my abandoning him after Garrett's death. For that, I still felt ashamed.

I commenced with an attempt at a smile and nodded my head in his direction.

"Of course. Hi. Good to…see…you."

His full lips flattened. His frown deepened. He visibly swallowed. He didn't respond.

He just looked at me and his stare felt like a branding iron.

"Oh—and this is Angelica, my granddaughter." Rose led me by the hand to where Nico held the small girl. Pride was evident in Rose's voice, but so was a trace of sadness.

I used the movement as an excuse to shift my attention away from Nico, and I smiled at Angelica as I approached. The small girl was dressed in a kid-sized hospital gown, and I knew better than to offer her my hand. Cystic fibrosis would make her extremely susceptible to pulmonary infection even though she was likely already on prophylaxis antibiotics.

Angelica smiled at me briefly then buried her face in Nico's neck.

"It is nice to meet you, Angelica." I kept my voice soft. "I'm actually here to talk to you and your—your—your dad about a research study that might help you feel better."

Curses!

I didn't know why I'd stuttered over "your dad," but I did know I needed to pull my shit together before shit got everywhere and shit got crazy.

"Oh, Lizzybella, Angelica isn't Nico's. Nico is her uncle." Rose leaned forward and her whisper assumed a wavering, watery quality. "Angelica was my Tina's."

I nodded in dejected and horrified understanding. On the tragedy scale, this news was an eleventy thousand. That's right: *eleventy thousand*. Not only did sweet Angelica have a chronic, life-threatening disease, but her mother was dead. Tina was Rose's third daughter. My father had told me of Tina and her husband's death last year in a freak car accident.

It was horrible and senseless, and I now felt the sudden need to drink some scotch and wade into a brooding sea of melancholy, or to read Edgar Allen Poe or the ending to *Hamlet*. Maybe I would top it all off with some YouTube videos of drowning kittens while listening to Radiohead.

"I see," was all I could say.

Again, without meaning to, my gaze sought Nico's. I found him studying me. I tried not to fiddle with my stethoscope; I hoped my eyes conveyed my condolences. Yet, I couldn't help but feel foolish and inadequate. I wasn't used to feeling foolish and inadequate—not since high school.

He made me feel foolish and inadequate.

At last Nico spoke. The sound of his voice—deeper than I remembered, raspy—made my spine stiffen in automatic response.

"We're in Chicago to see a visiting disease specialist, but we came to the ER because Angelica had a fever this morning. She's on the inhaled antibiotics since two weeks ago. I'm worried that…." he paused. His soulful eyes shifted from me to his mother then back to mine, and their intensity pierced me. "We're worried that they aren't as effective, and they did a chest X-ray downstairs, but we haven't heard anything about the results."

I motioned to the aptly depressing beige furniture and endeavored to slip into Elizabeth Finney, MD mode. "Here—let's sit down and I'll take a look at Angelica's chart."

Rose sat next to Nico on the couch, and Angelica moved from

his lap to hers. I deposited the consent forms on the table then crossed to the computer station mounted on the wall; Angelica's electronic medical record had two procedural tabs for April 1. The first was a full blood panel and the second was a chest X-ray. The actual image wasn't yet available, but the radiologist's report indicated that her lungs were negative for infection.

"Well, the good news is that the radiology report came back, and it looks like Angelica's lungs are currently free of infection. Her labs aren't in the system yet, but the attending physician will be able to review them with you before discharge." Unable to find a reason to loiter any longer with the electronic medical record, I crossed to them and chose the beige chair across from Rose. "The reason I'm here is to talk to you about a research study that Angelica might be eligible for."

Nico nodded. He leaned forward and placed his elbows on his knees, his hands tented before him. "Yeah, the nurses downstairs said that you guys were doing a study, and it might help with the symptoms—reduce the infections or something like that."

The hope in his voice was heartbreaking. I tried to distance myself from my history with him, with Rose, with this family, and review the study and consent forms with measured impartiality, just as I would with any other family.

But because I was unable to completely detach myself from the strength of memories and guilt—and, therefore, historical emotions—involving Nico, I kept my gaze fastened to Rose as I explained the study visits, risks, and benefits.

"Results thus far are promising; increase in mucociliary clearance, improved digestive and pancreatic function. But the study isn't yet fully enrolled. No definite conclusions can be made about long-term benefits."

Rose was staring at me as though I had three heads.

I reminded myself to slow down and use everyday terms, and to treat them like any other family. This was safe territory for me:

current research trends, the study, risk analyses.

What unnerved me was the realization that I still had unsafe territory where Nico was concerned. Since leaving high school, I was now used to venturing beyond the pale with abandon. I was not used to feeling like I needed to watch my words, determine where I looked, and control the inflection of my voice.

It chaffed. Each time I made a mental note to avoid his gaze my irritability increased. I didn't like this feeling. I didn't like the unresolved issues between us. What was unsaid choked me, and honestly, it pissed me off.

I started over. "This study is straightforward but also extremely intense: twenty-eight days of infusions administered every eight hours. This means that Angelica will have to return here to the clinical research unit every eight hours for twenty-eight days and receive medication via IV, in her vein, for half an hour. There are some documented adverse reactions. But, on the plus side, the study is not placebo controlled; this means that all patients will be receiving treatment."

Rose nodded her understanding and held Angelica tighter.

"You should take some time to read the forms and discuss them together." I studied Rose for a moment as she held her granddaughter to her chest. According to Angelica's chart, the little girl was four. She was very small for a four-year-old. She was also very shy and looked away every time I attempted to draw her out with a smile.

Rose sighed. It was a heavy, distracted, helpless sigh. "I just don't know…." She turned to Nico. "What do you think?"

Nico held his mother's gaze for a moment then glanced at his hands, studying them as though they might answer the question for him. He lifted his eyes to mine and targeted me with a pointed stare, sending another stabbing pain through my heart. If he saw me wince, he didn't make any outward sign.

He lifted his chin a notch, "What do you think we should do?"

"Read the study materials and take some time to think about it."

"No, that's not what I mean." Nico's eyes moved between mine and I was startled by the trust and vulnerability I witnessed in his gaze. "Will you be her doctor?"

"I…uh…." My head shook before I knew it was shaking. "No. The research nurses administer the infusions and conduct the study visits. And this is my last week in research rotation. It is a mandatory six-week rotation for all residents, and this is my last week. But the principal investigator of the study—Dr. Botstein—is a world-renowned pediatric pulmonologist. He is an excellent doctor. He will be assigned to Angelica."

Nico glared at me through his thick, black lashes. His left leg started bouncing. "Couldn't we request you?"

My involuntary headshake increased in speed. "No. Listen, you don't want me—really. You want Dr. Botstein."

"No, Elizabeth." He said my name slowly, stubbornly. His eyes narrowed for the briefest of moments then he leaned back against the cushions of the pitiful beige sofa. "I want you."

I set my expression to rigid, holding Nico's challenging glower, determined to win this staring contest.

I spoke first. "You're not thinking about this clearly."

"Whereas, you've won awards for clear thinking…."

"No." I gritted my teeth. "No one is perfect."

"Even you?" his tone was bitter, and his indisputably handsome face was marred by an ugly sneer.

"Especially me."

"That's not how I remember it."

My face flushed at the double-entendre and his eyes ignited with satisfaction. Some of the sneering ugliness was replaced with smug male arrogance. Even as I internally eye-rolled, I hoped that Rose wouldn't pick up on his complisult (compliment + insult)

I understood that he had every right to be angry with me. I was still angry with myself. But the timing of this conversation—his timing—was exceedingly not cool. This situation was not about him, us, or what happened eleven years ago between two grieving teenagers.

He was engaging in machismo ass-hattery, and I would have none of it.

I forced casual steadiness into my voice and redoubled my resolve to resist participating in his bait-fest. "You knew me a long time ago."

"I've known you all my life. We pulled pranks on my brothers, we had a monopoly game that went on for three years, we built a tree house in your backyard, our dads took us to our first Cubs game together."

"That was a long time ago."

"We used to have sleepovers…."

I flinched.

"I know you better than anyone." His words were a suggestive whisper, and patently false.

"Not for the last eleven years."

"Well…." He stretched his arms across the back of the sofa, his voice deceptively calm. "There's no time like the present. Let's get reacquainted. We can start with you treating Angelica."

"I'm not the doctor you want."

"You *are* the doctor I want." He grew adamant, louder, like someone who was used to getting his way by raising his voice.

"I'm not the doctor Angelica needs." I pressed my palm to my chest and held it there because my heart was once again hurting.

"You don't get to make that decision." His adamant became obstinate.

"In this case you should listen to me, Nico. I know what I'm…."

"I don't have to do anything. We've already established that you're not perfect." His obstinate became pigheaded. Usually I didn't mind a good old yelling match, but I had no desire to scare the little girl in the room.

"N–Nico." His name felt strange on my tongue because my voice was quiet, but I wanted to yell at him. I stuttered as my frustration peaked. "E–everyone makes mistakes."

It was his turn to flinch, and I thought I saw something resembling pain paint a shadow over his features; his voice increased in volume until it was a booming shout. "Well, one person's *mistake* is another person's-"

"Niccolò!" Rose's sharp warning was whispered, but it was enough to keep him from finishing the thought.

He clamped his mouth shut and shot to his feet, pulled both of his hands through his hair then drummed on his leg with restless fingers. His eyes flickered to mine then to the door.

"I need a cigarette," he mumbled.

He was gone before I registered that he was even moving, and the door shut behind him.

The room felt quieter and calmer without him in it. The beige didn't seem so dull. The fluorescent lights didn't seem so dim.

He'd always been a larger-than-life presence. Growing up in our small town it seemed everyone was drawn to him—everyone but me. When we played together as kids, he unsettled me; he made me self-conscious. He was too…magnetic. Even then, I didn't trust myself around Nico because I had difficulty saying no to him. I couldn't compete with his restless energy, and I didn't like being overwhelmed by it.

We'd just spent twenty minutes together, and already I was exhausted.

I rubbed the space between my eyes with my index and middle fingers. Frayed nerves began to mend, and I released a cleansing breath.

I didn't realize I'd been staring at the door until Rose interrupted my musings.

"It's so good to see you."

I blinked at her. "Ah, thank you, Rose."

"Are you Rapunzel?" A small voice sprang from Angelica's hidden face. Only her eyes and mop of brown hair were visible from behind the blue blanket.

My hand automatically lifted to my long, thick braid; my smile was automatic and immediate. "No, Angelica. But that was a very nice thing to say."

"Are you coming home anytime soon?" Rose cleared her throat, bringing my attention back to her. "Your father must miss you."

I nodded. "Well, yes and no. I'll be in town next weekend for the reunion, but my dad will be out of town. He and Jeanette are going on a cruise."

"Reunion?"

"Uh…." I cringed inwardly and outwardly and tried to stall by tucking loose strands of golden hair behind my ears. "You know, the high school reunion. It's been ten years."

Rose opened her mouth in understanding but no sound came out. She closed it, then opened it, then closed it. Finally, when she opened it again, she said, "Nico didn't say anything."

I shrugged. "He's probably not going."

"Why wouldn't he go? He should go."

I cringed again. There were some very good reasons why Nico shouldn't go, the most glaring of which was that he didn't actually graduate high school. The other obvious reason was why would he? He was a famous—albeit crude—and successful standup comedian with his own show. Why would he want to go to a high school reunion in Iowa?

I glanced at the door again.

Seeing Nico had been difficult—a great deal more difficult than I'd anticipated.

Yes, he was different from before—older, bigger, famous—yet he was still fundamentally the same person he'd always been. He was the same boy who branded me with the horrid nickname

Skinny Finney when I was ten. He was the same boy who broke every heart in high school. He was the same boy who held my hand at Garrett's funeral. He was the same boy who climbed into my window night after night the summer after Garrett's death.

And I still didn't understand him.

"He's not usually like that—with other people. He's not usually so...so abrupt."

Again, she caught me staring at the door. "What's he usually like?" I asked, genuinely curious.

"Well, you know," She swallowed visibly. She was stroking Angelica's hair. "He's always trying to make people laugh. But he can be intense with...*some* people."

My mouth twisted to the side and I offered good-naturedly, "Maybe I just have that effect on people."

She glanced at me and lifted a single eyebrow. "Conosco i miei polli[1]."

I gave her a small smile. Rose had a habit of responding to me in Italian at random intervals. I waited for her to translate, but when she did, I had the impression that the Italian did not match the English.

"I know my chickens, Lizzy. You don't have that effect on people—just Nico."

"Don't worry. I won't take it personally." I nodded my head toward Angelica. "I'm sure this is stressful for him."

"It is...." Rose began then stopped, her eyes moving over my face. "It is hard on him. But you still might want to take it personally. You know..." then the fox smile returned, "...just in case."

---

[1]Translation: I know my chickens

CHAPTER 2

Must focus on Dr. Botstein.

"...third time we've had to have this conversation, Dr. Finney, and I do not know how much clearer I can be about the severity of this situation..."

Must not think about Nico.

"...can't prove it was you, but switching the colonoscopy training with a porn tape was extremely unprofessional..."

Must not think about Nico's face.

"...seriously considering a formal reprimand for misconduct. And, honestly, that would be a shame and a waste of your talent, not to mention a disservice to the hospital..."

Must not think about Nico's exasperating hands.

"...believe in your abilities, your skill with diagnostics, your passion for your patients. This has to be the last time. I'm warning you..."

Must not think about Nico's maddening voice.

"...if I get the slightest indication that you're planning any more of these pranks, then, despite my personal feelings about the matter, I will be forced to request..."

Must not think about Nico's infuriating body.

"Have I made myself clear?"

Must appear to be contrite.

"Yes, sir." I nodded once.

Dr. Botstein exhaled through his nose in a way that reminded me of a horse. I had to bite the inside of my cheek.

Must not compare Dr. Bostein to a horse.

He shook his head, his voice abruptly and unexpectedly adopting a softer, paternal tone. "I don't understand why you do it, Elizabeth. Your attitude mystifies me. I've never seen someone with so much talent, who works so hard, who is so well respected and admired by staff and faculty, who just wants to throw it away like you seem to."

When I heard those words, I didn't have to appear contrite. I *felt* contrite, and ashamed. My gaze dropped to the floor. "I'm sorry."

He waited until I met his glare again; his eyes searched mine. Abruptly, he leaned back in his desk chair and flicked his wrist, dismissing me with an impatient, irritated wave. "Leave."

I didn't wait to be told twice and closed the door to Dr. Botstein's office as softly as I could. Once safely in the hall I closed my eyes and released a frustrated, yet quiet, growl. I couldn't understand how Dr. Botstein had ended up with the exploding latex gloves.

If I were honest with myself, the main reason for my frustration was that Nico didn't come back to the clinic room before I left. I was paged and had to leave Angelica and Rose before he returned. I didn't get a chance to say goodbye, and it was likely the last time I'd see him in person. I was perturbed.

Furthermore, I couldn't stop thinking about Nico Manganiello and his beautiful face, voice, and body—and his eyes...and his lips...and his....*better not go there*, I told myself, and changed the channel in my brain.

"How'd your meeting with your mentor go?" A voice that resembled nails on a chalkboard, only worse, sounded from my left. I contemplated pretending that I didn't hear her, but I dismissed the idea immediately. She was the type to pick, nitpick, and prod until noticed, and I was in no mood for her brain junk today.

"Hello, Meg."

"Hello, Elizabeth."

Meg was odious; nevertheless, we had a few things in common. Like me, she was younger than most second year residents. Also like me, she was fumbling through the concept of becoming a responsible adult at the age of twenty-six. Again—like me—she was trying to find her way outside the comfortable and safe confines of academia. Additionally, like me, she was of medium height and had long blonde hair and blue eyes.

Otherwise, we were polar opposites in just about every regard.

Where she was polished and stylish, I was messy. Where she was meticulous with every blonde tendril and plucked eyebrow, I was haphazard and messy. Where she embraced and wielded her inner femme fatale with practiced proficiency—batting eyelashes and casting about come-hither mojo—I just threw it all out there, wore a slutty dress, and was messy.

Putting it in *Star Trek Voyager* terms, I was the Belana Torres to her Seven of Nine.

I waited for a moment then opened just one eye. "Are you still here? What—no kittens to drown? No children to frighten? Can't locate that *eye of newt* you need?"

"Ha, ha, very funny, Dr. Finney. One would think you'd be a bit more repentant after getting your ass chewed out."

I opened my other eye and squinted at her. "What do you know about that?"

Her smile was wicked, as usual, and I knew. In that moment, I knew—Megalomaniac Meg had been the one to rat me out.

I breathed through my nose in a way that reminded me of a horse. "How did you know?"

"I saw you take the box of gloves into the room; it's April Fool's Day; the clinic room was assigned to Dr. Ken Miles. Honestly, Elizabeth, it doesn't take a genius to figure out that you were planning a prank."

"What did you do?"

She shrugged. "I switched Dr. Botstein's clinic room assignment with Ken's."

I closed my eyes again, my head falling to the wall behind me. "Go away."

Dr. Ken Miles and I had been flirting for two years. He was very bad at it. His attempts usually ended with me flinching. He also had the habit of picking his nose when he was fairly certain no one was watching. He also drank coffee with a lot of cream and sugar or combined with ice cream.

None of these were deal breakers because I didn't want to date the guy. I just wanted to hit that. Actually, I just wanted to hit something and soon.

I'd recently made up my mind and committed an unrepentant HIPAA violation when I scanned his last physical. He was disease free and had healthy cardiac and pulmonary systems. We would have a symbiotic and mutually beneficial relationship. It would suit me quite well.

"Oh, don't be a poor sport. You wanted to play an April Fool's Day joke on Ken—and, believe me, I completely get that—but I just couldn't pass up a chance to make your life uncomfortable."

"Why are you here?" I covered my face with my hands then rubbed my eyes. I decided my original plan of ignoring her held merit.

"I'm here because…" She shuffled her feet and cleared her throat. Finally, she continued. "So, I'm starting my research rounds next week."

I remained motionless.

She huffed. "I was told that a VIP patient came in today for the infusion study and that you met with them? Some kind of celebrity? Is this true?"

I shrugged noncommittally.

"Damn it, Elizabeth, will you just tell me who it is?"

I opened my eyes, not wanting to miss a moment of her discomfort, and tried not to snort at her question. I fully admit that when I scoff, I snorted. I feel strongly that scoffing should be accompanied by a sound that is scoff-worthy, and for me, snorting is that sound.

Her request for information—after openly admitting to me that she'd switched the clinic rooms—was very Meg-like. She didn't seem to comprehend the obvious: that her evildoer admission would color my response.

"Ah-ah-ah," I scolded in mock consternation. "That would be a breach of patient confidentiality." I knew that saying these words made me a hypocrite in light of my Dr. Ken Miles HIPAA violation, but I couldn't help it. She brought out the worst in me.

No way in hell or heck was I going to tell Meg about Nico. She would probably ask for an autograph, or request a picture, or propose a three-way. The way she spoke about celebrities was just strange. She called them by their first name and talked about what they did as though she knew them personally. It was weird.

"Oh, please." She rolled her blue eyes, crossed her arms over her chest. "I'm just going to find out next week. Why not just tell me now?"

I pushed away from the wall and faced her, my shoulders squared. "Aw, gee, Meg. I just can't pass up a chance to make your life uncomfortable."

My pager chose that moment to buzz at my hip. It was one of those perfect timing moments because I'd just said something witty and lasting. With a smirk on my face, I glanced at my pager and frowned.

CRU rm 410 asap; VIP peds cg1605 cf iv

Roughly translated, the message meant *Please come to the Clinical Research Unit, room number 410 as soon as possible. A VIP pediatric patient has arrived for protocol number 1605, cystic fibrosis infusion study.*

It was exactly the same message I'd been paged earlier in the day, just before I walked in on Nico, Rose, and Angelica. My heart skipped two beats.

"What?" Meg's eyes glanced between the pager and me. "What is it?"

I didn't bother responding. Instead, I turned away and walked in the direction of the staff elevators. I could feel her shooting daggers at my back.

~*~*~*~

Nico was the sole occupant in the room; Rose and Angelica were gone. He turned as I entered, and I stalled just inside the entrance. If being in a room with Nico—with his mother and niece as witnesses—was terrifying, then being in a room *alone* with Nico was alert level red.

Automatically, I took a half step back, and my wide eyes met his.

He spoke first. "Hi."

"Hi." I pointed over my shoulder with my thumb. "Do you want me to get one of the nurses?"

Confusion flickered over his features. "What for?"

"I...." I held my breath as I searched for an excuse to call in one of the research staff. "I thought that—I mean it might be helpful for your decision about the study if you talked to one of the nurses who administer the infusions."

He shook his head then stuffed his hands in his pockets. "No. I want to talk to you."

My eyebrows shot upwards. I'm sure I looked as dumb as I felt. "Me?"

"Yeah." He nodded slowly. "Come in. Shut the door."

Shut the door? Is he out of his mind?

I didn't move. I stood paralyzed with a Vulcan death grip on the doorknob. We stared at each other.

He was waiting for me to behave like a normal human being.

I was waiting for him to disappear and this nightmare to dissolve.

"Elizabeth..." his mouth quirked to the side, his brow furrowing in obvious confusion at my immobility. "Aren't you going to come in?"

"Yes." I didn't move.

Nico's smile widened, just a teasing of teeth behind divine lips, and he crossed the room until he stood directly in front of me. He reached for the doorknob, his hand closed over mine. It was warm and sent a shock wave of awareness coursing up my arm. Through his movements, our hands together pushed the door closed.

"Come in." His voice was barely above a whisper. He was standing so close that I could see the flecks of black and silver in his green eyes.

"Okay." I said. Panic caused by his proximity was enough to spur me into action. I averted my gaze from his and pulled my hand from the knob and his grip. I walked around him, gingerly choosing my steps so that I wouldn't accidentally make contact with his body.

Once I arrived in the middle of the small space, I felt lost. Should I sit? Stand? Lean? Cross my arms? Some combination of the above? I turned and found him advancing slowly. I backed up. My thighs met the arm of the sofa. I sat on it and hoped the near-trip seemed intentional.

"So..." I crossed my arms, uncrossed my arms, feigned nonchalance, and winced a little at the tight unnaturalness of my voice. "You must have questions."

He nodded. "I do. I have a lot of questions."

"Well, that's to be expected." I patted my lab coat, looking for a brochure. "I have a pamphlet on side effects associated with the study drug that might help."

He halted some four feet from my position and, once again, stuffed his hands in his pockets. "I don't have questions about that, not about the study."

"Oh?" My voice cracked.

The *oh shit* heartbeat was back. I held perfectly still and forced myself to meet his gaze. Eleven years of avoiding him—avoiding thinking about him, his show, that summer, that night, our history—caught up with me all at once.

He openly surveyed me; his eyes swept from my feet to the top of my head then back to my face. "You look the same."

"I—I do?" I glanced dumbly at the front of my scrubs then back to him. I didn't think I looked the same. In fact, I was pretty sure I looked completely different. I narrowed my eyes at him. For the first time since entering the room, my panic-fog began to clear, and if he didn't want to discuss the study, I wondered what he wanted.

"Except..." he motioned to my hair. "Except your hair. You used to have shorter hair."

Automatically my hand lifted to the braid. "Yeah, well, I don't have anyone trying to cut my hair during nap time, so it finally grew out."

The corner of Nico's mouth lifted just slightly at my small barb. "I'd forgotten about that."

"I hadn't." I responded flatly.

"How old were we?"

"When you cut my hair? You were five."

His face warmed with a smile. "You were four. I remember now."

The fact that he was smiling at the memory of cutting my hair awakened an old, long-buried injury. I did not return his smile. In fact, as I watched him silently reminisce, other memories from our teenage years turned my blood abruptly cold. I no longer felt flustered by his presence. I felt annoyed by his arrogance.

Furthermore, I realized that—notwithstanding his perplexing kindness the summer after Garrett's death, my resulting guilt, and all these years of separation—part of me still simply saw him as the boy who bullied me in school. Disliking, distrusting Nico was an instinctual response.

"What do you want, Nico?"

His eyes flickered to mine, and I witnessed a shadow of surprise pass over his gaze, likely caused by the sudden somberness of my tone. He studied me for a moment, and then he said something entirely unexpected.

"I want to apologize."

I stared at him. Really, we stared at each other, but then I glanced at my feet and inclined my head slightly forward, sure I'd misheard him. "You what?" I asked, my voice slightly raised as I lifted my eyes to his.

"I want to apologize. I'm sorry for my rudeness earlier. Seeing you was…unexpected. I was caught off guard. I reacted badly."

I attempted to shrug. "It's okay. I know you must be under a great deal of pressure with your niece."

"Yes, but no more than usual. I shouldn't have snapped at you, and I definitely shouldn't have yelled. I'm sorry. Do you forgive me?"

I frowned, felt abruptly hot, uncomfortable. I couldn't swallow. "Of course." I croaked.

We stared at each other again. His eyes darted over my face as though committing me to memory. The focus of his gaze made me feel like protozoa under a microscope.

I stood. It was an abrupt movement. I cleared my throat. "Well, if that's everything, then…."

"No. I also…" Nico's eyes looked directly into mine. He rocked forward on his feet. "I have a proposition for you."

My stomach tensed, but instead of running from the room screaming, I stood my ground and responded with, "What's that?"

"I think we should become friends."

My eyebrows met my hairline. "You want to be friends with me?"

"Yes."

"Uh…" I looked at the door behind him, the wall above his head, the linoleum floor. It all looked real, and I was pretty sure I was awake. "I don't—I don't understand."

Nico pulled his hands from his pockets and held them out

between us. "If we decide to do this study for Angelica, I'll be in town quite a lot." He watched me expectantly. When I didn't respond, his hands dropped. "I'd like to see you. Maybe…." He cleared his throat. "Maybe we could go out."

I'm sure I looked completely befuddled. I felt completely befuddled. Why would Nico *the Face* Moretti— or Nico Manganiello—want to be friends with me? "I don't understand." I repeated and, because my brain was on befuddlement autopilot, I asked, "You mean like friends with benefits?"

Did I just say that, or did I think it? Judging by the amused expression on his features, I guessed that I had said it.

Out loud.

I grimaced. "I mean, not that you…I mean I just don't…."

"No, Elizabeth." His eyes swept over me in a quick movement as though it were an involuntary reaction to my question. "Friends *without* benefits—just friends."

"Of course. I didn't mean…." I huffed to stop talking, and promptly leaned against the sofa arm. I peered at him from behind my lashes. He seemed to be earnest. Nothing in his expression hinted that this was a joke or that he was trying to make a fool of me. Nevertheless, my eyes narrowed with suspicion.

"Just friends?"

"Yes."

I shook my head. "Men and women can't be just friends. Haven't you seen every romantic comedy ever?"

"I have female friends." His face relaxed a bit, but his eyes were still guarded.

"I'm sure you do."

"I do." He lifted his chin a notch. "There is a clause that if the man grows up with sisters—and I grew up with three—then he is capable of having female friends."

I considered him and the strangeness of his request. In fact, our entire interaction was verging on *Twilight Zone* levels of absurdity.

Nico Manganiello didn't ask people to be friends, and he certainly never asked me for anything.

"Okay." I shrugged my surrender because I didn't know what else to do. I felt overwhelmed by him, his request, the gentleness of his voice, the sincerity of his words, the entire situation. It was weird and, as usual, he had an uncanny ability to discombobulate me in a few short moments. Since I couldn't think of anything else to say, I responded, "We can be friends."

He nodded once but didn't smile. "Good. That's good."

And for the third time, we stared at each other. The moment was the most surreal of my life. I watched his chest rise and fall with each breath. I noted that his eyes hadn't quite lost all their hostility despite the candor of our conversation. Although, I reflected, neither had mine.

I doubted that we could be friends.

I watched as Nico took a deep breath, as though preparing to say something of great importance. He got as far as "Elizabeth, I have to—" before my pager buzzed at my waist.

I pulled my attention from him and focused on the message. It efficiently told me that the ER was expecting seven trauma victims within the next five minutes, all with severe injuries. This typically meant a car wreck of epic proportions.

I frowned first at my pager then at him. "I have to go. There's been an accident, and I need to help."

"Okay." He nodded then pressed his lips together in a tight line, his soulful eyes tinged with a shadow of emotion I couldn't place.

I walked past him in a rush but paused at the door. I felt as if I'd left my stomach and a few select other organs still leaning against the couch. I glanced over my shoulder.

He stood just where I'd left him, his back to the door.

CHAPTER 3

My suspicions were correct; the injuries and overflow of patients were due to a car accident. I worked with the trauma team until my shift ended and then for a few hours afterward. Basically, I worked until I was kicked out.

But now, since there was nothing more I could do, I was determined to leave the ups and downs and all-arounds of the day behind me: the devastation of the car accident, my shaming encounter with Dr. Botstein, the failed prank, and Megalomaniac Meg's evil deeds. Furthermore, I needed to tuck Nico Manganiello and all my memories of him, along with all the pain and regret, back into their hiding place.

It was Tuesday, and Tuesday was typically the highlight of my week because Tuesday night was knit night.

I was forced to admit that the ladies of my Tuesday night knitting group had muscled their way inside my heart over the past two years. At first, I wasn't entirely comfortable with letting them all in at once; it made me feel like they were going to storm the castle and plunder the goods. But all attempts at holding off the siege of care and mutual respect vanished with the consumption of bottles and bottles and bottles of red wine, tequila shots, dirty jokes, and bonding over worsted-weight Malabrigo yarn.

Under the weight of the day, I staggered into the apartment I shared with my best friend Janie—although, since Janie's engagement, she was rarely at home—and flung my bag and coat and keys on the hall table. I left my hand-knit gloves, scarf, and hat on. I wanted to show off the finished matching set.

"*Ai-oh!*" Ashley bellowed at me from the living room, "Getcher butt in here, girl. Sandra said you finished the hat. I wanna see it." An immediate smile arrested my features, and I walked a bit steadier down the hall.

Ashley was always extremely successful at cracking me up. She was originally from Tennessee and had explained to me once— over several strong margaritas—that she'd moved to Chicago so her parents couldn't marry her off to "some redneck park ranger." Lucky for me, she was also a pediatric nurse practitioner at Chicago General, so I got to see her for lunch sometimes. Those were good lunch days.

I attempted a dramatic entrance, poking my head around the corner, the aforementioned hat on my head at a jaunty angle. I wagged my eyebrows and was met with whoops and hollers.

"I like that hat." Marie leaned forward in her seat, placed her elbow on her crossed leg, and gave me an approving smile; her curly blonde hair fell forward around her shoulders. Marie, out of our bunch of misfits, was the artistic one. She was a freelance writer and illustrator and was extremely talented. In addition, she was an excellent cook. My favorite knit nights were at Marie's apartment because she always cooked instead of ordering takeout. On those occasions, I usually slept over if I could manage it because she made amazeballs Belgian waffles for breakfast.

I pointed to my head and stepped around the corner. "You mean this hat?" If my grin were any wider, it would have split my face.

When Sandra saw the matching scarf and mittens, she stood up. "Shut. Up. You. Knitting. Prodigy." She pointed at me, her mouth open wide. "I can't believe how awesome that turned out. Let me see—get your skinny bottom over here." Originally hailing from Texas, Sandra was by far the loudest and most opinionated among us. Actually, at times, she and I tied for that title, but I liked to think she edged me out of the lead most of the time. Like me, she was finishing her second year of residency at Chicago General, but she was a psychiatry resident.

I hopped into the room and wiggled my fingers, a somewhat lame attempt at jazz hands, and crossed to Sandra. She met me halfway and immediately grabbed one end of my scarf for closer inspection.

"Is it fair isle? Where did you find the pattern?" Fiona turned in her seat and motioned both Sandra and me over. She placed her knitting to the side as I approached. Fiona was five feet two and reminded Janie and me of a pixie. Her hair was short, her lashes were long, and her wide dark eyes always seemed to sparkle with a knowing glow. She was our unofficial den mother, and we all loved her.

"It's based on the Mini Mochi Fair Isle Hat by Sandi Rosner. I just took the pattern and reworked it for the matching scarf and mitts." I handed a glove to Fiona and watched her inspect it.

"I know that pattern." Kat volunteered quietly. She brushed a length of brown wavy hair from her shoulder and reached for her margarita glass. Janie met Kat at her previous job where Janie— although highly skilled as an architect—had been under employed as an accountant for an architecture firm. Now Janie worked for her fiancé's company as a senior account manager, and Kat still worked as an executive secretary for the firm. Kat was sweet, kind, sincere, and very, very quiet. I didn't know her as well as I would like, but I had firsthand knowledge of how wonderful she was.

Janie strolled out of the kitchen carrying margarita glasses; she was balancing on stilettos that made her barefoot six-foot frame a towering six feet four inches. She and I shared a weakness for fabulously impractical shoes.

When she saw me, she smiled and lifted a glass. "Do you want a margarita? I'm making them with Limoncello and Petron."

"Yes. I will have margaritas." I returned her smile. I was very happy to see her. I hadn't seen her since last week's meet-up, and I missed my best friend.

Janie was my college roommate, and I loved her like the sister I never had. We'd bonded early over the fact that we'd both lost our mothers at a relatively young age, but there was our shared strangeness, too. I was a sarcastic, caustic tomboy who'd skipped a grade in elementary school, and Janie was a walking calculator and encyclopedia. We were a match made in heaven, and we both wore a size eight-and-a-half shoe.

"Ok, two more coming right up." She nodded in my direction then passed one glass to Ashley and the other to Sandra. She then wiped her hands on the Wonder Woman apron she was wearing. A fire-engine-red curl had escaped her loose bun and fallen in her face. She puffed it out of the way and returned to the kitchen.

Marie reached for Ashley's glass, took a sip, and smacked her lips together. "Oh…that's good. The limoncello adds something nice."

Fiona handed me back my mitt. "You do beautiful work." She smiled wistfully at my scarf. "I need more time to knit."

"Fiona," I said, leaning closer to her, "before I forget, I have something for Gracie and Jake in my room. Build-A-Bear Workshop was having a sale on the bear kits."

Her eyebrows jumped and her eyes lit with surprised pleasure. "Thank you, Elizabeth. But you didn't have to do that. You need to stop buying them toys."

"What are you two talking about?" Sandra called from her place on the couch.

Before I could give Fiona the warning glance that screamed *don't tell them!* she lifted her voice and announced to the group, "Elizabeth bought Gracie and Jake Build-A-Bear kits."

I grimaced and waited for what I guessed would come next.

"Wait…." Ashley lowered her work and frowned at me. "Do you know anything about the kits that were dropped off at the pediatric unit yesterday? We can't figure out who did it. There were like thirty of them."

Yes, I'd dropped off the bears. They were on sale. Kids love bears. Kids shouldn't be in the hospital. It was no big deal. I didn't want to discuss it. Sandra would likely call me Florence Nightingale, which would lead to all sorts of biological clock jokes. As a rule, I didn't mind teasing about my bad behavior, but I hated being teased—or evening admitting to—my good behavior. When attention was drawn to even an arguably good deed I felt like a fraud.

I didn't meet Ashley's scrutinizing eye-squint. I changed the subject.

"Fiona—Fiona—" I motioned to my teeth. "You have something in your teeth—right here." I pointed between my two front teeth.

Fiona did the standard lip-dance-frown-spit-swishing movement then picked at her teeth with her fingernail, "Well, thanks for nothing, everyone. Have I been sitting here this whole time with something in my teeth? Only Elizabeth has the decency to tell me."

Sandra snorted into her margarita. "Pshaw. I didn't notice a damn thing. And Elizabeth is OCD about that kind of stuff. I once spent the better part of a minute trying to remove a spec of pepper from my teeth. *No one* could see it except Ms. Microscope Eyes over there."

I shrugged. "Fine. Next time I won't tell you when you have a huge piece of parsley hanging like bunting between your incisors."

"I have some news that has nothing to do with Fiona's disgusting habit of storing food in her teeth." Ashley—seemingly ignorant to my Build-A-Bear subterfuge—winked at Fiona; Fiona responded to the wink with a deadpan expression.

"Oh. Does it have anything to do with Elizabeth's microscopic eyes?" Sandra wagged her eyebrows at me. I considered sticking my tongue out but decided against it as Fiona had turned her attention back to my scarf.

"No, surprisingly, it doesn't." Ashley's smile grew secretive and she paused, milking the dramatic silence. Finally, she said, "It has to do with a celebrity at the hospital today."

My eyes met hers and a chill ran up my spine. I schooled my expression and did an admirable job of not reacting.

"Was there a celebrity at the hospital? I didn't hear anything." Sandra regained her seat on the couch and began rifling through her project bag. "I hope it was someone good."

"There was and he is and you'll never guess who." Ashley glanced at each of us, her grin growing as her obvious excitement began to show.

Marie turned her work and rolled her eyes. "Just put us out of our misery."

"Okay, it was *Nico Moretti*!" Ashley smiled expectantly and excitedly.

"Whoa." Sandra and Fiona said in unison.

"Did you see him?" Even Kat appeared enthralled.

Ashley shook her head. "Sadly, no. If I had, I likely wouldn't have been able to contain myself, and you'd all be bailing me out of jail right now."

Sandra nodded her approval. "It would have been worth it. That guy…he's on my spank naughty list."

Marie lifted her right hand toward Sandra. "I approve!" she declared, and the two ladies gave each other a high-five.

"Did you hear anything about it, Elizabeth?" Fiona was eying me suspiciously, likely having discerned that I was being atypically quiet.

An image of Nico from earlier in the day flashed before my consciousness—the way he'd looked at me as though memorizing my face, his eyes brimming with sincerity and hostility—asking me to be friends. It was so strange and absurd, and it made me feel hot and cold: hot because he'd asked me to be friends and cold because I knew that it was impossible. I couldn't think about him. When I did, I felt tangled and out of sorts.

I cleared my throat and shrugged. Rather than lie, I decided to deflect for the second time that evening. "I actually got chewed out today by Dr. Botstein."

"What? Again?" Kat dropped her knitting to her lap. "What did you do?"

I unwrapped my scarf from my neck and claimed the seat next to her. "He was on the receiving end of one of my practical jokes."

Ashley laughed with a mouth half full of margarita. She swallowed quickly. "What was it this time—Mentos in his Coke? My favorite was the porn tape switch—they never could pin that on you. Of course there was the time you put 'I'm a wanker' in permanent marker on the bottom of Dr. Meg's coffee mug—she went around all morning like that, just drinking her coffee, what a moron."

Janie exited the kitchen holding two more glasses; she placed one in front of me and kept one for herself. I smiled my thanks and laid my scarf on my lap.

"I took an unopened box of latex gloves in the ER clinic and filled a few of them with lotion and rigged it to explode upon opening."

"So, Dr. Boty ended up with a face covered in mysterious gelatinous white goo?" Ashley looked as though she approved.

"I actually feel really bad about it. He was strangely nice to me afterward."

"That is weird." Ashley eyed me speculatively. "Dr. Boty is such a terror on the pediatric floor. I avoid him at all costs."

"I don't understand why you do these things. Why risk your career like this?" Fiona kept her voice low and addressed the question just to me; her expression was a mixture of concern and maternal frustration.

"I just—" Under her disapproving stare I felt ashamed again, felt the need to defend myself to her even if I couldn't do so earlier with Dr. Botstein. "It's the job. It's stressful. Kids come into the ER with gunshot wounds; babies come in sick, and I can do nothing to help them. I'm not complaining—I love what I do, and I feel like I'm making a difference but it's…it can be frustrating. The pranks, they help me—I don't know—keep things light."

"Obviously I have no idea what it's like for you, dealing with those issues every day, but it seems like you could identify a less self-destructive way of working through job stress." Fiona's expression softened. "I just worry about you. You need an outlet...you need...."

Somebody.

The word wasn't spoken, but the implication hung between us unsaid.

"Yes, well..." I cleared my throat and lifted my voice so the rest of the room could hear. "...it was an accident. I meant the glove prank for Dr. Ken Miles, but Dr. Botstein must've used the room first."

"He's kind of hot—Ken, not Dr. Botstein. Dr. Botstein seems like the kind of guy who would have a prematurely wrinkled bottom." Sandra nodded in assertion of her own observation and gulped the remainder of her drink.

"I concur." Ashley said, and lifted her glass. "But hopefully we'll never find out."

"Several breeds of dogs have wrinkles, like the Pug and Shar Pei." Janie sipped her margarita and licked at the excess salt on the rim.

We all paused for a beat, waiting to see if she would continue. Janie had an impressive habit of spouting trivial facts at odd times. It was one of the many reasons we all adored her.

"Janie, your left-fielding skills are very impressive. You are the most impressive left fielder I've ever met." Sandra surreptitiously reached for Kat's almost full margarita and took a sip.

Janie frowned. "You mean the baseball position?" She sat back in her chair and twisted the obscenely large ruby ring on her left third finger. "I've never played baseball."

"No, hun. I'm talking about someone who says stuff out of left field. I never know where you're going or where you're going to take me. I'm just happy to be along for the ride." Sandra blew

Janie a sincere kiss, which made Janie smile sweetly.

My heart twisted. Damn it, I missed Janie—a lot. I blinked away the sudden moisture and berated myself for this overreaction. Janie was getting married; she wasn't dying. I would continue to see her and talk to her—just not as often. I needed to get a grip.

Unfortunately, logic isn't a cure for loneliness.

Kat, seemingly just noticing that Sandra had swiped her margarita, began to sputter. "Did you—I can't believe—you stole my—Sandra!"

Sandra ducked her head and took a large swallow.

"It's ok. I'll make some more and bring out a pitcher." Janie stood and reached for Sandra's empty glass. "But since Sandra is being greedy, she has to come and help me."

Sandra stood. "Fine. It's a fair punishment."

"I'll come too." I took off my hat and bundled it together with my scarf and mittens and left the hand knit trio on my chair before following the redheaded duo into the kitchen.

Sandra strolled behind Janie and lovingly caressed the granite countertops as she entered the decently sized space. "I love this kitchen. It's a kitchen for cooking."

I shrugged. I wasn't much of a cooker. I didn't like to clean stuff up.

"I approve of this kitchen. I like the placement of the dishwasher relative to the sink and the refrigerator relative to the stove." Janie said, towering above both of us as she poured tequila and lime juice into the cocktail shaker. "Sandra, can you start squeezing more limes? They are in the bottom drawer of the fridge."

"These are really good margaritas, Janie. Well done." I smiled up at her as I poured salt onto a plate and coated the rim of Sandra's empty glass.

"It's the limoncello and fresh lime juice, I think. I also used agave nectar instead of sugar." Janie squeezed the amber-colored syrup into the shaker, replaced the lid, and shook the mixture with vigor.

"You should make these when we go to my reunion in Iowa next week," I said, screwing the cap back on the tequila.

Janie abruptly stopped shaking and stared at me with wide eyes, her mouth open slightly. She held very still. Sandra and I shared a concerned glance.

"Janie…? Are you ok?"

"I completely forgot. I completely forgot about your reunion." Janie slowly lowered the shaker to the counter. She appeared to be both distraught and preoccupied.

I couldn't help my frown. My heart sank. "Did you make other plans?"

"I'll…I'll find a way to—I'll think of something." She was staring over my shoulder in a way that told me she was trying to concentrate on a problem.

Sandra glanced between Janie and me. "What plans did you make? Maybe I can help?"

Janie sighed. "We're—Quinn and I—we're planning to go to Boston to see his parents. I was going to meet his parents, but…." Janie's hazel gaze met mine. "I completely forgot about the reunion. We planned the trip so long ago."

"I'm confused. Isn't Quinn estranged from his parents? Didn't they, like, disown him? Don't they blame him for his brother's death or some such nonsense?" Sandra picked up the discarded shaker and finished the task Janie had abandoned.

Janie nodded. "Yes, they did. I'm not sure if they still do. I called his mom a few weeks ago and introduced myself. I told her I was marrying her son and explained that I planned to give her a few grandchildren at some point."

Sandra's hands ceased mid-shake. "You did what?"

"Well, I know this separation from his family, from his mom and dad, contributes to his broodiness to a certain extent. I thought

I could offer them grandchildren in exchange for forgiveness."

I was not surprised. Janie was nothing if not practical. The plan made complete sense to me.

Sandra blinked at Janie, as though if she blinked hard enough, Janie might disappear or grow a tail. I took the shaker from Sandra's hands and finished the job of mixing the cocktail.

"I—I can't believe you did that. You're using children...."

Janie shook her head, "No. I'm not using children. We're going to have kids anyway, and I thought why not use the idea of these future kids to *persuade* his parents to make the right decision now?"

Sandra made a choking sound then leaned on the kitchen counter. "You're not going to—you're not going to use the kids, are you? Meaning later—once they're born—you're not going to manipulate his parents into..."

"No. Absolutely not." Janie appeared to be genuinely horrified by the thought. "I would never do that. I just—I just want his mom and dad to give him a chance. I just want them to make an effort. He's so...he's so...."

"Grumpy?" I supplied as I poured the margarita into Sandra's glass.

Janie tried to suppress her smile with a scowl. "No. Not grumpy. He's sensitive. He doesn't show it to many people."

I snorted. "You mean he only shows it to you."

She ignored me. "But he is. And he misses his family. And they're his family. And I want to meet them. I've never had a mother, not really, and his mom sounds great, except for the whole—you know—disowning her son thing. And why shouldn't my children have grandparents?"

I lifted Sandra's glass and took a sip. "They should. I completely support you in this decision."

Janie gave me a single nod of appreciation; "Thank you, Elizabeth. Your support means a lot."

Sandra was still frowning as she took her glass away from me before I could take another drink. "Well then, what about the reunion? I imagine it took a lot for you to get these people to agree to the visit, right?"

Janie looked from Sandra to me. She didn't respond.

The sinking feeling from earlier in the evening had morphed into full-fledged and sudden depression. I couldn't ask Janie to reschedule her trip to Boston. I knew how important it was to her to have a family. Her family was worse than having no family at all. Her sisters were criminals, and her father—although he meant well—was clueless and, honestly, similar in personality to dry paint. Her mother, when she was alive, was a terrible woman who'd abandoned her family whenever it suited her.

At least I had my dad and wonderful memories of my mother.

Janie deserved this. She deserved to have her husband's family know her and love her.

I stared at the counter and traced a design in the granite. "You should go to Boston." I finally said, meeting her gaze. "Really. Go to Boston."

She shook her head. "I can reschedule. You can't reschedule your reunion."

"I'll go." Sandra's declaration was a bit of a slurred shout.

Janie blinked at her. "To Boston?"

"No, Wonder Woman. I'll go to Elizabeth's high school reunion. I'll go with Elizabeth, and you'll be off to Boston with your McHotpants to make babies for those awful people."

Janie looked at me. I looked at Janie. I looked at Sandra. Sandra looked at me. Janie looked at Sandra. Sandra looked at Janie.

Sandra lifted her glass again, winked at me, and toasted us both. "To friendscorts. They're like escorts but without the cash."

CHAPTER 4

"For the love of chartreuse, can we please listen to something else?"

"No."

"Please oh please oh please oh please." She sounded so anguished and tortured.

"No."

"Damn it, Elizabeth. I've dropped three stitches and had to rip out two rows of this shawl. I can't listen to one more prepubescent boy say the word 'girl' or 'kiss' when you know he wants to say 'whore' and 'fu-'."

"Fine." I tightened my fingers around the steering wheel. "Pick something else."

Sandra bolted upright, placed her pile of knitting to the side, and grabbed my iPhone. "Oh, God, thank you so much. I know I said I wouldn't make fun of your music, but I honestly do not know how you can listen to that. I could feel my vagina shriveling with each neutered verse."

"Oh, come on!" Laughing, I glanced at Sandra from the driver's seat. "I saw you mouthing along with the last song."

"Yes, but much like a schizophrenic mouths wordlessly to themselves, or how you feel after stepping off that annoying ride at Disney World with 'It's a small world after all' stuck in your head for the rest of the day." She thumbed through my albums and her brow drew downward with each pass. "Well—you are a complete crackhead. Every single album on here is boy band shisterhosen."

Sandra, making no attempt to hide her disgust, pulled the audio jack from my phone and dumped it in the center console. She pulled out her phone and simultaneously plugged it in while searching for music. When she pressed play and a sultry, soulful voice reverberated over the speakers, her head fell back against the headrest and she closed her eyes.

"Oh, yes. God, that's the stuff." Her fingers flexed and unflexed on her knees in something akin to ecstasy.

We were just crossing the Mississippi River heading west on I-80. I promised Sandra that we would stop at the World's Largest Truck Stop so she could purchase an ear flapped trucker hat. Part of me wondered if the truck stop was the main attraction of the trip for her.

Acres of what were usually cornfields were barren on either side of the interstate. Large silver silos, red barns, and picturesque farmhouses dotted the landscape. Tall, leafless trees lined the road, stretching to the sky like brown bottlebrushes. It was near fifty degrees outside, and the sky hadn't yet decided if it wanted to be gray or blue.

"So…" Sandra's voice beside me was relaxed, almost dreamy. She recommenced knitting. "Is there anything I should know?"

I shifted in my seat. "About what?"

"About your high school dynamics. Is there anyone you're hoping will be there? Anyone to avoid? Who was prom queen, and do we hate her?"

"Well…let me see…" I shifted again in my seat and forced myself to loosen the grip on the steering wheel, and then I told a little white lie. "I don't really know."

If I were being honest, I would have said, *I hope everyone is there.*

"Don't know which part?" Sandra's head bobbed in time to the music.

"I don't really know about the high school dynamics." This, at least, was mostly true. I hadn't paid much attention to popular-people dynamics during high school. But I did know that I'd been universally invisible.

In my peripheral vision, I saw her head swing toward mine; she paused for a moment then said, "I call shenanigans."

I gave her a sideways glance. "It's true. I was kind of a—well, a loner."

And by loner, I really meant that I'd been a mean-spirited cranky-face who avoided my peers at all costs.

"Then why do you even want to go? We could blow the whole thing off and drive to Vegas instead."

"I did have some friends." I tried to defend myself, my face growing hot with the now grayish lie.

I did have some friends—or, more precisely, acquaintances—in high school, but I wasn't sure whether any of them would show up. The truth was, I really wanted to go to my high school reunion, but I couldn't tell Sandra why because most of my reasons were ten out of ten on the petty-insipid-twit scale.

Granted, part of me was curious.

However, a much bigger part of me wanted to go because I'd worked my ass off and was now a medical doctor. I wanted to lord it over all the people who were popular, beautiful, and barely knew I existed in high school. I was sure—crossing my fingers—that they were all failures of some sort. I wanted to introduce myself as Elizabeth Finney, MD—as in Medical Doctor. I practiced doing this in the mirror a few times before I'd left Chicago and felt good about my delivery.

My pretend conversation usually went something like this:

Them, surprised: *"Elizabeth? Is that you?"*

Me, caught off guard: *"Oh—hi. Yes, it's me, Elizabeth."*

Them, amazed and in awe of my beauty: *"Oh, my gosh—you look totally different."*

Me, humble smile: *"Aw, thanks!"*

Them, interested and dazed by my good looks: *"What are you up to now? Where are you working?"*

Me, politely responding with an air of modesty: *"What? What do I do now? Well, I'm actually a medical doctor."*

Them, completely blown away and fumbling over their words: *"Oh, my God! That's so fantastic! That's so impressive!"*

Me, laughing off the praise as though it makes me uncomfortable: *"Oh, I don't know about impressive, but—ha ha ha—I get by. What are you doing now?"*

Them, looking uncomfortable and ashamed: *"Oh? Me? Well...I pick through trash outside people's homes looking for recycled materials to take to the dump."*

It didn't matter if they were a materials scavenger or a train-hopping hobo; in my fantasies they were always less successful than I was. But mostly I wanted to go to my reunion because I now had C-cup boobs—ok, so they're a C cup on the third week of the month.

In high school, I was both short and impressively scrawny. Add to that my belligerent personality, and I was a double dose of teenage-girl fail. When I was fifteen, most people thought I was an eleven- or twelve year-old boy; my nickname—*Skinny Finney*—didn't help matters. New kids thought Finney was my first name.

Now, I had boobs. I was enormously proud of my boobs. I'd waited so long for them. But when they finally arrived with a vengeance after my sixteenth birthday, the summer before my senior year of high school, I was too despondent to notice or care.

I couldn't tell Sandra the true reasons without sounding like the raging, self-absorbed, shallow twit that I actually was at that time in my life.

Instead I said, "And I wasn't really into that stuff—group activities, team sports, and popularity contests."

"Well what stuff were you into? Living under a rock?"

I wrinkled my nose. "I was a tomboy in high school."

"Well, no shit, Sherlock. You're still a tomboy now except that you listen to tween music and have long hair. You're lucky you don't need to wear makeup. But you must've noticed which cheerleaders were hos and which guys to put onto your spank naughty and spank nice lists."

I rested my left elbow on the sill of the door and tugged at my bottom lip. If I were with Janie, I wouldn't need to explain that the reason I was detached during my last two years of high school—and any *Days of Their Lives*-type drama from ten years ago—was because of Garrett. Janie was the only person I knew in Chicago who knew my story.

Perhaps now was a solid time to test the sharing waters with Sandra.

I cleared my throat and repositioned my hands on the steering wheel. "So, there was this boy...."

"Ok, ok—good—good—this sounds promising." Sandra put her knitting aside and rubbed her hands together.

A small, saddish smile tugged one side of my mouth upward. "There was this boy; his name was Garrett, and he had big brown eyes and blond hair and just the best, warmest smile. He moved to my town when I was in fifth grade, right after my mother died, and I just...I just...." I swallowed. "I just fell for him."

"I didn't know your mother died."

"It happened when I was nine. Garrett really helped me through it."

"In fifth grade?"

I nodded once. "This isn't a happy story."

Sandra was quiet for a moment; when she spoke again, her voice was softer. "Go on."

I recognized it as her *shrink* voice, the one she used when speaking to someone upset and emotionally fragile with whom she was trying to reason. During one of our knit nights out on the town, she used the voice to convince a hoity toity maître d' that he, indeed, had lost our reservation, and that he, indeed, needed to set the thing to rights as soon as was humanly possible.

It worked.

We were impressed.

I was impressed.

She was using *the voice* on me now, and it was working.

"I fell in love with Garrett. I skipped a grade in elementary school, so he was a year older. But he was so easy to be around; he made me feel good, like I was important to him—you know? So gentle and kind, and sensitive. He was really there for me—you know? I just always wanted to be around him. We were childhood sweethearts, just like my parents were, and we were going to get married one day. But when he was fifteen, he...."

I started tugging at my bottom lip again. "We went to a party and both of us drank. He only had, like, two drinks, but afterward, he had severe pains in his neck and sides so his friend—uh—Nico—drove Garrett to the hospital. They discharged him almost immediately after he was admitted. I think they thought he just had too much to drink. But," I sighed, "a few months later, at the end of summer break, he was getting sick a lot—fevers with no other accompanying symptoms, that kind of thing."

I paused, waiting for the sting of tears that usually accompanied this part of the story, but to my surprise, when I spoke again, I was able to do so without a chin wobble or a voice waver.

"The doctor ran a complete blood panel, and he was diagnosed with Hodgkin's Lymphoma. He was sick our entire junior year, at first going through chemo, surgeries, then—later—just succumbing to the disease. He died in April—April thirteenth. He was stage...stage...." I cleared my throat. "It had progressed too far by the time he was diagnosed."

I heard Sandra exhale, and I exhaled with her. We were both silent for a long while. The World's Largest Truck Stop came and went. Miles of barren cornfields passed us by. I thought about the day Garrett died, and realized that today's weather was exactly like the gray gloominess of the day he slipped from my life and this earth forever. It gave me an odd feeling of being in the right place at the right time as I shared this story with Sandra on the way to my hometown that was full of so many memories good and bad.

At last Sandra spoke. "Well...that is some depressing and tragic shit, Elizabeth." Her voice was watery.

I glanced over at her and realized that she was crying; or, rather, she was trying not to cry. My eyes widened in surprise. "Did I just make you cry?"

"No, I'm crying because we missed the World's Largest Truck Stop." her voice was thick with sadness masked by an attempt at humor and sarcasm. "Yes, you did just make me cry."

I felt the first tingling of tears behind my eyes, and the chin wobble I'd been expecting earlier made its appearance.

"Oh no—don't *you* cry—" her tone became authoritative. "If you cry, I will be forced to beat you with my shoe, and you will not like it. I'm not wearing any socks, and my feet seriously stink."

I couldn't help it. I started to laugh. When I told Janie about Garrett, she didn't cry, but she held me while I did. It felt good to be held. It also felt good to laugh.

"Well, no wonder you weren't paying attention to high school dynamics or creating spank tanks. You were dealing with real life issues. I can't fathom what it was like for you, losing your mom then your first love like that."

I shrugged, but her words made an impact.

"Is that why you decided to become a doctor?"

"It's one of the reasons, yes. But also I really like it—I like the work."

"Why emergency medicine? Why not oncology?"

"Because both my mom and Garrett were misdiagnosed in an emergency room. If they'd been diagnosed correctly…."

"Ah." She nodded her understanding. "After Garrett's death, did you get some help? Did you go to therapy?"

I shook my head. "Afterward, that summer, I just kind of floated through stuff, not really noticing or paying attention. My dad decided to take me to Ireland at the end of the summer, and I completed the first half of my senior year there—which helped."

"He probably wanted to remove you from a place filled with

reminders."

I nodded. "Yeah. He took an adjunct teaching position at Trinity—or their version of an adjunct position—and I discovered an abiding passion for Guinness since the place we stayed was basically down the road from the Guinness factory. I think I did that brewery tour seventy times."

"Guinness is g-o-o-o-o-o-o-o-d."

Our apparent shared love for Guinness warmed my heart, and I glanced over at Sandra. She was watching me with a look that I could only define as restrained.

"What? What is it?"

"Do you—" She catapulted the words at me, paused, scratched her chin then turned as far in her seat as the seatbelt would allow. "Did you two—before he—did you…?"

"You're asking me if we had sex, aren't you?"

She nodded.

"No. Garrett and I never had sex. I was only fifteen when he was diagnosed and almost sixteen when he died. Besides, we wanted to wait until we were married, and then, when he got sick, I never thought he wouldn't get well until it was too late."

She expelled a loud breath. "That sucks."

"Yeah." I frowned. "Yeah, it sucks."

~*~*~*~

I soon discovered that Sandra was a badass.

Road trips can either suck monkey balls or, with the right person, they can be awesomesauce with cheesy fries. Sandra was that right person. She regulated the car temperature to make certain it was always comfortable; her music selection—although not my typical preference—was high quality; she ensured conversation flowed and waned at appropriate intervals.

And she was very skilled in the art of unwrapping my sandwich and arranging my french fries and ketchup so that I could eat effortlessly while driving.

Yes, we'd been knitting together for going on two years, and yes, I infrequently met her for lunch at the hospital. But our interactions until this trip rarely deviated beyond those situations. I'd been operating under and interacting with Sandra based on my initial superficial impressions: funny, smart, loud, and opinionated.

I should've known better that a person is never just funny, smart, loud, and opinionated without a whole lot of awesome behind it.

Furthermore, something about being trapped in a car together for five hours—the shared experience of synchronized pit-stop peeing and suffering through roadside fast food—will bond two people for life.

By the time we arrived at my childhood home, virtually all of my earlier melancholy from missing Janie was replaced with self-recrimination for being so narrow-minded. I was also experiencing newly minted good friend euphoria.

Sandra noted with a squeal that we were late as we exited the car and rushed into my childhood home. We hurried through showering and dressing; I realized I was excited about going to the reunion because I was going with Sandra and Sandra was badass.

I still missed Janie. I still lamented that she wasn't able to come. But I found I didn't need to be so diligent and determined about having a good time with Sandra. I was just simply having a good time with Sandra.

With Sandra's insistence and help, I wore my hair down in impressive loose curls over my shoulders which were left bare in my black and white polka-dot strapless dress. I loved this dress even though it wasn't at all my typical haphazard style. I wore a wicked black petticoat under the full skirt so it flared above the knee. I rounded out the look with red lipstick and borrowed—from Janie—black and white zebra print stilettos.

Sandra—always a bombshell—wore a long, clingy blue and white maxi dress and turquoise sequenced high heels. She left her short red hair down, falling in soft waves to her chin. Her eye shadow was also sparkly blue and I coveted her ability to apply makeup. All my attempts at eye makeup—other than mascara—left me looking like the loser in a bar fight.

We drove through the high school parking lot only one hour late and, despite my obvious bias, felt that we both looked amazing. Even though I had returned home with some frequency during the past decade to visit my dad—less often in recent years due to my crazy schedule at the hospital—I hadn't visited my high school since graduation.

Everything looked essentially the same except the trees were taller and the main building had recently been painted. I didn't feel much of anything—no nostalgia or twinge of apprehension—until I stepped through the doors and the smell of pencils and bread and Glass Plus cleaner slapped my brain backward in time.

Memories and accompanying thoughts and anxieties assailed me without warning.

I was suddenly thirteen, fourteen, fifteen, and sixteen all at once. I was short, angry, quiet, and flat chested. I was Skinny Finney trying to blend in with the lockers; I was sitting in the back of the classroom avoiding eye contact with all the kids in my class who were older, bigger, and louder.

I was looking at my past self through the one-way interrogation window of my current self, and it caused me to experience the strange sadness that accompanies helplessness. If only I could have told teenage Elizabeth that none of it actually mattered. It all seemed to matter so much at the time.

A half laugh, half gasp escaped my chest, and I paused just inside the door of the main entrance to catch up with the onslaught.

"What is it?"

I glanced at Sandra—her red eyebrows raised in confusion, her eyes wide with concern—and shook my head. "It's—it's nothing." In a daze, I walked a few steps forward and allowed the door to close behind me. "It's just really weird to be here."

Sandra smiled wryly, "Yeah. I haven't decided if I'm going to my high school reunion. I don't know if I should grace those people with the gift of my presence."

"Did you have a hard time in high school? Did you hate the prom queen?" I strolled forward feeling a bit easier and acclimated. I glanced at my surroundings; blue lockers lined gray walls. The floor was white and blue linoleum, peeling and scuffed.

"Oh, heavens no. I *was* the prom queen."

I stopped in my tracks and spun to look Sandra square in the eye. "You were the prom queen?"

She nodded; her grin was immediate. "Yes. I was the prom queen. Don't look so shocked."

"I'm not shocked. I'm...." I waved my hands through the air trying to locate the words as my feet automatically led the way to the gym. "I'm surprised."

"You're a doofus. Shocked and surprised are synonyms."

"No, not really. Shocked means that something is hard to believe; surprised means something is unexpected."

Sandra's eyes narrowed; their glittery green was intensified by the long blue and white maxi dress she was wearing. "You sounded just like Janie when you said that."

She was right. I did. The thought made me happy-sad.

"She's rubbed off on me despite my efforts to remain unaffected. I've spent all these years trying to wash off the stank of my own social ineptness—and, believe me, I had my own special brand of social incompetency—but I know I've adopted some of her mannerisms. She has this thing about words."

Sandra's expression was plainly skeptical. "In what ways were you socially incompetent?"

"I was really, really shy."

Sandra pushed my shoulder. "Get out. You? The queen of hospital pranks and hot man conquests? I call shenanigans."

"Are you surprised?"

"No. I'm shocked." She wagged her eyebrows, which made me laugh. "Why were you shy?"

"Actually, I don't know if I was exactly shy. Rather, I just had this overwhelming distain for the world and everyone in it."

Before Sandra could respond to this revelation, a super-duper cheerful voice interrupted our conversation with an exaggerated, "Hi there! How are you?!"

I hadn't noticed that we'd walked all the way to the entrance of the gym. Early decade dance music pumped through the open doors, specifically *Let's Get It Started in Here* by the Black Eyed Peas.

I blinked twice at the image in front of me. Stephanie Mayor, our class president, smiled at Sandra and me with extraordinary force as though trying to convey expediency. She stood behind a long, bare, rectangular banquet table covered in a navy blue tablecloth, and she looked exactly like her high school self. Even her hair—cut, color, and style—was identical to how it had been ten years ago.

The only difference was that instead of her usually casual cheerfulness, there seemed to be a radioactive, 1000-watt light of sunny glee radiating from her every pore.

"Hi—yes—hi." Sandra returned her smile with a bracing, unsure one of her own as if the force of Stephanie's grin had temporarily made Sandra question the intelligence of attending my high school reunion. "This is Elizabeth and I am her friendscort, Sandra. We would like our table assignment please."

Stephanie's eyes met mine, and I noted a lack of recognition there. Her brow wrinkled although her smile remained firmly affixed. "Hi…."

"Hi." I waited a moment for some kind of follow-through, like telling me where I could find my nametag or my table.

Sandra filled the silence. "This is the class reunion, right?"

Stephanie's eyes ping-ponged between us. Finally she asked, "Did you go to school here?"

I glanced at Sandra briefly then cleared my throat. "I'm Elizabeth Finney."

Stephanie blinked at me for several protracted moments, her brow comically low. I thought about pulling down my strapless dress and flashing her or slapping her across the face just to see if a Jerry Springer style wakeup call would make a difference.

"Oh! You—you're Skinny Finney! I remember you! But you look completely different, and your hair is really long now!" She cocked her head to the side and gave me a reproachful smirk. "You should have just said so!"

"Yes, what was I thinking?" I deadpanned my response, but she didn't seem to hear me.

"It's a good thing you caught me; I was just about to go in! I don't want to miss any of the excitement...." Stephanie's voice was muffled as she reached under the table and rustled through some unseen items.

It took her maybe a full four minutes to find what she was searching for. Sandra gave me a questioning glance, which I answered with a shrug.

"Here you go!" Stephanie bolted upright and handed me my nametag with a booklet. "Your nametag has your table number—and you cannot change tables, so please don't—and the brochure has a listing of—almost—" she paired the word *almost* with a clumsy double wink, "—all attendees with their contact information."

Sandra eyeballed her and crossed her arms over her chest. "Can I ask—what is with the stealth placement of the nametags? Why not just put them on top of the table and let people pick their own?"

Stephanie's mouth curved into a small O and, again, her eyes ping-ponged between us. "Oh! You don't know!"

We stared at her expectantly, waiting for her to continue. After a long pause, Stephanie leaned over the table and motioned for us to do so as well, even though we were basically alone in the hall. "We didn't know if we were going to have problems with people trying to get in since Niccolò is here. It was all very unexpected, and he has quite a security team with him but...."

I didn't hear anything else she said. The shock caused temporary peripheral neuropathy in my ear tips, fingers, and toes. I felt both hot and cold like a pathetic, melting ice sculpture. The anxiety was going to send me into cardiac arrest.

Sandra's attention moved from my face to Stephanie's. She blinked at us both. "Ok—what am I missing? Who is Niccolò?"

Stephanie chuckled. "Uh...only Niccolò Manganiello, AKA Nico Moretti, AKA *the Face*."

CHAPTER 5

"Wait, wait, wait...." Sandra held her hands up and catapulted a slightly hostile in my direction. "You mean that hot guy on Comedy Central who has that show where he tries to talk celebrities into getting naked, but mostly he just gets naked and they end every show with him Jell-O wrestling with hot ladies? You went to high school with *that* Nico Moretti?"

I didn't respond. I didn't get a chance.

"It's actually Nico *Manganiello*, but I changed my last name when I moved to New York."

Startled by his voice I instinctively half twisted toward the velvety sound. The first thing I noticed was that his unshaven stubble from last week had grown into a haphazardly trimmed, close-cut beard. Looking like sex on a stick—if sex were Italian and the stick had an unhealthy amount of charisma—he sauntered toward us.

His smile was big, open, and warm, but his eyes were shuttered and cold. Furthermore, they were focused squarely on me in a way that was all too obvious.

I experienced a head-on collision of involuntary sensations and recognized the strongest one for what it was: intense attraction. My chest swelled, my stomach flipped, my knees locked; my organs were competing in the lust Olympics. At the same time, I was immediately repulsed by the uncontrollable reaction of my body. I could only stare at his infuriating, omnipresent magnetism.

I was annoyed that I noticed how exceptionally fine he looked in a black suit, white shirt, and skinny black tie; his black hair was mussed with scientific precision. It was Hollywood-quality postcoital hair.

"Oh! OH!" Stephanie exclaimed with undeniable vigor. Then she giggled.

The sounds of her female flail were enough to snap me out of my haze. I straightened my spine and turned completely to face him, my chin lifted a notch. One of his eyebrows arched as though he was amused, and his smile shifted into a smirk.

He nodded at me once. "Hi, friend."

Sandra's head swiveled *Exorcist* style when she heard him greet me in such a familiar tone.

"Nico." I suppressed a Marge Simpson growl of frustration and instead returned his single nod with an air of what I hope passed for cool detachment. Awareness of his closeness made the surface of my skin hot beneath my curtain of hair from my neck down my back. I felt cold everywhere else. I fought the urge to shiver.

Ever the socially adept one, Sandra rolled with it and stuck out her hand. "Hey there, big guy, I'm Sandra."

Nico's eyes slid away from mine and he gathered Sandra's small white hand in his olive-toned, much larger ones. He didn't shake it. He just held it.

He was such an ass.

"Hi, Sandra." He bit his bottom lip, which made his smile crooked, small, and completely charming. He kept his voice low, intimate. I could practically hear seduction in it. "It's really nice to meet you."

Sandra's gave a breathy laugh and glanced at me with suppressed glee. I fought the urge to roll my eyes.

"What are you doing here?" My voice was accusatory because I meant it to be. It didn't make sense. He had no reason to be there, in Iowa, at my high school reunion. I narrowed my eyes. Maybe he would look less appealing and edible if I narrowed my eyes.

In truth, I didn't want to deal with him and my Nico-guilt; I wanted to be petty and childish instead. He was a reminder of my historical immaturity. His presence made me feel less justified in my self-indulgent endeavor to wow the graduating class with my perceived impressiveness. He deflated my bubble of adolescent angsty vengeance. This left me feeling silly and adrift.

One eyebrow lifted slightly higher in an attractive arch. "Well, I did go to school here…."

"But you didn't graduate." I cringed as soon as the words left my mouth. It wasn't my intention to be rude, but likely, the blurted words would be interpreted as a slight.

"No. I didn't graduate." His mouth twisted to the side. A flicker of what looked like bitterness burned beneath his cool gaze. "Some of us don't need to graduate three times in order to feel successful. Some of us don't need to graduate at all."

It was *exactly* like old times. We were standing in the hall of our high school trading insults and throwing hateful glares like grenades.

I blinked and flinched then opened my mouth to say something nasty, but Sandra interrupted just in time.

"I'm such a fan of your show, but you must hear that all the time. I especially love it when you have the girls do that game show skit, "Are You Smarter than a Bikini Model?" It's always fun when they make those guys look like idiots."

"Well, all the girls on the show are really smart and, honestly, the guys usually are idiots."

"I never miss it. Debbie is my favorite. I love that she leg wrestles; she's so strong. Thank you for the show."

His eyes twinkled. I've never seen anyone able to eye twinkle on cue quite like Nico. I suspected he must have perfected eye twinkling in front of a mirror at a young age.

"No, thank *you*. I never get tired of meeting fans. I *love* fans of the show."

I quietly snorted. It was a scoff-snort, but it must have been loud enough for him to hear because his eyes returned to mine as he released Sandra's hand.

"Do you watch the show, Elizabeth?"

I shook my head, disliked the way he said my name, looked everywhere but at his aggravatingly handsome face; I tried to sound bored instead of irritated. "Nope, can't say that I do, what with all the *graduating* I've been doing."

I felt his gaze on me for a very brief second. Then he said something entirely surprising and yet—for Nico—not at all shocking. "Right. Why would you? You've already seen everything up close."

Oh...my...God.

I heard Sandra's small intake of breath at my side.

My eyes widened and met his. Again, a spark of triumph was smoldering in his glare.

Nico was trying to bait me into a fight. He *always* used to do this in high school—the unkind nickname repeated at every opportunity, insults flung down the hall at my back, knocking books and folders out of my hands, introducing me as a boy to new students.

He was trying to get a rise out of me. He was *always* trying to get a rise out of me.

Freaking Niccolò Manganiello.

He'd been tormenting me from the moment he put a dead and road-flattened toad down my dress in Sunday school when I was four. Despite our mothers' close friendship and the time we spent playing together as children, my aggravation with him—and therefore avoidance of him—increased yearly.

In kindergarten, he cut one of my braids during naptime leaving me with long hair on the left and short hair on the right.

In third grade, he gave me what I thought was vanilla pudding but it turned out to be mayonnaise; of course I didn't realize it was mayonnaise until after I had a huge spoonful in my mouth and, of course, I couldn't spit it out because we were at his parents' restaurant for dinner. I still hated mayonnaise with an unholy fire.

In fifth grade, he gave me the nick name Skinny Finney, which stuck with me until college.

Worst of all, in sixth grade he became best friends with Garrett.

And through it all—the baiting when I was a kid and the persecution when I was a teenager—I couldn't seem to force myself to loath him like he'd apparently despised me.

I was so confused—his outburst at the hospital then later his apology followed by his request to be friends, and now his flirting with Sandra as well as the arrogant and flippant retorts. I had Nico-mood-swing whiplash.

I clenched my jaw and glanced over Nico's shoulder toward the door of the gym. I was officially flustered. I wanted to scream at him, indulge my instincts, give in to the spiteful verbal sparring match—as was our typical pattern. Instead I clamped my mouth shut.

I was determined to let the old habit die. I didn't want to be that person anymore.

My voice was a bit higher pitched than normal as I tried to literally and figuratively avoid the minefield of his last statement.

"Well, Sandra and I are going to head in, so…see you later."

I stepped to the side, hoping to walk around him, but he mirrored my movements, effectively causing me to collide into his chest. His hands lifted to my bare shoulders, and he held me in place. It was one of those moments where my body ceased listening to my brain.

My brain said, *Step away from the naughty hottie.*

My body said, *I like cookies.*

"Wait, where are you sitting?" He dipped his head such that only eight to six inches of air separated us, "Where's your table?"

Nothing is more frustrating than being attracted to someone who is a complete jerk—except for maybe also caring about that person despite continued abuses. I was such an idiot.

I cleared my throat, and my eyes—the traitors!—focused on his mouth. "We're, uh…."

Oh, my God, you smell fantastic.

"We're at table ten…I think," I stammered.

"You should sit with me—with us."

Sandra and I responded at the same time, talking over each other.

Me, shaking my head: "No, no, we're not supposed to switch tables, so…."

Sandra, nodding her head: "Yes, we'd love to. What table are you?"

Nico smiled warmly at Sandra. They both pretended I hadn't spoken. Matters weren't helped by his thumb dancing little sweeping caresses over the exposed skin of my shoulder, rendering me mute.

"I'm at table two, right next to the dance floor."

"Well then, we'll just see you inside." Sandra hooked her arm through mine, pulled me out of Nico's grip, and propelled me toward the gym. "But first we're going to go to the ladies room so we can talk about you."

The sound of Nico's laughter followed us only as far as the inside of the gym where it was swallowed by loud chatter and dance music.

Sandra leaned close to my ear and semi-shouted. "Where is the bathroom? Lucy! You have some *'splaining* to do."

I frowned—not at her, but at the entire situation—and pointed in the direction of the girls' locker rooms. She grabbed my hand and maneuvered us through the crowd. My carefully coiffed blonde waves tumbled over my shoulders in a messy mass.

No sooner were we inside did she open her mouth. I clamped my hand over it and with the other raised a finger to my mouth. Her eyes grew large and her eyebrows lifted. I motioned with my head toward the showers and silently asked her to follow.

Once we were tucked within the last stall in the last row, I closed the curtain then covered my face and breathed out forcefully.

"Please don't ask."

"Oh, girl, I'm gunna ask." She cut me off with a calm whisper. "And you're going to tell me, and you're going to describe every intimate detail—do they shave his chest? Because, on the show, he has no hair on his chest, and I think that must be because he is Italian. And what about his—"

"Stop. Please stop." I shook my head, my face still in my hands, and started to laugh. The sound was slightly frantic.

Sandra pulled my palms from my face and waited until I met her eyes. "Why are you so mortified about this? He is H-O-T hot. I would've thought you'd get T-shirts made that said *Yeah, I hit that.*"

"Oh, Sandra." I smile-frowned. "It's so complicated."

"Um, no it's not. It's simple, really. Nico Moretti—or Manganiello or whatever—still has the leg humpies for you."

I started laughing and shaking my head again. "No—it's not like that. He...he's...."

"No, girl, it is like that. It's *exactly* like that. I thought he was going to grab you by the hair and drag you away caveman style. Instead he manhandled you, just a little, and it was hot. I bet if we go to his table, he'll...."

"No, we can't do that. You don't understand. Nico was Garrett's best friend."

Sandra's mouth snapped shut and she blinked at me. "Wait...what?"

I couldn't believe this person was me. I was a grown woman, standing in a shower stall, whispering about high school drama. I didn't even do this when I *was* in high school.

I stepped back, leaned against the wall, and let my head fall against the tile. "Garrett and Nico were best friends."

"And you were..." Sandra lifted her eyebrows. "And you were the girl that came between them?"

"No. Not at all. Nico and I...we used to play together when we were kids, like, all the time. Our mothers were best friends, and he teased me *constantly*. But then my mom died the same year Garrett moved to town. The next year, by the time Garrett and Nico became friends, Nico hated me, and I didn't like him much either. He started all kinds of rumors about me when I was in middle school—just dumb kid stuff. He used to follow me down the hall whispering Skinny Finney—his nickname for me, by the way, which ended up being adopted by everyone."

"How did Garrett feel about this—about Nico's treatment of you?"

"Garrett would stand up for me. Sometimes they'd go weeks without talking to each other. Eventually, Nico would apologize, but always in front of Garrett. I knew he did it just for show. But I didn't want to be the reason Garrett and Nico fought. I always felt bad about it, like it was my fault."

"It wasn't your fault."

"I know, but I was an adolescent and I couldn't think of what to do, I didn't know how to process it, how to *not* overreact. But whenever we were in the same room together, it was like—I mean—we were always at each other's throats. I was shy with most people, but with Nico, I gave as good as I got. I was really mean. He was really mean. I couldn't stand him."

"Hmm...." Sandra tilted her head to the side, studying me. "You couldn't stand him?"

I looked up at the ceiling without really seeing it. What I saw was Nico next to Garrett's bed, the two of them playing their guitars. "That's not entirely true. I cared about him, about Nico. Even after—" I lifted my hands and motioned to the air around us. "—just everything. I mean, we grew up together. When we were kids it wasn't all bad. Sure, there was lots of teasing, but there were good times too, you know? And I thought he cared about me, as a friend, but the older we got the worse he became."

"You think he didn't care about you." It was a statement.

I nodded my confirmation. "How could he? How could he

possibly care about me and be so awful?"

"His treatment of you must have hurt."

"It did." I glared at her, didn't particularly like the fact that she was right, that it was still painful. I was a twenty-six-year-old adult whose feelings continued to be impacted by high school hurts. But, I supposed, that didn't make me any different than the rest of the general population.

Sandra sighed. "So, what happened? What changed?"

"When Garrett got sick, Nico and I started—we decided—to pretend to get along, to make things easier for Garrett. That year we took care of him—together. We didn't fight. And after Garrett died, Nico and I continued to hang out."

"Like go-see-a-movie hang out, or…?"

I tried to swallow again, but my throat was too dry. "He would climb into my bedroom window every night and hold me while I slept."

Sandra was exceptionally quiet; I couldn't even hear her breathe. I met her gaze and discovered that she'd turned into Shrink Sandra; she studied me with notes of detachment and supportive skepticism.

"Go on," said Shrink Sandra.

I didn't precisely know why but I did. "We—Nico and I—never spoke about it; not really. He just showed up one night at my window, and I let him in. He didn't say anything; he just hugged me and I cried, and then we lay down on the bed and I fell asleep. It was the first time I was able to sleep through the night since Garrett died."

I fiddled with the hem of my dress and recalled how it felt to wake up in Nico's arms. He had been watching me sleep. Just moments after I awoke, before I could form a coherent thought or thank him, he wordlessly kissed my forehead, extracted himself from my arms, and left the same way he came. That morning, after he left, I felt a measure of peace. I felt grateful.

But that night I wasn't able to sleep until he arrived.

"I think at first he came because he needed the comfort too. But then after a while I think he just felt sorry for me."

I stared past Sandra, remembering those months. I couldn't fall asleep unless he was there. If he was late, I would wait up for him. He was so warm and strong.

I began to resent Nico for having something I needed; I didn't like depending on him. I hated the fact that I started feeling something for him, this boy who'd tortured me in school, and only four months after Garrett had died. The thought of having feelings for someone was frightening enough without that person being Nico Manganiello.

But later, much later, I felt shame for taking him so completely for granted. I was a mess.

"How long did this go on?"

"Four months."

"And why did it stop?"

"I…" I took a steadying breath. "I can't believe I'm talking about this, in a shower stall, at my high school reunion."

Shrink Sandra's smile was warm but aloof. "Did you ask him to stop?"

"No." I shook my head. "I had sex with him. I lost my virginity…." It was hard to continue, mostly because I was going to admit out loud that I was a terrible person, but I forced the words past my tightening throat. "Then I went to Ireland for five months with my dad."

"How did he feel about you leaving?"

"I don't know."

"You didn't talk to him?"

"No. The week before, before the night we slept together, I told Nico I didn't want him coming to my room again. I didn't want him sleeping with me. I told him I was okay and that I didn't need him anymore."

"Because you started having feelings for him?" Sandra guessed.

I smirked at her mad-mind-reading skills and twisted the fabric of my skirt. "Because I started having feelings for him."

"And you never told him." Another statement.

I shook my head to confirm.

"Then you went to his house, climbed into his window, and—what—seduced him?"

I nodded my head to confirm.

"Why did you do that?"

I couldn't meet her eyes any longer. "Because I wanted to. I wanted my first time to be with someone I had feelings for. But I didn't care if he returned my feelings because I was being selfish. I used him."

Sandra sighed again. "Then what happened?"

"I left. I left him while he was asleep. When I was in Ireland, I sent back his letters unopened and didn't accept his calls. I cut him out."

Shrink Sandra studied me, assessing, frowning. I waited for her to point a finger in judgment or to shake her head in disappointment. Part of me wanted her to. I thought that maybe a good chastening might help me move past the guilt.

Instead, she asked another question. "What did he do when you came back? You finished your senior year here, right?"

"Yes. I was dreading seeing him. But when I came back, he'd dropped out of high school and moved to New York to become an underwear model."

"So, that night when you slept with him, was that the last time you saw him?"

I nodded, "Yes, well—yes, until last week." I glanced at my fingers. "You remember that he was the celebrity at the hospital last week that everyone was freaking out about. His niece might qualify for a clinical trial."

"And how did he behave when he saw you?"

"Sandra…." I glared at her. I didn't want to talk about it. I didn't want to discuss how he'd been able to fluster and disarm me so effectively eleven years after my monumental mistake. He was a big, old, gaping hole in my armor, and I didn't like thinking about him let alone discussing him.

"Elizabeth." Her eyes narrowed as well.

All it took was narrowed eyes and the inflection of her shrink voice.

"I don't know." I tried to be evasive and honest at the same time. "He was—I guess he was kind of hostile. Then, later, he apologized. He asked me to be friends."

"He asked you to be friends?"

"Yes. It was very surreal."

"I can imagine." She nodded slowly for a full ten seconds, still watching me through narrowed eyes. Then, Shrink Sandra was gone and she said, "Okay then. It's *High School Musical* time."

"What?"

"Well, we're not going to stay in here all night. I came here to dance and watch you make awkward conversation with your old classmates. I'm going to dance." She grabbed my hand and led me out of the shower.

The abrupt switch in topics gave me Sandra-personality-conversation whiplash. "But…but I can't—I can't…." with every thump of my heart it rose higher in my throat. "I can't go out there."

"Yes, you can." She grinned over her shoulder. "And we're going to sit with *the Face*."

~*~*~*~

I didn't notice much about my surroundings as we wound through the tables to the one nearest the dance floor. I was too busy chiding myself for being an idiot. This was something I used to do a lot when I was younger and really an idiot. All my blustery intentions of stunning everyone felt ridiculous and insipid, because they were.

Because I was.

I was ridiculous and insipid.

I decided that all plans for vapid high school maneuvers were to be abandoned ASAP. I felt both better and lost. With no plan, I wasn't quite sure what to do.

Hoping that this part of my personality—perhaps like most people—was regulated only to situations involving high school, I made a silent pledge to redouble my efforts to be brave, honest, and self-effacing.

This would be difficult.

Every person clustered around Nico's table was aiming stares with toxic intent in our general direction. Well, almost everyone. Well, all the women.

Regardless, Sandra approached with the confidence of one who is certain to be welcomed. She sauntered right up, placed my nametag at an empty seat, and hooked her bag on the back of a chair.

Nico was standing at a different table nearby leaning close to a tall blonde. I recognized her as one of his on again, off again high school girlfriends, Shelly Martin. She was mostly in profile. He whispered something in her ear that made her laugh. It wasn't a forced laugh. It was genuine and contagious. People in their sphere were attempting to lean closer to be part of the conversation, pressing themselves into his space.

I was reminded that he was irresistible to just about everyone.

"Okay then—start introducing me to people." Sandra grinned, her eyes dancing around the crowd.

I grimaced at the thought, but feeling strangely better now that my sins had been confessed and my foolhardy plan abandoned, I surveyed the room. My gaze landed on a boy from my sophomore trigonometry class who I'd despised: Brace Wilson. He was on the swim team, and he barely kept up the grades required to be a top athlete. He always tried to look over my shoulder during tests and frequently asked to copy my homework.

Swallowing my pride I marched over to where he stood with a woman I assumed was his date. I decided that now was a good time to practice redoubling my efforts to be brave, honest, and self-effacing.

"Hi, Brace—" I paused a beat, giving him time to identify me, and then I stuck out my hand. "It's good to see you again."

Brown studied my face with teetering recognition. "Oh, hi…uh…."

"I'm Elizabeth—but you probably remember me as Skinny Finney." I smiled.

His eyes grew several sizes. "Oh, yeah. I remember you—we were in math together." To my complete astonishment, he hugged me. "You were so nice." Brace released me, but he kept a hand on my shoulder as he turned to the woman at his arm and said, "She used to let me copy her homework. Finney is the reason I didn't fail that class."

The woman's eyes were warm and friendly. "He is still terrible at math. I'm Belinda."

I shook hands with Belinda, introduced Sandra, and then found myself engaged in an easy conversation with Brace and Belinda.

They were married. Brace joined the army after high school then left after four tours in Iraq. He now drove semi-trucks. Belinda was a nurse. She was pregnant with their first child.

Soon our foursome was joined by more members of the swim team. Sandra was flirting with a local farmer while I was reacquainting myself with people I used to hate but now couldn't remember why. I was talking to Daniel—the class valedictorian, now a software engineer in Palo Alto with three kids and one more on the way—when I felt a warm hand close around my upper arm.

I turned toward the owner and found Nico standing next to me, studying me.

A hush fell over our small group, and Nico's attention drifted from me to the rest of the faces. All eyes were on him. Everyone was smiling expectantly, eagerly. No one said anything.

It was eerie—like, now that Nico was there, he was expected to provide witty conversation and entertainment.

Dance, monkey, dance.

"Hi, everybody."

"Hi, Nico." In unison.

"Is everyone having a good time?"

"Yes." In unison.

I frowned at Sandra, looking for someone with whom to share unspoken communication, but found her to be under the same spell as the rest of the group. My frown deepened.

"I was hoping someone could tell me how I got here."

Crowd: *Grin, grin, grin.*

"I mean, one minute I'm in New York eating a hot dog and holding a brunette," then, as though speaking only to himself, "or was that holding a hot dog and eating a brunette…."

Nico: Comedic pause.

Crowd: *Chuckle, chuckle, chuckle.*

Nico: Head shake.

"And the next minute," he slid his arms around my waist, and pulled me back to his chest, "I'm in Iowa holding a blonde, but I'm still hungry."

His hands moved with familiarity, resting on my stomach. If he'd been anyone else, I would have stepped out of the embrace, but for some reason, he seemed to have all of us under some kind of hex or enchantment or voodoo mojo.

My brain told me it was the celebrity cloud. My heart told me it was just Nico being Nico.

"What I really want to know is…" He leaned close to my ear

and glanced over my shoulder; I could tell he was looking down the front of my dress. "…what happened to the hot dog?"

Crowd: *Laugh, laugh, laugh.*

It wasn't what he said so much as how he said it. He possessed showmanship, swagger, confidence, and just the right shade of weirdly laudable chauvinism.

I was just a prop. I felt my face flame, and I tried to step out of his arms.

"Whoa—you're not going anywhere until you return my hot dog."

"That's what she said," Sandra supplied, indicating her chin toward me, and the whole group roared with laughter.

I felt the reverberations of Nico's laugh at my back and knew his intent before he turned me to face him. He didn't look at me as he tucked me under his arm and led me away from the group. They all seemed satisfied with his little performance and happy to have basked in his witty banter, even for a short time.

I clenched my jaw and willed my feet to stop.

Brain: *Stop, feet.*

Feet: *I like cookies.*

My feet kept moving.

I was equal parts mortified, annoyed, and confused. Nico's hold on me was not entirely related to the strong arm over my shoulders. Nonsensically, I knew I still felt guilty about my behavior as a sixteen-year-old, and due to years and mountains of remorse, I felt indebted to him. I felt I owed him.

I hated it.

So I allowed myself to be led past his table to the dance floor just as the first notes of *True* by Spandau Ballet drifted out of the speakers. I struggled against an eye roll.

I was slow dancing in my high school gym with the most popular guy in school, and suddenly I felt like the protagonist in a 1980s Jon Hughes movie.

CHAPTER 6

Nico placed my hands behind his neck and skimmed his long fingers down my bare arms to my waist, sending shivers and goose bumps racing over my skin. He pressed my body to his tall, lean form, and we swayed to the music.

I swallowed.

He smiled at me. It was an irresponsible, dreamy, devastating sex-on-a-stick smile.

I swallowed again.

Nico was a good dancer. I never danced with him while we were in school, but I remembered watching him dance with other girls at homecoming or at our high school prom. He was one of those guys whose rhythm and corresponding movements fused effortlessly with the music, as if the music took its cue from him and not the other way around.

I was at a loss. Part of me—the part that endured a half decade of merciless teasing—wanted to glance around the room and feign boredom. Another part of me—the part that was held every night for four months—wanted him to hold me close, stroke my back, and tell me I was forgiven for treating him so shamefully.

Both parts were trapped in the quicksand of his gaze and the web of his body. He seemed content simply to look at me. We traded stares for several long moments. I felt hot.

One of us *needed* to say something, and I realized it wasn't going to be him. I tried to think of something to talk about but felt every topic was a minefield of either innuendo or historical baggage. I finally settled on something most people would want to know.

I cleared my throat before I said, "So, your show."

He blinked at me, almost as though my voice startled him, then his lips twitched. "My show."

I cleared my throat again. "Well…how is your show?"

"I thought you didn't watch it."

"I don't."

"Then why do you want to talk about it?" His twitching lips turned into a small, challenging smile.

"I don't watch it, but I know *of* it." I cleared my throat for a third time. "It's hard not to know of it, what with all the stripping of celebrities and objectifying of women."

His grin grew rueful. "So, you haven't watched, but you're ready to judge it?" He nodded with exaggeration. "That makes sense."

"Aren't you even a little ashamed?"

"There is nothing wrong with the show." His hand slid from my side to the center of my back as though to hold me in place.

"You don't think there is anything wrong with objectifying women?"

"I don't objectify women."

"Your show does."

"I disagree." He said.

"So—bikini models wrestling each other in tubs of Jell-O…?" I lifted my eyebrows and waited for him to concede. "What is the definition of female objectification then?"

"There is nothing wrong with men looking at or appreciating beautiful women." His eyes swept over me. I ignored the implication and successfully suppressed the rising heat that accompanied it.

"There is. There is when being looked at is a woman's sole purpose."

"You mean like art?"

I scoff-snorted. "You're comparing your show to art?"

"Yes…and no. The women on my show are definitely comparable to art. I admit there is a wrong way and a right way to do things. I feel like my show does things the right way."

"It must be hard for you to work in an industry where there is so much confusion about what is *porn* and what is art." I smiled sweetly at him.

"Yes, well—" an edge was discernible in his voice, which told me he was not pleased with my comparison, "—it must be hard for you to work in an industry where the fundamentals are based on Nazi research, leeches, and bleeding people."

I stiffened and stumbled, but he countered my misstep flawlessly and held me tighter. His eyes glowed.

It felt just like old times. We were teenagers again engaging in a game of spitefulness. I hated it.

"You're right." I deadpanned. "It really is a worthless, ignoble profession."

"No." His hand resettled on my back and he lifted his chin; his soulful eyes focused on me, intent and earnest. "It's a very noble profession. It suits you well."

My blush of embarrassment was annoying and immediate. I couldn't respond to his compliment with a cutting remark, so I just stared at him. We traded stares again for several long moments. I felt hot—once again—and an irrepressible urge to say something. It needed to be nice, damn it.

I didn't like that he'd had the last word, and it was a nice last word, and he was—therefore—kinder, more forgiving, and more mature than I was. I wrinkled my nose at the ridiculous thought but was powerless against it.

I wanted to be the nice one.

I wanted to show him that I was just as ambivalent to him and our past together as he seemed to be. I was a grown up. I was mature. I had on my big girl fancy panties. I could be the better person, even if it killed me.

I bit my tongue to stall my words because I wasn't sure what they would be. I only knew they would be honest and nice and, honestly, that combination scared me. I also knew whatever came out would be an attempt at nice-one-upmanship, which meant I would likely compliment—

"You are very funny," I finally said.

Nico frowned and flinched slightly. His hand loosened on my back. "I wasn't being funny; I was being serious."

I nodded. "Oh, I know. I believe you—what you said. It was very nice. Thank you." I cleared my throat for the eight thousandth time. I really was going to have to get something to drink, like maybe vodka. "And I meant what I said. You are very funny. You're a funny…person."

His eyes narrowed, and he studied me through dark lashes. "Ok."

"I mean it."

"Ok."

"No, really. I may not watch your show, but—" I took a deep breath. I was going to admit to something I had no intention of admitting to anyone, ever. "—but I may have seen or caught part of—well, it was on while I was walking by—your standup special…thing…." Finally, I huffed and just owned it. "I saw your New York to LA standup special on HBO last year. It was funny. I laughed."

The truth was I ordered HBO for the month when I learned he was going to have a standup special. I couldn't wait for it to come out on DVD or Blu-ray; but I would *never* tell him that. I was officially ridiculous.

His stare and expression betrayed befuddled amusement as I struggled to speak; then, finally, comprehension and something like smug satisfaction. It was in his smile, the way he stood a little taller, the twinkle in his eye.

"What was your favorite bit?"

"The one about universally funny concepts."

He waited then prompted, "Specifically…?"

My jaw flexed. "Specifically about interpretive dance and synchronized swimming, about how synchronized swimming is funny if attempted by anyone but a professional, and then you paired it with interpretive dance. I like how you...you're just a very physical comedian, and it was funny." I rolled my eyes again. "Don't get a big head about it."

"Too late. Dr. Finney thinks I'm funny."

I warred bravely against my own grin. "I saw it in the middle of the night after a long shift."

I used to watch it in the middle of the night after my long shifts.

"But when I remember this conversation later, I'll tell myself that you watch it every night before you go to bed." His voice was both teasing and intimate.

"Whatever." I shook my head and turned my face away, but I saw nothing because he was everywhere I looked. "Believe what you want."

Leisurely, Nico brushed his soft beard against my cheek then dipped his mouth to my ear and nuzzled the space beneath it, his hot breath on my neck as he whispered, "There's nothing wrong with having fun."

His movements and words caused an electrical shock of awareness to course from the tip of my head to the center of my belly.

I jerked away, glared at him. "I know that."

"Do you?" He smirked, his fingers flexing on my back as he held me tighter. "When is the last time you had fun?"

"Last Tuesday."

"Oh, yeah? What did you do?"

"I went to my...knitting...group." I realized, just as the words left my mouth, how lame and sedate that sounded. He probably pictured me sitting in a reindeer sweater drinking tepid peach and mango tea while exchanging cocktail recipes...*doh.*

Non-knitters just didn't understand the dynamics of a knitting group. It wasn't just a good time or a fun time; it was the best time.

"O-o-o-oh, ok. I didn't realize that you are part of a knitting circle. I stand corrected." His smirk intensified; it was an intensa-smirk, and his eyes glowed with plain enjoyment at my expense. "You have fun scheduled for every Tuesday night."

I glowered at him. "It's not like that."

"Then tell me about it."

We engaged in a staring contest for several stanzas of the song—a whisper of a smile on his features, a frustrated glower on mine.

I felt the need to escape his eyes and run from the room.

My hands moved from his neck to his chest and pushed against him. Before I could move even an inch he covered one of my hands and pressed it to his heart. His other hand pressed into my back and held me in place.

"The song is almost over." His expression turned serious, his eyes beseeching, his body tense. "Stay with me."

Stay with me.

Nico's words set off a gathering thickness in my throat. I could only press my mouth into a line and nod.

Stay with me—it was what I said to him the first night, the first time he climbed into my window, the first time he held me while I slept—and then every night thereafter.

I wondered if he remembered. I wondered if that was why he said it. It didn't matter; not really. The song would be over and he would walk away, and Sandra and I would go back to the farmhouse, and I would try to forget this dance ever happened.

He pulled me closer and held me tighter, his chin against my temple as his hand held mine over his heart in a firm grip, his other hand and arm completely wrapped around my middle. He was holding me as we danced.

The once-habitual feelings of familiarity and the sentiments of comfort, safety, and serenity were now laced with confusion, uncertainty, and anticipation. Most troubling was how good he felt, and how my body curved and bent and molded to his without my consent. These sensations reminded me of the last time we'd held each other.

These feelings, and the fact that he would never return the sentiments, were why I'd left him.

Ending notes of the song filtered through the speakers, but I heard nothing. I was immersed in Nico quicksand and sinking deeper with every beat of his heart as it thudded against me with masculine urgency. I blinked against a perplexing stinging in my eyes.

Then, Beyonce sang, "I'm feelin' *sexy*," and I was promptly yanked out of my vortex of warm and fuzzy Nico quicksand.

There were a number of contributing factors to my rude awakening, and they occurred all at once:

The tempo of the music escalated from slowmo *True* to the substantively more upbeat *Naughty Girl*.

Three women appeared out of nowhere—or rather, what felt like nowhere in that moment—and surrounded us.

Two of the women grabbed Nico's arms.

One of the women said very loudly and very close to my ear, "Come on, Nico– we want to dance!"

Nico, looking a bit stunned, turned toward the very loud woman, and I was forced to step back; the group of three was hip gyrating, arm waving, and hair flinging with wild abandon. I lifted my own arms to protect against incidental bodily injury and glanced around the room. I was startled back to reality when I realized that Nico and I were in a room full of people. For the past several minutes, it had seemed as though he and I were alone.

I scanned the perimeter of the dance floor looking for Sandra. My eyes met those of a tall, brown-haired man that I didn't recognize; he was watching me openly. Disconcerted, I glanced to his left and met the gaze of a medium-sized woman—also watching me. It was at that point I realized everyone in the room who was not currently dancing—and even some who were—was blatantly watching me. It didn't seem to occur to them that openly watching a person was strange.

Someone pinched my elbow and I turned to find Sandra at my side. She was shaking her booty. Next to her was a man I almost recognized, and he was booty shaking with the best of them. She flung a toothy smile at my frowning face and leaned into my ear.

"Hey—you remember this guy?" Sandra indicated with her thumb toward her dance partner. "He said you two were lab partners in biology."

I brought the tall semi-stranger back into focus, and once my brain started working again, I was surprised that I could confirm he was indeed Micah Becker. "Yes—oh, my gosh, hey, Micah—nice to see you."

I extended my hand to him and he gave me a lopsided grin. He accepted my hand and—instead of shaking it—he twirled me. "Elizabeth, it's so good to see you—I didn't recognize you until Sandra told me who you were."

"Oh—" I stumbled through the twirl then, once I was certain I wouldn't trip, and then I gave his hand a firm shake and released it. "Good to see you too! You look a lot different…also."

I didn't really remember much about Micah because we'd barely spoken during high school. He'd been even quieter than I was. I remembered that he wore flannel shirts every day with jeans and Doc Martens. His hair had been a buzz cut in high school, and his blue eyes had always been hidden behind large glasses.

Now his black hair was stylishly cut, his blue eyes were no longer concealed, and he stood a good six inches taller. The dress shirt he wore, although not as fine as Nico's, clearly signaled that he had a decent body. In fact, I could barely see the seventeen-year-old kid in the booty-shaking man before me.

"Dance, girl." Sandra bumped her hip against mine and smiled at Micah. "Do you think you can handle both of us?"

Micah turned his smiling blue eyes to Sandra. "No—I'm pretty sure I can't, but I'd like to try."

My mouth dropped open. *Who is this person?*

This was not the Micah I knew. This Micah was confident and sorta handsome. It's amazing what ten years and nice clothes can do for a person.

Or, maybe more precisely, it's amazing what maturity and adulthood can do for a person.

Sandra threw her head back in laughter and grabbed my hand as she encouraged me to dance. I complied, a little dazed at first, still feeling lingering gazes from the crowd. I kept my eyes on Sandra and Micah and the floor, because every time I glanced around the room, I found people watching me.

However, without any conscious intent to do so, my gaze eventually sought Nico. He was still surrounded on all sides by women wielding sharpened elbows. Instead of just the three, he'd amassed six or seven, and he was smiling at them, all of them. But it didn't look like a welcoming smile; it looked like a beleaguered, pacifying smile.

They had him cornered on one side of the dance floor, and I noticed his movements were somewhat restricted; the pack of she-wolves appeared to be pressing in on his personal space with increased audaciousness. Their slutty one-up(wo)manship made me inwardly cringe and outwardly chuckle.

Micah stepped into my line of sight and grinned at me; I grinned back. He reached for my hands and I allowed him to turn my back to his front, with Sandra behind him. We made a Sandra, Micah, Elizabeth sandwich.

He was a pretty good dancer—not as good as Nico, but still decent—and I permitted him to place a hand on my hip as we continued our booty-shaking good time. We turned and I was facing Micah's back, Sandra at his front, which—once again—allowed me a pretty good view of Nico's harem.

I expected to get another chuckle from the she-wolf antics but instead felt a bolt of fury. Nico was now surrounded by at least fifteen women, two of whom were pulling his shirt from his pants; he'd grabbed their wrists. He was no longer smiling. He did not look amused.

Before I fully comprehended my intent, I was across the dance floor like a shot. I used no subtlety to push through the crowd of crazed women. I innately know that I could (wo)manhandle these females in a way that he could not —with hair pulling and scratching and smacking and eye poking.

There were a few exclamations of "Hey!" and "Ow!" and "What the…?" and "My foot!" and "That's my eye!"

I ignored their screechy protests, but—despite my aggressive attempts—an impenetrable barrier remained. Through the crush of bodies, I could see that more women had placed their hands on him, squeezing his bottom and+ grabbing his tie. They'd tugged his jacket back by the collar in an attempt to pull it off.

The dark frown marring his features mirrored my own.

"Get the hell off of him!" Frustration made my hands shake.

Only one woman seemed to hear my shouted command, and she merely smirked at me.

I glanced around the room expecting to see other outraged faces and was astonished to find—among those who were paying attention to the spectacle—only expressions of amusement. One person even had his phone out and was apparently either recording or taking pictures. I thought about asking Sandra and Micah for help, but before I could turn, I witnessed one of the women snake her hand around and try to grab Nico in the crotch.

His dark frown turned furious. He looked murderous.

I gasped. I struggled to find words that would make them stop before he used physical violence on them, and chaos descended.

I needed to do something shocking, something no one could ignore. I could only think of one thing.

I found the nearest chair, climbed on top, and yelled at the top of my lungs, "THE CHILD IS YOURS!"

Everything stopped.

Well, the music continued, but everything else stopped. Everyone was looking at me, including the pile of grabby females—and Nico.

I took a deep breath. His gaze tangled with mine, and I saw the precise moment that he comprehended my words. Before I lost the crowd's attention, I climbed from the chair and charged through the circle of still stunned women.

I grasped Nico's wrist and pulled him through the parted red lipstick sea. I marched him off the dance floor. He gently slid his wrist out of my grasp then enclosed my hand in his. I didn't know where to go. He must have sensed my hesitation because he soon took the lead and his pace immediately quickened.

We were nearly running when he pushed through the double doors that led outside. Darkness and cold wind greeted us. My teeth chattered, but I didn't know if it was from the cold or the aftereffect of adrenaline from my outburst.

His long steps carried us to the football stadium. Nico easily found the spot where we could squeeze through. The passage led to the hollow space beneath the bleachers, and the wind died as we entered the manmade cavern. Soda cups, water bottles, and napkins littered the dirt.

Nico paused just inside and glanced at me. He withdrew his hand, slipped off his jacket, and placed it over my shoulders. I watched him as he did this, his face illuminated only by horizontal bands of light shining through the bleachers from the full moon and the quilt of stars overhead. His eyes searched mine as he tugged the collar of his jacket and we stood in silence, starting at each other.

He looked expectant, tense, agitated.

His gaze drifted to my lips. He licked his.

The small movement made my heart race, and I broke the

silence with a rush of words. "God—that was crazy! Those women were completely crazy." For no reason at all, I hit him on his shoulder. "Why don't you have security guards?"

"Elizabeth." He swallowed the end of my name. "Do you…did we…do you have something to tell me?"

"Yes. You need to hire yourself some security." I nodded at the assertion. "I don't think those women were going to stop until they had you naked—"

He closed his eyes briefly, shook his head, and interrupted me. "Forget about that—what about the child?"

"The child?" I frowned at him. "Nico…there is no child. I said that so those psychos would back off."

He blinked at me and seemed to be holding his breath; his eyes were impossibly large. He released the lapels of the jacket and took a step back.

"There is no child." He sounded skeptical and surprisingly angry.

"Of course there is no child. I was trying to keep twenty crazy females from tearing your clothes off." I straightened my dress needlessly before adding. "You're welcome, by the way."

His voice rose and he tucked his shirt back into his pants with jerky movements. "Then why didn't you yell 'FIRE'—or, 'Look—the aliens are here!' —anything else that wouldn't have given me a heart attack! Why did you yell 'the child is yours'?"

The vehemence and volume of his voice took me by surprise. I didn't respond immediately, but when I did, I tried to sound soothing and calm. "It's illegal to yell 'fire' in a crowded room. I didn't want them to freak out. I just wanted them to stop—"

He turned away. He stuffed his fists into his pants pockets and stomped to the slanted wall created by the bleachers. He turned. He glared at some unknown spot beyond the slats.

"I didn't think…I wasn't trying to—did I—did I embarrass you?" I thought I might suffocate on guilt.

"No. I wasn't embarrassed at all. It's just, for a minute I thought...." He shook his head as though to clear it. In the shadow and half-light of the moon, face in profile, his features appeared as though carved from granite. I allowed myself to look at him and really see him. He looked tired. In school, when I knew him, he never looked tired. He'd been bursting with restless, aimless, infectious, enigmatic energy.

As an adult, I was discovering that he radiated a level of magnetism that was difficult to ignore, but it felt more controlled, directed, harnessed. The effect was potent and heady when he focused the laser beam of charisma on a single person, as he'd done with me earlier.

Nico stirred and crossed the space with measured steps until he was just inches from me, his attention focused on the dirt at his feet. "If there is a child, then I want you to know that we would get married."

It took me a moment to comprehend his words; when I did, I choked, "What?"

"I will marry you...."

"What is this, the nineteen fifties? Are you for real? Are you seriously...?" I released an exasperated sigh then rubbed my forehead with cold fingers. "No. We would not get married, and there is no child, so there is no reason to have this conversation."

"Yes. Yes, we would get married. I could move to Chicago."

"Oh, my god, no. We would not. Your show is in New York. Why would you move to Chicago?"

"I could move the show for a few years. We could always go back to New York, or even LA, if you wanted to." He made it sound like it was all so obvious, like I was an idiot. He'd always done this to me.

I pointed at his chest. "This is so typically you, Nico—male chauvinism with a truck load of arrogance."

"It's not arrogant to want to take care of my family."

"We are not your family. You don't even know me, and the child would be ten by now and likely—GAH!" I threw my hands in the air, determined to end this ridiculous, pointless argument before we started picking out china patterns and debated the merits of Le Creuset bakeware. "I don't know why we're discussing this. We're not getting married, and THERE IS NO CHILD."

A muscle ticked at Nico's temple; his jaw flexed. He was silent for a moment, and then said, "We would talk about it."

I blinked at him, momentarily speechless, then found the words. "You are an insane person. You were just assaulted by a group of raging female horn dogs, and all you want to do is argue with me about a theoretical marriage and a non-existent child. You need to get a grip."

Nico shifted a step away. He returned his gaze to the dirt and released an audibly shaky breath. "Damn."

I studied him for a moment. He appeared to be genuinely upset, and it occurred to me that perhaps the groping from earlier had truly affected him. Instinctively, I touched him on the elbow then withdrew my hand. "Hey, hey…are you ok? Those women really were crazy, and they had no right to touch you like that."

He nodded; his eyes met mine for an instant then darted away. "Yeah. I'm fine. I've had worse."

"Worse?"

"Groping."

"Oh." For some reason, the thought of women, or men, groping Nico made me want to shoot a machine gun. "How much worse?"

I didn't know what possessed me to ask the question; I was obviously an anger-masochist.

"Well," he gathered a slow, deep breath; his chest visibly expanded before he said, "a few years ago, I was charged with assault when three women in a club stuck their hands down my pants."

I choked on my own breath. "Wait—what? Why were *you*

charged with assault?"

He appeared to be stalling, as though struggling to avoid telling me something unpleasant. "I elbowed one of them in the face and broke her nose." He swallowed and didn't precisely roll his eyes. "It was an accident."

My eyebrows shot upwards. "Were you convicted?"

"No, but she won a civil suit."

"What a freak."

"She's crazy."

The comment, seemingly offhand, sounded strangely meaningful and loaded, especially because he said she *is* crazy, not was. "How crazy?"

He wiped a hand over his face. "She actually…she's a bit of a stalker."

"A stalker? You have a stalker?"

Nico grimaced, obviously uncomfortable discussing the subject. His tone was flat. "She hasn't attacked me, but she has…."

"Except for sticking her hand down your pants."

"Mostly she sends a lot of hate mail."

My mouth dropped open. "Your stalker sends you hate mail?"

He shrugged as if it was no big deal.

"Only you would have a stalker that sends hate mail. Is that why you just stood there tonight instead of tossing those crazy ladies off of you?"

Nico kicked a soda cup to one side.

Just when I thought he wasn't going to respond, he said, "I wanted to, believe me I did, but I don't hit women."

I studied him; his expression was stern, and he was seemingly unwilling to say anything further, as though that were explanation enough for not administering a smackdown on the pack of she-wolves.

I studied him as I brought the sleeves of his jacket to my cold nose and breathed into them to warm it. His jacket smelled like him—his expensive cologne and light traces of cigarette smoke and mint—and, of course, the headiness of the scent aggravated my muddled mind even more.

I loved the smell of his cologne; I hated the smell of cigarette smoke; the mint was unexpected, and I didn't know how to feel about it.

"I'm going to have to insist that you hire some security to deal with the nutters, especially the hate mail whack-job."

"I have. I do."

"Where are they tonight?"

"They were there."

"What the…? You should fire those assho—er—clowns. Or I can do it if you want."

He did meet my eyes then, and his mouth was curved in a quizzical smile. "You want to fire my guards?"

"Yes." I answered honestly.

I enjoyed firing people when they were bad at their jobs. It felt somehow satisfying to be the angel of darkness, the necessary evil, the harbinger of doom. Someone needed to do it, and I didn't mind dirty jobs.

"No, that's ok." His smile grew but the bemused expression remained. "But thank you for the offer. It's…it's hard finding a good team. I like my privacy, and security guards know all your business whether you like it or not. I'll just call the agency and get new ones."

I glanced at my feet and considered the scene on the dance floor and my reaction to it. What bothered me almost more than the grabby ladies were all the people who witnessed what was happening and just stared and did nothing, like it was ok for Nico to be groped without his consent.

What a bunch of freaks.

"I will do it, you know. I will fire them for you if you want."

"I know you will. But I don't want to have to find another trustworthy agency."

"You're going with the same agency?" I shifted on my feet, bracing them apart. "Why do you think the next team they put on you will be any better? You should go with a different agency."

Nico's eyes narrowed, a smile dancing over his expression. "You're just as bossy as I remember."

I echoed his narrowed eyes, but not his smile. "I'm not bossy. I've never been bossy. I'm just always right."

"Not always."

"Mostly always."

Then, he laughed. It started as a small burst of laughter that turned into a tumbling landslide. It rolled over me and did lovely things to my stomach. I felt lighter and heavier at the same time. I brought his jacket sleeves back to my nose to hide the curve of my mouth.

His display of merriment receded, leaving him with shining eyes and a wide smile; his teeth looked stark white, likely due to the dark beard framing his mouth. I liked his beard. It made him look a little wild.

"Ah…Elizabeth." He shook his head then lolled it to one side, his eyes moved over my face. "I've missed you."

"How could you miss me? This is the longest civil conversation we've had since I was four."

"I even miss our conversations that were arguments."

"They were all arguments."

"Not all of them."

"You're right—sometimes we didn't talk."

"I miss those times the most."

His open appraisal and direct manner were confusing; I didn't know if he was being sardonic or sincere. I never could tell with him, so I always erred on the side of caution. I decided to rebuff his maybe praise with sarcasm. "You're just saying that because moments ago I was the Kevin Costner to your Whitney Houston."

"And I will always love you," Nico said.

The sound I made was part snort, part laugh as I faced him. "Yeah right, you're hilarious…." but the words caught in my throat as I met his gaze.

He was staring at me solemnly with no hint of sarcasm and no twinkle of mischief. In fact, his eyes were devoid of twinkle. The twinkle had been replaced by a cool heat that felt like a bucket of ice over my head.

"I, uh…." I took an automatic and unsteady step backward, and my heart felt as if it would escape my chest.

"Elizabeth." He shifted on his feet then braced them apart; his eyes moved to my mouth. Nico energy filled the expansive cavern of bleachers. I heard buzzing in my ears.

"I need to tell you…."

ALERT ALERT ALERT!

"Can it wait? Because—because I basically left Sandra in a room full of crazy strangers." I gained a step backward, then another.

I was out of practice. Avoidance, like any skill, required practice. My excuse for avoiding him and the next words out of my mouth sounded lame even to me. Nico opened his mouth to respond, but I'd already turned and was walking quickly toward the opening.

"We've seen what they're capable of—I should go get her," I called over my shoulder.

After a short delay on his part, which afforded me a head start, I heard Nico's footfalls follow. I quickened my pace until I was nearly running and didn't stop until I reached the front of the main building.

Nico's steps were just behind me; an anxiety riddled, warning, electric shiver raced up my spine as I grabbed the door handle to the main entrance and yanked it open.

"Elizabeth, wait!" Nico called from just behind me.

"Elizabeth, hey," Sandra called from just in front of me.

"Sandra!" I bounded into the safety of her sphere, relieved, anxious, and wanting to leave this epic confusion of a high school reunion as soon as humanly possible.

Nico caught my arm and spun me to face him. "Will you just wait a minute?" His expression, if I were reading it correctly, was a mixture of hope and hurt. It knocked the wind from my lungs.

"There you are." Sandra's voice, then hand on my arm, pulled me away from Nico's soulful expression. The rescue was not a moment too soon. His eyes were a black hole, and I felt myself being stretched until I thought I would break.

I blinked at her, at the room, at life in general. I blinked against the tight feeling in my middle. I blinked against the burning sensation of Nico's stare; I could still feel it moving over my face.

I gripped her hand like a lifeline. "Here I am." I hoped she read the SOS clearly on my features.

"I was looking for you," she said. "I wondered if...." She glanced between Nico and me, her pleasant expression becoming somewhat perplexed, but no less pleasant. "I wondered if you would...."

"Yes. We should go." I nodded.

She released a breathy laugh. "No, I meant, Micah and I—"

"I shouldn't have left." I interrupted her and pulled my arm from Nico's grip. "Let me just get my purse."

Before I could make my escape, Nico stepped into my path.

"Wait—"

My heart thump, picking up pace with his words. I fought against the urge to close my eyes, cover my ears, and say, "La la la, I can't hear you!" in a singsong voice.

I settled for not meeting his gaze as he sighed then continued. "Before you leave, I promised my mom, I promised Rose, that I would invite you to breakfast at the restaurant tomorrow.

Obviously, you're both invited."

Again, Sandra and I spoke at the same time.

Me: "Oh, no, we need to get an early start back...."

Her: "Oh, yes, we'd love to. We don't have to be back 'til late. What time should we be there?"

I cringed. I noted that she was smiling.

Again, as though I hadn't spoken at all, Nico addressed Sandra. "That's great. I'll tell her to expect you both around, say, ten?"

I didn't even attempt to contradict but instead allowed Sandra to nod vigorously. "Yeah—yes, we'll be there at ten."

"Good." He said. I felt him hesitate for a moment before taking a step back and out of my path. "See you then."

Sandra beamed at him. He lingered. I knew he was looking at me, but coward that I was, I just couldn't meet his gaze. One more painfully long second passed then he walked around us and back toward the gym. I waited until I was sure he was gone, and then I led Sandra by the hand in the direction of Micah. He was waiting for her at the edge of the hall.

"You can loosen your grip on my hand now before you break something."

"Oh." I immediately released Sandra's hand and rubbed my suddenly sweaty palm against my skirt.

"What did I interrupt between you two?" Sandra handed me my purse.

"What? Nothing. Nothing is going on." The words were a little too loud, a little too fast, a little too false. I was out of breath and recognized that it had very little to do with my spurt of exercise.

"Ri-i-i-ight...anyway...." Sandra leaned closer to my ear. "Micah wanted to get out of here and get a drink. I was thinking of going with him, but after that outburst of yours, and now that I know you were trying to escape naughty Nico, I'll just blow off Micah."

I shook my head. "No, you should go. I'm good. I'll just head back to the house and take advantage of this very rare sleep opportunity."

Sandra wrinkled her nose and brought us to a halt. "I'm staying with you."

"You came with me to see the world's largest truck stop, and I couldn't even make that happen. Go with Micah. I'm just going to go to sleep when I get home."

She wasn't convinced. "Are you sure?"

I could tell she didn't believe me, so I decided to yawn for good measure. "Yeah." *Big yawn.* "Yes. Now go and have a good time."

Sandra reached for and squeezed my hand. She gave me one last scrutinizing gaze before she left to join Micah.

As soon as she turned, I bolted for the door, not wanting to give her an opportunity to change her mind, not wanting to interact with any more of my high school acquaintances, and not wanting to chance another interaction with Nico.

CHAPTER 7

Boy bands are sent by God to aid women of all ages in their quest to avoid reality, but specifically to trick young women into believing that males think about topics other than sex.

When I listen to boy bands at a loud volume, I can almost forget about stress, sadness, life and death, and the unfairness of both. The innocence lures me into a superficial, cotton candy world, and it feels so good to be mindless, worriless, unburdened, new, and blissfully ignorant.

Bursting into the front door of my childhood home, my shoes came off first, then my dress. I left both at the bottom of the stairs and rushed up the steps in my strapless bra and underwear. Upon reaching my room on the third floor—which was actually the attic—I placed my phone on the docking station and simultaneously pressed play. Opening bars of "You Don't Know You're Beautiful" by One Direction filled the expansive space. I cranked up the volume until I couldn't hear my own thoughts.

Contentment that accompanies the avoidance of worry eased my tense muscles, and I sighed, closing my eyes. Eventually I bebopped around the room—pulling on pajamas, brushing my teeth, using my hair brush as a make-believe microphone—until I was ready for bed.

But I didn't go to sleep. Instead, I rested on the quilt and stared at the ceiling, listening to the music, trying to believe the words even though I knew they were all lies.

A shadow moved across the wall in my peripheral vision, and I bolted upright in bed, eyes wide and searching.

I spotted him immediately.

Freaking Nico.

His expression betrayed his thoughts about my music choice,

and he hurried from the window to the speaker dock. He groaned with dread and couldn't hit the pause button fast enough.

"I can't believe you still listen to boy bands."

My hands were white knuckled, gripping the sheets. I closed my eyes and shook my head, "Nico! What the hell? You scared me."

I meant to breathe out a relieved sigh but I couldn't—likely because I didn't feel relieved. Instead, I just kept gulping in air and had to force myself to stop before I ended up with the mother of all hiccup attacks.

"Sorry." His steps sounded purposeful on the wood floor as he crossed to the bed. I felt the mattress depress under his weight. This small action made me scramble to my feet and launch out of the bed.

"What are you doing here?" I went to the docking station and claimed my phone, navigated to the clock alarm feature, and set the alert for nine o'clock.

"You have excellent taste in everything except music."

"That's why you're here?"

"No, I'm just stating a fact. Your taste is excellent except for music."

"How would you know that?"

"Because I know you."

I didn't turn, but I accepted the bait. "You don't know me very well anymore. I could have terrible taste in a lot of things. For example, I like that shirt you're wearing." I gestured to his New York Yankees T-shirt then met his gaze. "See? I have terrible taste."

His smile was crooked and sincere and adorable, and it annoyed the heck out of me.

He ignored my insult. "I think you listen to these bands—and I use the word *band* lightly with a great deal of disrespect—because you're trying to hold on to something that's been gone for a long time."

I lifted my chin. "You're talking about Garrett."

Surprise glinted in his gaze and flickered over his expression, giving him pause. His gypsy eyes searched mine. He stood and walked to me slowly as though not wanting to frighten a skittish creature. "So…you can say his name now."

I shrugged. "Yes. I can say his name now."

Nico studied me for a moment then scratched his chin. "The last time we were together…"

I lifted my hands to my ears but didn't exactly cover them. Instead, I waved them around my head and turned away. I crossed to the small white vanity where my baseball cards were neatly stacked. "I don't want to talk about that. I don't want to talk about what we…what happened."

He was silent for a moment then I heard him release a small breath. When he spoke, the timbre of his voice was lower and gruff with suppressed emotion. "I was just going to say, the last time you couldn't say his name."

"Well, I can now." I picked up the baseball cards and started thumbing through them absentmindedly. "Garrett. Garrett Thompson. Garrett P. Thompson. Garrett Patrick Thompson."

It was true; I could say his name. It was easily done. I could say it and with no residual ache, only a weird numbness where something else used to be.

Oftentimes I wished there were a corporeal mark to demarcate the before and after of Garrett Thompson in my life. Once or twice, I'd gone to a tattoo parlor looking for a design to brand my skin, to prove what his prematurely extinguished existence did to me. At least a physical wound would provide proof of the hurt.

"He's been gone for eleven years." Nico's voice—sabulous, strained—was closer than I expected. He'd crossed the room while I was pretending to look at my baseball cards.

I attempted an unhurried saunter to the window; my objective was distance.

It was unseasonably mild for April, and the sky was clear and moonless. I affixed my attention upward. Every star felt within reach, hovering just inches above my window. The soft and relatively moderate spring breeze teased the white eyelet curtains. If it were summer, the wind would be rustling the corn. At times, a strong gust mimicked the sound of the ocean breaking against the shore.

Again, Nico's voice was closer than I'd anticipated, and this time it was quieter and softer. "I don't know if you—eleven years is a long time."

I glanced over my shoulder, startled by his gentle tone. Inexplicably, I couldn't quite draw a full breath, so I whispered, "I know that."

"I miss him too."

"I know you do." I nodded.

"Elizabeth...." In my peripheral vision, I saw his hands lift; he hesitated then placed them gently on my shoulders and turned me to face him. "Do you...?"

"I'm not in love with him anymore, ok?" I clenched my teeth, "I'm not. I was just a kid—*we* were kids."

What I didn't say was that whether or not I was still in love with Garrett was completely irrelevant. I wasn't capable of loving anyone—nor did I want to. That part of me was forever broken because I would never take the risk again. Loving was a kamikaze mission that only ended in misery.

His handsome mouth lifted, a rueful tilt that ended with his lips, and he pinned me with a searching gaze. "What's with the boy-toy bands?"

"Well, Judgey McJudgerton, maybe I just like boy bands. Maybe I feel they are misunderstood and their collective artistic contribution to society is undervalued. Where would modern hip-hop be without 'N Sync and the emergence of Justin Timberlake as a solo artist?"

"But you don't listen to Justin Timberlake, you listen to 'N Sync."

I tried and failed not to grumble. "It's all the same."

He shook his head. "No. You're a purist; you always have been. Boy bands are the high fructose corn syrup of music. It's the only thing about you that isn't real. It doesn't make any sense."

I narrowed my eyes and ignored the way his thumbs were brushing over the bare skin of my shoulders because it was confusing, and every time he did it, I thought of his expression at the reunion after he said "and I will always love you."

I didn't want to think about that. "It's not the only thing about me that doesn't make sense."

"Oh yeah? What else?" He surveyed me openly through thick lashes and shifted a half step closer into my personal space.

I shrugged out of his hold and leaned against the windowsill, trying to gain distance. Nico's omnipresent restless energy, charisma, and handsome face were proving to be more than I could resist. That hole in my armor was stretching to accommodate him. I didn't want to accommodate him. I wanted him to leave my armor intact.

Therefore, I decided to ignore his question. "I think you're biased."

"About what?"

"About everything."

"Explain."

I remembered this, the one word command: Explain.

Growing up I was used to his mother saying this to her children, and because Nico heard it all the time, he said it to Garrett and me. It was how his family communicated. Some people found it off-putting. I just knew it was part of who he was.

"Of course you think I'm trying to hold on to something. The truth is you're jealous of my excellent taste in music. Have you even heard of One Direction? Have you listened to their songs?

You can't say you don't like something if you've never tried it—because that makes a lot of sense." My attempt at deflection, to use his own words against him from earlier that evening, only served to increase my blood pressure and his skepticism.

"I don't need to eat cotton candy to know that it will rot my teeth...."

"Shut it, Nico." His patronizing retort sent a jarring wave of anger down my spine. I pushed away from the sill and stalked around him, further annoyed by my sudden juvenile outburst.

I couldn't figure out why I was so angry. An irritating and spectral voice told me it was because he knew me so well. I didn't want him to know me.

I shoved the spectral voice over the side of a cliff, rationalizing my violence by internally asserting that spectral voices were shrewish and should be ignored or murdered.

I felt a surge of stubborn resolve and spun on my heel. I charged him, caught him off guard, pointed at his chest, poked his sternum, and proclaimed, "You say I'm a purist, and you know what, you're right." I fisted my hands on my hips and tried to straighten to a height greater. "I *am* a purist. And I think boy bands sing about the purest form of love and devotion—the *idea* of it. The purest form of something is the idea of it. They sing about something they can't possibly know anything about. Once you know what falling in love is, what it requires in order to be sustained, it becomes infinitely less...less...less...." My arms flailed about in a circular motion as I lost my mental wrestling match with the English language.

Nico lifted his eyebrows and prompted, "Less convenient?"

I scowled and poked him again. "No. Less alluring, less likely, less possible, less obtainable."

He grabbed my finger and held it suspended between us. "I disagree."

"You disagree about which part?" I didn't want to be huffy, but

I was. I was huffy and eyerolly and crabfacey. None of it, however, seemed to be off-put-y because he stalked closer and held— commanded—my gaze with his.

"You had one experience that ended tragically. Have you even tried to love anyone since then? Have you tried again?" His earnestness and honest openness felt...weird and...disorienting. I tried to glance over his shoulder, but he moved to intercept my glare. He nodded as though confirming a suspicion. "Yeah. I thought so."

To keep from frowning I pinched my lips together. "You don't know anything."

"Is that why you left?"

I stiffened.

His eyes moved between mine, his voice growing both softer and more severe. "Is that why you left me, that night?"

My heart thumped painfully in my chest. I couldn't answer; my throat was too tight.

"Why did you send back all my letters? When you left, why didn't you take my calls?"

"I...." I breathed the word, but didn't know what to say. I should've apologized, but instead I said, "We were just kids."

"Did I scare you, that night? Did I do something wrong?"

My heart thump became a gallop. "No. It wasn't you, but...but...that was so long ago. Why are we talking about this?"

Nico gathered a deep breath, his eyes searching mine. He dropped his gaze to our hands and shifted them in order to hold my palm in both of his. "Because I've missed you." Nico flinched and cleared his throat immediately after saying the words.

"Nico, you didn't even like me. How could you miss me?"

"That's not true. I always liked you. I admired you." Again, his gentle words and his ardent expression were contradictory

I frowned, flummoxed. I tried to respond but instead blinked, and my mouth expelled a strange, breathy sound.

"Nico…what…that…we…you and I…we were never…you never…."

I watched him close his eyes, take a deep breath, and then meet my confused stare with an extremely steady, heady, ready one of his own.

He didn't speak. He just looked at me. Rather, he allowed me to look at him, and I knew.

He thinks he loves you.

A jarring bolt of shock, almost painful in its intensity, accompanied the realization and sounded between my ears with a high-pitched ping. This was followed by a more precise and distressing realization.

He thinks he's in love with you.

The sound, the ping, increased in volume. I abruptly pulled my hand from his, and to my relief, the shrill squeal was replaced with rushing silence.

"Elizabeth…." Nico stepped forward as though he were going to reach for my hand again.

"It's late. You should go." Eyes wide, I shook my head then crossed my arms protectively over my chest.

I noted that his gaze strayed to my mouth. He didn't make any move to leave.

I tried to laugh lightly. "I don't know how late you people New York City stay up but, it's got to be one in the morning by now and I…" I faked a yawn badly and borrowed a word from Sandra's repertoire. "Well, shisterhosen, I'm tired."

He let out a man-sigh, which is a cross between an exasperated growl and a belligerent huff. "You're leaving tomorrow."

I swallowed the building thickness in my throat and shifted another step backward. "Yep."

"Elizabeth…."

I swung my arms and clapped my hands because I was having difficulty standing still. "All the more reason why I should be getting to bed now and you should go home."

"I have to tell you something." He cleared his throat, and I seized the momentary pause to escape.

"Damn it, I need to pee. You can see yourself out!"

His staying hand reached for and held my arm just above the elbow; his touch was light, but it was enough to still my movements. He tugged me toward him. "Wait—don't...don't do that."

"Pee?" I pointedly avoided his eyes but didn't try to shrug out of his hold.

"No—please stop...." He man-sighed again, and when he spoke, his voice was raised, and the words came out in a staccato avalanche. "You have to know that I'm in love with you—you have to know that I've loved you since we were kids, since before I can remember."

I closed my eyes against the lava-like onslaught and willed myself someplace else. His words, his expression, his voice—they burned me, and it hurt.

He started again, speaking as though he were doing his utmost to maintain a calm exterior. He looked furious but his voice and words were gentle. "I know that...." There was a pause, a strained swallow, and then he continued. "I know that it was Garrett, that you chose Garrett. I know that." I felt his free hand encircle my other arm just above the elbow. "I didn't want to like him, but I did; he was my best friend and I never begrudged him that— meaning, you. But, the summer after...."

I opened my eyes and stared at his chin. A long moment passed. My face was stiff and numb, like granite.

"And when I saw you in Chicago, even though I thought I was over it, over you—I knew I still . . ." He swallowed. "I'm still in love with you." I felt the angry hesitation and frustrated indecision in him just before he released my arms. He took a step backward. "I just wanted you to know."

I drew in a steadying breath, still not able to meet his eyes. "What do you want me to say?"

A long moment passed. Then he laughed lightly, his reply both sarcastic and defeated. "I guess nothing."

I finally found the courage to lift my gaze to his, but he wasn't watching me anymore. He was staring at the floor. His jaw ticked like a bomb.

"Well, now. That's done." His tone changed, became more *the Face*-like and less Nico-like, and his eyes darted around the room as though searching for something. He patted his pockets, scratched the back of his neck, and gained another step away from me. "If you'll excuse me, I have to go find Shelly Martin and get to work on plowing that field."

He turned away from me, the sexual innuendo a blatant defense mechanism. He walked to the window.

I wanted to do something, but I was truly paralyzed. He had one foot over the ledge and on the roof before I stumbled, both figuratively and literally, toward him, "What—what are you doing? You don't need to use the window. Why are you leaving out of the window? You'll break your neck! Would you please use the door?"

He held his hands up and slipped out of the widow, moving with fluid grace, jogging the length of the roof. I'd just reached the opening when he swung to the largest branch of the oak tree. I held my breath as he picked his way down then landed like a cat on his feet.

I wanted to call to him but didn't know what to say.

So I didn't.

Instead, I watched him walk away.

CHAPTER 8

Sandra was taking her time getting out of the car. She had the passenger side mirror down and was running her pinky finger along her bottom lip to smooth her lipstick. I sat next to her with the driver's side door open; one foot was in the car, one foot was on the pavement. I used the opportunity to stare at the red brick building in front of us that housed Manganiello's Italian Restaurant.

Nico was inside that building, and I had no plan.

I didn't consider myself a control freak, but I always liked to be armed with a plan, especially when facing a boy—no, a man—who'd just declared his love for me the night before. And not only was it love; it was a lifetime of *unrequited* love.

"Hey—Elizabeth? Are you ready?"

My lashes fluttered as I was yanked from my contemplations. I nodded, "Yep. Guess we should get inside."

I made no move to exit the car.

My father and I dined at Manganiello's Italian Restaurant at least three times a week when I was growing up; it was the only time either of us ate a hot meal (as long as microwaved leftovers aren't counted), and the restaurant was one of my most favorite places on earth.

Sandra was watching me. I could feel her hesitate as she studied me. "Is there anything wrong?"

Weary was how I felt as I looked at the building now; weary and worried. *The big deucey Ws.*

My heart raced at the thought of seeing Nico; it was pounding so hard I could feel the pulse and throb of blood rushing through my veins in the palms of my hands and at the back of my neck.

I shook my head. "Nope."

That was a lie. Everything was wrong. Niccolò Manganiello was in love with me—or thought he was. I couldn't fathom it. Reality had tilted on its axis, and everything in the world was now a different color. All of our previous interactions, all of his teasing, everything that made me hate him while we were growing up required reassessment.

I had so many questions, the first of which was how could he spend his childhood being so mean and spiteful to a girl he supposedly loved? How could he spend years goading me, needling me, bullying me if he cared about me?

"Is this about your outburst at the reunion last night? Are you embarrassed?" Shrink Sandra said.

I shook my head. "Nope."

I wasn't embarrassed about standing on a chair and yelling, "The child is yours." I wasn't even embarrassed when I did it last night.

I was embarrassed about how I'd behaved when he told me he loved me. His confession of love reignited the guilt surrounding my abandoning him after we slept together and how I'd treated him afterward: I had basically cut him out of my life.

His confession last night further served to intensify my guilt. I didn't know it at the time, but when I slept with Nico and gave him my V-card, he was in love with me. If I'd known then what I knew now…if I'd had any idea, then maybe….

I shifted in my seat and sighed heavily, my eyes narrowed at the red brick in hesitant speculation.

I didn't want to see him—well, I was pretty sure I didn't want to see him. And I was certain we'd already spent more than enough time together over the last fourteen hours—well, more or less enough time. I was planning to absolutely ignore him once we walked inside the restaurant—well, absolutely ignore him in the general sense.

Gah! Make up your mind.

I administered a mental kick to my backside and suppressed a growl, not wanting to raise additional suspicion.

"What did you and Nico talk about when you disappeared last night?" Shrink Sandra said.

"Stuff...things." I shrugged. I didn't want to talk to Shrink Sandra. I needed a friend, not a shrink. I needed to talk to Janie. But Janie was in Boston climbing all over her fiancé Quinn, and I was in Iowa avoiding confrontation.

Maybe I do need a shrink.

"He told me he has a stalker."

Sandra flinched, opened her mouth, closed it then opened it again. "He has a stalker?"

I nodded.

"Is he ok? Does he have security?"

I nodded again but said, "His security sucks."

"Obviously. Last night he was nearly mangled. I hope he plans to do something about that."

"I'm going to try to talk to him about it today." I tapped my fingers on my thigh. "Maybe I can talk to Quinn, and get him to persuade Nico to switch security firms."

Sandra sighed. "Sounds like a plan. Ok then, let's go inside. I'm hungry!"

I bit the inside of my bottom cheek for courage and led the way to the front entrance, wiping my sweaty palms on my jeans.

As soon as I opened the door to the restaurant, the smell of divinity enveloped me. Ah, yes...this was what I imagined heaven would smell like: garlic, basil, and fresh baked bread. The smell was one I associated with my childhood. My nose was on sensory overload, and I was forced to blink against the darkness when we stepped inside.

I heard Sandra's immediate gasp, and then whispered—almost moaned—a rapturous exclamation. "What is that heavenly smell? And why is it so dark in here? I can't see a thing."

Before I could respond, a booming voice swallowed all other sounds in the room. "Yeah, because that's what everyone wants to do on their day off—go to the place where they work and cook for thirty people. Yeah, this makes complete sense."

I recognized the voice as Nico's oldest brother, Robert. I blinked again. The room was finally coming into focus, and I was in a time warp. Navy vinyl benches, gold carpet, silk flower arrangements that were just a little too big for the dark wood tables, the jukebox that played only the Rat Pack, with Frank Sinatra was currently crooning about his funny valentine to complete the atmosphere.

I squinted, looked for, and found a fresh ball of mistletoe tied just above the archway between the two dining rooms.

I hadn't been to the restaurant in eleven years, but everything was the same. I half expected an eight-year-old Nico to rush out and take us to our table, or a sixteen-year-old Nico to ignore me in favor of chatting politely with my dad, only to pull my chair out too far when we got to the table ensuring I fell to the floor, landing on my ass.

Robert's voice, still booming, cracked through my reflections. He exited the swinging galley door that led from the kitchen to the dining room.

"Because if I were a secretary and my youngest brother came to town, I'd invite the entire family to the office, make them coffee, then clean up after they leave. Yay. Sign me up."

"Robert." Rose's warning was sharp and immediately effective.

Neither son nor mother had noticed us yet. I could hear sounds of children and adults working feverishly in the kitchen, with pots banging and water running as they cooked and cleaned for a steady flow of customers.

Rose appeared to be absorbed in reprimanding her tall son. "You don't see your brother for three weeks and this is how you behave? Shame on you, Robert Vincenzo Manganiello. And I want us all to sit in the dining room, not back in the kitchen."

"What? Why sit in the dining room? There is more than enough room at the kitchen table."

"Because I want to do something nice for your brother, that's why. And I can't arrange it if we're all back in the kitchen." She reached up and pinched his chin. "Don't question your mother."

His big shoulders rose and fell with a sigh. "Fine…fine. I'll go finish the manicotti."

Sandra bumped her shoulder against mine and leaned into my ear, "Manicotti for breakfast?"

I nodded and shrugged. I couldn't form an opinion about having manicotti for breakfast in my present state of panic.

Either Sandra's question or my awkward movements alerted Rose to our presence. She glanced over, her smile immediate; her eyes were large and excited, as though seeing something delicious.

"Lizzybella, my beauty—it is so good to see you." Rose charged toward us and engulfed me in a tight hug.

I tried to speak but found the task impossible. Words were caught in my throat. I was choking on apprehension, guilt, and anticipation.

Rose didn't seem to notice. She released me and promptly pulled Sandra into a hug, "I made Nico promise. I told him you better come and visit me while you are here."

Sandra was engulfed in a motherly hug. "I'm Sandra," she said, somewhat stupefied, when Rose finally released her.

"Of course you are, dear." Rose smiled at Sandra and patted her hand then turned her attention back to me. "Now Lizzy, please go to the kitchen and help get the settings for the big table out here. Robert, Franco, Milo, and Manny are in the back. I'm sure they want to say hi."

Rose dismissed me by linking her arm with Sandra and pulling her in the direction of jukebox. I watched them stroll away, leaving me by the front entrance. I shook my hands to force them to relax, hoping to shake off some of my nerves along with them. I glanced at the galley door to the kitchen, still feeling weary and worried, but resolved to get through this moment by playing the part of a mature adult.

I stepped forward when Franco and Milo—two of Nico's brothers—burst through the swinging door. In their hands were large trays of food and, as was typical, they were arguing with each other.

"No, no—over here. Robert said over here," said Milo, the tallest and second oldest, indicating a long buffet table with a tilt of his head.

"That's stupid," said Franco, third in the family. "Why don't we just put it all on the big table? Why are we doing this buffet style?"

Milo shook a head full of dark curls. "Robert said that Ma said that Nico is—you know what, don't ask questions, dummy. Just put the food down."

Distracted by his rant, Milo let his tray slip, and I quickly moved forward to assist. His large green eyes widened when I stepped in front of him, steadying the tray.

"Well, hello." Milo tried to balance the tray with one hand as he reached his other out to me. "I'm Milo."

I frowned at him, "Yes, Milo, I know. It's me—Elizabeth Finney."

He blinked at me, clearly startled, then grinned, "Oh, hey. I didn't recognize you." He openly studied me, perhaps trying to find the waifish teenager in the woman who stood before him. "Nice to see you again," he said with an approving smile.

Milo was twelve years older than Nico and therefore thirteen years older than me. I knew him only as a heart-breaking teenager when I was in elementary school; then, later, as a serious and studious graduate student turned physics professor who visited his family intermittently.

He indicated a long table in the smaller dining room. "We're taking these over there. Can you go in the kitchen and start bringing out the silverware?"

I stepped to the side, and he winked at me as he passed. Just like the restaurant, he looked exactly the same. Even though he had to be nearing forty, he still looked like a twenty-something graduate student.

I turned to Franco and gave him a small smile. "Hey, Franco."

Franco's smile mirrored my own, small and shy. He was by far the quietest member of the Manganiello family. He was ten years older than Nico and used to play with us when we were kids. He allowed us to help him fix his trucks or tinker around with strange machine parts. Franco Manganiello was the reason why I knew how to change the oil in a car. When I left for college, he'd just opened his own auto repair shop.

I'd be lying if I didn't admit that, while growing up, I had hero-worshipped Franco Manganiello.

He nodded at me once then carried the tray over to the long table. With no new excuses presenting themselves for delaying my trip to the kitchen, I took a deep breath and plowed through the swinging door.

I was greeted by a scene of chaos.

Children were everywhere—running around, playing with pots and spatulas, "helping" the adults put the finishing touches on dishes of food, wrapping silverware in napkins, or poking each other with the butter knives. A cluster of kids was busily pairing crayons with coloring books at one of the far tables, and that was where I found Nico.

He was bent over a coloring book; a little boy was on his right, and a little girl was on his left. He looked just really, honestly, achingly adorable. A small frown of concentration pulled his dark brows low over his eyes, and a memory of a seven-year-old Nico— in the same spot, doing the exact same thing—spurred stirrings and symptoms of nostalgia within me. My heart and stomach engaged in a fencing match as they struggled with conflicting emotions.

I was still staring at him when he glanced up and did a double take. I held my breath. His gaze tangled with mine, like thorny vines. If I looked away first, the thorns would draw blood. I didn't want to draw blood. I wanted to gently disentangle him from my life. I wanted him to move on from whatever fake memories and feelings he'd imagined to be real. I wanted to pretend that the last twenty-four hours had never happened.

Except, the last twenty-four hours did happen, and I couldn't forget. I didn't want to look away, and a growing part of me liked being tangled with him and his thorny vines.

"Elizabeth—the silverware." Milo knocked my shoulder as he rushed past, and I automatically turned toward his voice.

The moment was over, but I could still feel Nico's eyes on me. I thought about meeting his gaze again, and I really wanted to. But if I looked at him again, if I allowed our gaze to tangle, then it wouldn't be fair to him. So I kept my attention focused on Milo and his rushing about.

Milo crossed to the counter and I followed him to receive into my outstretched arms a stack of dinner plates with forks, knives, and spoons piled on top of them.

I spied Robert, the oldest of the Manganiello children, instructing a teenage girl on the appropriate ratio of parsley to parmesan cheese. I realized the girl must be his daughter, the same daughter who was only four the last time I saw her. This realization made me feel each of my twenty-six years and then some.

Milo made introductions to any member of the family I didn't know. This included Robert's wife Viv and their five children; Franco's wife Madeline and their three children; Christine's husband Sam and their six children; and Manny's wife Jennifer and their three children. It was explained to me that Lisa—Nico's second sister—couldn't come, as she was a busy and important attorney in Chicago and hardly ever made it to family events.

I was thankful for Lisa's absence and the fact that Milo was still single—fewer names to remember.

I tried to make mental notes in order to remember names, pairing spouses and children with the Manganiellos I knew; after a while, I just accepted the fact that I wasn't going to remember everyone's name. So I did a lot of smiling and nodding and calling little girls "dear" and boys "cutie."

Through all of the introductions and handshakes and smiles, the back of my neck itched and tingled. I could feel Nico's gaze intermittently follow my movements. I didn't want him to see my confusion or my lack of a specific plan, so I went with my de facto plan—pretend everything was fine, feign ignorance, and act normal.

I didn't mind that Milo appointed himself as my handler. Once he seemed to be satisfied with the introductions, we left the kitchen with stacks of plates, cloth napkins, and silverware and set to the task of setting the large table in the dining room.

"We'll put the silverware and napkins around the table but leave the plates on the buffet." Milo announced, indicating with his chin toward the long buffet table in the smaller dining room where he and Manny had already placed some of the food.

My attention moved to the indicated table but snagged on the sight of Sandra and Rose with their heads together, engaged in deep conversation by the jukebox. This sight made me frown. This sight also made the back of my neck itch and tingle.

I kept my eyes on them as I placed the flatware. Rose had her hand on Sandra's arm. Sandra bent her head lower to hear something that Rose said. Rose laughed at something Sandra said. It all looked very benign and was therefore extremely suspicious.

"Do forks go on the right or the left?" Milo's question pulled my attention away from Sandra and Rose. I blinked at him then at the settings I'd just placed. Some places had two knives and no forks; some had all spoons.

"Oh, I've made a mess." I immediately moved to remedy my mistake.

Milo laughed, and it caused a twinge of awareness between my shoulder blades. He and Nico had the same laugh. Except for Milo's curly hair, they also looked a great deal alike.

"Don't worry about it. It's actually something I would do. In fact," Milo winked at me—again—and with a crooked smile, a smile that looked a lot like Nico's, he added, "I think I've done that before."

I returned his smile with a grateful close-lipped one of my own and realized that his green eyes were twinkling at me. This gave me pause. Perhaps the eye twinkling was simply genetic and hard-coded into Manganiello DNA.

"Why don't you take the dishes over; I'll finish with the place settings...if I can remember which side the forks go on." Milo glanced at the table and moved a fork to the left then the right.

I grabbed a stack of plates and called over my shoulder, "Forks go on the left; knives and spoons on the right."

"Thanks..." I heard him respond distractedly. "I think you're right."

Milo reminded me a lot of my father. They were both distracted in a way that might be misconstrued as lofty. Since both were professors—Milo a professor in the physics department at NYU and my father a professor in the agriculture department of Iowa State—I guessed that the behavior was not unusual for tenured faculty.

I stacked the plates at the start of the buffet then ferried over another pile while keeping one eye on Sandra and Rose and another eye on the door to the kitchen. I was waiting for Nico to emerge, wondering if he were going to speak to me or if he'd also decided to go with the de facto plan of acting as if everything was normal.

I didn't have to wait long to discover the answer.

Nico exited the swinging kitchen door carrying a stack of medium-sized plates just as I'd set down my last load. I immediately stiffened, straightened, and averted my eyes to the buttery croissants on the buffet table. I needlessly shifted the platter containing the croissants and fiddled with the edge of the tablecloth.

He stopped at the end of the table. "Hi."

I failed at swallowing again and lifted my eyes to his. Even at this distance, I could see that his eyes were twinkling.

"Hi? Oh, hi." I wondered at my ball of nerves. I didn't even recognize myself. Who was this girl who was anxious around a man? I hadn't been anxious like this around a man since—ever, and I hadn't been anxious around a boy since—well, since Nico.

He set the plates on the table—at the other end—then sauntered over to where I stood. I tried my best to cease fiddling with the croissant dish.

He halted just in front of me, planted his feet, and crossed his arms over his chest. "I'm glad you decided to come."

"I said I would." My eyes were darting all over the restaurant. I forced myself to settle down and meet his gaze directly. When I finally did, I began to understand why my subconscious preferred to look everywhere else. It was trying to defend me from his soulful gypsy eyes, big and brownish green, so large and open and mesmerizing.

A small, playfully wry smile pulled his mouth to one side. "Actually, you said you couldn't. I believe it was your friend who said you would."

"Well, I'm here now," I managed to choke out.

"Yeah, you are." His expression turned serious and thoughtful as he added, "I like seeing you."

The words knocked the air from my lungs, and I could actually hear my own heartbeat; it was as clear as though I was listening through a stethoscope.

"I like seeing you too." The statement was out of my mouth before I realized I'd said it or thought it.

He blinked at me in obvious surprise; it made his eyes widen and his brows lift. "You do?"

I nodded. I nodded because it was true, but I felt a pang of guilt because I didn't know what it meant.

He shifted an inch closer, but before he could speak, Robert's booming voice reverberated from the galley door. "All right, everyone, the food is hot, and it's time to eat, so stop what you're doing and circle around the big table."

Someone shouted, likely a teenage boy, "God's neat—let's eat!"

"Your grandmother does not approve of such jokes, Lello." Rose's authoritative voice reprimanded.

"Hey, guys." Sandra, seemingly out of nowhere, was suddenly standing at my elbow. She tucked her arm through mine, drawing my attention from Nico. "I'll need some introductions at some point, but for now, let's get a move on so we can get some grub."

Not waiting for my response, she pulled me toward the big table, and I allowed her to lead me away. It was a relief actually. I hadn't meant to be so honest with Nico and was trying to decide if I regretted it.

After a great deal of blustering and bustling, the buffet was laid, the large dining room in the main restaurant was set, and the Manganiellos—plus Sandra and I—had said grace and were now lined up to pile our plates with food.

I kept stealing glances at Nico. Two of his nephews were monopolizing him, speaking excitedly and animatedly in the way that only children do. I realized that I hadn't yet seen Angelica— Nico's niece, Tina's daughter. The realization made me frown, and I craned my neck, glancing around the room.

My attention rested on a constellation of small children at one end of the big dining table; they were laughing, roughhousing, shouting, and just generally behaving like small children. Angelica was not among them.

I skimmed the crowd then finally caught sight of her. She was sitting on Christine's lap—Nico's oldest sister—holding the same blue blanket that she'd been gripping at the hospital. The four-year-old looked like her cousins, but she wasn't laughing, shouting, and having a good time. She was sitting very still, holding her blanket to her cheek, and though her face was a mask of indifference, she was watching her cousins with loneliness in her eyes and sadness beyond her years.

The image pulled at my heart, and I felt equal measures of frustration and resolve—frustration because there was nothing I could do immediately to improve her quality of life, and resolve because, even if she didn't enroll in the study, I would find a way to do something for her.

With my plate in hand, I planned to select a seat near Angelica. I made it to the large arch that separated the two rooms when my path was abruptly blocked by Sandra and Rose.

"Oh!" I rocked backward to keep from spilling my food.

"Hey, Elizabeth, Rose was just telling me the funniest story about you and Nico from when you were kids." Sandra placed her hand on my shoulder and pulled me about a foot and a half forward as though positioning me to her liking.

I braced myself for the story and attempted a polite smile. "Is that so?"

"Niccolò. You come over here now and speak to your mother." Rose caged me in on the other side and bellowed to her youngest son.

I took a deep breath and glanced over my shoulder. Nico left his plate at the buffet and, rather reluctantly, I observed, walked over to where we stood. I closed my eyes briefly so that neither of the ladies witnessed my eye roll. I was sure whatever the story was would be an attempt to horribly embarrass me, Nico, or—more likely—both of us.

He sauntered then stopped a few feet away, his eyes moving from me to Rose then back again.

"Come over here." Rose motioned with her hand. "Listen to your mother."

Nico took two unenthusiastic steps forward and stopped just adjacent to where I stood, his arm almost touching my shoulder. "Yes?"

"Oh, look," Rose and Sandra took three shuffling steps backward. Nico's mother clasped her hands and rested them against her cheek. "You're standing under the mistletoe."

I blinked at her then noticed where Nico and I were standing— under the arch that separated the two main dining rooms. My eyes lifted upward and, sure enough, we were standing under a brand new bunch of mistletoe. It was even tied in place with an obscenely wide red ribbon.

"I must've forgotten to take it down after Christmas," Rose said. The statement was, of course, a lie.

The restaurant was famous for keeping the kissing bough up all year. I glanced briefly at Nico and found him glaring at his mother. Growing up with this family, I'd witnessed that expression with a great deal on each of the Manganiello children's faces when dealing with their mother.

His stunned embarrassment quickly escalated to mortification when it met a healthy dose of anger. His scowl told me that this setup was just as much of a surprise to him as it was to me.

"You didn't forget, Ma. In fact, not surprisingly, it looks brand new."

"Well, I can't very well have old mistletoe up, now can I? Anyway, you and Elizabeth are standing under the mistletoe now, and it's tradition."

Nico turned to me. He looked unhappy. He shook his head.

"Just ignore her."

"Don't be a dummy, Nico." Milo walked past Nico and purposefully bumped into his shoulder, then he winked at me. "If you don't kiss her, I will."

"No one is going to kiss her," Nico growled.

"Someone has to," Robert called over his shoulder from the buffet table. "It's bad luck if you don't. She's standing directly under the damn thing."

Nico's eyes lifted briefly to the greenery above our heads then closed. I was rooted in place, holding my plate of scrambled eggs, manicotti, and melon. I watched the emotions that played over his features—annoyance, frustration, and exasperation.

"Fine." Before I knew what was happening, he'd already brushed a kiss against my cheek, his eyes avoiding mine. He turned away.

I swallowed what tasted like bitter disappointment. But it couldn't have been bitter disappointment because I didn't actually want Nico to kiss me. I also noticed that I was sweating.

"No." Milo placed his hands on Nico's shoulders and turned him to face me again. "That wasn't a kiss. If you can't do it then, like I said, I will volunteer."

"Fatti i fatti tuoi[2], Milo." Rose snapped happily at her son.

"I am minding my business," Milo said in his defense. "I'll make it my business if Nico is unable to get the job done."

I heard Sandra laugh. I glanced in her direction. She was standing next to Rose. They were both grinning at us—like foxes. If I'd had any doubts up to this point, I now knew that this was a setup. I narrowed my eyes at Sandra, hoping to convey my disapproval. She answered my scowl by lifting an eyebrow and widening her grin.

A silent communication passed between us in the span of a

---

[2]Translation: Mind your own business

single second

Me: *I can't believe you did this.*

Her: *Whatever. You know you like it. Mount that stallion.*

Me: *You shouldn't have put him on the spot.*

Her: *Then you should just kiss him and get it over with—but use tongue or else you'll have to do it again.*

At this point everyone had stopped eating and talking and was staring at us. But these weren't like the freakish stares of last night; most of these people had known us our whole lives and loved Nico. I noticed his sister, Christine, who appeared to be debating whether to intercede.

Gritting my teeth, I faced Nico again. His eyes were cast downward; he seemed to be exceedingly interested in my plate of food, but his jaw was ticking like a bomb.

Someone needed to do something.

I could do this. I could kiss Nico, on the mouth, to everyone's satisfaction, and walk away unscathed. I could put on my big girl pants and just get it over with.

I swallowed, held my plate to the side, gained a step toward him, tilted my chin upward, and captured his mouth with mine. He jolted, and I knew he hadn't been expecting the contact. His mouth was soft and full, his bottom lip in particular. I lifted my head a fraction of an inch, and pressed my lips more fully against his. Abruptly, as though he'd just woken up, he took control, and my eyes drifted shut.

CHAPTER 9

His hands lifted to my waist, pulled me firmly against him. Nico's fingers gripped my body with a building force that echoed the pressure of our mouths. He tilted his head to one side and tasted my top lip. I think I went a little insane in that moment and everything—the restaurant and everyone in it—ceased to exist.

It was the kind of madness that peaks all at once. It crashes like a tidal wave, leaving no time for thought of the past or future or of consequences. I couldn't think of a single thing I'd rather do than kiss Nico Manganiello.

I wanted to kiss him for the rest of my life.

I wanted to sell all of my worldly goods and spend all waking hours with his hands on my body and his mouth on mine.

When I parted my lips in response to his teasing and answered his exploration with my own, and when I nipped his—let's just face it—incredibly juicy bottom lip, his tongue swept into my mouth. He was delicious. I tasted intense need, and I endeavored to press closer. The muscled torso I'd watched a dozen times on television was hot and hard against my stomach and chest. One of his hands fisted in my hair and I stood on my tiptoes; the friction of the movement made one or both of us moan—I can't remember which—but I didn't care.

And then I dropped my plate.

The loud crash of the dish hitting the floor made me jump. Both Nico and I turned toward the sound and an involuntary, strangled yelp erupted from my throat. I gripped his arms; then, when I realized what I'd done, I covered my mouth with my hand.

I turned my wide eyes to Nico. He wasn't looking at me. He was looking at the plate on the floor; his gaze was unfocused, his breathing heavy. One of his hands was still gripping my waist; the other had released my hair and rested on my mid-back.

"Well…that was one hell of a kiss." Milo's voice seemed to rouse Nico. He blinked at the floor then gazed at me, his eyes searching mine. His hands fell away; then he pulled one through his hair, leaving it adorably tousled and askew. He took a step backward.

But I didn't want him to take a step backward. I wanted him to kiss me again. I wanted to wrap myself around him and hold him close and tousle his hair, and the realization of this want scared the ever-loving crap out of me.

I gasped. My cheeks heated. I diverted my eyes to the broken plate and mess of manicotti on the floor. I knelt next to it and tried to clean it up with the paper napkin I'd also dropped.

Rose tugged at my elbow. "Don't worry about the plate, dear."

"I've made such a mess." I tried to focus all my attention on cleaning as wild thoughts bounced around my brain.

I was bargaining with myself as if I had an angel and a devil perched on my shoulders hammering out a deal where they both got what they wanted. The angel wanted to treat Nico with respect, keep his heart safe, not take advantage of him, and not lead him on.

The devil wanted to watch Nico unbutton my pants with his teeth.

"Let me help you." Nico bent down to assist, and my gaze flickered over him. He was watching me intently, his soulful eyes a precarious mixture of hope and weariness.

Two other sets of hands made quick work of the cleanup; I was about to volunteer to grab a wet towel from the kitchen but someone was already there—one of Nico's nephews—wiping up the lingering bits of tomato and cheese.

"I'll just go wash my hands," I muttered to no one in particular, and made a dash around the circus of Manganiellos.

I was sweating and my hands were shaking; I needed a minute to myself. I felt justified in escaping to the women's room at the back of the restaurant. Once inside the small space, I rinsed my hands then leaned heavily against the countertop.

I studied my reflection, but in my mind's eye, all I saw was Nico.

He was so…disconcerting. His willingness to be vulnerable with me was unsettling. The openness of his emotions, simmering just beneath the surface, was something I couldn't recall ever seeing in him in the past.

Or, maybe, as a kid and a teenager, I just saw what I expected. Maybe I never really looked at him. Maybe the real Nico was there all along, and I was just blind to him.

The sound of the door opening yanked me back to the present. Nico slipped inside and slid the lock behind him; our eyes tangled in the bathroom mirror.

"Hey…." He said.

"Hey."

Staring commenced.

Unrequited love was typically my favorite kind of love. The non-reciprocal nature of it appealed to me in much the same way boy bands appealed to me; it was theoretical love because it was untested—hopeless in its one-sidedness yet tragically inspiring.

Being faced with Nico's presumably real feelings for me forced me to reexamine my affinity for unrequited love.

His love—or, rather, my knowledge of it—hung like a winter coat around my shoulders, tight around my neck, and it made me feel heavy all over. I still couldn't swallow. I kept attempting to swallow, but instead I could only manage a half swallow.

Maybe I was coming down with something.

"I didn't know that she was going to do that." He said, breaking the silence.

"I know. I believe you." I said.

Staring recommenced.

My eyes drifted to his Adams apple. I noted that he also seemed to be experiencing swallow fail.

Maybe we were both coming down with something.

"You kissed me," he said.

I pressed my lips into a line and rolled them between my teeth to keep from licking them.

I had kissed him. I glanced at the counter. I'd kissed him and really, really liked it. I wanted to kiss him again, often. I turned and tossed my loose hair over my shoulder. I leaned against the countertop and crossed my arms, and bravely met his gaze.

"Yes. I did," I said.

His eyes surveyed me, narrowed with palpable confused hopefulness. "Why did you do that?" Nico mimicked my stance.

"Because we were standing under the mistletoe."

He blinked, rocked backward on his feet. "No other reason?"

I considered lying. I considered telling the truth.

Lying would be easier, less messy, and not at all who I was anymore, at least not who I wanted to be. Telling the truth would likely cause one or both of us a measure of difficulty ranging from awkward to painful.

But hadn't I spent the last ten years becoming a person who embraced confrontation instead of running from it? Hadn't I passed advice to others proffering the merits of problematic honesty over an easy path paved with avoidance and half-truths?

I wasn't a hypocrite—well, everyone was a hypocrite, but I was trying hard to be less of one.

I made one more attempt at swallowing and succeeded.

I lifted my chin and said, "I kissed you because I wanted to."

He blinked at me again, and this time he rocked forward on his feet. "You wanted to?" I watched him try to swallow again, unsuccessfully. I made a mental note to check his lymph nodes. "Does this mean…." He sighed then glanced at the wall. "Did you think about what I said last night?"

I nodded. "Yes. I've thought about it. And I think you're

wrong."

He stared at me, his eyebrows suspended on his face. I witnessed the exact moment his expression changed from confusion to frustration. "Wrong? I'm wrong?"

"I think you just think that you're in—in love with me." I squeezed my eyes shut for a moment, summoning courage; the words were difficult to say. "I think it's misplaced and you're confused, and you think this way because you never got over your best friend's death, and I'm the closest thing to Garrett."

He scoffed then frowned. Frustration morphed into something resembling fury. "Really?"

"Yes, really."

"You don't believe me?"

"I just don't understand how it could be possible. I think you're misremembering…things."

"I'm misremembering being in love with you since before I can remember?" His voice was lethally low, as though it was a great burden to keep from shouting.

"Nico, come on. You were always so mean to me. You teased me every time I saw you."

"Yes, you're right of course. Boys never pick on girls they like."

"Well, it wasn't just teasing—it was *mean* teasing, hurtful teasing. You cut my hair, gave me the nickname Skinny Finney, told new students that I was a boy, pushed me into the boy's bathroom and-"

"Yes. I remember doing all of that." His words were an impatient whisper; he rubbed the space between his eyebrows with his index and middle finger.

"Do you understand how awful that was? How mean you were?"

His expression softened slightly, and he took a step forward. "I wasn't trying to hurt you."

"Then what were you doing? If you had this great big love for me, then why did you bully me?"

He appeared to be genuinely pained. "I didn't bully you...." He released a tortured sigh. "I didn't mean it to be bullying. I was a kid who liked a girl, and the girl wouldn't even give me the time of day."

"That makes no sense."

"You wouldn't talk to me unless I made you angry." His frustrated growl echoed against the mirror and tiles.

"I thought you hated me." This comment was said mostly to myself. Apparently, I was feeling suddenly introspective.

"I never hated you...I never...." Nico closed the rest of the distance between us; his hands lifted to my shoulders then slid down my arms. His features were anguished when he shook his head and said, "I'm sorry. That's not true. I did hate you. I hated you because you wanted to be with Garrett instead of me, and I wanted you so badly." His fingers flexed on my arms. "But I was a kid. I was a stupid kid."

"Nico, I. . ." My vision blurred, and I realized that tears were gathering in my eyes. "You make it sound like I chose Garrett over you. You're wrong. You're so wrong. Don't you understand? You were never an option."

Nico winced as though struck, his hands tightened on my arms as his eyes dimmed. "Why? Because you couldn't—because you can't-"

"Because of how you treated me. Because I never *knew*. I can honestly tell you I had absolutely *no* idea." My voice wavered and I cleared my throat. "God, you were so awful."

"I know, I know—I'm sorry." He shuffled closer, his eyes apologetic; he hesitated then pulled me against his chest. I didn't resist, and I allowed him to hold me. "I'm so sorry."

I blinked against the stinging moisture and just allowed myself to be held. One of his big palms petted my hair from the crown of my head to the middle of my back.

When I was certain I'd escaped the crying jungle of danger, I pushed against his chest. He released me from his embrace, but his hands lingered, still on my arms.

"This is nuts." I sniffed then glanced at him. "This is completely nuts."

The corner of his mouth hitched and his eyes seemed to be memorizing my face. "It's the truth."

I shook my head. "No, Nico." I licked my lips and still tasted him there—tasted our kiss. "Nico, you may have felt something for me once, but that was a long time ago—eleven years ago. Believe me when I tell you that I'm not the same person." I shrugged out of his grip and stepped to the side. "I'm not the quiet, well behaved Elizabeth Finney that you remember."

"I don't remember you ever being well behaved."

I ignored him. "I'm different now, and you…." I lifted my hand, motioned to his height, breadth, face, everything. "You are different."

He leaned his hip against the counter and sighed. "I hope I'm different. I used to be a complete dick."

I laughed and sniffled again then wiped my nose with the back of my hand. "The point is, my point is, you don't know anything about me." I shook my head. "You aren't in love with me."

His gypsy eyes lost their twinkle in favor of scorching intensity; likewise, his expression became serious and impatient, and his tone harsh. "You don't get to tell me what I feel. I was the one left behind."

I grimaced and clutched my folded hands to my chest where his words pierced. "I know."

"You don't know. You left."

"Nico…I don't know what to say."

"There is nothing you can do about the decisions you made when you were a teenager except learn from them. Just like there is nothing I can do about the mistakes I made—the way I treated you, how I reacted after you left—except not make them again."

I eyed him warily, not entirely sure that I wanted to know the answer to my next questions. "What do you mean? What did you do after I left?"

He exhaled a short, mirthless laugh. "Typical impulsive teenage behavior: I picked fights. I failed out of high school. I moved to New York, moved in with Milo, and was completely self-destructive."

I wanted to comfort him—both the teenage Nico I left behind and the man who stood in front of me now. Instead, I clenched my hands into fists and watched him silently.

"I can't be sorry about it." He said these words mostly to himself. "If you hadn't left, I might still be the jerk I was before. I did a lot of stupid things, but I learned from them. I changed. I'm different now. And I know you're different now too."

I nodded, pressed my lips into a line, and glanced at the counter. Nico and I might both be different, but it sounded like he'd changed for the better whereas I'd changed for the worse.

"But, Elizabeth, even though you've changed, I still know you. You're brilliant and you're—" he cleared his throat, "you're beautiful. You care about others, strangers, and you take care of them. You're still loyal and honest and generous."

"I'm not generous."

"You are generous. None of that has changed."

"Nico…."

"You're also stubborn and bossy, and you lose your temper almost as fast as I do."

"Nico, no." I shook my head, stared at a spot on the counter between us.

"You kissed me."

"Because you're insanely hot!"

He smiled. "You think I'm insanely hot?"

My head lolled to the side and I gave him my very best *bitch, please* scowl. "You know you're hot. You could've had any girl in high school. You used to be an underwear model. So don't pretend you don't know that you're alert level red."

His smile grew. "We should talk about this in greater detail. What about me, precisely, is alert level red?"

I hit him playfully on the shoulder. "Really, seriously, you don't know me. You wouldn't like me if you did. I'm spiteful and petty. I'm immature. I'm lazy."

"Everyone is." He shrugged.

"No. Listen to me." My frustration with his willful blindness was mounting, building itself into a skyscraper of aggravation. I needed him to understand without spilling too many specifics that the Elizabeth he thought he knew didn't exist anymore. Garrett's sweet, kind, pure, naïve, wilting flower was a memory.

"The girl you knew, the girl who left you and went to Ireland, she doesn't exist. Ok?" I glared at him through my eyebrows and pressed my hand to my chest. "The woman before you now is shallow, conceited, and selfish. I use people. I'm kind of a terrible person."

He looked like he was trying to contain laughter. "How so?"

"You'll just have to trust me on this."

"I'm not that trusting."

"Ok, then. You want to know?"

His smile was wide and clearly amused. He was adorable. My brain melted a little. I steadied myself to tell him, but in that moment, looking into his eyes, faced with his smile, I couldn't continue. I didn't want him to know. The thought of him knowing the truth about me felt like the worst thing in the world.

Therefore, the truth caught in my throat.

But it wouldn't be fair to him. Avoiding the truth would postpone the inevitable. I needed to give him honesty. His eyes—those puppy dog, gypsy, soulful eyes—were going to keep looking at me with worshipful allegiance unless I was completely honest.

His eyes twinkled, his gaze caressed my features, and his admiration was practically tangible. It felt like an uninvited third person in the bathroom. When I didn't immediately continue, he filled the silence. "You can't tell me that I don't know you. I see you. I see you better than you see yourself. And you are beautiful."

His lovely words coming from his lovely mouth said with his lovely voice made my insides melt to mush.

Maybe just a little longer.... A traitorous voice that sounded nothing like mine pleaded from behind the curtain of my subconscious. The entreaty had the opposite of its intended effect.

I stood taller by straightening my back, picked a make-believe piece of lint from my jeans, and cleared my throat. I would prove to him that he didn't know me at all.

"I use people."

His confident smile slipped. He frowned. "What?"

"I use men."

"What do you mean, you *use men*?"

I shrugged, but my heart was galloping and I felt abruptly nauseous. "I use men for sex. I pick a guy, have sex with him, and when I'm done, I toss him aside."

I know I sounded heartless, cold; but I did so purposefully. In order to save his heart, he needed to understand that mine no longer functioned; that after losing my mom and Garrett, I wasn't interested in loving or being loved by anyone. I endeavored to hurt him a little now because I refused to prolong his hope.

Nico straightened and crossed his arms over his chest again. "Explain."

"Ok, then. I'll spell it out: I pretend to like a guy and use him for sex. When I get tired of having sex with him, and I always do, I stop returning his phone calls, and I blow him off." When I finished, I noted that my stomach hurt.

Nico watched me, a plain assessment, and his frown became

more severe. "You haven't...?" He shook his head. "When was the last time you dated someone you actually liked?"

"Garrett." I didn't hesitate. My response was immediate. He flinched. My hands were cold and clammy.

"Jesus." He sighed. However, instead of appearing disgusted by my proclamation, his gaze softened and he shifted closer. "I wish we could have...."

"Haven't you been listening? I'm trying to be honest with you. I'm not looking for love, I'm not even capable of it. I'm completely toxic. I'm a user. I have no interest in having a relationship. I have no interest in men other than using them to play 'hide the salami.' So, *see me*, Nico. See me for who I am and not who you want me to be." I was annoyed by the lingering look of sympathy he was casting in my direction. I rubbed my forehead with damp and shaking hands. "Forget it. This isn't going to work."

I moved to the door and unlocked it. I was unrepentant in my honesty, but in that moment, I recognized that a big part of me wished things could be different. I wished I were different. He crossed to my position and held the door shut. I tried yanking the handle, but he was too strong. After several fruitless attempts, I smacked the door with my palm—a childish display of frustration—and turned my flashing blue eyes to his now stoic face.

"What?" Feigning anger was really the only thing keeping me from bursting into tears. "Don't like what you see? What is it going to take for you to let me out of here?"

His face was like granite as his eyes moved between mine. He was still frowning. He opened his mouth as though he were going to say something, but ultimately, he moved his hand from the door and stepped out of my way.

I tried to make my face rigid, severe, and acrimonious as I tugged open the door. "I did warn you."

I searched his expression for the judgment I hoped would be there and found only pity. His pity dually pissed me off and sparked my mortification. Gritting my teeth, I walked past him out the door and into the dining room where everyone looked like him, talked like him, and laughed like him.

I couldn't wait to leave.

CHAPTER 10

Indefinable emotion cast the next several moments in a fog of gray grumpiness. Sandra, after one look at my expression, made excuses for our hasty departure. I said nothing. I allowed her to steer me through the crowd of Manganiellos with a plastic smile pasted on my features.

Just as we were nearing the front door, Nico shuffled into the dining room looking like a kicked puppy. I blinked against stinging moisture as the beginnings of an inexplicable, epic cry fest forced my chin to wobble. I clenched my teeth and bit my tongue to hold back the deluge.

Sandra led me to the car. Rose followed us out.

I could tell that Rose was disappointed, but I couldn't think clearly enough at that point to pacify Nico's mother. I promised, with a head nod, that I would visit the next time I was in town.

We drove in silence for several minutes, my hands flexing and gripping the steering wheel intermittently as I replayed my encounter with Nico no matter how hard I wanted to forget it. I wasn't paying much attention to where we were going. When I ran a stop sign, Sandra made me pull over so that she could drive. As soon as we switched seats and my seatbelt clicked into place, the tears started to flow.

It was a messy cry—a snotty, snorting, sobbing cry. It felt like someone was trying to pull my lungs and stomach from my body. And, damn it all, I wasn't sure why I was crying, which only made me cry more.

Sandra, bless her, drove in circles until I was ready to give directions to the interstate.

"Oh, Elizabeth." She sighed and reached for my hand as we climbed the ramp to I-80. "I'm so sorry."

"It's ok." I hiccupped. "I don't know why I'm so upset."

Sandra cast me a sideways glance and offered a small smile. "Let me know if you want to talk through it."

I nodded and pulled tissue from the glove compartment. I didn't want to talk about it—not with Sandra, and maybe not with anyone. I just wanted to forget the last twenty-four hours.

That would be my plan A.

But, try as I might, I couldn't stop thinking about Nico and his expression when I told him how I'd used guys. This recollection caused new tears. I kept seeing how his eyes changed from worshipful to pitying, and for several moments, I really felt like I was going to be sick.

Miles of empty cornfields passed by in a blur, and I tried to console myself. I silently repeated that I'd done the right thing. I'd been honest with him. It was in his best interest that I'd dispelled any residual delusions about me.

I would only disappoint him.

We continued in this way until my eyes stopped leaking. Sandra didn't push me for details about what happened in the bathroom, and she voluntarily turned on the Backstreet Boys as driving music.

I knew she felt bad. At some point, I would need to knit her something nice to prove I wasn't upset with her. I really wasn't upset with her. I understood her motives, and part of me—the part of me I was trying really hard to disregard—was quite euphoric to have kissed Nico.

The rest of me was gorging itself on pity party pie.

I didn't consider myself broken, because I wasn't broken. I was merely content to be shallow, and I actually really hated that about myself. Nico would never want to touch me again now that he knew what I was like. He deserved better.

As my breathing normalized, I found myself touching my lips, remembering, daydreaming. Sandra was kind enough to disregard my wistful sighs. Instead, she made jokes about the apocalypse and finally having a chance to see the World's Largest Truckstop as we neared the state line.

The actual apocalypse occurred as we were on the exit ramp.

My cell phone rang. I glanced at the number. I made a face. "Ugh. It's Meg." My voice was still nasally and thick. I had a cry headache.

Sandra made a face that mirrored mine. "I like that you call her Megalomaniac Meg. The description fits her like a pair of bike shorts."

I smirked my agreement and rejected the call.

My cell phone rang again. I glanced at the number. I made a face. "Ugh. It's Meg again." I rejected the call.

Sandra laughed. "She thinks you two are besties."

I tried to chuckle then sighed and sniffled. "Nah. She knows what's up. She's my nemesis. We're on the same page."

My cell phone rang again. I glanced at the number. I frowned. "What? It's Meg—again."

"Do you want me to answer it? I could tell her you're in the bathroom and seem to have a nasty case of gastroenteritis." We pulled into the truck stop parking lot. Like the rest of the World's Largest Truckstop, the parking lot was truly massive.

"Yes, please, if you don't mind. I don't particularly wish to speak with her right now."

Once we parked, Sandra slid her thumb across the touch screen and brought the phone to her ear. "Elizabeth's cell phone answering service, this is Sandra. How may I direct your call?"

Almost immediately, Sandra held the phone away from her ear; Meg's indecipherable screeching filled the car.

"Ah, take it off speakerphone!" I winced and covered my ears.

"It isn't on speakerphone. She's banshee screaming."

I took the phone from Sandra and held it a safe distance from my ear as I yelled into the receiver. "Meg. You have to stop screaming—what is the problem? I can't understand you."

"Oh, my god! Elizabeth Finney—you are in so much trouble! Why didn't you tell me you had a child with Nico Moretti?"

I held the phone away from my ear and in front of me. I stared at the screen. The sound of Meg's continued expletives blasted from the small device. I stared at it. I just stared at it. I couldn't think.

How did Meg know about Nico?

I glanced at Sandra who was wide-eyed and horrified.

"You didn't…? Did you call Meg and tell her about Nico?"

"Hell, no." Sandra held her hands up. "Your secret is safe with me."

"How did she find out?" My palms started to sweat. I glared at the phone. It felt suddenly dangerous. Tentatively, I brought the speaker to my mouth, and when Meg paused in the middle of her enthusiastic screeching to take a breath, I interjected. "Listen. Meg, listen to me. What are you talking about? What did you hear?"

"It's all over the place. I saw the article on Yahoo Celebrity Stalker and watched the YouTube video just seconds ago."

"What are you talking about? What YouTube video?" I stared at the sign for the World's Largest Truckstop. I had the abrupt sensation of being trapped in a Mel Brooks movie.

"Don't pretend you don't know what I'm talking about, Elizabeth. It's the YouTube video of you dancing with Nico Moretti then later yelling at the top of your lungs about HAVING A CHILD WITH THE MAN!"

I choked. I actually choked on air.

Sandra pulled the phone from my hand and handed me a bottle of water. Between coughs, I motioned for her to hang up the phone. When I caught my breath, I set the bottle of water between my thighs and gripped the dashboard. I was in a Mel Brooks movie. I was certain of it. I couldn't have been more confounded if someone had jumped in front of my car wearing a giant pretzel and singing "It's Springtime for Hitler."

"I couldn't understand her. What did she say? How did she find out?" Sandra sounded as perplexed as I felt.

I shook my head. My voice was now both nasally and raspy due to my recent coughing fit. "She said there was a YouTube video of Nico and me dancing, and then…" I swallowed another gulp of water, "…then later the video shows me announcing to a room full of people that I—that he and I had a child together."

Sandra covered her mouth and gasped; her green eyes were wide with disbelief. "Oh, my god. Someone must've been recording at the reunion." She shook her head, stared unseeingly out the windshield. "Oh, my god."

"Maybe it's not that big of a deal. Maybe no one will care and it'll be a little blip."

She was already shaking her head before I finished my sentence. "No, Elizabeth. This is a big deal. Have you followed Nico at all? Have you followed his career or his personal life?"

"No." I hadn't followed him. In fact, I'd more or less purposefully avoided his personal life and stories about him in the news.

"Elizabeth." She turned in her seat and unlatched her seatbelt to face me better. "He's notoriously private. Like, he never talks about his personal life or his family. He's never been photographed off set with a woman who didn't work on the show. It's to the point where a lot of people assume he doesn't *like* women."

"He likes women."

"I know. I saw him kiss you, remember?"

I didn't respond. I just tugged on my left eyebrow.

"This is not going to blow over. People are going to think you have a love child with Nico Moretti. And you're a doctor. That's not a typical attention-seeking type of profession if there is such a thing. You appear to be a credible person."

Love child with Nico. That was a strange concept to think about.

It made me feel all kinds of warm things I couldn't define.

We sat in stunned silence for an interminable period; the engine was still running. I abandoned plan A and wallowed in my memories, rewinding the last twenty-four hours. I played back all my Nico interactions that could have been recorded.

Sandra placed her hand on my forearm, rousing me from my remembering; "Elizabeth...what are you going to do?"

My throat hurt. I shook my head. I couldn't think, so I answered honestly. "I don't know. I don't know." And, because I really didn't know, I said it again. "I don't know."

~*~*~*~

When I arrived home Saturday evening, I decided to redouble my efforts to ignore all thoughts and feelings associated with the kiss under the mistletoe and the resulting bathroom fiasco as well as the viral YouTube video.

Upon arriving to my apartment, I flipped on the TV. This was a mistake. An entertainment TV show was airing the grainy clip of me climbing the chair and belting out my confession. I continued watching just long enough to hear the commentators bad-mouth Nico's alleged abandonment of our love child.

For a brief moment—despite the danger involved—I wished I'd yelled *fire!* instead of *the child is yours.*

I felt sick with remorse at what I'd done, especially since Nico was now paying the price in the court of public opinion. I wanted so badly to apologize for my ridiculous outburst, but I felt fairly confident that he'd never want to see me again, so I figured it didn't matter anymore.

Disgusted, I flipped off the TV and listened to boy bands loudly. I organized Janie's comic books. I ordered Marie a set of Addi Click knitting needles that she'd been lusting after for a *just because* present. I alphabetized my records. I read FARK.com for an hour then searched *AskMetafilter* for questions related to odd yarn materials and recycle crafts: plastic grocery bags = plarn; T-shirts = tarn.

I busied myself. I was getting more practice at avoiding.

However, even without turning on the TV, life post Nico/love child/apocalypse quickly became less than pleasant.

The fallout of the YouTube video began to take shape. My voicemail filled up first. After the fortieth text message, I called my cell phone provider to remove texting ability from my phone and change my number. The change would take twenty-four to forty-eight hours. After another twenty minutes of rejecting phone calls from unknown numbers, I finally turned the damn thing off.

Then I made the mistake of checking my Gmail account. I had seven hundred new messages.

How did these people find my contact information so quickly?

Throughout all of this, Nico was never far from my thoughts. I worried about him and the trouble I'd caused him. His security guards were absolute crap. Then there was the psycho stalker he'd mentioned. And now I had an email account full of obsessed crazy people. I wished I'd been successful talking him into switching security firms. I kicked myself for not giving him Quinn's number when I had the chance.

With these concerns for his safety also came daydreams. More than once I found myself caught up in a fantasy about him, about our brief time together over the weekend: dancing at the reunion, later in my room, telling me he loved me, at the restaurant, his hands on me, his mouth on mine, the way he looked at me like I was the only person in the world.

The daydreams were wonderful and awful and confusing. Every time I slipped into one, I wanted to cry again. I was officially a crying female.

I made a concerted effort to focus on the not-so-bad aspects of the whole situation, otherwise known as *it could have been worse* or *look on the bright side* or *at least you're not a hobo.*

I thanked my lucky stars that the quality of the video was spotty at best, though it was clearly me. The idiot who posted it on YouTube listed my name beneath the clip. However, on the bright side, he or she never got a full shot of my face. The amateur videographer seemed to be mostly preoccupied with capturing Nico.

I also thanked my lucky stars that I never felt the need to set up a facebook account or other form of social media. My ambivalence to social media was another way that Janie had rubbed off on me. I didn't have friends other than my small circle, and I didn't much care for *connecting* with people. Therefore, the only picture of me linked to the video was my high school graduation photo.

I thanked my lucky stars a third time that I now looked almost entirely different. My teenage self could have passed for a picture of a younger brother.

The weird celebrity stalkers had my name, a dark video of me, and my high school yearbook photo, and that was basically it. I felt some measure of relief for my own sake, but I struggled with how to make things right for Nico. I told myself that I'd overreacted, and the likelihood of it all blowing over was almost certain.

I was wrong, but it took me until lunch on Sunday to understand the depth and breadth of the situation.

When I returned to work on Sunday, I braced myself for…something. Meg had the day off. Everyone else appeared to be oblivious to the Nico/love child/video/apocalypse. That or they were too polite to mention it. I was able to go about my day with no disruption, which helped me feel calmer and more relaxed about the kerfuffle.

Ashley and I had made a date the week prior to meet for lunch Sunday afternoon. Since the day was unseasonably nice for April in Chicago—at forty-nine degrees and sunny—we bundled up and decided to eat on the stone patio benches in the garden, a small green space beside the hospital, but presently the area was more brown than green.

"So…." she openly studied me as we settled on the cold bench. Ashley took a bite of her carrot. It snapped with staccato perfection. "How was the reunion?"

My lids drifted shut as unbidden images of Nico—at the restaurant, blocking my way, holding the bathroom door closed, his expression full of hurt—flashed before my eyes. I rubbed my forehead. My heart thudded painfully for three or four beats.

"Can we save this conversation for Tuesday? I know the ladies will want to hear all about it, and I just don't think I can tell the story twice."

"That good, huh?" Ashley smiled then continued her carrot munching.

"That…strange." I handed Ashley a peanut butter cookie. As was my habit, I always brought her a cookie when we had lunch together. She always brought me mango soda.

I'd just unwrapped my egg salad on pumpernickel when Ashley stopped chewing her carrot. She blinked then squinted at a bush some distance away, at the end of the hospital garden.

"What the…?" she tilted her head to the side, looked behind us, then glared at the bush again. "Elizabeth."

My mouth was watering and I was starving. I grunted, "What?" then stuffed a quarter of the sandwich in my mouth.

"There's some weirdo in the bushes over there taking pictures of us." She pointed to the edge of the garden.

I wrinkled my nose and squinted in the direction she indicated. Sure enough, a weirdo was in the bushes taking pictures of us with the largest lens I'd ever seen. I stared at the lens and the weirdo as I chewed my sandwich.

Ashley set her lunch to the side and stood. "I'm going to ask him to please stop taking pictures."

"You're going over there?" I managed to ask through my mouthful of sandwich.

"Jeepers, yeah. I don't want to have pictures of me eating

carrots just floating around out there for all those carrot fetish people to leer at."

I watched her saunter over to the man with the camera and took another bite of my sandwich. She was about halfway to the weirdo before it occurred to me that the weirdo might actually be paparazzi and that I, and not Ashley's propensity for eating carrots, was the real purpose of their photographic endeavors.

I tried to yell at Ashley to turn around but then abandoned the plan, the unchewed egg salad and pumpernickel a sound barrier. I was forced to swallow a painful and inadequately masticated lump of sandwich, which I washed down quickly with water, and then I stood and shouted at her to come back.

But I was too late. She was already talking to the man.

CHAPTER 11

Ashley was pointing to his camera. She was very calm. He pointed to me. She cocked her head to the side and laughed. He shook his head. She shook her head. He pointed to me again and then lifted his camera to take a picture.

Shrugging her shoulders she sauntered back to our bench, her expression a mixture of quizzical amusement and befuddlement.

"That guy has his horse switched with a raccoon." She reclaimed her seat.

"Horse?"

"He's plain nutters."

I cleared my throat; it still ached from the large swallow. "What did you talk about?"

"Remember last week when I told you all about that celebrity in the hospital—Nico Moretti?"

I nodded slowly and the queasiness that accompanies dread gripped my stomach. I turned sideways on the bench to keep the man with the camera from getting a clear shot of my face.

"Well, that guy over there thinks that you're Nico's *secret luvah.*" Ashley waved her eyebrows at me and grinned, emphasizing her mispronunciation of the word *lover* in a way that made me think of sweat, labored breathing, and porno mustaches from the seventies. "I told him he was nuts."

I wasn't hungry anymore. I wrapped up my uneaten sandwich and put it back in my lunch sack along with my untouched mango pop. "Oh, my god…."

Ashley's grin waned. Her hand holding the carrot hovered in the air, halfway to her mouth; "Hey. Elizabeth? Are you ok, hon?"

I fanned my fingers at my temple, trying to hide my face. "Oh, Ashley. I have to tell you something."

I motioned for her to pack up her lunch and then I stood abruptly. She stared at me for a long moment, hesitated, but eventually complied.

I gripped her hand and pulled her back into the hospital, through the corridors, and into the doctor's lounge. It was lunchtime, and most people opted to eat in the cafeteria or offsite. We basically had the space to ourselves other than a few dozing docs on the couches.

We sat at a table in the corner and I kept my voice low. "Ok, so, here's the deal." I squeezed my lids shut to work up my nerve. "I know Nico Moretti."

"You *what?*" Ashley shook me slightly; when I met her gaze, her blue eyes were open so wide that they nearly popped from their sockets.

"Shhh." I covered her mouth with my hand. "I'll tell you, but you have to be quiet about it."

She nodded without a word, her face serious and eager. She traced a cross over her heart then brought her fingers to her lips for the universal sign of *my lips are sealed.*

I left most of the personal, sentimental, touchy-feely emotional stuff out, but even so, halfway through my story about the reunion and Nico and our shared past, Ashley pulled out her cell phone and searched YouTube for the video. She gasped, covered her mouth, and stared at me with wide, shocked eyes.

"You had a love child with Nico Moretti?"

"Shhh." I glanced over my shoulder. No one was paying attention to us. "No. I did not have his love child."

"But you still know him? You're involved with him?"

"No. Yes. I mean…." I twisted my fingers. "Yes, I know him. We went to school together. He was best friends with my boyfriend, Garrett. He helped me after Garrett died." I gritted my teeth. "We slept together once. But there was no baby."

"This is inconceivable." She shook her head slowly as she hit the replay button on the video and watched it again, mesmerized. "I can't believe this."

"It's over. He never wants to see me again."

"He said that?"

"No—not precisely, but I'm pretty sure it's true."

"After you rescued him from those dance floor hoochies? You'd think he'd be grateful you stepped in, even if you did tell the whole world that you and he made a baby."

"I didn't tell the whole world, it was never meant to be recorded. I couldn't think of anything else to distract them."

Ashley pursed her lips. "Why didn't you yell *fire*?"

"Because it's illegal and dangerous to yell *fire* in a crowded room. Besides, he wasn't angry about that." My scalp was suddenly itchy.

"What was he mad about?"

"He told me that he loved me, and I…."

"He said he loves you?" Ashley covered her mouth with her hand after shouting the sentence. We both glanced at the couches but found the inhabitants still slumbering.

"Sorry." She lowered her voice to a whisper and said, "When…how…ok, just tell me what happened. When did Nico Moretti tell you he loved you?"

"It doesn't matter. I told him how I indiscriminately sleep with men then stop returning their phone calls."

Ashley placed her hand on my knee. "Hon, you don't indiscriminately sleep with men. I have known you for going on two years, and I've never seen you whore it up."

"I do. I have."

"So you go up to random men on the street and request sex?"

"No. It's not like that."

"What's it like? How many guys have you slept with?" Ashley crossed her arms under her chest. Her eyebrows were disbelieving umbrellas over skeptical blue eyes.

"Four."

"Four?"

"Yes. Four."

"Including Nico Moretti?"

"Yes. Four including Nico."

She chuckled and shook her head. "Four a whore does not you make."

I blinked. "What?"

"Sorry, sometimes when I try to rhyme I end up sounding like Yoda." She cleared her throat. "Sleeping with four guys is hardly loose goose territory."

"But it's how I do it; my intentions are selfish. I use them, I have sex with them, and then I stop taking their calls."

"And how long have these relationships—"

"They weren't relationships."

Ashley held up her hands. "Fine, how long do these meaningless orgies last? How long have you been with each of your four sexual partners?"

"With Nico it was just the once but with the others…." I shrugged and sighed. "I don't know—maybe a couple months each."

"And have you been with more than one guy at the same time?"

"You mean like a three way or do you mean two guys, different days?"

"Either."

"Well, actually, it's neither. I've only been with one guy at a time."

"Oh, dear." She shook her head and clasped my hands in hers. "Elizabeth, I don't know how to break this to you, but you've been having relationships with men."

"No, no I haven't. I've been using them."

"Yes, yes you have. You have been in exclusive relationships with these men."

"I haven't."

"You have. You've been dating them."

"I paid for all my own meals."

Ashley's eyes danced as she laughed again. "It doesn't matter who pays for dinner, dear. A date is a date. You've dated four guys, engaged in relations, then ended the relationship when you no longer wanted to pursue it." She tightened her grip on my hand when I tried to pull away. "It's called breaking up."

"No, you're wrong. I never had any intention of dating them. I didn't want a relationship with any of them. I didn't even like them."

"But you like Nico."

I hesitated then decided to be honest. "Yes." I breathed the word out, finally allowing myself to hold her hand in return. "Yes. I do like him. But I'm so different now, and he—he's some famous comedian. It doesn't matter anyway because I told him that I use men that I don't like for sex."

She glared at me through narrowed eyes. "You were purposefully trying to scare him away."

"No…" I narrowed my eyes at her, mirroring her expression. "I was trying to be honest. And if my honesty makes him realize that he is wrong about me, then so be it."

Ashley's mouth was curved in a frown of plain disgust. "You are pushing the poor guy away."

"He doesn't love me, Ashley. He doesn't even know me."

"Do want a relationship with Nico?"

I hesitated again. I didn't know the answer to her question because I'd never considered the possibility, not even that summer when we were teenagers and he held me as I slept. The idea that Nico Manganiello would want a relationship with me—then or now—was beyond my comprehension. More than that, the idea of dating him felt wrong *because* I liked him and cared about him.

I'd already experienced my one great love. It wouldn't be fair to Nico if I led him on and made him hope for a future that wasn't possible, that I didn't want, and that I wasn't capable of.

I decided to deflect rather than discuss these thoughts with Ashley. "You don't understand what he was like in high school. He was *the guy*. Everyone had a crush on him. He was hot and smart, and he oozed charisma. There was much swooning whenever he walked into a room."

"What does that have to do with anything?"

"He's a celebrity. And he has a terrible security firm. He needs better security."

"Again, what does that have to do with anything?"

"I've already had my great love."

Ashley blinked at me, waited to see if I had more to reveal, then she shook her head slightly. "What are you talking about?"

"I've already been in love." I glanced at my watch. Much to my annoyance, I still had another fifteen minutes before lunchtime was over.

"It's like you and I are having two different conversations. I asked you if you wanted a relationship with Nico, and you didn't answer the question."

"Because I don't know how to answer it."

"Well, that's an answer. You could have just said, 'I don't know, Ashley. I don't know if I want to have a relationship with dreamy Nico Moretti even though I like him and he's a great guy and he loves me and over half the population of the United States wants to get in his pants'." She mocked me in a high-pitched North Dakota accent, which was surprisingly good considering she was from Tennessee.

My mouth pulled to the side. "I do not sound like that, and, really—over half the population?"

"More like three quarters. I know some straight men who would switch teams to take a bite out of that apple arse."

"Oh, my god." I hit her thigh. "Ashley!"

"What? It's true. I know I'd like to take a look at his knackwurst."

"What are you two talking about?"

Ashley and I stiffened and automatically turned toward the owner of the voice. I met the dreamy—yet dull—gaze of Dr. Ken Miles with an expression that I was sure looked guilty.

"Oh, hey, Ken. I didn't see you come in." Ashley didn't look guilty. She looked pleased. I scowled at her.

"So who were you two talking about? Was it me?"

Ashley kept her face turned toward Dr. Ken Miles but her eyes slid to me. "Actually we were talking about a friend of Elizabeth's from high school. She just recently made contact with him again, and he wants to get together, so…no. Not you."

It took all my Jedi power to keep from smacking Ashley at that moment. She knew my plan for Dr. Ken Miles. She knew he was my best hope for getting laid in the foreseeable future. She knew she was interfering with the potential for an orgasm, maybe several if I was lucky.

Friends don't pussy submarine friends. Not cool.

"Old friend?" Dr. Ken Miles turned his pale blue eyes to mine. He appeared to be interested and his voice held a slight edge. It was a good sign and a bad sign.

I shrugged. "Oh, yeah, well—you know. I went to my high school reunion this weekend and ran into some people."

Dr. Ken Miles was chewing gum and holding a half-finished milkshake. He set it down and pushed blonde curls to one side of his forehead then crossed his arms over his chest. "Yeah. I saw that…."

I stared at him for a beat. When I spoke, my voice cracked. "You saw what?"

Dr. Ken Miles's eyes narrowed, moved between mine; his jaw opened and closed as he kneaded the gum between his molars.

"The YouTube video with you and that comedian guy. Meg showed it to me yesterday."

Shitzerhozen! Megalomaniac eyebrow-tweezing Meg.

"Oh. That." I laughed. I knew it sounded insincere and forced. I grimaced.

He smiled at me in return. It looked insincere and forced. "I didn't know you had a kid."

I rolled my eyes and released a long sigh. "I don't. I didn't. I was trying to be helpful."

"See? She was trying to be helpful," Ashley said sweetly.

"I was, Ashley." I shot her a stealthy death stare despite the forced smile on my face. "As I was just explaining, Nico and I were acquainted in high school. One of his closest friends was my boyfriend. At the reunion there were some intoxicated women who were harassing him, so I tried to diffuse the situation by yelling something to shock the ladies out of their inappropriate behavior."

Dr. Ken Miles had pulled up a chair next to me while I was speaking. He obviously wanted to hear more, but his expression was still guarded. "Why didn't you yell *fire*?"

Oh, for the love of god!

"I actually explained that too." My smile was waning, and I worried that it looked more like a growl than a grin. I wondered how many times I was going to have to explain the legality of screaming *fire* in an occupied room. "It is actually against the law to yell fire in a crowd of people. You know, what with all the panic and trampling to death and whatnot."

"Hmm..." Dr. Ken Miles leaned back in his chair, his long legs stretched out in front of him. He studied me speculatively. "So, you two hooking up now or something?"

"That's a very personal question, Dr. Ken." Ashley's Tennessee twang reminded him that she was still there. "Unless you have a stake in the dairy farm, the milking pen is none of your beeswax."

Dr. Ken Miles frowned at Ashley's untoward metaphor, his eyes moving over her in plain contemplation. He responded with a vehemence I wasn't expecting. "Shouldn't you be getting back to work, nurse?"

Ashley and I shared a look of silent communication

Me: *That was weird.*

Her: *What was all that about?*

Me: *I don't know. Kinda douchey though.*

Her: *Yes. My sentiments exactly.*

"Well…" Ashley stood from her chair slowly, keeping her eyes on me. "I suppose that is my queue to leave."

I glanced at Dr. Ken Miles, glowering at his rudeness, then back to Ashley. "No, no—you don't need to go."

"Actually, Dr. Ken is right. I need to get back. You two have a nice chat." She stressed the word chat and issued me a wonky stare as she left.

I frowned at her back then shifted my attention to him, challenging him to speak, but I didn't wait.

"That was really rude, Dr. Ken Miles."

"Yeah, well, she did need to get back." He ground the gum between his molars. "I'll apologize to her later, ok? I just wanted to talk to you alone."

I studied his pretty face. Decided to let it go, for now, but I tucked it away as another reason why I disliked him.

He issued me a flat smile. "So, then you had a nice time at your reunion?"

I nodded. "It was different from what I expected, but not unpleasant."

"So…." He opened the lid to his plastic cup and spit the gum into it. Gross. "I heard about your latest prank."

"Really? From who?"

"Dr. Botstein."

"Huh." I shrugged. I was just happy he'd dropped the Nico

babygate scandal so fast. "Really? Was he still mad?"

"He asked me if I thought you should be disciplined."

"What? Why would he do that?"

"Because I'm the chief resident." Dr. Ken Miles looked a little affronted that I would even ask the question.

This annoyed me. I decided to cover my annoyance by flirting. Maybe I could kill two birds with one stone: disguise my irritation that Dr. Botstein had consulted dull Dr. Ken Miles on my antics, and push my getting laid agenda.

Thoughts of getting laid made me think of Nico.

My stomach flip-flopped. For a single second I entertained the possibility that my strange, chaotic, messy, tangled feelings for Nico were just a byproduct of engorged hormones. Maybe all I needed was a nicely built partner.

But I wasn't that stupid.

I couldn't convince myself that Dr. Ken Miles was a suitable substitute for Nico any more than a Pinto was an adequate stand-in for a Ferrari. I wanted to be touched, kissed, held, caressed—and I wanted Nico, but I couldn't use him in that way. I liked him too much.

So I flirted with Dr. Ken Miles.

"I guess it's a good thing then that you and I are such good friends. Besides, the prank was meant for you, and it *was* April Fool's Day." I leaned forward and batted my eyelashes in his general direction. Rebalancing my hormones was a top priority, but I might have slathered on the flirt a little too thick.

Dr. Ken Miles cleared his throat and shifted his attention to the plastic milkshake cup in his hand. "I didn't know the prank was meant for me."

"How am I expected to contain myself around you on April Fool's Day?" I ran my index finger down the length of his arm. I was bracing myself for one of his poor flirting attempts, but it didn't really matter. I didn't care if he was bad at flirting.

"I thought you'd like to know that I stood up for you to Dr. Botstein."

My eyes widened with genuine surprise. "You did?" Maybe Dr. Ken Miles was likeable after all.

He nodded proudly. "I did."

"What did you say?"

"I told him that there was no way to definitively prove that it was you who planted the box of gloves."

I felt badly for Dr. Ken Miles. He wasn't a bad guy. He was just boring.

"I'm sorry, Dr. Ken Miles. I admitted it to Dr. Botstein when he confronted me. But, thanks for trying to cover for me."

"Oh." He looked disappointed, and then his expression suddenly changed to aggravated. "Elizabeth, I think…we need to talk."

I sat up a little straighter and watched his growing somberness through narrowed eyes. "Is there something wrong?"

"Yeah, there is, actually." He glanced around the lounge then set his cup on the table and leaned closer to me. "If it had been anyone else, anyone but you, I would have told Dr. Botstein that I didn't think a hospital was an appropriate place to play pranks." His jaw ticked before he continued. "As this is your third time acting so unprofessionally, I would have told him I thought you needed to be held accountable."

"Ok." I withdrew my hand from his arm and placed it back on my knee. "I—guess, thank you for not saying that to Dr. Botstein."

"This doesn't change how I feel about you. In fact, I'd like very much for us to be more than friends, if you want to know the truth. But if you keep behaving in immature and reckless ways…."

"Immature and reckless?" I could take a reprimand from Dr. Botstein, who I respected and admired, but I had difficulty accepting a lecture about maturity from Dr. Ken Miles, who was not much older than me. "Now, wait a minute. I was playing a harmless prank on April Fool's Day. It's not like I was…."

"Switching a training video with a porn tape?"

I didn't respond. My aggravation was alert level red. Dr. Ken Miles had laughed when I pulled the porno tape prank, and now he was using it as ammunition.

He breathed through his nose, his mouth clamped shut, his nostrils flaring. My eyes shifted to his flaring nostrils.

His flaring nostrils were just...aggravating.

In fact, everything about Dr. Ken Miles in that moment aggravated me—the leftover milkshake with a gob of gum floating on top, his prettiness, his lack of humor, his hall monitor goody-goody attitude.

I shifted my weight to stand and his hand reached out to still my movements. "Where are you going?"

"I'm leaving. I have work to do."

"I just told you that I want to be more than friends, Elizabeth. I think I deserve a response."

I scoff-snorted. "You also just told me that you think I'm immature and reckless. I think you'll excuse me if I need some time to process this new information first."

Dr. Ken Miles leaned forward, his voice lowering to a harsh whisper, "This is why I haven't acted on my feelings, Elizabeth. I can't be with someone who is incapable of behaving like an adult."

"Says the guy who is always attempting a clandestine nose excavation." There—I said it before I could stop myself. I knew it was childish to reference Dr. Ken Miles's constant nose picking, but I was angry and reacting as such.

He blinked and flinched visibly. "What?"

I rolled my eyes. "Nothing. Thanks for your honesty." I forced a smile and nodded vigorously. "Mind if I go now?"

His eyes looked straight into mine, cornflower blue and wide with disbelief. He released my arm abruptly, sniffed, and glanced at his shoes. "Fine. Go."

I stood and walked blindly out of the lounge, past the still dozing doctors on the couch, and into the corridor.

Plan *hide the salami* with Dr. Ken Miles was officially on hold.

~*~*~*~

I was in a terrible mood, and Janie was still in Boston with Quinn.

Stupid Quinn.

Quinn the friend usurper.

Actually, I liked Quinn. He reminded me of me. And I knew he'd be great to my best friend. But that didn't make the time she was gone any less difficult to bear.

Usually, when either of us were feeling the funk, Janie and I would drink mojitos and watch movies based on comic books—her choice—or 1980s Jon Hughes movies—my choice.

Instead, I went to bed early Sunday night, tossed and turned, and had two dichotomous types of dreams: disturbing dreams about Nico being in danger or frustratingly fantastic dreams about Nico and me *en coitus.*

The worst of the nightmares, although I couldn't explain why, involved me running through a crowd trying to find him. Every time I thought I'd found Nico, it turned out to be Dr. Ken Miles. I would turn away from him and continue my search just to find Dr. Ken Miles again. I experienced a high degree of interdream anger and despair.

I needed to contact Nico about his security firm. He needed to hire better guards. His lack of appropriate security was interrupting my sleep. Thoughts of him naked were also interrupting my sleep, but I couldn't do a thing about that except enjoy them while they lasted.

I woke up for my early morning shift feeling hung over. The worst kind of injustice is doing nothing to deserve a hangover and waking up feeling like you have a hangover.

Still yawning by the time I walked into the hospital, I noted that the ibuprofen I took for my headache seemed to be working. I allowed myself a moment of optimistic contemplation—Monday could only be an improvement over Sunday.

I was so distracted by my bad dreams and trying to figure out a way to get Nico's security team replaced as well as the unfairness of my undeserved hangover that I didn't notice the buzzing of my pager. It vibrated off the shelf of my locker while I was pulling on a freshly laundered lab coat over faded teal scrubs.

As I retrieved it from the floor, I felt a twinge of disappointment; the day was already starting with a hectic bang and my shift hadn't technically started yet. I'd arrived to work early. I wanted to spend a few minutes drinking coffee and eating a doughnut. Instead, now abandoning my plan for ten minutes of peace, I gathered a deep breath and glanced at the message.

CRU rm 410 asap; VIP peds ready cg1605 cf iv

I stared at the message.

Oh, shit.

Roughly translated, the message meant *Please come to the Clinical Research Unit, room number 410, as soon as possible. The VIP pediatric patient is ready to enroll on a clinical trial, protocol number 1605, cystic fibrosis infusion study.*

I stared unseeingly at the empty contents of my locker. My mind was in a blank panic. A moment later the original message was followed by a second message that was infinitely more cryptic: *!!!!!!*

Well, I wonder who it could be I thought drolly as I mentally prepared to trudge to the Clinical Research Unit.

Nico had returned with his niece.

They'd decided to enroll her in the study.

CHAPTER 12

The weight of dread heavy on my shoulders, I moved in slow motion to the clinic room. The thought of seeing Nico filled me with despair. Certainly, all the admiration I'd seen in his beautiful green eyes the last time we were together would undoubtedly be replaced with disgust, pity, or some combination of the two.

Granted, I acknowledged that my reaction made no sense. I'd basked in Nico's admiration for an extremely short period, less than twenty-four hours to be exact, in a total of three encounters. But I couldn't help feeling dread at seeing him against, just as I couldn't stop fantasizing about him.

Even if I'd been the type of person who believed falling in love more than once in a lifetime wasn't a crazy stupid thing to do, Nico wasn't interested anymore. He also wasn't my type.

He was hot like lava and sexy like cake. *Wait...like lava cake. Nice.*

He was annoyingly witty and intelligent.

He was thoughtful and kind to his family.

He was too likeable, too charismatic.

Ok, he was my type, damn it.

But, I reminded myself, *he is also the Nico Manganiello who made my childhood hell and....*

I paused, actually stopped walking, and was struck by the complete lack of anger I felt toward him now. Yes, the memories still chaffed; yes, his actions years ago were still hurtful to think about.

However, Nico's apology, my own mistakes and regrets, and relief from finally knowing the reason why I was harassed, all mixed together to produce a mysterious mystical forgiveness, as follows:

[Nico's Heartfelt Apology x (My Mistakes + My Regrets)] + Reason Why = Magical Forgiveness

I leaned against the wall and searched my mental grudge inventory. His name was missing. I was no longer angry at Nico.

"Huh." I said to the empty hall...*weird.*

Haltingly, I continued down the corridor to the CRU, trying to find some reason to dislike him. It took me seven steps to remember that he was a comedian who made his living trying to get celebrities naked on television. I used this as fuel and allowed myself to get worked up.

He was frequently naked on his show; there were mostly nude women parading around and giggling for god's sake—*giggling, half-naked women.* How could I ever respect someone who thought that was ok? How could I respect myself if I condoned it?

It doesn't matter anyway. He's never going to be interested in you now, so stop confusing yourself, weirdo.

When I rounded the corner to the Clinical Research Unit nurses' station, I was so lost in my internal nonsensical struggle that I didn't immediately see Dr. Botstein and Nico huddled together by the door to room 410 or Meg hovering in front of the nurses' counter.

I was nearly upon them when Dr. Botstein's voice pulled me from my musings, causing me to stumble over my own feet. "Ah. Here she is."

I looked from Nico to Dr. Botstein—who was smiling. It was freakish and bizarre to see Dr. Botstein smile. It made me immensely uncomfortable so I opted to look at Nico instead.

"I...."

I didn't know what to say, so I met his stare directly. Where I predicted a pang of sad embarrassment, I was met with a shock of hot awareness. Nico wasn't looking at me with pity or disgust. His gaze held mine hostage, and he was eye twinkling like a champ.

I'd been gaze-hijacked.

"I...."

Then he smirked, his lids lowering to half-mast. There he stood—twinkling, hot lava, sexy cake, sex on a stick, obscene levels of charisma.

Freaking Nico.

I sighed. It was a weak woman sigh. It was the sigh of a female helpless and ensnared by the hypnotic gaze of the guy she fantasizes about.

I'd never been so happy to hear the sound of Dr. Botstein's voice; it was a hard sharp slap to my cranium. "Dr. Finney, I believe you are acquainted with Mr. Moretti."

"Hello, Elizabeth." Nico nodded his head once in my direction.

"Nic—I mean, Mr. Moretti. Good to see you."

Nico smiled at me, caught his bottom lip between his teeth. My breath hitched, and then my stomach flipped at the simple action. His effortless and playful sexiness was mind-muddlingly maddening.

"I think it's ok for you to call me Nico. Dr. Botstein is aware of our relationship."

"Our...?"

"Yes, well, Mr. Moretti already explained the nature of everything." Dr. Botstein returned his attention to Nico. At this point Meg crossed to stand next to me, and nudged me with her elbow. I ignored her as Dr. Botstein continued. "We're just pleased that you've decided to enroll your niece in our clinical trial."

"You have?" I was surprised.

Most of Nico's nimble playfulness waned with a shift in the conversation to serious matters; his expression turned sober. "Yes. My mother and I called Dr. Botstein last week and talked through our questions."

"You did?" I asked.

Meg nudged me again with her elbow. Again, I ignored her.

"Yes, Dr. Finney." Dr. Botstein said, exhaling his impatience. "I saw no reason to discuss the matter with you as I wasn't aware that you knew the family. Besides, your research rotation *was* set to end tomorrow. Obviously, it will be extended."

"It will?" A troubling thought immediately arrested my attention. I was worried that the decision to enroll Angelica in the clinical trial had something to do with me, or more precisely, it had something to do with Nico and me.

"Yes. Obviously." Dr. Botstein said, looking at me with a blank expression as if my slow comprehension required infinite patience.

Meg elbowed me again, this time with a great deal of force. I turned slightly to give her the stink eye, but before I could, I found her glaring at me with unfettered displeasure. *She* was giving *me* the stink eye.

Hag.

Dr. Botstein continued. "And, obviously, everything will be done under my strict supervision. I have complete faith in Dr. Finney, of course, but as I explained last week, the infusion schedule is rigorous. Since you've opted out of an admission to the CRU, bringing little Angelica back to the hospital every eight hours for the next twenty-eight days will require a great deal of dedication."

Nico nodded. "We understand."

"Wait." I pulled my attention from Meg's death stare. "I don't understand; why is my research rotation being extended?"

"Because, Mr. Moretti and his mother requested that *you* treat the patient during the study period."

Meg finally spoke, her voice false and chipper. She glared at me and said, "But don't worry. My research rotation will start as scheduled, and the research nurses will conduct the other patient visits as usual. I just won't be taking care of Angelica—seeing as you are such good friends with the family."

I stared at her, my eyebrows meeting my hairline. "I'm going to do what?"

Dr. Botstein shifted, pulled his pager from where it had been clipped to his scrubs. "Excuse me." He glanced at the screen and *tsked*. "It looks like I'll need to get this. Thanks so much for coming in today. Dr. Finney will get Angelica started on the paperwork and screening tests; it's all very run-of-the-mill. Please call me—day or night—with any questions. I'm here to help."

"Thank you. We appreciate everything." Nico said as the two men shook hands.

With a curt head bob in my direction that seemed to convey both annoyance and respect, Dr. Botstein turned and stalked away from us. He pulled his cell phone from his pocket and barked orders to some faceless person on the other end.

My eyes locked again with Nico's, and I noticed that I was holding my breath as if I were waiting for…something. Silence stretched. Nothing happened—well, nothing other than the unwavering intensity of his gaze, my resulting increase in heart rate, and our lengthy staring contest.

Someone cleared a throat very loudly and I turned toward the sound. The clinical research nurses were sitting behind the nurses' station, pretending to work but obviously eavesdropping on the entire conversation. They both peered at me with Cheshire grins. I glanced at my feet, attempted to gather my wits.

I sensed that Meg was about to nudge me again with her sharp elbow, so I sidestepped the movement and advanced on Nico. I felt an acute need to speak with him alone. Despite his and Dr. Botstein's assurances, I wanted to make sure Rose and Nico had made a fully informed decision about Angelica's treatment.

And, if I were being completely honest, I just wanted to be alone with him—preferably in some enclosed space where I could smell him.

"Can I talk to you for a moment?" My eyes shifted to the clinic room where Rose and Angelica were visible through the open door. I gave the pair a small smile of greeting then returned my attention to Nico and added, "Privately?"

"Sure." He didn't frown, but he didn't smile either. However, his eyes dropped to my mouth and lingered there.

"Ok—here." I grabbed his hand. "Come with me." I pulled Nico after me, not stopping to consider why I'd decided to hold his hand when a simple gesture to follow would have sufficed. It wasn't because I desired contact with him, loved the shock of awareness that spread through me where we connected, craved it like a drug addict in need of a dopamine fix…nope, none of that.

I led him to a vacant infusion room down the hall. I pushed him inside. I ignored the curious glances from Meg and the nurses as I shut the door.

Gathering a steadying breath, I turned to face Nico and was fully prepared to interrogate him about his reasons for moving forward with the research study. Instead I found him just behind me, less than three feet away, and his proximity rendered me stupid.

I could smell him. He smelled quite good. Therefore, when I met his gaze, I could only manage to breathe out one word. "Hi."

"Hi," he said. He was leaning against the wall with one shoulder, outwardly relaxed and wholly at ease.

Curses!

And he was looking at me funny.

Not angry or disappointed. Not worshipful either.

He looked interested, like I was something new and curious—like he was readying himself for something amusing as well as potentially important.

As usual, the intensity of his focused attention made me feel unbearably self-conscious; my lashes fluttered under the weight of it. "What? What is it?"

Nico shrugged. The shrug did little to decrease the concentrated sharpness of his funny look. "You tell me. You're the one who wanted to talk privately."

It might have been my imagination, but the room felt abruptly smaller after the word *privately* passed his perfectly formed mouth.

"Oh. Yes. Well." I cleared my throat and tried to mirror his relaxed posture, resting my shoulder against the wall and crossing my arms. "There are actually a few things I'm hoping we can discuss, starting with your decision to enroll Angelica in the study."

Mild amusement abruptly transformed into somber concern; he frowned, his posture less relaxed. "Is there something we should know about the study? Is it dangerous? Do you think we made the wrong decision?"

"No, it's nothing like that. I just want to make sure you're making the decision for the right reasons. You shouldn't feel pressured or swayed by any factor other than what you think is right for Angelica."

He nodded somberly. "Dr. Botstein didn't try to sway us one way or the other. He just laid out the facts. We all talked about it this last weekend."

"Who is *we all*?"

"Everyone. Well, everyone you saw on Saturday. It was a family decision. We just want Angelica to get better. You saw how she was at the restaurant, sitting on Christine's lap watching all the other cousins play. She's not…" he glanced at the ceiling, "I just want things to be better for her."

I studied him and my chest hurt a little. He appeared every inch like a tortured parent, and his vulnerability was heartbreaking. A need to protect him welled up within me. I didn't like seeing him so upset and seemingly helpless.

"Why are you here?" I felt compelled to ask this because it seemed unfair that he should be shouldering this burden for his family.

"What do you mean?"

"Why are you here instead of your sister Christine or your brother Robert? How can you take so much time off from your show and from your life in New York?"

He considered me for a moment; the tightness in his features indicated that the topic was difficult for him to discuss, but he seemed relaxed in my presence. "Tina and I were close, and I'm Angelica's godfather. She left my mom custody, but I think Angelica needs a male role model too—a father figure."

"But Robert, Manny—they all live in town and already have kids. They know how to be a father. Wouldn't it make more sense for them to fill that role in her life, and be here for her?"

"No." The corners of his mouth tugged downward, and the muscles at his temples ticked. Nico's typical charismatic energy felt muted and restrained, and he looked like such a grownup. I was struck by how adult-like he seemed—responsible, trustworthy, thoughtful, careful. Everything about him screamed *I have my shit together*.

"But you're missing so much work, and that can't be good for your career, not to mention the upheaval to your personal life."

"Those things don't matter."

"But the burden of caring for a special needs ch-"

"I love her, Elizabeth. I want to be here. She is not a burden; she is my family, and I love her." The rising heat behind his words and the flashing of his eyes demanded that I drop my questioning.

My gaze slid to the infusion chair in the corner, mostly to avoid his. "Ok." I sighed, feeling repentant for pushing him but still frustrated by my helplessness to ease his burden. "I'm just trying to understand you better."

"Why?"

A smile pulled at my mouth, and I glanced at him through my lashes. "I guess because I feel like I don't know you anymore, and I'm curious."

His expression mimicked mine—albeit with a smaller, somewhat sad smile—and his gaze moved slowly over my features. "Elizabeth, I don't think you've ever known me. Not really."

His words were soft, almost resigned, absent any residual frustration from my meddling. And they were doing things to me—the sound of his voice more so than the actual words—that made me feel both warm and adrift.

"That's completely preposterous."

His mouth hooked higher. "You're blinded by stubbornness."

"You're just jealous that I'm always right."

"Not always."

"Mostly always."

"There is no such thing as *mostly always.* It's either always or not always," he said.

"Well, you mostly always used to say things that made me blind with rage."

"And now?"

"And now…." I allowed myself a brief moment to study him. His gaze was wary, but it betrayed interest. "And now I feel like I'm mostly always the one saying the wrong thing."

His gypsy eyes, searched my gaze, before he whispered, "Not always."

We engaged in another staring contest. The frequency of our staring contests was verging on ridiculous. But I couldn't help it. I liked staring at him, and I liked it when he stared at me. His eyes caused a delicious pleasure pain to spike in my chest. I could see myself becoming addicted to the feeling.

This thought paired with an igniting heat behind his eyes stirred me from my Nico-trance. We'd drifted closer to each other without me realizing it.

I stiffened then took a step back and blurted, "The video."

His brow dipped into a V as though he was confused by the

sound and the meaning of my words. But then, as understanding arrested his features, a slow grin claimed his mouth. "Ah, yes…" he also shifted a step backward and had the decency to appear contrite, "…the video."

I tucked loosened strands of hair behind my ears then clasped my hands in front of me, hoping their grip would quell the earlier tinglings and longings and stars still buzzing around in my head. I tried to mentally swat them away and focus. "So…the video…on YouTube…of me…and you…where I said that thing."

He nodded again. "Yes. I'm aware. I was there."

"Yes, of course. And I realize this is my fault. No one forced me to hop on that chair and yell crazy things at the top of my lungs." I took a faltering step toward him. "And I know I have absolutely no right to ask you for help but, is there—do you think there is anything you can do to make these people back off?"

"Are people bothering you?"

"A bit."

"What happened? Did someone approach you?" He advanced a half step and we were again close enough to touch.

"Not really."

"Not really? What does that mean?"

"Well there was a photographer taking pictures of me yesterday while I was eating lunch."

"Damn."

"How did they find my phone number so fast? And my email account is completely full. Half the messages are from newspapers and bloggers I've never heard of, and the other half are from crazy women who want to…." I grimaced and shoved my hands into the pockets of my lab coat. "Well…let's just say they wish their child was yours."

He gave me a mirthless smile. "Just so you know, I really appreciate—really appreciated—what you did. You're right. You didn't have to jump on that chair. But you're also wrong; you do have every right to ask for my help."

"Are you sure about that?" I didn't agree with him. I truly felt I had no right. "Because, I wouldn't blame you if you gave me the middle finger salute and walked out of here."

Nico wrinkled his nose. "Why would you say that? Why would you even think that?"

"Because...." I searched his eyes, hoped to convey without actually admitting the internal frustration and dissidence I'd been living with since he'd appeared last week—actually, perhaps even longer than that. "Because I saw a segment on *Showbiz Weekly* this weekend, and they were crucifying you over what I yelled at our reunion, about you and me having a child. If I've caused you any problems, I can't tell you how...."

Nico waved away my concern. "Are you kidding? I have fake baby drama all the time. Every month there is a blog or trashy newspaper claiming that I've left some poor woman abandoned with eight kids, my very own octomom. Don't worry about it."

I wrestled with my guilt then finally blurted, "I haven't been very nice to you."

His expression softened. "Elizabeth, in your own misguided, crazy, PMSing woman way, I think you've been trying to be nice."

My mouth fell open. "Hey."

"You're just not very good at being nice. It's not a strength of yours."

"I can't believe you just said that."

"You should work on it. You should compliment me more; tell me I look pretty."

I hit him on the shoulder even as I laughed. "You're an idiot."

"And you're beautiful."

I stopped laughing. I couldn't look away from his eyes—and, believe me, I tried. "You can't do that."

"What?" His tone was soft, like a caress.

"You can't say things like that." My hand waved through the

air, floundering. "If we're still going to be friends, you can't keep breaking out the charm canons." Realizing what I'd just said, and what I'd implied—that I still wanted to be friends—my face and neck warmed with embarrassment, but thankfully, not a full-fledged blush. "That is, if you still want to be friends."

"Did I say I wanted to be friends?" He assumed an expression of mock thoughtfulness, eye twinkle alert level red. "When did I say that?"

My heart fluttered as though he'd yanked it toward him. "Yes..." I cleared my throat in an effort to subdue my silly heart. "It was last week. I believe you said, 'I want to be friends—just friends'."

"Ah, yes. Friends without benefits, right?" His eyes narrowed, again with mock seriousness. "Do you still want to be friends without benefits?"

I nodded my response because I didn't trust myself to speak.

"Hmm...ok." His smile was small and sly. "What am I not allowed to say? That you're beautiful?" His voice was still soft, like a stupid caress.

The heat spread; I wrestled like a Klingon with the urge to blush. "Yes."

"You don't tell your friends when you think they look nice?" The eye twinkle was like a bullet.

"It's not the same." I huffed. "Don't do it."

"What do you typically do with your friends who are girls? Since you seem to eschew males from that circle."

I needed to get control of this conversation before he had me wobbly legged and falling into his arms like an idiot. "Talk about sex."

He paused. His smiled widened. "Ok. We could do that."

"Really?" The single word was a disbelieving squeak; my plan to obtain control had officially backfired.

"Yeah. It might be nice for you to have a man's perspective.

What else?"

"Uh…we drink, cuss, and knit."

"Well, I think I'm definitely down with the drinking and cussing, but I'll need your help with the knitting." His full-fledged charming smile was back, but he hadn't lost the residual appearance of a responsible adult male.

"You're going to learn how to knit?" My eyebrows bounced upwards again.

"No. Knitting is for girls. I'm going to learn how to crochet. But…" he dipped his chin to his chest and issued me a look that meant business, "…since we're going to do this, I have a request of *my friend.*"

I stiffened. "What's that?"

"I'm going to give you music homework."

I stared at him. "Say what?"

"I'm going to give you music to listen to, not boy bands, but lots of different artists and genres, and you have to listen to it." He shrugged, hands still in pockets. "We can talk about it when we hang out."

The request sounded benign—suspiciously benign. "Fine," I stated as though I had won an argument. I couldn't think of a reason to object, but I didn't want to appear to be too accommodating, "Then I have a friendship stipulation."

"Why do you get two?"

"It's less of a stipulation and more of a request."

"Fine. Let's hear it."

"Will you please let me fire your security guards?"

He sighed, scratched his neck. His gaze was sheepish. "They are pretty bad."

"I know someone who has a security company. He owns the building where I live—well, part of it, my floor anyway, and is engaged to my best friend. He has a division that provides private security, and he's kind of a badass wizard. They are very discreet, and you don't have to worry about your privacy at all. Please, will you just talk to him? You'll like him. He's really bossy, just like me, and mostly always knows best, just like me."

Nico smiled but then quickly suppressed it. He shrugged again. "Fine. That's fine. Give me his number." Nico handed me his phone.

I released a breath that I wasn't aware I'd been holding, feeling relief down to my bones as I programmed Quinn's number into Nico's cell. I couldn't stop my large smile. "This is great. And you will not regret it. You should call him today, or I can call him."

"I'll call him."

"You promise? You'll call him today? If you don't call him today, I'll find out."

"Yes. Yes, today." He rolled his eyes but I could tell he was enjoying my bossiness. "Do you worry about me?"

I didn't want to lie, but I didn't want to tell the truth either, so I settled for a statement that applied to all of humanity. "I don't want anyone to get hurt."

"Even me?"

My response escaped before I had a chance to disarm it. "Especially you."

His eyes lit, burned brighter. "Why?"

Curses!

"Because..." My brain was failing me. I flailed, resorted to making a few weird scoffing and *tsking* noises, raised my hands and lowered them, then said something true but not the entirety of the truth; so, once again, avoiding. "Because I really like Angelica. She seems like a sweet girl and has already lost quite a lot in her short life. I wouldn't want her to lose you too."

"Hmm...." His expression betrayed his skepticism. "She likes you too."

"She does?"

"Yes. She does. Why wouldn't she?"

"Kids usually don't. I'm not generally great with kids. My friend Fiona's kids refer to me as 'that strange lady'."

"What a coincidence—that's what Angelica calls you too."

I gave him my very best *I am not amused* face. He, of course, thought this was hilarious. His laughter eventually became infectious, and soon we were both laughing.

"Funny, funny guy."

"Smart girl."

"Somehow I don't believe you when you say that."

Nico studied me for a moment, and then he swayed forward, his voice velvety, his eyes dreamy. "You should. You should always believe me. I will always tell you the truth."

My stomach dropped to my feet and the room tilted a bit. I could only nod.

My silence seemed to fuel his amusement. He glanced at the floor then shifted a bit closer. His tone was silky, measured. "Still friends?"

"Yes…friends." The words almost caught in my throat.

CHAPTER 13

As Nico and I exited the infusion room, I felt listless. I drifted aimlessly in a cloud of confusion and self-recrimination. I floated distractedly on the despondency that accompanies getting exactly what you want then realizing what you want is stupid.

Nico, apparently a gentleman, held the door open, and I walked out. Therefore, I saw Dr. Ken Miles first. He stood tall and fit and pretty, and leaned against nothing. Rigidly upright, he glared at something behind me.

Dr. Ken Miles's stare darted to mine. I frowned at his plain hostility because, honestly, I was perplexed by his presence. He had no reason to be on the fourth floor. He had no business in the CRU. Furthermore, he had absolutely no right to needle me with pale blue eyes rimmed with accusation.

I drew in a slow breath, preparing myself for a temper tantrum of some sort, and shuffled over to where he stood—then I saw it, just over his shoulder. It was a smirk. More precisely, a Megalomaniac-Meg smirk.

When Brutus betrayed Caesar, I'm sure that all the people in the general vicinity were shocked out of their brains. I'm guessing Rome collectively voiced baffled disbelief when the news spread. Millennia later, it's still a big deal—maybe one of the biggest *oh snap* moments in the history of forever.

Meg's readiness to monkey-wrench me wasn't at all shocking. Rather, it was annoying in its expectedness, and most of my irritation was focused inward. I really should have seen it coming. Placing trust in her was like placing trust in the Borg. You just didn't do it.

I closed my eyes against an epic eye roll and paused some feet away from Dr. Ken Miles and Meg's smirky face. Nico halted at my side, his bicep brushing against my shoulder as he crossed his arms. I glanced at two nurses who were watching Nico with rapt attention. I almost asked if they were planning to pass out popcorn.

Dr. Ken Miles's jaw was clenched, and he was smiling with his mouth only, which he had too carefully shaped into a grim line that curved just enough on the ends to consider it a smile. It gave him the air of someone who'd just tried cocaine for the first time or was making a halfhearted attempt to control anger.

Everyone was looking at me, waiting for me to speak. I imagine I might have looked a bit like a petulant teenager when I lifted a single eyebrow and prolonged the thick silence. Finally, and with great reluctance, I sighed.

"Hi, Dr. Ken Miles."

His features were pinched, and his eyes bounced between mine as if he was measuring my response before I gave it. "Meg called me."

"Oh? Did she need a consult?"

"No. Do you want to introduce your friend?" If a man could sound prissy, it was Dr. Ken Miles, and he perfected prissy in that moment.

"Sure," I said woodenly, knowing this was a complete farce. I turned slightly toward Nico and indicated to him with my hand. "Nico, meet Dr. Ken Miles. Dr. Ken Miles, meet Nico."

Neither of them extended a hand to shake. I was nearly blown over by the gusting funnel clouds of testosterone.

"I know who you are. You're that funny guy, right? That guy from that show—I can't remember the name of it." Ken's eyes moved over Nico as though sizing him up. It was all rather weird and vexing.

I allowed myself a brief glance at Nico. He shrugged. "Yep. That's me."

"Huh." Dr. Ken Miles's grin morphed into another weird smile as if he smelled something bad but was trying to disguise his discomfort with a smile. "You should do something funny then."

"Excuse me?" Nico sounded distracted, as though he hadn't really been paying attention to the conversation up to that point.

"You know," Dr. Ken Miles rebutted, and then he crossed his arms over his chest and braced his feet apart, the X-ray he carried dangling from one hand. "You should do something funny, right now. Say something funny."

"I don't know if I can make you laugh, but I guarantee I can make you uncomfortable."

I glanced at Nico again. A whisper of a smirk hovered over his lips. I was both surprised and impressed by the continuing nonchalance of Nico's tone paired with the not-at-all veiled threat of his words. It was…attractive.

Dr. Ken Miles's eyes narrowed for a beat then he flashed a sharp, white grin and chuckled. "Yeah, ok…."

I briefly thought that he was going to challenge Nico's assertion, but after a protracted moment, Dr. Ken Miles shrugged, seemingly worked to clear his throat, and looked away.

I felt Nico shift behind me. I felt the heat of him at my back, and then his hand tugged my elbow and turned me to face him. "I'm going to get out of here."

I searched his eyes and found them shuttered. "Ok." I experienced a swallow misfire; they were becoming quite frequent. "I'll arrange for the screening tests…for the study…for Angelica. Is tomorrow too early?"

"No. It's fine." Nico's frown deepened as he studied my face; the soberness in his eyes made him look older. "I'll see you later."

I nodded once, but before I could speak, he leaned down and placed a soft, lingering kiss full on my mouth; then he turned away and walked to the clinic room where Rose and Angelica were waiting. My fingers automatically lifted to my lips and touched them, my brain not quite able to process what had just occurred.

Dr. Ken Miles's voice brought me back to the present. "Can I speak with you for a moment—privately?"

Déjà vu.

I stared at Dr. Ken Miles for a beat. My mouth felt strangely sensitive and hot.

I knew I was expected to answer, even though I wanted to just stand in place and touch my lips all day. I eventually said, "Yeah, ok, fine."

He motioned with his chin toward the infusion room I'd just exited. I ignored Meg's glare as well as the nurses' curious stares. It felt a little ridiculous marching back into a room I'd just vacated, but I walked through the door anyway, tucked myself into the farthest corner of the small space, and faced him.

Dr. Ken Miles shut the door and issued me a stern, scolding expression, as though he expected an apology; not even my father looked at me that way. "Well?"

"Well what?"

"I thought we were on the same page, Elizabeth."

"What page would that be? Because you're on a weirdo page and I'm not comfortable with weirdo pages."

He sighed. "We've known each other for, what—eighteen months? We're both ending our last year of residency. We've sown our oats."

"Did you just say *sown our oats*?"

"We've been building toward something. The two of us together make a lot of sense."

I opened my mouth, released a confused puff of air, and frowned. "Yesterday you said I needed to grow up, and now you're, what? Wanting to pee on my leg to mark me as your property?"

"Is that what this thing today is all about? You flirt with me non-stop over the past year; you play practical jokes on me……"

"I play practical jokes on everyone."

"Are you mad at me about something?"

"No." I rubbed my forehead with my fingers. "No, Dr. Ken Miles."

"Why do you do that?"

"Do what?"

"Why do you always call me Dr. Ken Miles? Why don't you just say my name?"

"I don't do that."

"Yes, you do. You've done it since we met."

I stared at him unseeingly. "I don't...." My eyelashes fluttered as I thought about his complaint. I realized he was right. I did almost always think of him as Dr. Ken Miles.

I suddenly realized that I hadn't really ever thought of him as having a name like a person has a name. I'd thought of him as a project—a target. He was Dr. Ken Miles, not Ken or just Dr. Miles, and I had planned to eventually cross him off my *I'd do that* list.

I huffed. "Fine, Ken, I'm not upset with you, ok? I'm just trying to enroll a patient on the Cystic Fibrosis study. I don't know why Meg called you." That last part wasn't true. I *did* know why Meg called him: because she was a raging eyebrow-tweezing horn-dog rhinoceros who was trying to embarrass me in front of Nico...yep, that summed it up.

Dr. Ken Miles lifted his chin. "I want to be exclusive."

"Um...what?"

"You and me. You've been flirting with me for months. I know you're interested in me." To his credit, the words were plainly spoken with no hint of cockiness or arrogance.

"Oh, for the love of...." I sighed and glared at the ceiling.

He crossed the room to my corner in three short steps then rested his hands on my shoulders. "Let's stop pretending. I know it's what you want too."

"Ken, listen, I...." I huffed again, and recognized that I would likely end up hyperventilating if I didn't reign in my huffs and puffs.

I was trapped. I was cornered, and the only way to break free from relationship doom with Dr. Ken Miles was to tell him the truth. He would either be disgusted, which would send him running, or intrigued, which would give me the option of getting laid by a very nice-looking, disease-free Dr. Ken Miles.

I gritted my teeth and braced myself for his reaction, and then I said, "The thing is, I did want you. I wanted your body."

He smiled. I'm sure he thought it was a dazzling smile. "I want you too."

"No. Listen. I wanted to use you—your body—and have sex a few times, maybe weeks, maybe for a few months, and hopefully there would be oral involved. But, hey, I was willing to accept just the basics—and no butt sex. I don't do that. I've seen enough rectal tears in the ER to last a lifetime. However, just so we're clear, I was never interested in dating you."

He frowned. "You wanted to use me for sex?"

"Yes."

"Like friends with benefits?"

"No, like benefits with no friends—no friendship."

"Are you...are you still interested in that kind of arrangement with me?" Dr. Ken Miles's expression was inscrutable.

The irony of this conversation was not lost on me. A small shiver raced down my spine as my thoughts automatically recalled a vision of Nico and the words we'd exchanged just moments ago, words of mutual respect; then I thought of his soft yielding lips on mine when he kissed me goodbye. My stomach dropped and I experienced a brief moment of vertigo.

I wasn't an idiot. My tangled feelings for Nico were more than a need to exorcise pent-up sexual frustration. Furthermore, I knew that engaging in benefit sessions with Dr. Ken Miles wouldn't erase my desire for Nico. I just hoped it would dull the building ache a little by scratching the most pressing itch.

I reflected with some optimism that maybe after a few sexual encounters with Dr. Ken Miles, I might be able to interact with Nico without massive, crush induced, fumbling female failure. Then maybe I could get some sleep.

"Yes." I nodded. "Yes, I'm still interested."

And, really, why not? Dr. Ken Miles was still disease free, and he had a really nice body. Hopefully, he knew how to use it.

Dr. Ken Miles studied me, his hands on his hips. "Do you really think that once we start dating…?"

"It wouldn't be dating."

"Once we start whatever, do you really think that you won't want to get serious? Do you think you can resist getting serious with me?" To his discredit, he appeared to be completely perplexed by the notion that someone would want him only for his fine body and not his insipid little mind or potential bank account.

I recalled his propensity for frappuccinos, his secretive nose picking, his hall monitor-like behavior, his complete lack of humor, and his most recent prissy jealousy attack.

I schooled my expression to be as serious as a heart attack. "I'm pretty sure I can contain myself."

~*~*~*~

Synchronizing schedules with Dr. Ken Miles was like trying to pee upside down: nearly impossible, horribly uncomfortable, and entirely frustrating. When we emerged from the infusion room, we had three trysts scheduled. The first one was scheduled for three weeks from Thursday; it was the first evening we both had off where neither of us already had plans.

For our first meetup, Dr. Ken Miles insisted—and I reluctantly agreed—on taking me out to dinner before commencing with the benefits portion of the evening. I wasn't happy with the concession, but he, in turn, agreed that we would only have to share the one meal together for the duration of our interactions. If I didn't want to watch him eat in the future, I wouldn't have to. It seemed like a fair trade.

The rest of my Monday workday was fairly benign. I encountered only a few broken bones, cuts, and cases of the flu in the emergency room. I avoided Meg, ate in the doctor's lounge, and knit a baby hat. Between large projects, I frequently knit hats for the newborns. They are fast and thus give me a sense of completion, and I have the pattern memorized. It also gives me a little thrill to see the hats on the infants when they leave the hospital.

I was able to leave the hospital on time after my double shift was over, which was a rarity. I wasn't looking forward to my evening alone in the apartment. It would likely be spent trying to drown out fantasies of Nico and the weird shortness of breath I was beginning to associate with thoughts of him.

I pulled on my coat, hat, and gloves. Now that I was no longer busy with the day's tasks and with taking care of others, the first inklings of decisional doubt and regret began to plague me. I had a vague impression that was quickly morphing into a very large, Godzilla-like monster of a feeling that I'd made a monumental mistake agreeing to a benefits-only relationship with Dr. Ken Miles.

I was wrestling with myself about the decision. From one perspective, it made a lot of sense: sex, no feelings to hurt, total honesty, itch scratched. But, from a different perspective, the perspective that liked to pretend from time to time that I was a decent human being, the agreement was making me feel like a piece of foolish poo.

The internal stubborn versus pigheaded struggle for dominance warred within me as I distractedly strolled to the hospital exit, and it followed me outside, but my brain froze as soon as I stepped onto the pavement.

My paralyzed state wasn't due to the biting April wind that pelted my face as one might guess. Rather, it was due to the crowd of photographers loitering along the length of sidewalk outside the main ER doors.

I locked eyes with one of the crowd and he, only hesitating for a split second, lifted his camera and started snapping pictures as he jogged toward me. His sudden movement alerted the rest of the paparazzi. The first man's head start was soon usurped by a younger, seemingly more athletic photographer.

I heard one of them shout, "It's her—Nico's girlfriend!"

Thankfully, my wits returned before they reached my position. I backed up three steps and darted back into the ER, jogged through the double doors marked S*taff Only*, and stepped into a vacant clinic room. I shut the door behind me and leaned my forehead against the partition.

I was wrong. Mondays were so much worse than Sundays.

CHAPTER 14

I escaped from the hospital by hitching a ride with one of the ambulances; they dropped me at my train stop. The evening alone at my apartment was much how I'd envisioned it: trying to repress Nico fantasies.

The next eighteen hours were split into two distinct segments.

The first twelve were spent in a cyclic wish-wash of excited expectation, then anxiety-riddled dread, then excited expectation. I couldn't wait to see Nico again when he brought Angelica to the hospital. I even contemplated wearing makeup and doing something with my hair that day.

I also dreaded the encounter and felt as if I would need to explain Dr. Ken Miles's behavior and my relationship with him. I planned to be honest, but then I seriously wondered for the first time in a long time if honesty was overrated.

The remaining six hours occurred after Angelica's clinic visit and screening tests. Rose brought her in. Nico was not with them. When I realized he wasn't coming, I felt a foolish amount of disappointment. Rose explained that he'd gone back to New York to tape several shows and do some publicity interviews.

Rose spent most of the visit scrutinizing me with her intrepid, foxlike gaze. The lady was difficult to evade. Every so often, she'd ask, "Are you ok?" or "Is there anything you want me to tell Nico?" or "He'll be back soon."

In my defense, after the initial letdown, I was able to conceal and tuck away my disappointment.

I endeavored to take excellent care of Angelica, this little girl that Nico loved. I used a butterfly needle—smallest gauge—when drawing blood, and I insisted on conducting the entire exam myself. I told her all the kids' jokes I knew, surprising myself with the vastness of both number and subject matter.

Before Angelica and Rose left, I was rewarded for my efforts with a small hug and a shy smile from Nico's niece. The simple display of gratitude did strange things to my brain and heart, and made them both swell in unison. I started mentally sizing her up for a hand-knit kid's sweater that I'd placed in my Ravelry queue two weeks ago. At the time, I'd added it for no reason at all other than I loved it; but now I was happy that I did. It would look lovely on her, maybe in purple hypoallergenic yarn such as bamboo or possibly linen.

She was really very lovable for a kid. I made a mental note to discuss her illegal levels of cuteness with Nico when he returned.

If I get a chance…if he wants to see me.

Just before they left, Rose gripped me by the arm until I met her gaze. She smiled at me, but it was only because I'd known her my whole life that I discerned the penetrating quality of her gaze masked behind a motherly façade.

She pressed a CD case into my hand and leaned in close as though to share a secret. "Oh. I almost forgot. Nico asked that I give this to you."

I glanced from the CD to Rose then back again. Written on the disc in handwriting that I recognized as Nico's were the words *Good Music*; then, in all capitals, *LISTEN TO THIS.*

"Oh. Thank you." I turned the plastic case over needlessly, suppressing a smile and an excited fluttering in my stomach.

"You're supposed to listen to it." Rose said, still watching me.

I nodded, placed it in my lab coat pocket. "Yes. I see that."

"You should listen to it."

I glanced at Rose and gave her an obligatory smile. "I will."

"Promise?" she pushed.

"Yes."

"Soon?"

"Rose!"

"He'll be back this week."

I pressed my mouth into a firm line as she eyeballed me. After a long moment, she sighed.

"Tra il dire e il fare c'è di mezzo il mare[3]." Rose rolled her eyes heavenward, turned, and left.

"I will cross that ocean and listen to it!" I said with a grin at her retreating back, referring to what she had said in Italian: "Between saying and doing is the ocean." Her matchmaking attempts were as subtle as a fire alarm. If she knew what I was like, and knew who I really was, she wouldn't want me for her son.

I spent the rest of the workday oscillating between the extremes of happiness that he'd made me a mix-tape—in the form of a CD—and stomach-twisting restlessness.

I wanted to see him. I didn't want to see him.

I couldn't wait to listen to the CD. I didn't want to listen to the CD.

Maybe being friends wouldn't be so bad. I didn't want to be friends.

The last time I'd felt such a dichotomous, swirling mixture of emotions was the night I'd snuck into his room and handed him my virginity. It had felt like I was in a boat and that boat was both sinking and flying, but not floating. Nothing made sense, and I was preoccupied by my nonsensical indecision.

Therefore, I forgot until just before my shift ended, when my knitting bag stared at me from my locker, that it was Tuesday knit night with the ladies. For the first time ever, I considered skipping, making an excuse, and calling in sick and muddled.

Instead, mostly because I knew Ashley and Sandra would have a conniption fit if I didn't show up, I switched my phone from airplane mode to cellular mode. I'd been keeping it on airplane mode since Sunday so that no calls could be received. If I left it on

---

[3]Translation: Between saying and doing is the sea

cellular mode for any length of time, it started ringing and buzzing uncontrollably with journalists and crazy horn-dog stalker women. That just wore down the battery.

I called Ashley and arranged to have her pick me up from a lesser known entrance to the hospital, just in case any weirdoes with cameras were loitering at the entrance to the ER. She owned a car and insisted on driving to work every day using the excuse that, since she was from Tennessee, she didn't trust public transportation.

This made no sense to me, but I had to admit that Ashley was oddly unique in that almost nothing she said made a whole lot of sense, but she was one of the wisest people I knew.

I exited the hospital and pulled my scarf over my mouth and nose to stay warm while I waited for Ashley's green pickup truck. I surveyed without seeing the parking garage, and to pass the time, I counted the number of white cars and then the number of blue. There were a lot more white cars than blue cars.

Movement to my left snagged my attention, and I glanced at an approaching woman. She was dressed in a fancy jacket, wore fancy sunglasses, fancy boots, and her hair was also fancy—pulled back with sleek intricate braids at her temples. She approached me; she slowed then stopped.

She didn't say anything at first; her face was expressionless. She just looked at me. I wasn't wearing any sunglasses, and my eyes moved between the giant lenses of hers, then to the ground, over my shoulder, then back to her.

"Uh…can I help you?"

She shifted her weight from one foot to the other. "You are Elizabeth Finney?"

Bah. Fancy reporter.

I glowered at her, my hands fisted in my mittens. "Listen, lady, I don't know who you are, but I'm not interested in chitchatting about much of anything with anyone. So, please just leave me alone."

Her mouth hooked to the side in a mirthless smile. "You're short."

My eyes narrowed further in an attempt at a Dirty Harry squint. "And you're fancy. And the sky is blue. And the sidewalk is gray. Go away."

She withdrew an envelope from her fancy bag and held it out to me. "Niccolò Moretti is a scumbag and so are you. You both deserve to burn in hell." The sleek and slightly scary stranger poked me in the chest with the envelope. "Take this."

"Ok...." My hands automatically closed over the envelope. I was so shocked by her words I would have accepted a hissing viper.

Even so, she took a step closer, her nose flaring. I assumed she was giving me a once-over from behind her dark glasses. "You're nothing," she hissed.

I blinked at her then released a confused breath. "What was that?"

"You're nothing special at all. There is nothing remarkable about you."

"Ok...." Her presence had been odd up to this point; now she was seriously scaring me. My eyes shifted to the left and right looking for an escape. "Thanks for that."

Ashley's horn honked twice, startling the fancy stranger. She jumped backward and almost toppled over in her fancy boots. I took the opportunity to dart around her and jog—in my sensible shoes—to Ashley's truck.

I locked Ashley's doors as soon as I closed the passenger side, lifted my eyes, and found that the stranger had turned and watched me depart. She was now staring at the truck. "Go! Go! Get out of here!"

"Who is that?"

"Just get out of here." A chill spread through me. The woman was standing perfectly still. "Go!"

"Ok! Ok! You're freaking me out!" Ashley put the truck in drive and peeled out of the garage.

I held on to the dashboard. "Hey, slow down, Miss Fast and Furious—look out!"

Ashley swerved, nearly hitting a pedestrian, and merged into traffic, almost hitting a car.

"Why are you driving like a maniac?"

"Because you're scaring the poo out of me, that's why." Her hands tightened on the steering wheel, and she stopped short at a yellow light. The driver in the car behind us pressed on the horn until the light turned red. Faintly, as though from a great distance, I heard someone yell an expletive.

"All right. It's all right. We're all right..." I was shaking, and my jaw was clenched. I forced myself to relax and take a deep breath. "We're all right."

"Who was that woman? And why do you look like you've just seen the ghost of Attila the Hun? And what is that?" Ashley pointed to the envelope in my hand.

I stared at it dumbly for a moment then dropped it to the floor of the cab as if it were poisonous. "I don't know. That lady gave it to me."

"What is it?"

"I don't know."

"Well, who is she?"

"I don't know!"

"WHY ARE YOU YELLING?"

"I DON'T KNOW!"

The driver behind us honked his horn again causing us both to jump. Ashley grimaced then pressed on the gas gingerly and slowly accelerated to the speed limit. We both ignored the passing car as the driver gave us the middle finger.

"Ok. Let's just get to Sandra's apartment. We'll...drink some wine, do a little knitting, and you can fill the ladies in on your very colorful week."

I nodded, still staring at the envelope on the floor. "What should I do with that?"

Ashley thought for a moment then said, "We'll ask Fiona. She'll know what to do."

~*~*~*~

We arrived at Sandra's apartment in one piece. I kept stealing glances at the envelope, rationalizing that it was too thin to be a bomb but freaking myself out with all the other possibilities. We ended up leaving it in the car, deciding that we'd wait until Fiona advised us on what to do next.

As soon as Sandra saw us, she knew that something was amiss. She accepted our coats, pushed wineglasses in our hands, and shoved us toward the living room where everyone from our group but Janie was chatting happily, waiting for us to arrive. Janie was still in Boston and wasn't set to return until Thursday.

"Ah, Elizabeth, Sandra tells us you have some peculiar news." Fiona glanced up from her stitches, and her ready smile slipped as her eyes moved over my face then Ashley's.

"Are you two ok?" Marie's voice sounded from the couch. I walked over to the empty spot next to her and sank into the comforting cushiness.

"Elizabeth had a colorful week," Ashley announced in a deadpan voice, and then she gulped her glass of wine, finished it, and held it out to the room for someone to pour another. "And I almost killed a person driving over here. How are all of you?"

This proclamation was met with stunned silence, their eyes bouncing between Ashley, me, and one another.

Fiona finally spoke, ending the game of eyeball Ping-Pong. "Ok. Well then. Why don't we start at the beginning? Elizabeth, tell us about your colorful week."

I nodded then gulped the contents of my glass, finished it, and placed it on the table. "I'm going to need some more wine. Also, if anyone has some cashmere yarn I can pet, or even alpaca, I'd really appreciate it."

"Good idea. Yarn fondling always calms my nerves. Make that two balls." Ashley clinked her wine glass against mine.

The next forty-five minutes were spent filling the ladies in on the general story of my life during the past week, but I left out the more sordid and personal details.

I did tell them about Megalomaniac Meg, closing the deal with Dr. Ken Miles, and the resultant date for our first benefits session.

Several times during the story, Marie poured me a new glass of wine. I had to cut myself off at the third glass because I needed to be sober enough for a double shift the next day.

When I finished telling the tale, the ladies heaved a collective sigh, and the room plunged into a prolonged period of silence.

Unexpectedly, Kat was the one to speak up and ask the question that was probably on everyone's mind: "What was in the envelope?"

"I don't know. Ashley and I decided to leave it in the car."

"This lady could be Nico's hands-in-the-pants stalker," Marie added. "It could be anything."

"Or she could just be another stalker and not the hands-in-the-pants stalker. Nico could have several stalkers." Ashley hiccupped halfway through this observation then nodded at her own assertion. "Hot celebrities usually have more than one stalker. I read that somewhere."

"That's a cheerful thought. Here, have some more wine." Sandra poured Ashley another glass then turned to Fiona. "What should we do about the envelope?"

I half smiled. Neither Ashley nor I had said anything about consulting Fiona regarding the envelope. It warmed my heart that, by default and universally, we all looked to her to provide us with guidance in times of chaos and absurdity.

Fiona sighed. "The cautious part of me thinks that you should call the police, just in case it's something dangerous. The curious and impatient side of me says that we should just open it."

We all nodded.

"My two sides tell me the same." Kat offered.

"Well then." Sandra put the bottle of wine down on the table. "Give me your keys, Ashley. Since I'm a little cautious but mighty curious, I'll go open it."

Ashley handed Sandra her keys and hiccupped.

Sandra pulled on her coat and gloves, and then marched out the front door wearing leather-soled fuzzy slippers and no hat.

We all waited. I tried to start a knitting project but couldn't concentrate. Through my wine-induced cloudiness, I had a sudden spike of adrenaline and shot to my feet. "I should stop her. I'll— I'll call the police. What if, what if it's—"

Sandra entered the apartment at that moment carrying the envelope in one hand. Her face was grim. She motioned for me to join her.

As I approached, she pulled a picture from the envelope and handed it to me. I glanced at it then sucked in a sharp breath. It was a picture of Nico and me walking out of the infusion room after our friends-without-benefits conversation. She'd first used a black sharpie to scribble over my face then some kind of sharp object to scratch at my image.

"There's more." Sandra flipped the photo over.

On the back of the picture was a very lengthy handwritten letter. The script was sporadic. In some places, it was large; in others, the writing was small. In some places, she'd used capital letters; in others, she'd written in cursive. Certain words and phrases stood out, such as *I love you*, or *be with me*, or *I hate you*, and *I'll die without you*. Mostly it just appeared to be a crazy, scrawling blob of indecipherable script.

I released a breath I didn't actually know I was holding. "She's bonkers."

Sandra nodded. "You should probably call the police now."

~*~*~*~

I ended up calling the police from my apartment when I got home. I explained the situation as much as was feasible over the phone and with a great deal of reluctance. I was passed from person to person until someone offered to take down my information and schedule a phone call with a detective the following day.

Things progressed much faster the next day. The detective, it seemed, had looked me up on the Internet, seen the YouTube video, and offered to come down to the hospital to collect the picture. Detective Carey Long met me just inside the ER clinic and praised both Sandra and me for not touching the photo without gloves; she also admonished me for opening it at all.

"Have you informed Mr. Moretti about the incident?"

I winced a little. "No. He's in New York."

Detective Long gave me a disapproving frown. "Do you have any way to contact him? He should know about it. Tell him as soon as you can."

I promised I would. I was then instructed to call her if I saw the woman again, and I was given strict orders to always have a walking buddy.

Before the detective left, and just after we shook hands, she dropped her official persona and said, "I'm a big fan of the show." She gave me a polite smile then departed.

I stared at her retreating form until it disappeared around the corner, wondering how a smart, seemingly capable woman like Detective Long could be a fan of Nico's misogynistic show. For that matter, how could Sandra be a fan of his show?

I didn't have much time to meditate on this disturbing fact because I was paged with the results for Angelica's screening tests. They came back positive, and she was officially eligible for the study. I felt a twinge of relief on her behalf. The results thus far looked promising, and I was very pleased for her and her family.

My next call was to Rose to inform her of the results and to work out the next month's calendar. Administering Angelica's infusions at the hospital every eight hours for twenty-eight days meant that my schedule for the next month would be completely rearranged.

We settled on the timing of her infusions to be at 6:00 am, 2:00 pm, and 10:00 pm This meant I would have to be at the hospital at these times regardless of whether I had a shift or not.

But I didn't care. I could give up four knit nights over the next four weeks with no complaint if it meant a lifetime of improved outcomes for a patient. No big whoop. Besides, other than knitting, my social life was basically nonexistent and had been since before college. Now with Janie missing in action, making kissy face with Quinn Sir Handsome McHotpants von Fiancé, I was free as a bird.

You can't miss what you don't have.

Of note, I didn't count my future benefit sessions with Dr. Ken Miles as part of my social life. They fell more into the *recreational* category, like seeing a movie or window-shopping.

Speaking of window-shopping, Wednesday evening I pulled together a first day infusion survival kit for Angelica. I'd noticed earlier in the day that her blue blanket had a *My Little Pony* patch; therefore, I purchased a purple purse with an obscene amount of lace and fringe and filled it with pony paraphernalia. I also packed pineapple slices for after the infusion.

When Rose and Angelica arrived Thursday, I tried to hand the purse off to Rose, but she waved me away.

"Lizzy, what is wrong with you?" She gave me a mother stare, the kind that says *where is your common sense?* "You went through all that trouble to put this together for Angelica, and you want *me* to give it to her? Why can't you take credit for your good deeds?"

I groaned. I complained. I didn't want to give Angelica the purse because just the thought of doing it made my hands damp. Rose held fast, and in the end—with sweaty palms and a nervousness I didn't really understand—I gave Angelica the purse.

She loved it. Her smile was brilliant. She squealed with happiness, and her eyes twinkled in a way that reminded me of Nico. It made my knees wobbly and my heart melt.

The infusion portion of the visit was uneventful, which was a big relief to everyone. When it was over, while one of the research nurses was taking Angelica's vitals, I pulled Rose to the side and asked her to have Nico give me a call when he had a free moment. I didn't want to tell Rose about the fancy stalker lady because I didn't want to worry her unnecessarily, but I did need to inform Nico about the issue.

After Rose and Angelica departed, the stars aligned such that I had the remainder of the day off. From 3:00 pm until Angelica's 10:00 pm infusion, the time was mine to spend, and I knew exactly what I wanted to do.

It was high time for a panty dance party.

Sometimes, when I had an afternoon off, instead of going to sleep right away like I ought, I liked to dance around my apartment wearing nothing but underwear…usually sexy underwear…sometimes paired with high heels. I'd introduced this concept to my best friend Janie some years ago, and she'd joined me on more than one occasion. We'd bonded over lip-synching to 'N Sync and bobbing to the Backstreet Boys.

Even I, Elizabeth the tomboy, wanted to feel beautiful, feminine, and desirable every once in a while, even if no one was there to see it. It made a difference in my mental wellbeing. This behavior was usually precipitated by periods of dressing in nothing but scrubs. I felt like an asexual blob of teal cotton and sensible shoes.

I left the hospital with a panty party plan in mind.

I'd perfected a method for avoiding the paparazzi by tucking my hair into a hat, changing into civilian clothes, and leaving via one of the lesser known back doors. If the photographers were loitering around my train stop, I crossed the street and walked to the next closest stop several blocks away. I kept a vigilant eye out for the fancy stalker.

I arrived at the apartment without incident.

A certain amount of preparations were required in order to maximize the benefits of my plan: I needed to take a bath, shave everything that could be shaved, lubricate my legs and body with fancy lotion, apply light makeup—just enough to make me feel girly—paint my nails, and brush my teeth. I blew out my long hair, and it fell in soft waves over my shoulders.

Once I felt clean and pampered I pulled out a full set of pink and black lacey lingerie; thigh highs, pushup bra, garter belt, lace panties—the works—and strolled over to the stereo in the living room in stocking clad feet. I felt and smelled fantastic.

I briefly considered listening to the CD that Rose had given me from Nico, my music homework, but quickly dismissed the idea. I wasn't in the mood to broaden my horizons, and I'd already spent too much time fantasizing about him recently. I was in the mood to dance like a crazy person and enjoy being in my own skin.

The first few beats of "As Long As You Love Me" by the Backstreet Boys reverberated through the speakers. I allowed the cotton-candy, feel-good rhythm and lyrics to carry me off on the pink bubble of sublime happiness and true love. I slid around the polished wood floor, I spun on my tiptoes, I tossed my loose hair from side to side with wild abandon, all while mouthing along with the song and meaning every syllable. I jumped up and down on the couch during the chorus and felt the fantasy of the words to my bones.

It was during one of these jumps that I caught sight of a figure standing just inside the entranceway.

Startled beyond reason, I spun, sucked in a gasping breath, and lost my footing. I fell ass over ankles off the couch and landed with an unforgiving thud on the area rug in front of the sofa. I also made a weird yelping, moaning, screaming sound. The figure ran toward me; his face half amused, half concerned.

And that's when I realized that Nico Manganiello had been watching my panty dance party.

CHAPTER 15

When I opened my eyes, I found Nico kneeling at my side. His forehead was creased with worry. It took me a moment, only a moment, to realize his hands were on my body. One hand cupped my face; the other moved from my hip slowly down my thigh.

"Elizabeth? Are you ok?"

"What are you doing here? How did you get in?" I rolled onto my side and toward him; my hands automatically clutched my bottom. It hurt.

"Janie gave me the key. Are you hurt?"

"Where is Janie? And why did she give you a key?"

"I'm looking at…wait, are you sure you're ok? Did you break anything?"

"No, but my bottom is going to be sore tomorrow." I rubbed the painful curve of my backside.

Nico released a breath, sat back on his heels, and gently pushed my hair from my face. His fingers threaded in the long strands, and he carefully brushed the waves over my shoulder. "I can massage it for you if you want."

I glared at him and his teasing face. Stupid handsome face. Stupid twinkling eyes. Stupid kindness.

God, I wanted him.

"No, thanks. I'm sure I'll recover without you needing to get all handsy."

He half smiled and his eyes decided to choose that precise moment to lazily scan my scantily clad body. He loitered for a prolonged moment on the straps that held up my lacey stockings, and then his eyes traveled up to where my bra snapped together between my breasts.

"See anything you like?" I meant for the words to sound biting and sardonic, but the breathy quality to my voice might have derailed my intent.

"Mmm. Yes. Quite a few things." His gaze felt like a touch; his eyes were heavily lidded; his tone was all velvet and soft and soothing.

"Hey…buddy!" I was surprised by the tremor when I spoke. I removed my hands from my bottom and tried with no success to conceal everything that was exposed. "Do you mind? Eyes up here."

"I'm not finished."

I stared at him for a shocked second then shoved him. "Nico!" I rolled away, my face flaming as I grabbed the only thing nearby that could shield me from his scrutiny—a sofa pillow. I held it in front of my torso as I stood. It was ineffectual.

A wide, crooked grin spread over his features and he chuckled—actually chuckled—and watched me from his position on the floor, on his knees. "I've seen you before."

I officially lost the war against my mortification and felt crimson heat spread to the tips of my ears.

"That was…that was a long time ago, and this is different."

He nodded in agreement, his eyes unapologetically moving over me again. "You're right. This is very…different." Nico straightened from the floor and stalked to where I stood.

"What are you even doing here? How did you get in?" Again, I sounded winded. But I was determined to shift the conversation away from me and my lingerie before his scorching stare made me lose all self-control and my panty party turned into a depanting party as I tore all his clothes off.

I needed to remember that this guy, adult Nico, was a nice guy; smart, sweet, funny, deserving of all good things. And he loved me—or at least he used to; I was equal parts unwilling and incapable of returning those feelings. I was many things, but I would never knowingly hurt him—not again.

Therefore, Nico Manganiello and every ounce of his hotness were off limits.

Off. Limits.

Which was what I kept repeating to myself as our faces inched closer together. The twinkle in his eyes heated to an inferno of desire. A small whimper passed my lips.

Nico whispered, "Elizabeth. . ." His blazing gaze on my mouth.

Just then, I heard voices from the entryway, and turned in time to see Janie and Quinn rounding the corner.

"...the second penthouse makes the most sense—oh!" Janie stopped short, her hazel eyes growing wide then moving over me in curious appraisal. "Elizabeth. I didn't expect you to be here."

Quinn, Janie's fiancé, glared at me. In fairness, Quinn may not have been glaring. But his gaze was always ice cold, and his mask of perpetual aloofness was firmly in place. He indicated in my general direction with his chin. "Why are you dressed like that? And whose crappy music is this?"

I mentally face palmed.

"Janie, could you turn off the music?" I asked, not willing to sashay mostly naked over to the stereo.

"I'll get it." Nico gave me a last lingering look then left me. He stood from the floor, took my phone off the iPhone dock, and crossed to our trio. I felt his eyes on me the entire time; he stood just to my right, still studying the black and pink lace openly. I turned a little and readjusted the pillow, hoping to appear not at all affected, but I failed. In truth, his gaze was making me hot...and bothered.

Janie clasped her hands together and pointed at me with both index fingers. "You were having a panty dance party, weren't you?"

"A what?" Quinn shifted his glacial blue eyes to his fiancé.

"From time to time Elizabeth and I like to dress in our underthings and dance around the apartment." She smiled at me.

"Once these two leave, I'll join you."

"Wait—what?" Quinn no longer looked aloof. "You're going to dance around in your underwear?"

"Ideally it will be lingerie of some sort. Cotton underwear won't suffice. Luckily I have on the nice set you bought me in London." Her tone was explanatory and serious—typical Janie.

Quinn's expression shifted from incredulous to wounded. "Why do I have to leave?"

"Because, unless I'm mistaken, I imagine Elizabeth wouldn't feel very comfortable with you being here while she is dressed in her underwear."

"We could all stay here and have a pants-off dance-off," Nico offered with a careless shrug. His mouth tugged to the side in a way that told me he was seconds away from bursting into laughter.

"No!" Quinn and I responded at the same time and with an identical amount of vehemence.

I finally found my voice and added, "Wait! What is going on? I thought you and Quinn were in Boston. And how did you get in the apartment?" I addressed my last question to Nico.

"You gave him my number," Quinn replied unhelpfully.

"I'm moving in," Nico supplied with cheerful easiness. "We're going to be neighbors."

"What?" I almost dropped my pillow.

"It was actually my idea, Elizabeth," Janie said. "Nico explained about his issues with security, the whole mess. Additionally there is the rigorous schedule with his niece and the research study to consider. If Nico moves into the building, then it will help with both problems. This building already has top-notch security, and the firm will be supplying personal guards wherever Nico goes. And now you don't have to go down to the hospital every eight hours, and neither does Angelica. She can meet you at the hospital if you're already down there for a shift, but the rest of the time you can just go upstairs to Nico's penthouse and treat her there."

"But...." I closed my eyes. "But I can't treat her in an apartment. The study drug is in the investigational pharmacy, and I need an infusion chair and a lot of other equipment."

"Just give me a list." Nico brushed my curtain of hair over my shoulder; I fought the urge to lean into his touch. "I'll have it ordered, whatever you need."

I glanced from Nico to Janie then back to Nico again. I'd lost the game, and I didn't even know I was playing. "Fine, fine. I'll pull together a list."

"Ok, then. It's settled." Janie turned her smiling face back to Quinn.

"There is one more thing," I announced, even as I reflected how awkward this conversation was going to be with me in my underwear. "I was approached at the hospital on Tuesday by a woman."

Like flipping a switch, Nico's stance and posture became alert and intent. "What woman? What happened?"

I glanced between Nico and Quinn. "She approached me after work and gave me a picture of the two of us from Monday. She'd...uh...marked up my face. And she wrote you a letter on the back of the photo." Nico's eyes closed and then he turned and cussed severely, his expression thunderous. I told them the entire story, from start to finish, during which Nico paced the room like a caged animal.

I addressed my last comment to Quinn. "I don't know how she could have taken the picture. There was no one on the floor except for staff."

Quinn nodded. "We'll have to get you a guard." Then he turned to Nico. "Do you have any idea who this woman is?"

Nico's hands were on his hips and he was watching me, his expression rigid. "Yes. I know who she is."

"Did you call the police?" Janie placed a comforting hand on my shoulder.

"Yeah. I met with them yesterday," I said, then I offered to Quinn, "My contact is Detective Long. I'll get you her information."

He nodded once. His jaw ticked. "We better let the hospital know too."

Janie rubbed my arm. "I understand now why you need a panty party." Her smile was warm and reassuring.

I huffed a laugh and glanced at myself.

"I'm sorry, Elizabeth." Nico's words were softly sincere, and my eyes tangled with his. "I'm sorry you had to go through that."

I endeavored to shrug, but the heat of his gaze was wreaking havoc on my motor function. "'S ok." I slurred, swallowed, then tried again, "It's ok. I'm really fine."

His frown intensified at my words. "I wish you'd called me when it happened."

"I don't have your number."

"You could have gotten it from my mother."

"I told your mother to have you call me. I didn't want to invade your privacy if you didn't want me to have your number."

His eyebrows jumped on his forehead and he stalked to my position. "Well…from now on, consider my privacy your privacy. You can call me anytime, ok? In fact, call me every day."

My eyes flickered to Quinn and Janie. I readjusted the pillows. "I'm not going to do that."

Nico, now just inches from my face, shook his head; his eyes moved over my face with gentle deliberateness. "I wish you would."

Everything about him at that moment made my internal organs bleed hearts and flowers and puppies and kittens and hot chocolate and hot apple cider and red wine and campfires and *Star Trek* and yarn—my favorite things. I flushed scarlet under his focused, exploding charisma.

Janie squared her shoulders and spoke with authority to both Quinn and Nico, effectively pulling me out of another Nico trance. "Now you both need to leave. Elizabeth and I will be down here dancing in our underwear, and you two can go upstairs and finish your tour of the penthouse where Nico and his family will be staying."

Quinn's eyes abruptly heated and swept over Janie's curvaceous form; then he actually groaned and muttered to no one in particular. "This is so unfair."

Nico leaned even closer and whispered in my ear, "I agree with Quinn. How am I supposed to concentrate with you down here?" I was still beating down my blush.

"I guess you'll just have to suffer through," I offered, even as I shivered.

His smile was crooked and immediate. "You have no idea."

~*~*~*~

"I like him!" Janie, true to her word, stripped to her underwear and bra as soon as the door clicked behind Quinn and Nico.

"Who?" Still dazed, I flopped myself on the couch, tried to sort through my feelings and the fact that my panties were literally on fire. If the combination of embarrassment and lust could kill a person, I would have been dead.

"Nico. Mr. Manganiello. He's nice."

I glanced at the red lacey bra and panty set Janie was wearing. It was a nice one. It looked brand new.

"Yeah. He's nice." Then I sighed. He was nice. He was *really* nice. And it was a seriously bad idea to think about how comprehensively nice he was now. I sighed again thinking about the way he looked at me when he first came in. I could get used to that look coming from him. I could probably grow addicted to it.

I felt an intense need to change the subject. "When did you get back from Boston?"

"Just today, this morning actually. Nico called Quinn last night and made arrangements to meet us today, to arrange private security, and that's when I suggested his family move into the second Penthouse." She walked to the stereo, picked up my discarded phone, and scrolled through my playlists. "Have you abandoned your plans with the Dr. Ken Miles?"

"No…not really. Not yet. Maybe. I don't know." I didn't want to think about Dr. Ken Miles at that moment. I was semi-enjoying the after effects of Nico's shameless stare.

Janie was silent for a moment then said, "Nico seems like a really nice person."

I stared at Janie and cleared my throat exaggeratedly to get her attention. "You already said that."

"Yes. I just wanted to reiterate the fact that he is a really nice person."

"And why do you want to reiterate that fact?"

Janie turned, still holding my phone, and met my gaze directly. "Because I'm ninety-seven percent certain he is in love with you."

I considered her for a moment; there was an almost disapproving coolness in her gaze. "Why ninety-seven percent?"

"A three percent confidence interval is standard."

"Why would you think he's in love with me?" I tried to sound confused but failed. As soon as the words left my mouth, I knew I sounded defensive.

"You know what I'm talking about."

"No, I don't."

"Yes, you do. He's *the* guy. He's the guy from Iowa—Garrett's best friend. He's the one you were friends with as kids, then hated, then didn't hate, then lost your virginity to. I just met him this afternoon, and I, the queen of missing the obvious, couldn't help but notice. He talked about you nonstop. Quinn found it irritating, but I thought it was charming. Also, he looks at you like he wants…well, like he *wants*."

My heart rate increased, and I couldn't help the breathless

question, "What did he say?"

"He talks about you like you invented penicillin—like you…like you're an angel. It's rather disconcerting, to be honest."

I frowned. "Because I'm so awful?"

"No. You're not awful; what a ridiculous thing to say." She gave me a severe, annoyed scowl before she continued. "It's disconcerting because he's so smitten and you don't…well, you know. You don't have relationships, after what happened with Garrett."

I covered my face with my hands and sighed deeply. "Oh, Janie. I don't know what to do."

Janie crossed soundlessly to where I sat and claimed the spot next to me. She placed her hand on my back. "What's wrong? Did I say something wrong?"

"No, but I've really missed you." I sniffled and suddenly felt like crying again.

I was officially ridiculous.

"I'm here now. Do you want to talk about it?"

So I cried.

"What happened?" Janie pulled me to her shoulder and held me as I leaked all over her. We sat on our couch in our shared apartment, in our fancy bras and lace panties, and I quietly cried on her shoulder. I'm sure that weird didn't even begin to describe what we looked like.

I didn't cry for long. The tears were actually more of a quiet sob than a cry, and I reigned in my wobbly chin admirably. Janie left briefly to fetch tissues and tequila. When she returned, I unloaded the entire story and left absolutely nothing out.

Janie listened thoughtfully. When I told her about his confession then his kiss, she took a shot of tequila then offered me a shot. I refused it since I would need to be back at the hospital at 10:00 pm to administer an infusion for Angelica.

When I finished my tale of both woe and *whoa,* we sat together in silence. She appeared to be deep in thought, and I was completely spent. After rehashing the entire story, I thought I might feel better about things, or at least less muddled. If possible, the opposite was true.

Finally she spoke. "You know I'm bad at this."

"At what?"

"I'm not good with relationship advice."

"I'm not in a relationship."

"Right. I should have been more precise. I'm not good with giving advice about men."

"I don't need any advice. I don't—I can't lead him on. I can't get involved with him."

I felt her curious and concerned gaze. "Before you make up your mind, I will ask you a question. You don't have to answer out loud, but you should answer honestly to yourself."

I drew a steadying breath and closed my eyes. They were scratchy. I rubbed them with my fists. "Ok. Go ahead."

"When was the last time you were happy?"

My chin wobbled and my nose stung again. I swallowed and bit my tongue to stem new tears.

She added. "I've known you for over ten years."

"Are you saying people need to be in a relationship to be happy?"

"I think relationships, whether friendship or something else, are a contributing factor to happiness." Janie placed her hand on mine and pulled my fist from my eye. "You and I have been happy together, and our relationship has helped both of us. I hypothesize that love plays a key role in happiness."

I scoffed at this notion. "I don't need someone to love me in order to be happy."

"I agree. I don't think you need someone to love you. But I do think maybe you need someone to love."

I opened my eyes and brought her kind face into focus. My eyes blurred with tears. "I love you, Janie."

She nodded. Her smile was watery. "I love you too, Elizabeth. But I've learned something this past year."

I sighed, sniffled, tried to lighten the mood by sounding weary. "You're going to tell me what it is, aren't you?"

She nodded again, gave a tearful laugh, and then squeezed my hand. "I've learned that the more people I love—and I mean really, really, completely, unconditionally love—the happier I am."

~*~*~*~

Quinn Sullivan—Janie's fiancé—was the most efficient man in the universe. If I didn't know better, I would have thought he was a wizard—an irritable, stubborn, taciturn wizard. In the span of a few hours, after learning from Nico that I'd been harassed by paparazzi and that my phone was theoretically not useable, and that my email was clogged, and that I'd been stalked by the weirdo lady, Quinn waved his magic wand and solved the majority of my problems.

Quinn arranged for a car to take me to the hospital every day along with a very discreet, effective guard to assist with untoward photographers and to keep an eye out for the crazy fancy stalker.

Quinn had his people clear out my email and apply a new spam filter that miraculously caught the bad but released the good.

Quinn provided me with a new cell phone, a new unlisted number, and all my old contacts already programmed in—including a few new ones, like Nico.

Not that I called him.

Janie's non-advice advice increased my decisional paralysis. She made sense. But I remembered what it was to love someone—really, completely, unconditionally love that person—and then watch him turn to dust and disappear.

I'd also watched my father struggle with my mother's death for years.

For some people, the cut is too deep and the broken bones never heal. They don't get stronger; they remain in an immunocompromised limbo.

Others are immunoresistant, meaning, they are incapable of sustaining a new (love) infection because their body, heart, and mind are vaccinated against it.

I believed my father and I fell into the second category. We'd been vaccinated.

After my mother's death, my father told me repeatedly as I grew up that she was it for him. She was the love of his life. He had loved her and could never love another. I didn't appreciate his perspective until Garrett died and I knew, I knew to my bones, that my father and I were just alike. We were built the same way.

Regardless, I'd actually hoped to see Nico, but he was not at the 10:00 pm infusion with Rose and Angelica Thursday night. His mother explained that he'd flown back to New York earlier in the evening. She didn't know when he would return.

Feeling bereft from this news, I ended up giving Rose the list of equipment needed in order to complete the study visits at the new penthouse where Rose, Angelica, and Nico would be staying for the rest of the month. I also spoke to Dr. Botstein about the study drug; he, in turn, promised to solicit approval from the study sponsor to allow us to take the drug out of the investigational pharmacy and store it at my apartment.

Several days passed in this way: double shifts in the ER, polite but awkward interactions with Dr. Ken Miles, not-so-polite interactions with Meg, study visits at the hospital with Angelica and Rose three times a day, to which I was carted back and forth by Quinn's guards. I saw Janie in passing a few times, as I was coming or she was going. When I wasn't at work, I was knitting or reading the latest medical journals, or listening to music loudly and, more often than not, fantasizing about Nico Manganiello.

I began to look forward to the study visits with Angelica and Rose. I enjoyed seeing them and visiting with them. I enjoyed taking care of Angelica and easing Rose's fears. On Friday, we met for lunch before the infusion, and we decided that we should continue doing so for the rest of the month when my schedule allowed.

Rose informed me during the 6:00 am infusion visit on Saturday morning that all the equipment from my list would be at the penthouse by that afternoon. With approval from the study sponsor in hand to take the drug offsite, I made a plan to stop by their apartment once my shift was over.

Much to everyone's excitement and relief, I was able to complete Angelica's Saturday evening study visit in the comfort of their apartment rather than having to migrate back to the clinical research unit at the hospital. I was doubly relieved because it meant I wouldn't have to go back to the hospital at 6:00 am on Sunday, which was my day off.

The alarm woke me up at 5:15 Sunday morning. It pulled me out of a really nice dream; Nico and I were on a private beach someplace. All my dreams recently, good and bad, seemed to involve him. It wasn't something I struggled against. I accepted it, and even looked forward to sleep partially because of it and partially because sleep is awesome.

My plan was simple: I would take a shower, pull on some scrubs and slippers, administer the infusion, come back home, go back to bed, and hopefully reenter the dream exactly where I'd left off: Nico shirtless and walking toward me. Yum.

I used the key Rose had given me on Saturday to enter the penthouse around 5:45 am, still yawning and feet trundling as I closed the door behind me. It smelled like coffee and baked goods. My stomach rumbled.

I walked past and took note of two suitcases by the entranceway but thought nothing of them. I made my way soundlessly into the living room where we'd placed the infusion chair and other needed supplies. Rose was there and Angelica was curled on her lap, still asleep. A *My Little Pony* cartoon was on the TV.

Rose met my gaze and gave me a hazy, sleepy smile. "I'm going to let her sleep for a few more minutes. There is coffee in the kitchen if you'd like some, and apple fritters."

I scrunched my face at her. "How long have you been up?"

"Not long." Rose pressed a kiss on Angelica's forehead. "Go get something to eat. I'm hungry just looking at you. You're like skin and bones, working all the time."

I lifted an eyebrow but did as I was told and turned toward the kitchen in search of apple fritters. Rose liked to tell me I was skin and bones, but I was not. I was a size eight and healthy with a pleasant tummy pooch in the middle. I liked to think it made me cuddly.

I slipped my hand under the shirt of my scrubs and was scratching the aforementioned pooch when I walked into the kitchen, to the coffee machine, and stopped, immobilized.

Before me was the sight of Nico, shirtless and in black boxer briefs, making apple fritters. He was standing at the kitchen table spooning apple goo into a waiting dough shell. Flour speckled his chest and stomach. I noted his stomach was pooch free.

Watching a shirtless Nico Manganiello bake was something that belonged in *Playgirl* magazine.

The scene was practically pornographic. Between the smell of coffee and apple fritters, the still lingering arousal from my Nico beach dream, and finding him in the kitchen all hot and domesticated, I thought I might orgasm on the spot.

I certainly would if he touched me.

Don't   let   him   touch   you!

CHAPTER 16

I stared at him and his...everything. Just...freaking...everything. And I might have drooled a little bit. In fact, I know I did, because I felt a bit of drool fall to my arm. It was enough to wake me from the Nico domestic porn trance. I wiped my arm and hand on the pants of my scrubs and—with every ounce of self-control I had—I tore my gaze from him and his...fritters.

As luck would have it, Nico appeared to notice me at the exact same moment. "Hey, Elizabeth. Want a fritter?"

"Uh, nope." I noted that the color of the kitchen walls were pale grey.

He crossed to me holding a golden pastry. "Sure you do." I lifted my eyes at his approach and was slapped in the face with the unrealness and unfairness of his perfect physique.

"No. I'm good. Really." I turned slightly and backed up, unthinkingly trapping myself between the island counter and the sink.

He lifted the pastry to my mouth and said, "Open up."

I leaned backward over the sink, my arms flailing, and forced him to stop his advance. "Hey buddy, you want to...put that junk away?"

Nico glanced down at his black boxer briefs. "What are you talking about?"

"The torso of magnificence and thighs of splendor. You want to cover up?"

Nico placed the fritter on the counter to his side; his other hand rested on his chest and he issued me a soporific smile. "Torso of magnificence?" His hand moved down the front of his chest, over the ridged plane of his abdomen then slowed just above the elastic of his briefs and hovered there. I watched the movement of his hand as though it were a snake ready to strike....

Bad, bad, bad analogy!

"Am I distracting you, Elizabeth?"

"No, no you're not. You're just—you just shouldn't walk around half or mostly naked when people are out and about. That's all I'm saying."

"Do you have a problem with male nudity?"

"I don't have a problem with male nudity." I shook my head. "I have a problem with your male nudity—in this apartment."

"This is my apartment."

"Yes, I know. But there are women and children in this apartment, in the other room watching cartoons."

"She's my niece."

"I know that."

"And my mother."

"Yes, I'm aware of that fact as well, but I'm not related to you."

"No, you're not, are you." His grin was less lazy and more focused

"No…I'm not." I was trapped in his gaze for a moment, and I might have swayed forward a few inches before catching myself and averting my eyes. "I'm not, and we've already established that fact, and I'm going to leave the kitchen now." I tried to move past him but he shifted to the side; my arm made contact with his bare chest, and I recoiled as though burned.

"Well, let me just get out of your way," he said though he purposefully filled the entire space between the two counters, ensuring that I would have to touch him and his torso of magnificence—if not his thighs of splendor—in order to pass.

"Very nice…very nice…." I rolled my eyes at his antics and attempted to navigate a path through the small space without rubbing against his impressively proportioned and well chiseled body.

"You know, maybe you would be more comfortable if you took your clothes off." Nico shifted and caught me against the counter between his arms; his hands rested on either side of my hips. "I think if you took your shirt off, then you wouldn't feel like things are so uneven." He was the only person I'd ever met who could swagger while standing still.

"Would you please just—please just move out of my way."

"I mean, you don't have to take your bra off; you could just take your shirt off."

"Oh, really? Did you want me to administer the infusion to Angelica with no clothes on? Would that be appropriate behavior?"

His grin intensified. "Elizabeth, I can think of many things I want you to do without your clothes on, but administering an infusion to my niece is near the bottom of the list."

"Oh? Ok, what other things can you think of that would be near the bottom of the list?"

"Let's talk about the top of the list."

"No." I forgot for a moment that I was trapped and found myself thoroughly enjoying the unexpected turn of our conversation. "I want to talk about the bottom of the list first."

"Ok…at the bottom of the list of things I want Elizabeth Finney to do with no clothes on is…" Nico glanced at the ceiling, his eyes unfocused as though deep in thought, then he abruptly returned them to me. "…Hug another guy."

"Really?"

"Yeah. That's near the bottom of the list."

I placed my index finger on my chin. "Well, what about…washing a car?"

"No, no—that's high on the list. Very, very high."

"Oh, it is?"

"Lower on the list would be something like cleaning up poop."

An involuntary laugh burst forth. "Ok. I can see that. I can see why that wouldn't be so great."

"How about you?"

"How about me what?"

"What would you like me to do with no clothes on?" His eyes were intense and intent as they searched mine.

Heat swelled within me, and I knew—beyond a shadow of a doubt—that he wasn't asking; he was offering. I held my breath and knew that any response would likely result in us getting naked on the counter.

Teetering on the precipice of ruin, I was sure he saw the silent answer to his offer. I was sure because it was plainly observable in my eyes, my shallow breathing, my parted lips, and the thundering of my heart. However, just as his fingers slipped under my shirt and brushed against my stomach, Rose's voice sounded from just beyond the kitchen.

"Elizabeth, it's almost six, and I think Angelica is awake enough for you to start."

We quite literally jumped apart. I jumped up onto the counter and sat very awkwardly on the edge of the sink, and Nico jumped to the far side of the kitchen, back to his station by the apple fritter assembly line. I can't say with certainty whether he managed to accomplish the task with one giant leap, but I do know that one minute his knuckles were searing my skin, and the next minute he was across the room spooning apple goo into dough.

Rose shuffled in, still in her bathrobe, and meandered to the coffee pot. "I turned on another cartoon, just until the procedure is over. I think I'll send her back to bed after we're done." Rose, either purposely ignoring the tension in the room with an impressive display of acting ability or completely blind to it, sleepily moved to the refrigerator and pulled out some cream.

Meanwhile, in an attempt to surreptitiously rein in my rapid heart and raging hormones, I pointedly stared at the counter across from me and counted the number of spatulas in the utensil container. There were eight. Who would ever need eight spatulas?

I was not looking at Nico and his flawless olive skin. I wasn't looking at the gracefulness of his movements, the way his back muscles bunched and flowed, or the fact that he had the most perfect man-butt in the history of all time.

Period. End of story. Goodnight.

"Lizzybella, where is your coffee? Do you want cream?" Rose was suddenly standing in front of me, eyeing me with open concern.

I blinked at her dumbly then released the breath I'd been holding for maybe over a minute. Gingerly, my feet touched the ground as I slipped off the edge of the sink.

"I...." I released another breath. It was audibly shaky.

She glanced between Nico and me and muttered in Italian, "Chi ha l'amore nel petto, ha lo sprone nei fianchi[4]."

Nico's shoulders tensed.

I frowned. "Pardon me?"

"Are you feeling well?" Rose pressed her hand to my forehead.

"Yes. I'm fine."

Without turning around, Nico joined the conversation. "I was just asking her the same thing. She looks hot." He stressed the T and I was immediately frustrated by the calm in his voice and the double meaning of his words.

Freaking Nico!

"I'm fine." I said and politely refused Rose's offer of cream. "I don't take anything in my coffee."

"Hmm. Nico takes his black too. I can't drink it like that. I need it a little sweet."

"Elizabeth is already sweet," Nico mumbled, just loud enough for us to hear, and my chest constricted at his sweet sincerity. I wanted to evaporate and disappear. I hated that he did this to me.

"Yes she is. She is an angel."

Rose's agreement caused me to grown inwardly. The blood

---

[4]Translation: Who has love in the chest, has the spur in the hips

pumping in my veins felt anything but angelic. It felt downright sinful.

Anxious to leave my fan club, I ducked my head, darted around Rose, and said over my shoulder, "I better get started."

"What about your coffee?" Rose called after me.

"I'm wide awake!"

Nico caught my eye as I passed. Instead of a smug smile, his features were solemn and sober, and his eyes were hot with intent and promise.

It stung me with an awareness that lingered and made me cognizant of where the worn cotton touched my skin, and it was the reason I took a cold shower as soon as I returned to my apartment.

~*~*~*~

My palms were actually sweaty as I approached the penthouse for the 2:00 pm infusion. I needed to never be alone in the same room with Nico ever again. My skin was still on fire, and I was honestly worried what I would do if presented with any opportunity to maul him.

But when I entered, he was nowhere in sight. Angelica was coloring, Rose was knitting, but Nico—Rose explained—was out with Quinn, Janie's fiancé. This thought made me frown.

Quinn and Nico, roaming around Chicago together...no good could come of it.

Rose invited me to stay and knit, but I hastily declined. I administered the infusion, conducted Angelica's daily exam, then rushed out of the penthouse, worried that I might run into Nico if I dawdled. Arriving back to my apartment, coming face-to-face with the silence of solitude, I immediately regretted not staying with Rose and Angelica.

So I took a nap and, predictably, dreamt of Nico and his...apple fritters. I may or may not have been licking the sticky sugar and apple juice from his bare stomach to his collarbone, and he may or may not have been bringing me to bliss while forcibly restraining me.

I awoke hot and sticky and with my legs, middle, and arms tangled in sheets—which explained the *restraint by force* portion of the dream—and decided I needed another cold shower.

I stumbled across Nico's mix-tape CD when I was getting dressed. Man scrawl stared at me from the inside of my underwear drawer where I'd unthinkingly placed it for safekeeping. At first, I ignored it as I rummaged around for some very white cotton underwear and a sports bra.

I dressed myself in yoga pants and an oversized T-shirt with a chemistry joke about methane inscribed on the front; crude chemistry jokes were my favorite, followed closely by *Star Trek* puns. I pulled my hair into a tight ponytail and attempted to busy myself—and hopefully center myself—with some yoga.

But thoughts of the CD in my underwear drawer, touching my underthings, kept me from focusing. After fifteen minutes of mental arm-wrestling while trying and failing to do a firefly pose, I stomped over to the drawer, pulled out the CD, and pushed it into the player connected to our stereo.

I waited, breathing hard for no apparent reason, hands on my hips.

Freaking Nico.

The first notes of the first song startled me. A single cello followed by a group of violins played in abrupt unison—one over the other—and created a solid yet stunted rhythm. Then a woman's voice, thick and rich and familiar, sang the opening words.

As the song unfolded, a heady modern bass beat reverberated in the background. I recognized the song and the singer—Shirley Bassey singing "Where Do I Begin"—and further recognized that it was a remix, and that the remix was masterfully done, resulting in a solid, modern, edgy reimagining of an old standard.

I walked back to my exercise mat now feeling curious. Music, quality music, flowed over me, and I easily centered myself. I spent the next half hour doing yoga, holding poses somewhat longer than typical. I strained to listen to the words of the songs and held my breath in anticipation of what would come next.

Some songs I recognized, some I didn't. They ran the gamut of decades and musical genres. I repeated a few—like the Cars' "My Best Friend's Girl"—and I would have skipped a couple of them if I'd known the words ahead of time.

The most distressing song—and one of the songs that I'd never heard before—was a very low-key pseudo-rock song about the last days of a person's life from the perspective of the one left behind.

The line just before the chorus, and the chorus for that matter, caused a lump to form in my throat. The singer stated, "Love is watching someone die," which was then followed by a chanting response of "Who's going to watch you die?"

It gave me chills and instantly made me think of Garrett and his last months, hospice coming to his house, sitting with him the week before he died, watching him sleep. Musically, the song was remarkable and beautiful, and I loved everything about it other than the words. I had no desire to hear it again.

There were a total of seventeen songs. I stopped my yoga poses for the last two and lay quietly on the couch listening to the music. The last stanza of the Drifters' "Save the Last Dance for Me" marked the end of the CD.

When the CD ended, I didn't get up. Instead, I lay on the sofa and stared at the ceiling, with only the faint sounds of Chicago traffic marring the silence. Nico was right. The music he'd selected for the CD was *good* music. I missed good music.

I walked to the stereo and hit Play again.

~*~*~*~

I listened to the CD over and over for the rest of the day— another attempt at yoga, doing laundry, bills, checking email, knitting two more newborn hats then starting on Angelica's sweater, eating Chinese takeout—but I always skipped song number six, the one about being left behind.

When 9:45 pm rolled around, I wandered up to Nico's penthouse.

I felt strangely satisfied after spending the afternoon listening to good music, and I was excited to see Nico. I knocked on the door before I opened it with my key, hopped in and bounced to the living room. All the hopping and bouncing—quite unlike me—betrayed my anticipation.

I heard noise coming from the kitchen so I called out to let anyone in the vicinity know that I'd arrived, and then I crossed to the infusion chair to prep the space for Angelica.

"Hi, Elizabeth! I'm in here. Just give me a minute to finish up," Rose called from the kitchen. A moment later, she came out holding a plate full of biscotti and a cup of tea. "Well, these are for you. Let me go get Angelica. She's been asleep for the last few hours."

"I'll get her." I offered, and I moved toward Angelica's bedroom without waiting for a response. "Isn't Nico here?"

"No, but he should be right back. You just missed him when you left earlier. He and Angelica have been playing My Little Pony all afternoon, bless him. They wore each other out, I think. And now he's gone to the market before it closes." Rose set my tea and biscotti on the coffee table.

"You sent him to the market? Won't he be recognized?"

She tossed her hand in the air to wave off my concern. "I need fresh sweet basil. The least he can do for his mother is help out around here once and a while."

"Why not just send one of the guards?"

"They wouldn't know sweet basil from oregano. He'll be fine. He likes to do it." With that, she walked back to the kitchen; a moment later, I heard the unmistakable sound of dishes being done.

I found Angelica asleep in her room, her face covered with a night mask connected to her breathing apparatus. I carefully picked up her small body in my arms and wheeled the apparatus after us. It would be ideal to interrupt her sleep only briefly while administering the study drug.

One of her small hands rested on my chest over my heart as I carried her. I smiled and felt warmed by the contact; I deposited her gingerly in the living room. Rose sauntered out of the kitchen just as I finished the infusion and took Angelica's vital signs. Rose handed me a blanket, which I used to wrap up the little slumbering patient, and I carried her back to her bed.

Before I left her room, I kissed her on the forehead. Something about a sleeping Angelica, likely a fairy dust she exudes while dreaming, makes leaving her without a kiss completely impossible. I also loitered by her bed, watched her sleep, brushed her hair from her face. Then, telling myself I was being ridiculous, I kissed her hand and left.

As soon as I emerged from the hallway, I glanced at my watch. It was 10:45 pm.

"Come sit next to me and have some tea. I made these cookies just for you." Rose patted the sofa beside her; she held a cup of tea and was wiping crumbs of biscotti from her bathrobe.

I wanted to stay. I hoped Nico would come home soon so that I could talk to him about the CD. I liked the idea of chatting with Rose and catching up on all the Manganiello gossip. I liked her biscotti, and I loved peppermint tea.

I had a dark, empty apartment downstairs full of nothing interesting, so I stayed.

At first, Rose talked a bit about the family and the restaurant with swift precision. She made her way through all her children— in order from oldest to youngest—and focused a bit longer on those who were not married, who were career minded.

It was the tea and cookies that ultimately led to my downfall.

Rose had successfully distracted me with yummy treats and, therefore, I didn't realize until it was too late that her not so subtle hints—about community and family and love being much more important than work—were leading to a stealth attack.

"Take for example you and Nico."

I stopped chewing and stared at her, likely resembling a deer caught in semi-truck headlights. She smiled like a fox and continued.

"Nico is twenty-seven now, did you know that? He may not realize it yet, but he's ready to settle down with the right girl and start a family. I feel certain that the two of you have been brought back together for a divine purpose. I always said to your mother that the two of you were meant to be."

I gulped my tea, swallowed a large chunk of the almond cookie, and glanced at my wrist where I wasn't wearing a watch. "It's getting really late, Rose, and I have to get up early for Angelica's next infus...."

She placed a staying hand on mine and held me hostage with her clever eyes and authoritative posturing. "No. You're going to stay with me for a minute. I want to talk about this with you. You might think it's none of my business, but Nico's happiness, *your* happiness—these things are my business. I love you and care about you. I held you when you were a baby...."

"Rose...." I closed my eyes and hoped she'd yield to the pleading within my voice.

"I'm not going to leave it alone until you explain to me why you don't like my son."

My eyes flew open. "I do like your son!"

"Is it me? The family?"

"No. You know I love your family."

"You think you're too good for him? Because you're a doctor?"

"God, no! It's the other way around. He is definitely too good for me."

"Nonsense. At least be honest with me."

"I am. I'm being honest." I set my cup down and turned to face her more completely. "I know you think I'd be good for your son, but I promise you, I wouldn't. He deserves so much more, so much better than me. He's...." I let my face fall into my hands. "He's such a bright shining star of awesomeness. He's sweet and clever and so damn funny. He needs a girl whose name can be blended with his to form one of those Hollywood super-couple combinations—like Benifer or Branjelina. Our name together is Nicabeth or Elizaco. That's awful."

"What are you talking about?"

My hands fell to my lap and I shook my head; I met her silver-green eyes directly. "I'm not for him. I'm not like him. I'm ordinary; my feet touch the ground. And, honestly, I haven't worked through all my issues."

"Elizabeth Finney, you are extraordinary. And for heaven's sake, no one ever works through all their issues. Perfection is the definition of boring."

"But I carry baggage. I'm stubborn and selfish, and I've hurt him."

"And he still loves you."

"But he shouldn't. He shouldn't love me after what I did."

"What did you do?"

"I can't tell you."

"Because I'm his mother?"

"Because I don't want you to hate me." I answered honestly then latched on to my selfish self-preservation as another reason Nico and I were not suited. "See? I'm a coward. Surely Nico deserves better than that."

"Yes. He does. He does deserve better than that."

I searched her gaze. Before I could respond, she continued.

"But you also deserve better than that. I don't know what happened to make you feel so down on yourself, so undeserving of happiness, but I can tell you that your mother would be appalled."

I studied my fingers, unable to hold her gaze. "I'm not down on myself. I just don't want...I don't want...."

"Happiness? Someone to love you? Is this why you try to hide the fact that you make all those baby hats and wanted me to give Angelica your gift last week? You don't want someone to care for you?"

"Yes."

"Why not?"

"Because he's not Garrett." My heart was carried out of my body through a loud exhale. My stomach actually cramped.

"Oh, honey...." She *tsked*. I felt her sympathy, though my stare was firmly affixed to my hands.

"That's not exactly right...I just don't ever want to—it's like—" I turned my eyes to the ceiling. "I know it was a long time ago. I know it's been eleven years, and I can honestly say that I'm not carrying around my love for Garrett like it's a burden. It's not holding me back; it's keeping me grounded. I remember loving him, and I remember the good. But I can't do that again. I can't do that again with anyone."

"Because you're afraid?"

"No." I pressed my fingers to my chest. "Because *I* can't. Because I don't think I'm actually capable of returning those kinds of feelings. If I tried to love Nico and found that I couldn't, I...I just can't bear the thought of hurting Nico again...not again."

Rose was silent until my eyes lowered and met hers. She was watching me with a sober smile. Her pretty eyes were framed by lines of wisdom and grace.

"You are stubborn," she said.

"I am."

Rose breathed in through her nose, glanced over my shoulder as though clearing her vision, then leaned forward. "Let me just say something, and you don't need to say anything—ok? Just listen."

I nodded, not sure what to expect from this woman I'd known and respected and, honestly, admired my whole life. I felt like I was letting her down. But, I'd rather deal with her moderate disappointment now than incur her wrath by breaking Nico's heart.

"Dio li Fa, poi li [5]Accoppia." She paused after making this proclamation in Italian. I stared at her blankly; she smiled swiftly. "Despite what you say, I do know that you and my Niccolò will make each other very happy. In fact, I think part of you is already in love with him too. Why else would you be fighting so hard to protect his heart?" She held my gaze, and I fought a chin wobble. "I think you push him away mostly because you fear getting hurt, losing someone else, like you lost dear Garrett. He really was a beautiful boy...but there is something else you need to know. Since you've been so honest with me, I feel I should be honest with you."

"Ok...?"

"I have to warn you that I'm going to be working relentlessly to get you and Nico married."

I frowned then blinked. "Um...what?"

She placed a well-manicured hand over mine and squeezed. "One day you'll find out what it is to have children. You will want to give them everything their hearts desire, especially when it's good for them. His heart wants you, Elizabeth. It has always wanted you. Since the two of you were children, his heart has known that you are *the one*. The two of you *belong* together. And I have watched him struggle with his heart all his life.

"As you know, I love to spoil my children and the people I love. So, again, yes, I know you two will be very happy together when it happens, and that is wonderful. But also, selfishly, as a mother's prerogative, I think he deserves to get everything he wants, and if that just so happens to be the lovely, clever, stubborn daughter of my dearest friend—God rest her beautiful soul—then so be it."

---

[5]Translation: God makes them, then mates them

I opened my mouth to respond but couldn't. I gaped. I stared at this woman as though seeing her for the first time, and I really *looked*. I really *saw* her.

She was completely insane.

The sound of the front door closing startled me from my disturbing realization. The accompanying sound of Nico's voice announcing his arrival made me jump to my feet.

"Ma, I went to three places, and no one has fresh sweet basil, so I got regular basil instead." He stopped short as he entered the room and glanced between Rose and me. His eyes gradually narrowed into a suspicious squint and eventually came to rest on his mother. "What's going on?"

"Oh, just female talk." Rose stood, waved off his misgivings, and covered a yawn with the back of her hand. All previous crazy-lady vibes had abruptly evaporated. "Can you see Elizabeth back to her apartment? I'm going to bed."

To my surprise, she embraced me in a short hug and gave me a kiss on the cheek as she left.

"Don't worry about the basil, Nico." She called over her shoulder, not turning. "I found some in the refrigerator when I was cleaning up."

CHAPTER 17

Nico, despite my protests, walked me back to my apartment. Really, it was a short walk: down his hall, an elevator ride to my floor, and down my hall—barely enough time for me to gather my wits.

But Nico filled the time with easy and entertaining commentary on his frantic nighttime search for fresh sweet basil. We slowed as we approached my door and he was animatedly wrapping up his story.

"...at that point I thought about just buying a Sharpie and writing the word *sweet* across the top of the container. I would have, too, if there was any chance she'd fall for it."

"You were right not to do it. She is far too clever..." *and conniving.*

Nico stopped me by tugging on my hand. "Oh, hey, how did Angelica do today?"

"Really good, actually. How was she when you two were together?"

"You mean this afternoon? When I was Twilight Sparkle and she was Rainbow Dash and I lost the Pony Town ice-skating championship?"

I patted him on his shoulder. "I'm sure you gave a good effort. Maybe you can try again tomorrow."

"Thank you. I appreciate your sympathy. But..." Nico paused and seemed to survey all of me at once, and then he leaned a fraction closer. "I won't be able to try again tomorrow because I'm flying out early for New York in the morning."

"Oh...but you just got here." I wondered if I looked or sounded as disappointed as I felt. "That's too bad."

"Yeah." He agreed, watching me closely.

"When will you be back?"

"Next Tuesday."

"Oh." I was certain I both looked and sounded as disappointed as I felt.

We stood in melancholy silence for a long moment. I studied him, committed his jade green eyes to memory, etched in mental stone how it felt to be near him and hear the sound of his voice.

"Well," he abruptly broke the protracted silence, "where can I kiss you?"

What?

"What?"

He lifted his fingers to my face and tucked a few loose strands of hair behind my ears. "Where can I kiss you goodbye?"

My stomach did a backflip, and I responded stupidly, "In the hall...?"

"No, Elizabeth. That's not what I meant. Where—on your body—am I allowed to kiss you? Where do your other friends kiss you?"

Thoughts of Nico's lips all over my body bubbled into my consciousness. I had trouble thinking of places where I *didn't* want him to kiss me.

Finally, I managed to croak, "Well—they don't."

"That's not true. How about your cheek?"

I shrugged, completely flabbergasted by our conversation, my mouth suddenly dry. "Yeah, I guess I've been kissed on my cheek by friends before."

"Good." He smiled. "We'll start there."

Then, he deliberately moved into my personal space.

I wanted to hold my ground but instead my feet—the traitors!—move me backward as he approached until my back met the wall behind me. His gaze held mine, a soft smile stealing over his features, and when I could escape no farther, he halted as well. His body was everywhere yet didn't touch mine. He braced an arm just to the right and above my head then bent slowly, slowly until his lips were even with my cheek.

Hot Nico breath fell on my neck. Even the air vacating his lungs carried his confounding magnetic charisma, and I struggled to suppress a shudder. He kissed me, an infuriatingly chaste peck, then straightened but didn't move away. My hands dug into the unyielding wall at my back.

"Was that a good friend-kiss?" Nico's eyes searched mine, the earlier smile diminished to a residual insinuation of one.

He must've been pleased with what he saw in my answering glare because he started to laugh. It was a low, rumbly sound and—had I not been all wound up—it might have been infectious. His eyes danced with tangible amusement.

I released an unsteady breath and forced myself to nod, my body buzzing with awareness, and I untangled my gaze from his.

I didn't want to play this game.

Did I want him? *Heck yeah.*

Did I like him? *Heck to the yeah.*

Did I even adore him a little bit? Adore how sweet he was with his niece, how thoughtful and kind he was with his mother, with me? Adore how smart and witty and steady he was? Respect him?

Hells yes!

For all those reasons, I didn't want to play games.

I wiped my hands on my yoga pants and navigated around his imposing form with the swiftness that only comes from being small. I worked on unlocking the door to my apartment.

The sound of his laughter tapered off from behind me, and I could sense the moment when he detected that I was not amused.

I'd just finished unlocking the deadbolt when his hand closed over my shoulder. "Hey, Elizabeth, I was just teasing you."

I nodded again. "I know." I worked on the second lock.

"Are you…are you mad?"

"No." I wasn't mad. I was sad, disappointed, and frustrated—

mostly with myself.

His hand slid to my arm and turned me to face him. "I'm sorry if I did something to upset you."

My eyes stayed on the door. "You didn't."

"You're lying."

"I'm not."

"You are."

I clamped my mouth shut and swallowed. I felt his eyes move over me, assessing. Finally, he let me go, but he didn't move away. "You can tell me anything. Anytime."

I couldn't stay my bitter smile. "Unless you're in New York, you mean?"

Curses! That wasn't fair. I immediately regretted my words.

He shifted, braced his feet apart. "You have my number. You know you can call me whenever you want."

I glanced at the keys in my hand. "I'm tired and have to be up in a few hours, so…I'm going to head in and get some sleep."

Nico stuffed his hands in his pockets, his eyes searching mine for understanding; finally, he nodded and stepped away. "Ok. Goodnight then. I'll see you next week."

"Ok…goodnight." I mirrored his head nod and slipped into my apartment. I successfully won the battle with myself to close the door behind me without capturing another mental snapshot of him as he retreated to the elevator.

My head fell against the door, and I briefly considered watching him walk away through the peephole. It didn't occur to me until 2:00 am as I tossed and turned in my bed that I'd missed my chance to talk to Nico about the mix-tape and tell him how much I loved it, and to say thank you.

Maybe I should call him in New York and tell him.

As I dozed off, I ignored all subconscious whisperings related to the rationalization of questionable behavior, and I succumbed to another Nico-apple-fritter fantasy.

This time he was licking me.

~*~*~*~

I was in a *mood*.

That is what my dad called it when I behaved in a morose manner. I'd snapped at Meg at least ten times during the first two hours of my workday and literally flung myself into a broom closet to avoid Dr. Ken Miles. It was only Tuesday, and I was already missing Nico terribly. I'd only seen him twice on Sunday, and both times were short interactions.

I felt Nico's absence like a pulled tooth. I mourned it.

Every time I slept, my dreams were filled with Nico. I began listening to the CD almost obsessively—even track six—and could sing along word-for-word with each of the songs. However, I hadn't yet called him. I stared at his contact information on my telephone screen a few times, but I hadn't yet grown the nerve to dial his number.

Matters weren't helped by increased attention from the media. They now swarmed the entrance to the hospital and apartment building. I was thankful for the underground garage to my apartment more than ever. On Monday, a few photographers posed as patients and tried to get admitted to the ER.

The ease with which the media seemed to infiltrate the hospital was disturbing to me for another reason. Nico's stalker had been able to navigate to the Clinical Research Unit seemingly with ease, take pictures of Nico and me by the nurse's station. If the paparazzi could deftly sneak in giant cameras, then how easy would it be for FancyBoots to come and go as she pleased?

I was just thankful that no new pictures of Nico and I had been leaked to the press.

Presently, I sat in my apartment on my big sofa —stewing in my mood—knitting. I was finishing Angelica's sweater, and it was Tuesday knit night. We'd all agreed, for the time being, that it made the most sense to have knit night at my apartment; at least until paparazzi and stalkers were no longer a factor.

My next planned project was a new scarf—a man scarf. I was going to use a silvery jade green cashmere; the color reminded me of Nico's eyes.

Sandra discussed her recent first date disaster with the group, a topic that typically amused us all. She had more first dates than Janie had comic books—and that was a helluvalot. Tonight I was only half listening. Nico's mix-tape CD was playing in the background, distracting me with thoughts of him.

"...and so he finally admitted that he wasn't over his ex-wife. So, bad news—there won't be a second date. Good news—I think I have a new patient."

The ladies laughed good-naturedly. Sandra had a talent for adorable self-deprecation that I admired.

I cleared my throat to get her attention. "Whatever happened to Micah? From my reunion? You two seemed to get along well. Doesn't he live in Chicago?"

"Ah! Manly Micah! Yes. He was fun...." Sandra pulled out a length of yarn and adjusted her work in progress.

I waited for her to continue. When she didn't, I pressed her further. "Did you get his number?"

"Ha! Actually, no." Sandra sent me a Mona Lisa smile. "He spent most of the evening talking about you. Did you know he had a crush on you in high school?"

"Me?"

"Yeah, you, dummy."

"I find that hard to believe. I was such a nothing back then."

"Why would you say that?"

"Because I was. I was small and scrawny and sarcastic."

"Well, he said you were shy, pretty, and smart."

"Did he talk about me the whole time?"

She shook her head. "No. We spent some time working through issues with his father. He is still very angry with the man."

I noted I wasn't the only one glaring at Sandra with disbelief.

She glanced up from her knitting and was somewhat startled to see us all watching her, dumbfounded. Her eyes darted around the room. "What? What did I say?"

"You are a freak of nature, Sandra. Can't you ever go out on a date with a guy without turning into his shrink?"

"This is why you're such good friends with all your ex-boyfriends." Marie singsonged the words, her eyebrows lifted high on her forehead.

"And what, pray tell, is wrong with being friends with your ex-boyfriends?" Sandra didn't sound upset so much as perplexed.

"Nothing except it's not just ex-boyfriends. It's every guy you've ever gone on a single date with. How many have you collected? Like thirty?" Ashley shook her head as though disgusted. "You'll never find a steady beast with a strong back, partner, if you keep shrinking and exploding good advice all over the place."

"I agree." I mumbled behind my needles.

"You shut it!" Ashley turned slightly in her chair, her refined wrath now focused on me. "You don't get to talk. You have, quite possibly, the funniest and sexiest guy in the world wanting to give you multiple orgasms—and I don't mean the cocktail—meanwhile, you've retired him to the friend pasture. Ugh! You disgust me."

Sandra and I shared a glance and Marie cleared her throat.

"Ashley...." Fiona's soothing entreaty sounded from beside me. "What is wrong, dear? Why so testy?"

Ashley closed her eyes, rolled her lips between her teeth, and breathed out through her nose. After a long moment, she spoke again. "I'm sorry, ya'll." She brought her fingertips to her forehead and pinched the bridge of her nose. "It's been a long week."

"Do you want to talk about it?" Kat's quiet voice carried from the couch.

Ashley shook her head but she answered regardless. "It's my

biological father."

A collective sigh of understanding spread through the room, and she didn't really need to say anything else.

Ashley referred to her dad as her biological father. She had no other father, and the man was present for her childhood, still married to her mother, but Ashley despised him. When she was fourteen she'd started calling him "my biological father" because it annoyed the "jeepers" out of her family.

"Do you want to talk about it?" Kat's quiet voice was soothing.

"No. I honestly don't. I'm just sorry I'm behaving like a jerk." Ashley's mumbled self-recrimination was barely audible.

Maybe partly out of curiosity but most likely to change the subject, Sandra lifted a finger in the air and addressed her question to Janie and me. "So, what music is playing? Is this some kind of eclectic, unrequited romance, love song-themed Pandora station?"

"No. I believe it's a CD." Janie glanced at me.

"Yeah, it's a CD." I confirmed her response without looking up from Angelica's sweater. I would likely finish it tonight. Then, if I spent all my free time on the scarf, I would finish it before Nico returned next week.

"Where did it come from?" Sandra crooked her head to the side. "Is it yours, Janie?"

She shook her head. "No. It's Elizabeth's."

"Elizabeth's?" Marie asked; her disbelief was obvious. My propensity for exclusively boy-band albums was infamous.

"Actually..." I sighed, paused, half-contemplated making up some story but then—feeling tired of playing pretend—decided to tell the truth. "It's Nico's. He made it."

"What do you mean *he made it*? Did he make it for you?" Sandra sounded honestly mystified.

I nodded.

"Like a mix-tape?" Kat said.

I nodded.

"Nico Moretti made you a mix-tape of love songs?" Ashley repeated, as though to clarify.

I shook my head. "No…not of love songs…just good music."

The room fell into a suspended hush. I glanced at my friends and found that I was the only one knitting; everyone else was staring at nothing in particular and listening to the sorrowful, regretful, passionate sounds of *One Love* by U2.

Kat caught my eye. She was frowning. "What other songs are on the CD?"

My heart fluttered a little and I shrugged. "They're all good, like the Cars' "My Best Friend's Girl." My dad used to play that song all the time."

"Oh, my god…." Sandra stood and crossed to the stereo.

"What? What's wrong?" I sat up in my chair.

Sandra pressed the Back button and started the CD over. She played only the first twenty or so seconds of each, and then skipped ahead to the next song when someone named the song and artist.

"Where Do I Begin," Shirley Bassey; "Swing Life Away," Rise Against; "I've Got a Crush on You," Frank Sinatra; "My Best Friend's Girl," the Cars; "Mr. Brightside," the Killers; "What Sarah Said," Death Cab for Cutie; "The Scientist," Coldplay; "Everlong," Foo Fighters; "Wild Horses," the Sundays; "One Love," U2; "Criminal," Fiona Apple; "Bleeding Love," Leona Lewis; "Again," Janet Jackson; "I Think That She Knows," Justin Timberlake; "Let's Get it On," Marvin Gaye; "Let's Stay Together," Al Green; "Save the Last Dance for Me," the Drifters.

Sandra stared at me as though she expected something, expected me to say something in specific. I turned my work, and—feeling compelled to speak—offered. "It was nice of him, to do…?"

"*Nice* of him…?" She gaped, her expression both horrified and incredulous. "Elizabeth, listen to this CD. I mean, really *listen…to…it.*"

I glanced around the room. Everyone was on the edge of her seat, except of course Janie, who looked just as confused as I felt. I was inexplicably embarrassed. "I have listened to it."

"No. You haven't." Sandra exhaled loudly. "'My Best Friend's Girl'…'Mr. Brightside'? Hello! This CD is the story of you and Nico. This CD is his way of telling you how he feels. Wake up and smell the obvious for Thor's sake!"

"Oooh!" Janie, finally seeing what I was missing, met my gaze directly. "I get it! 'Swing Life Away' is like when you were kids, and 'Mr. Brightside' is—he's jealous."

"'What Sarah Said' by Death Cab for Cutie, that's when Garrett died." Fiona caught my gaze. "Love is watching someone dying." She quoted the song.

I gawked at her. I'd been rendered speechless, and I felt as if I'd been punched in the stomach. I couldn't decide if they were right. Furthermore, if they were right, I couldn't decide how I felt about it. The only thing I felt certain of was the sensation that I was drowning.

"The next three are about the summer he stayed with you after Garrett's death." Sandra nodded, picking up steam. "Then, 'One Love'—that's obvious. 'Criminal'—that's when you left him after…."

"Stop!" My heart was racing. "Just…just stop." I gathered up my knitting, and crossed to the CD player. Without a word, I ended the music before Shirley Bassey could croon the words "where do I begin?" one more time.

I was hot with a surge of unidentified feelings. I took the CD out of the player and left my group of friends staring at my back as I hurried to my bedroom and shut the door behind me.

I didn't turn on the light. Instead, I paced back and forth in the dark, wringing my hands.

Lyrics from the songs competed for my attention as they pounded through my brain.

My first reaction was anger, toward him. When I turned that over in my head a few times and realized it didn't make sense, I then directed the anger inward. After a few laps around my room, the anger dissipated—unable to gain traction—and I felt bereft and unbearably alone.

I *needed* to talk to him. I needed to ask him about the CD.

I needed to call Nico.

A light tapping on my door yanked me from my contemplative kerfuffle. I turned just in time to see Fiona and Janie peek their heads into my room.

"Elizabeth? Are you...?" Janie squinted at me. "Are you ok?"

I walked to the door and opened it a bit, and motioned for them to come in. "Yes. I'm ok. I'm fine. I just—" I rubbed the space between my eyes with my index finger and thumb. "I'm just feeling somewhat ridiculous at the moment."

Fiona walked over to me and engulfed me in a hug. Janie, without hesitating, followed suit, and we stood in my room, a hug tripod.

"Whatever you decide about Nico is your business." Fiona's soft voice helped melt some of the cold rigid anxiety in my bones. "But, no matter what, no matter if you tell that sexy Italian dreamboat to hit the road and no matter if you quit your job to become a belly dancing figure skater, there are six women here who love you and support you in all things." Fiona pulled back, snagging my gaze with her large, elfish eyes. "No matter what."

~*~*~*~

The first and only person I called after the ladies left and I finished Angelica's 10:00 pm study visit was my dad. I needed to hear his voice.

I knew he and Jeanette would be back from their two-week cruise by now. With all the media calls, I had not yet let him know about my change in phone number. We were long overdue for a chat.

He was so reasonable, so logical, so honest, so everything I'd always tried to be. If anyone could help me see reason, set my feet on the ground, and find a clear path, it was my dad.

The house phone rang three times before someone answered, and that someone was not my father.

"Um, hello?" A sleepy, female voice sounded from the other end.

I glanced at the clock on my nightstand; it was 11:00 pm I winced.

"Hi, Jeanette. I didn't realize how late it is. I'll call back tomorrow."

"Oh! Elizabeth, honey, don't apologize." I heard rustling on the other end as she adjusted the phone. "Your dad is so worried. We haven't heard from you."

"I know. Things have been a little strange."

"Let me go get him. He'll be so happy to hear your voice."

"Thanks, Jeanette." I picked at a frayed hole in my jeans, breaking the white cotton threads that ran horizontal and twisting them between my fingers.

"Elizabeth? Are you ok?" My father's steady voice soothed my nerves. I gathered a deep breath.

"Yes. I'm good. I'm fine. I just wanted to call you and give you my new cell number, and explain why I've been missing in action, see how the cruise was. But I can call back tomorrow."

"No. It's fine. I'm still up working on a grant proposal for the department. The cruise was really great…just a minute." I detected soft voices then a door close, the distinct sound of my father sitting in the chair behind his desk. It always squeaked. "What was I saying?"

"The cruise."

"Yes, yes, the cruise. Listen, Elizabeth, there is something I've been needing to talk to you about. I really wanted to do this in person, but with your schedule and mine, I think the phone is probably just fine."

I frowned. He sounded suspiciously hesitant, somber even. This sounded serious. I braced myself. "Are you ok? Are you sick?"

"No, no—nothing like that. This is good news. At least, I think it's good news—great news in fact."

"Oh. Good." His words only served to increase my disquiet. *Great news?*

"Well, you see, the thing is…." I heard him huff. It was the kind of huff that is accompanied by a smile—a huff-laugh. "I asked Jeannette to marry me, and she said yes."

I opened my mouth with no intention of speaking. It was just open—wide open. To say I was shocked was a gross understatement. My mind was blown. I thought for a moment that I was dreaming.

"Elizabeth?"

This was the man who'd said that my mother was his soul mate: his one true love. This was the man—throughout my entire childhood—who told me there was one right person for him, no one else, and that person had been my mother. This was the man who regaled me with stories about them, how they met, how they fell in love, and how much they loved me.

But this couldn't be the same man, because he was about to marry someone else.

"Elizabeth? Are you still there?"

"Yes! Yes, I'm here." Inexplicably, my eyes stung. "God, dad, I'm so happy for you." I looked at the ceiling, blinked away the moisture, and swallowed the sudden bitterness in my throat. "Congratulations."

"You can see why I've been trying to call you. It happened while we were on the cruise and," he huff-laughed again, "I just can't believe she said yes."

CHAPTER 18

I called Nico on Wednesday.

Learning about my father's engagement felt like taking the red pill in the Matrix. Everything he'd told me—about him, his unwavering love for my mother, about soul mates and true love—everything felt like a lie. I knew he'd meant well when he'd told me those things, and I knew he believed the sentiments at the time.

But that didn't change the fact that he'd lied.

The rug had been pulled out from under me, my balloon had been popped, the wind had vacated my sails, and—for maybe the hundredth time in two weeks—I felt adrift, unanchored, and unsteady.

I spent the day talking myself in and out of calling Nico. I rationalized that I had two very good reasons for calling him.

First of all, I couldn't be one hundred percent sure, but I thought I saw the fancy stalker lady in the hospital on Wednesday afternoon. I only saw her from the back, and it was in the crowded cafeteria, but I was almost positive the fancy stalker was back.

This excuse didn't really work because I'd immediately told my assigned guard, Dan, about the incident. Dan contacted Quinn. Quinn, most likely, had already told Nico.

However, my second excuse was perfectly sound. I reasoned that it was appropriate for me to call him about Angelica's progress. He was likely wondering why I hadn't called about it already. I figured any further delay in calling would be unprofessional on my part.

Yeah. That's the ticket. Unprofessional.

The first time I called Nico it was just after Angelica's 2:00 pm clinic visit. I had a shift at the hospital, so Rose and Angelica drove to the clinical research unit for the infusion. Seeing them made me miss Nico, and I called him on a whim before I could talk myself out of it.

It rang four times then went to voicemail. I didn't leave a message.

The next time I called Nico was during my dinner break. One of my patients had been listening to "Mr. Brightside" by the Killers on his iPhone. The aggressive melody carried through the teenager's headphones. The song reminded me of Nico and his mix-tape CD.

I let the phone ring twice then I hung up before it went to voicemail.

The third time I called him, I was just leaving the hospital at midnight, on my way home. I was sitting in the backseat of a large black SUV, one of Quinn's cars that drove me back and forth to work.

The phone rang only once before I pressed the end button.

I stared at the screen and laughed at myself. I was such a coward when it came to this man. I hated it. I hated how uncertain I felt. I hated how I couldn't stop thinking about him and his stupid funny jokes. I hated how he invaded my dreams—during the day and at night.

I was a mess.

The phone vibrated, causing me to jump and drop it. I fumbled on the floor of the car for the phone and glanced at the screen. It was Nico. I shut my eyes tight.

Gah!

I swiped my thumb across the screen and brought the receiver to my ear, grimacing as I did so, because I was a coward and, honestly, very much afraid of hearing his voice.

"Hello?"

"Elizabeth?"

My heart leapt to my throat. "Nico?"

"Yes...."

The hairs on the back of my neck stood at attention. Damn him and his damn freaking sexy voice!

"Um…Hi."

"Hi."

Silence.

Nico spoke first. "Are you ok? One of Quinn's people told me what happened with that woman who—"

"No. I'm fine. It probably wasn't even her—nothing to worry about, really."

"Ok. Good. So…what's up?" He sounded friendly and casual, as if I called him every day.

"You called me."

"Yes, but you called me first; three times actually. Are you sure you're ok?"

"Oh yeah. Everything is fine. I was just going to check in with you about Angelica."

"Is she ok? I talked to Ma this afternoon, and she said that Angelica seems to be doing a bit better."

"Yes. Yes, that's true." I wiped my free hand on the knee of my scrubs; it was damp with sweat, as was the one that held the phone.

"Good. That's good."

I heard voices in the background, muffled banging, and then someone shouted.

"Well, you sound busy. I should let you go."

"No. I'm not busy. I don't need to go."

"Oh. Ok." I switched the phone so that I could wipe the sweat off my other hand. "How are things going in New York?"

"Good. Crazy. Busy. I've been taping two shows a day."

"Wow. That seems like a lot." I eased into my seat, relaxing a bit as the conversation settled on the benign topic of his show.

"Yeah, well, I want to take some time off after this week and spend a few days in Chicago next week."

My stomach did a backflip. It took me a moment to recover from the news. "You'll be here all next week?"

"Well, starting Tuesday."

My stomach did a front flip. I had a stupid grin on my face. "I'm sure Angelica will really like that. She misses you."

"I miss her too. But, it's not just Angelica that I'd like to spend time with."

My grin widened. I knew where he was going with his last statement, but I wanted to torture him a little. "Well, your mother misses you too."

He chuckled. It was a man chuckle, and it made my heart squee. "I'm sure she does. But you know I was talking about you."

My stomach did a side flip. "Me?"

"Yes. You. Maybe when I get back we could go out, catch a movie, see a show—you know, friend things."

I laughed. "Nico, I can't even leave my building without photographers chasing me down. The two of us out together might incite a riot. How are we supposed to go out to a movie?"

"In disguise. We'll wear wigs and dress up like an old married couple. Of course, I'll have to cop a feel to keep up with the ruse."

"Ha! Yes. Because I've never seen an old married couple out in public without one of them copping a feel."

"Copping a feel, making out, heavy petting, wild sex in public places—old married couples are really a PDA menace, but I'm willing to commit to the disguise if you are."

My head fell back to the headrest as my laughter filled the car. "You are a funny, funny guy, Nico."

"Well, it is my job. Speaking of which—just a second." He must've placed his hand over the phone because there was silence for a short moment. When he came back to the phone, the background noise was gone. "How's work going? What have you been up to?"

"Bah. That's boring. You don't want to hear about that." I

didn't want to bring the lightness of the conversation down with my daily statistics: two shootings and a car accident.

"I do; otherwise I wouldn't have asked. How is work? Anything interesting in the ER today?"

I shifted in my seat, crossed my legs. I thought about unloading on Nico. In truth, I wasn't used to talking to someone about my day, not anymore. Janie and I used to swap work stories before she met Quinn and virtually disappeared.

"Well, how was your day?"

"No—I asked you first. I want to hear about everything. Start at the beginning."

"What is considered the beginning?"

"Waking up."

"Ok."

"Don't skip anything."

And I didn't. I didn't skip anything. I told him all about the young kid who died in the ER while I was trying to intubate her and how angry and sad it made me. We covered my day, his day, Angelica's clinic visits, his feelings on different brands of tequila, my unhealthy yet abiding obsession with goldfish crackers and *Star Trek Voyager*, his plans to travel to Italy, my plans to eat a deep-dish pizza on Friday, the perfect pizza toppings.

It felt indescribably good to unburden the day and then discuss topics of absolutely no importance to anyone but us. I stayed on the phone with him as I changed my clothes and brushed my teeth. I lay in bed and argued the merits of learning a foreign language at a young age—we both agreed it was a good idea.

We were still talking at 2:00 am when I heard him yawn on the other end. It was a stretch-yawn, and I shivered involuntarily at the thought of his big body stretching next to mine, relaxed and sleepy.

"Nico. We need to go to sleep. It's two here, which means it's three there."

"Just a little longer."

I closed my eyes and pictured him next to me, talking in my ear. "I have to be up at five forty-five for Angelica's infusion."

He groaned. "Ok. Get some sleep. When are you calling me next? Tomorrow?"

"I have a double shift tomorrow."

"Don't you have breaks?"

"Yes. I have a dinner break at six in the evening."

I could hear the smile in his voice. "Perfect. Call me then. We'll have dinner together."

"Ok." I answered his smile with a shy one of my own. It was ridiculous and girly, but I couldn't help it. His sleepy, teddy bear voice gave me the warm fuzzies.

"Oh, and Elizabeth?"

"Yeah?"

"What are you wearing?"

"Uh, my pajamas. Why?"

"What do they look like?"

He was a dirty bird. Two could play at this game. "Actually..." I stretched. "...I'm naked."

This statement was met with silence. I opened my eyes and stared at the ceiling. "Nico? Are you still there?"

"Yep." His voice sounded strained.

I laughed lightly. "Are you ok?"

"Yeah. I'm great. I was just thinking about the fact that we're wearing matching outfits."

An image of naked Nico flashed into my mind, big and hard and smooth, nestled between soft cotton sheets. I stopped laughing. I swallowed.

"Sweet dreams, Elizabeth."

"Sleep tight, Nico." I choked.

I hung up the phone, no longer tired.

I didn't sleep a wink.

~*~*~*~

Over the next several days, my sleep and knitting suffered because, when I wasn't working, I was talking on the phone with Nico. During my breaks we either spoke or texted. Our discussions put me in a good mood, and I even successfully ignored Meg's attempts to draw me into a petty fight.

For the first time in my adult life, I was counting the hours between phone calls with a man.

Who was I? Who was this silly, giddy girl?

I didn't dwell on it.

Friday night, late, after I unloaded on Nico about a case of domestic violence that I'd treated earlier in the day, I brought up the topic of my father's impending nuptials. It was a very graceful conversational transition.

He said, "Geez, that sucks," in response to the story about the patient.

And I said, "So my dad is getting married."

"Oh." He paused; then, "Wait, what? Really?"

"Yeah. Really." It felt nice talking to someone who understood what this meant.

"I can't believe it. To who?"

"To the baker, Jeannette."

"Ah yes. The woman my mother has been referring to as the child. Well, good for him…right?"

"Yeah…right."

"I thought you liked her."

I shrugged my shoulders then realized he couldn't see me. "She's nice."

"Are you happy about this?"

"Yeah…"

"You don't sound so sure about that."

"It's just—do you mind if I talk about this?"

"Yes. Please. Talk about whatever you want as long as you talk."

"So, here's the thing: I don't know how to feel about this because growing up, my dad…it's just…." I released a measured breath. "Everything he said about him and my mom feels like a lie now."

"Why? Because he found somebody else? It's been, what, fifteen years?"

"But that shouldn't matter—not if you really love someone. It shouldn't matter how much time has passed."

"You know he is allowed to move on with his life. If she is good people, then you should be happy for him."

"She is good people, and I don't have any problem with him moving on with his life. It's just that, growing up, he used to tell me about how he met my mom, how he knew at first sight that she was the one for him and that there was never going to be anybody else. They were childhood sweethearts, and now it just feels like he's saying, 'Okay, that was then, this is now—time to marry somebody else.' I mean, does he really *love* her? You see what I mean?"

I heard Nico take a deep breath; I could sense the hesitation in his voice. "Can I tell you a story?"

"Is it already story time?" I snarked.

"Smartass. I should send you to bed with no story."

"No, no. Please do. And you can picture me, chin resting neatly on the back of my folded fingers, listening attentively, gazing at you adoringly as you tell me a story."

"I will picture you that way. It's actually how I typically picture you whenever we speak on the phone. Also, you're usually naked."

"Shut up and tell the story already."

"Ok…." He briefly chuckled at my mixed message, cleared his throat, and began. "Once upon a time, there was a boy who fell in love with a girl when he was very young."

My heart skipped a beat and my stomach tumbled. "Nico...."

"Just listen. This might be very enlightening. So, he fell in love with this girl, and he didn't know how to talk to her, because she was better at him than everything, and she was smart, funny, pretty...."

"Nico!"

"Let me finish!"

"Ok, fine, but if you name her Elizabart and him Nici then I'm hanging up the phone."

"I will call him boy A and her girl A."

"Wait, is there more than one girl?"

"Yes. There is more than one girl."

"I'm not so sure I want to hear this story."

"Would you please just listen?"

I frowned at the thought of more than one girl, but tried to hide my displeasure when I responded. "Fine," I deadpanned.

"Good. Okay, so boy A, girl A, boy A is in love with girl A, but doesn't know how to talk to her so he teases her."

"Got it."

"Time goes by. She falls in love with boy B. Therefore, boy A became very upset with girl A."

"Why didn't boy A get upset with boy B?" This was a question that had been bothering me. I wondered, since his reveal in my room in Iowa some weeks ago, why I'd had to shoulder the brunt of his wicked behavior. Why had Garrett been exempt?

"Well, because boy A really liked boy B. Boy B was hard not to like because he was a good person, also funny, and really nice. A good guy, you know? They got along really well. Anyway, boy A wasn't upset with boy B. Boy A was upset with girl A because girl A chose boy B over boy A."

"First of all, girl A didn't choose boy B over boy A. As I've pointed out previously in the bathroom of your family's restaurant, girl A didn't know boy A was even a letter."

Nico man-sighed. *"Can I finish the story?"*

"And secondly, this is confusing and it's sounding a lot like a math problem. Please tell me boy A doesn't leave Boston on a train traveling at sixty miles per hour."

"Very funny. You're a natural comedian—did you know that? You should quit your day job and try the standup circuit."

"No, I could never do what you do. I can't get up in front of people like that."

"What are you talking about? You stood up in front of our entire high school reunion and—wait, stop trying to distract me from the story. Where was I? Oh yes, boy A was very mean to girl A and did everything he could to make girl A miserable, and it worked. But it didn't make boy A happy; all it did was make him miserable too. And so he took his frustration out, part of it, by sleeping around and going out with girls S through Z."

"Whoa. That's a lot of girls."

"And then…well, things happened, and we skip forward in our story a few years. Boy A lost touch with girl A, and he thought for a while that she was going to be it for him—that he was never going to find anyone else, and that he was just going to be with girls S through Z, and he knew that they were just placeholders, stand-ins for girl A. But then one day, he met someone else. We'll call her girl B."

He paused and I became aware that I was gripping my sheet, my hands were sweaty, and I couldn't speak because my throat was tight with some unknown yet terribly unpleasant feeling. I wanted to tell him to stop talking, that I didn't want to hear any more of the story, but I was paralyzed and fascinated.

I also needed a moment to process the fact that Nico had dated other people over the last eleven years.

Of course he has dated other people over the last eleven years. It's been eleven years, fruitcake!

"Boy A met girl B and fell in love with her."

"How is that possible?" I blurted, my voice a pitch or two higher than usual, ripe with complaint. "How is that possible if you were still in love with me?"

"Elizabeth, it is possible to love more than one person at the same time. That is a possible thing."

I didn't want to be yelling but I was. "Well maybe boy A wasn't ever really in love with girl A, or maybe he doesn't know what love is or, maybe boy A's feelings for girl A were shallow and it wasn't really love."

"No, Elizabeth. Love is not one single definable thing, it doesn't work the same way for everyone. Over these last eleven years, I watched my father die of lung cancer and my niece orphaned when her parents were killed in a freak accident. Maybe boy A realized that you have to find happiness when and where you can, and that falling in love isn't a once-in-a-lifetime occurrence, because if it is, then he was doomed to be miserable at seventeen. Maybe boy A was tired of being miserable." He didn't sound upset. He didn't even sound defensive. But he did sound somewhat exasperated.

I meditated on what he'd just admitted. I'd sent the family a sympathy card when Nico's father died. He'd been a larger-than-life figure—just like Nico. He'd been funny like Nico too, and bighearted.

Of course he would move on—or try to. It was what normal people did. I'd systematically rejected him for months after I left. Of course he believed the door was closed on us, I'd all but slammed it shut in his face.

The thought of Nico going through life unloved caused me a measure of physical pain. Despite my preconceived and conflicted feelings on the matter, I almost found myself rooting for girl B.

"Back to the story. Boy A fell in love with girl B. And they were very happy for a long time."

"How long?"

"For three years, actually."

Three years.... "What happened?"

He sighed. Somehow, I knew his eyes were closed. "She was there before he became famous. She supported him through all the trials and errors, before he had an HBO special, before he had a show. When things started heating up in his career, when he went from small time to big time, she couldn't deal with the attention. She didn't like having her picture taken, and she didn't like the lack of privacy. She asked him to give it up."

I waited for him to continue. When he didn't, I prompted him with a question to which I already knew the answer. "So did he?"

"No. He didn't."

Then I asked a question to which I didn't know whether I wanted to know the answer. "And did he regret it? Picking fame over her?"

"He didn't pick fame over her. He chose his career and his dreams over her. But, yes—yes he did regret it."

I felt a little sick to my stomach and realized that I was seething. I was upset. I was angry with this faceless girl B for issuing him ultimatums and leaving him when he is so obviously amazing.

What a feckless twit! I raged inwardly. It was at this point that I realized I was truly mentally disturbed.

Regardless, I forced myself to ask the next obvious question. "So why not just give it up and go get her?"

"Because she is now married and lives in Long Island with her three kids and engineer husband...and because there were other reasons why they split. The fame was really the last straw. He doesn't regret his choice anymore but he has learned from it."

"You think you would still be with her if you hadn't become famous?" I picked at a thread on my comforter and braced myself for his answer.

"No. Ultimately, she wanted something different from what I wanted. But that doesn't mean I loved her any less. It just means we weren't compatible in the long term."

"Then why do you regret picking your career over her? If it was going to end anyway, then it doesn't matter now."

"Because it doesn't mean anything—all the fame, the money, the recognition, the accolades—it doesn't mean anything to me without family, and without having someone to share it with. It's not really success."

"But if…." I closed my eyes and rested my cheek on the cool cotton blanket. "But if you believe there is more than one right person for you, then why not just move on to girl C?"

"Come on, Elizabeth. Finding girl C, being who I am, what I do…." He sighed. "I guess it's possible." I almost threw the phone, but then he continued. "But honestly, I don't really want to."

"Why not?" I held my breath.

"Because one of the reasons girl B and boy A would never have worked is because I'm—he's still in love with girl A."

I squeezed my eyes shut and felt a burst of something potently warm spread through my limbs. But then a sudden thought halted the delightful feeling. "Is he still in love with girl B?"

"No."

"But he is with girl A? He still loves her? That seems strange."

"I don't think so. You should know better than anyone how hard it is to let go of someone when you've loved them most of your life."

"But I did. I let Garrett go."

"Have you?"

Have I?

Have I really?

I waited for a stab of pain or an ache. Again, I felt only a numbness where something used to be. I answered honestly. "Yes. I have. I'll always love him, but I'm not carrying a torch for him like I used to, like I did for years. I don't think about him hourly or even daily—not anymore. I don't…pine for him." *Like I do for you.*

GAH!

I hoped he didn't detect my unspoken words, because I wasn't quite ready to admit them to myself let alone to him. I needed to spend more time in my petri dish to culture in the bacteria of possibility. Or, in *Star Trek* Borg terms, I needed a cycle in a maturation chamber.

We were silent for a moment. I was about to ask him if he believed me, but Nico surprised me by continuing his story. "So, back to boy A and girl A. I haven't told you the end of the story."

"There is an end?"

"Technically not an end—just a final statement. Boy A, although he's pretty sure girl A is for him, isn't certain that he is for her."

"Why do you say that?"

"Because, if he were for her, wouldn't she have already done something about it?"

"Maybe she needs time." *Stop speaking. Stop talking right now.*

"Maybe...." He didn't sound certain, and I was feeling borderline mortified and completely confused. I was worried any additional conversation might cause me to lead him on. I didn't want to lead him anywhere false, especially to hope.

I abruptly sat up. "Well. Thanks for telling your story, and the take-home message, I'm surmising, is that you like to tell math problems disguised as stories."

"No, the take-home message is that your dad is allowed to have a girl A and a girl B. In fact, he's allowed to have a girl C, D, E, and F. He's allowed to have an alphabet of women. And so are you."

"Oh, I bet you'd like it if I had an alphabet of women."

"I'm not going to lie; it's something I might warm up to on a cold night. But you know I meant that you have an entire alphabet of people for you—and not people who you can use, but people out there who want to share a life with you. Maybe not what you and

Garrett had, but something new; something great. Don't give up on your alphabet." I could hear the teasing in his voice, which had grown raspy and sleepy during our long conversation.

"Don't give up on my alphabet." I smiled. "I will keep that in mind."

"Life is alphabet soup, Elizabeth. Eat that soup."

~*~*~*~

We spoke again on Saturday—three times in fact. I didn't have much time to think about our discussion before we were on the phone with each other again. The calls also had the maddening effect of placing a virtually permanent, ridiculous, goofy grin on my face. I didn't even see Meg. She may have been working, she may even have talked to me at one point, but my good mood was impenetrable.

I kept meaning to bring up the mix-tape, but I always got sidetracked by something he said. It always felt like we never had enough time to talk. Therefore, when Nico brought it up during our Sunday lunch conversation, I was a little blindsided.

"You haven't mentioned anything about the mix-tape."

"Oh!" I jumped then fidgeted in my seat, "Yes…the tape."

"Did you listen to it yet?"

"Yes. I listened…to it."

"Well, what did you think?"

"I think…" I paused to gather a breath, but also to stall. If the ladies were right, and I was one hundred and ten percent positive that they were, then what was I supposed to say about the tape? What right answer could I give?

I settled for honest and benign. "I think that it is full of some really good music."

He was very quiet for a long moment then he said, "I feel like this is a huge step forward for you to have admitted that."

I released a breath. "I never said I didn't like good music; I just said I preferred boy-band music."

"Which song did you like the most—wait, actually, which songs did you not like?"

"Um...."

"Were there any songs that you didn't like?"

"I don't know that I didn't *like* them so much as...this is hard to talk about."

"Yeah, I thought it might be."

"Well, the song, I guess, that was the most difficult to listen to, even though I recognize that it's a really good song, is the one by Death Cab for Cutie about someone dying."

"Ah, yeah. I thought that might be the one you were going to say. I was hoping you were going to mention a different one, but, yeah—that's a really good song."

"It is."

"It actually helped me. When it came out, it helped me work through some issues."

"You use music to work through issues?"

"Don't you? Doesn't everyone? Music helps us feel things that we're not ready to feel, or that maybe we're blind to."

I decided to avoid the implications of his last statement in favor of the simple truth about me and music. "No. I don't use music for that."

"Right. Obviously. Because nobody is using boy bands to work through issues unless it's about copping your first feel or dealing with morning wood."

"Nico!"

"Because what issues could boy bands help you work through? Lingering questions about how to remove a bra? Hey, when did the boy with a premature ejaculation problem arrive to the party? I'll give you a hint: he came too early."

I barked a laugh, and I knew he was smiling as he continued. "You listen to boy bands to avoid issues."

He was right, of course. The fact that he knew me so well didn't at all surprise me, although it did make me uncomfortable. I didn't have anything to say in response to his probing, so I decided on the silent approach.

I should have known him better.

"Elizabeth?"

"Yes."

"Are you being quiet because I'm right?"

I squirmed a little. "Yes."

"Is there any possibility that over the course of this conversation you will actually say the words, 'Nico, you are right'?"

"No. That's not going to happen."

"Even though I'm right?"

"I'm always right. You don't see me going around ordering people to tell me so."

"Almost always right."

His teasing rejoinder made me smile and melt a little. "Fine. I'll admit that what you said was true."

"So you're fine with saying, 'Yes, Nico,' and you're good with saying, 'That's true, Nico,' but you are physically incapable of saying, 'Nico Manganiello, you are right'—is that correct?"

"That is correct." God help me, I was giggling. "First of all, you know I've never been able to pronounce your last name."

"If you'd let me touch your tongue while you tried to say it, I bet we could fix that problem."

I decided to pretend he hadn't spoken although my body was having difficulty ignoring what he'd said. "And secondly, I could maybe say a word that rhymes with 'right', like 'Nico, you are light or blight or sight or bite'."

"Nico, you are bite? That doesn't make any sense. How about, 'Nico you are bright'?"

I was laughing as I said, "I don't think I can say that either."

He was laughing as he asked, "Why?"

"Because it's a compliment."

"So now you're incapable of complimenting me?"

"I've complimented you! I told you that one time that you are funny."

"Mmm-hmm…why is it so hard for you to say nice things to me about me?"

"Because I'm so used to saying mean things about you to you…." I glanced around the doctor's lounge; no one seemed to be paying me any attention. Regardless, just in case, I lowered my voice. "Call it sixteen years of it being drilled in my head—by you—that you are the Romulan to my Vulcan."

"You and your *Star Trek* analogies."

"I'm trying to get used to this new kinder, gentler, softer Nico."

"Softer?"

"Well, smoother."

"Oh my stars! Did you just—was that a compliment? Did you just call me smooth?"

"Did you just say, 'Oh my stars'?" I laugh-snorted.

"I'm just shocked you complimented me. I'm going to write this day down so I can remember it. Dear Diary, today I was complimented by Elizabeth Finney. I think she's starting to like me. When oh when will she let me feel her up?"

I laugh-snorted again. "Very funny. That wasn't at all smooth by the way. Just be happy I called you smooth and not slick or…or charismatic."

"Hmm, I don't at all mind slick…we should spend more time discussing that, and you think I'm charismatic?" I could almost see the devastating small smile that accompanied his question.

"Oh, please. You know you're charismatic. Your superhero name would be Captain Charismatic. Your superpower would be stupid exploding charisma. I mean, you walk into a room and people, everyone, can't keep their eyes off you."

"You don't think my TV show has something to do with that—

the fact that they recognize me?"

"No. It's you. If you put a paper bag over your head, people would still be looking at you. Before you were famous, when we were in school, it was the same way. You were always so visible, and I was always so…invisible." I hadn't meant to say that about myself. It just came out, and honestly, it startled me. I swallowed a strange thickness in my throat.

"You were never invisible to me." Nico's voice was insistent, and for some reason, I felt that he was frustrated with me.

"Sometimes you made me wish that I was invisible to you." I stared at the toes of my comfortable shoes, lost in an unpleasant memory from high school; specifically when Nico introduced me to a new class member as *Skinny Finney, the brainiac boy everyone cheats off of.* There were so many hurtful things about that moment that I had difficulty settling on just one.

"Well…" Wisely he decided to sidestep my last comment. "I can compliment you."

"Please don't." I sniffled, surprised to find my eyes tearing up a little. I blinked away the beginnings of unwelcome emotions.

"Why not?"

"Because…." I closed my eyes. "Because it makes it hard to talk to you."

"As incapable as you are of complimenting me, I'm physically incapable of not complimenting you and how amazingly smart you are."

"Nico."

"Listen, you are. I remember in high school, we had classes together, in specific biology, and you ruined the curve."

"I liked biology. If you'd put me in public speaking, I would have gotten an F."

"The other thing I can't help complimenting you about—and that I wish I'd brought up at the reunion when we were dancing— is that you are funny."

This statement caught me by surprise. I never really thought of myself as funny—sarcastic, yes; funny, no. "I'm funny?"

"Yes. You are very funny."

I twisted my free fingers in the hem of my scrubs. "...really?"

"Yes. You're witty. I love how witty you are. I love talking to you because you're going to say something intelligent and hilarious. I love it."

Warmth suffused my cheeks at the thought of Nico, *the Face*, calling me funny. He was, after all, an expert on the matter. In addition to being charismatic, he always seemed to know the right thing to say. It was aggravating and sexy.

"I like talking to you too." My voice was small because my words were sincere.

I could feel his exploding charisma through the phone. "Was that a compliment?"

I rolled my eyes but my smile widened. "Yes. Fine. I complimented you. I love talking to Nico Mangenigelino or however the heck you pronounce your last name. Are you happy now?"

Blast of charisma. "I'm getting there."

CHAPTER 19

That night I pondered the fact that I'd been avoiding speaking with Nico about his fancy stalker. It felt like an unpleasant, heavy topic, like a rusty car or unmanageable box of poo. Whenever he asked me how I was doing in relation to the pressure of paparazzi or the stalker, I changed the subject. I didn't want to talk about it.

But we were having such a good time during our conversations. I loved them.

In fact, it dawned on me just as I was drifting off to sleep on Sunday night that I loved hearing about his day—not because it was exciting but because I loved being *there* for him. I loved being his sounding board, offering support and helping him reason through issues and problems. I loved giving him that part of myself.

All of this added together meant that I was letting him in. In fact, he was already *in*. He'd breached my fortress walls, he had a mancave in my citadel of seclusion and we were picking out curtains for the barred windows. The thought was both thrilling and terrifying.

I needed to decide what to do, what to say to him when he returned. Instead I rolled over in my bed, pulled the covers with me and, again, ensconced myself in avoidance. I justified my avoidance by reminding myself that we were just friends. I didn't need to make any decisions because there were no decisions to make. I could just enjoy the conversations for what they were: two friends talking on the phone.

And that was a load of horse manure.

I didn't want anything to change. I also loved how much we laughed together; we shared the same sense of humor, as sick and twisted as we were. I loved that jokes that might make others cringe sent us both into long, breath-stealing, stomach-cramping bouts of laughter.

Therefore, I didn't particularly want to dwell on any modification to our relationship that would likely ruin it; and I didn't want to discuss the stalker while we were joking about the phallic qualities of pasta.

However, on Monday, I saw the fancy stalker again, and this time I knew for certain that it was her. She was sitting in the ER waiting room, and I spotted her from behind the discharge counter. Sure enough, she was wearing fancy shoes, fancy sunglasses—which was really weird, considering that she was indoors—and a fancy trench coat—also weird.

I hurried to the doctor's lounge, the only place in the ER with cell phone coverage, and dialed the direct line of Detective Carey Long, the officer who'd come the last time. I also paged my guard, Dan. By the time I made it back to the discharge desk, the fancy stalker was gone. In the chair where she'd sat was another envelope.

I didn't touch it and I didn't open it. I waited for Detective Long to arrive and gave her the honor. She picked it up with official looking tweezers and placed it in a plastic bag then promised to let me know the contents as soon as she could.

Before she left she suggested to Dan that he follow me all day—stand outside clinic rooms—rather than walk the halls of the floor. She also recommended to Dan that Quinn's security team alert the hospital security team about the issue and circulate a picture of the fancy stalker so that staff and providers could keep an eye out. Dan informed Detective Long that they'd already taken that precaution but would circulate her picture again.

Before she left, she reminded me to tell Nico about the incident.

I decided to notify Nico of this latest episode in person. He would be home Tuesday, just one more day, and I would be able to draw him aside and describe the situation face-to-face. I didn't want him to become twisted in knots about it while he was in New York, as he was prone to do.

My Monday shift ended at 4:00 pm and, after trying but failing to reach Nico on the phone, I decided to take Rose up on an earlier offer of dinner and a movie with her and Angelica. It gave me an opportunity to give Angelica her new sweater, and Rose, although crazy as a loon, was still an amazing cook. I was hoping to pick up some tips. Since my father had never cooked, I'd never learned.

But I wanted to. Marie from my knitting group had taught me to make Belgian waffles and a few simple dinners. I could always use additional instruction and practice. Rose did not disappoint.

She was making ravioli from scratch. Angelica was sitting at my elbow, seemingly perfectly at ease. This was remarkable because I wasn't typically a kid magnet. In fact, kids seemed to sense my apprehension and usually—from a radius of at least six feet—cast disapproving and/or suspicious glares in my direction.

But, with Angelica, we'd developed an easy rapport since I'd shared my inventory of kids' jokes and given her the pony purse a few weeks ago. She was easy to like. In fact, I noted with some reluctance, she was easy to love. The fact that she adored the sweater I knit her didn't hurt matters either.

"What is that?" Her little munchkin voice pointed to my poorly constructed square of pasta.

"It's ravioli."

"No it's not." She shook her head, reached for a slice of pineapple, and popped it in her mouth.

"Well, what does it look like to you?"

"It looks like Pinky Pie's alligator." Her mouth was full of pineapple and a little juice dribbled down her chin. Instead of gross—which is what it should have been—she pulled off effortless adorableness.

Rose was making two kinds of ravioli. The first was your traditional wheat and egg pasta filled with ricotta cheese plus other top secret ingredients. The second was a wheat free, egg free, dairy free dough filled with a rice cheese substitute and vegetables. Angelica's disease meant that every meal was full of substitutions and omissions.

But pineapple was always on the menu.

I blinked at her. My eyes moved back to the pasta. It did indeed look like the shape of an alligator. "You mean Pinky Pie from *My Little Pony?*"

She nodded then wiped her hand on my shirt as though it were the most natural thing in the world. This caused me to blink at her again. "Did you just wipe your hand on my shirt?"

Angelica turned her wide, green eyes to mine and then she laughed. It was an answer of a sort. It was a *yes, I just wiped my hand on your shirt,* but, more than that, it was a *yes, I wiped my hand on your shirt, but I'm sure you don't mind because now I'm going to giggle with extreme cuteness and make your forget about the impropriety of using people's garments as hand towels.*

It worked. I opened my mouth in mock outrage. "I can't believe you just did that!"

This caused Angelica to laugh harder, her eyes bunching at the corners, which made her look even cuter. More pineapple drool tumbled from her mouth.

Rose watched our exchange with an approving smile up to that point. Her smile morphed into an expression of mock outrage—mirroring mine—when Angelica leaned over and wiped her mouth on Rose's shirt.

"Angelica!" I could tell, and so could Angelica, that Rose's indignation was as bogus as mine. "That's a no, Angelica!"

The small girl's giggles only increased with our fake reprimands. This game of human napkin continued for a while and ended with me pretending to use Angelica's hair to dab at the corners of my mouth. At this point Rose sent her off to the bathroom to wash her hands and face.

We both watched her go with a smile on our lips. But, as soon as she was gone, I felt Rose's eyes shift to me.

"You know, that is a sign that she likes you; she's comfortable with you."

I quickly glanced at Rose then refocused my attention to the butchered ravioli I'd abandoned. "I am glad. I want her to be comfortable with me."

"For the study? So she doesn't fear the visits?"

I shook my head. "Well, yes. I don't want her to fear the visits. But that's not the main reason I guess." I frowned at the pasta, finally decided it was beyond repair, and tossed it in the trash. I cut out a new square and tried repeating the filling procedure.

"Then why?"

I responded although I was somewhat distracted by my previous pasta-fail as well as my current attempt, which was also shaping up to be a past-fail. "She is so easy to like. She's brave and sweet and smart. She's also illegal levels of cute; that smile of hers could melt metal. And she's important to...."

I swallowed the end of the sentence, realized a little too late what I'd been about to say. I tucked my chin to my chest and redoubled my effort to focus on the ricotta cheese.

"Yes. She is very important to Nico. That's true."

I discerned the teasing behind Rose's words, and I struggled against the heat of embarrassment. Luckily, Angelica chose that moment to reappear. She held her hands out in front of her as though to prove she'd washed them.

Surprisingly, Rose said no more about my slip, and we spent the rest of the time in lighthearted conversation. Angelica had a great time laughing at my sad attempts to make the pasta. Most of my shells ended up torn, wonky, or in the trash; regardless, Rose was patient and kind and kept the red wine flowing. I may have purposefully disfigured a few of my attempts in order to sustain Angelica's giggles. She had a great laugh.

We were feeling pretty happy and loose by the time dinner ended. I cut myself off at two glasses around five thirty, conscious of Angelica's looming infusion.

After the treatment, I stayed for Monday movie night. But halfway through the movie—Angelica's current favorite, *The Secret of Kells*—the distinct sound of someone messing with the lock of the front door made my stomach cramp in fear. I stiffened and stood, placed my finger on my lips to silence Rose and shook my head.

Nico wasn't due back until the next day, and the guards always announced themselves.

I felt an immediate and fierce surge of protectiveness for both Angelica and Rose.

"Call Quinn," I whispered to Rose. "Tell him there is someone trying to get in the apartment."

After the envelope left at the hospital, I felt certain that the fancy stalker had found her way into the building. I didn't know how she'd managed to get past all the security, but I knew I wasn't going to let her into the apartment. There was no way in hell she would have an opportunity to hurt Angelica or Rose.

I rushed into the kitchen and grabbed a cast-iron frying pan. As quietly as I could, I tiptoed to the front door and heard the bone-chilling sound of someone turning the lock. I tightened my grip on the pan and prepared to knock out the intruder.

When the door swung open, I lifted the cast iron and met the startled expression of Nico—wide eyes, hand on chest, audible gasp. He took a step back into the hall.

"Jesus, Elizabeth!" He breathed out, still gripping his chest. "You scared the shit out of me."

My arms fell to my sides, the pan to the floor, and I raced into his arms and hugged him tightly around the neck. "You scared me too."

He hesitated a moment then returned my hug, holding me with

equal force. "What the hell is going on? Is everyone ok? Where's Angelica? Are you ok?"

I buried my face in his neck and breathed in the comforting smell of his scent. He smelled like his cologne and mint. Faintly I registered that the scent of cigarette smoke was missing.

"You weren't supposed to be home until tomorrow!"

"I caught an earlier flight." His hand rubbed a circle over my back.

"Oh god! I thought you were the fancy stalker."

His hand stilled. "Fancy stalker? Wait…what?"

"Uncle Nico!" Angelica's small voice carried to my ears, and I released my stranglehold on his neck. I stepped out of his embrace, which he reluctantly allowed, and shuffled to the end of the entryway, giving his niece plenty of space to welcome him home.

I stood at the end of the hallway and watched the homecoming ritual unfold as I tried to calm my frayed nerves while avoiding eye contact with both Rose and Nico.

Angelica was embraced first.

"I missed you, Uncle Nico." Her typically diminutive voice sounded unusually fervent.

"I missed you too, muffin," was Nico's muffled response, his face obscured by her mop of hair. After a long moment, Angelica pulled away and smoothed her hands over his cheeks. Nico asked about her day, about the status of her dolls, about the antics of Pinky Pie on *My Little Pony*.

Next, still casting stern looks in my direction and still holding Angelica with one arm, he hugged Rose and gave her a kiss on the cheek. She returned his kiss then inspected his face and clothes.

"Are you eating anything at all in New York?"

"Yes, Ma."

"What are you eating? Not much, that's what. You'll come in and eat now."

"I already grabbed something at the airport." Nico glanced at the ceiling but then his gaze snagged on mine, and he frowned.

"That's not food, Niccolò. You'll eat again. Elizabeth and I made ravioli," Rose said.

"That's not true. Rose made ravioli. I watched." I held my hands up.

"No." Angelica rested her head on Nico's shoulder and gave me a small grin. "You did make some, but they all went in the trash."

Feeling a bit calmer, I wrinkled my nose at her. She laughed.

Rose exhaled loudly and took Angelica from Nico's arms. "I'm not going to stand here and argue about the ravioli when Nico should be eating it instead. And you," she held Angelica close, "should be in bed." Rose turned and winked at me as she carried Angelica out of the entryway.

Nico watched his mother and niece depart then his eyes found and held mine. We stared at each other, as was our habit, and I realized how deeply I'd missed seeing him. He had reentered my life a few weeks ago, we'd spoken on the phone every day for the last five days, and he'd only been gone a week, but I missed him. I clasped my hands in front of me, my fingers wound tightly together, to keep from blurting out the truth of it.

"Hi, friend." His voice was both teasing and concerned.

"Hola, amigo."

"Do you want to tell me what happened?"

I returned his interrogating stare with an ashamed, evasive, shifty-eyed, stalling shrug. "Sure...but first, you should probably get something to eat."

"No, Elizabeth." His face was suddenly granite. "Did she come back? Did she approach you?"

I was caught. "She didn't approach me. But she did show up today."

He cussed. His voice rose and he checked himself; he pulled his hands through his hair, mussed it to perfection. I placed my hands on his forearms to pull his attention and focus back to me. "Calm down. Just calm down—it was really nothing, ok?"

Nico's eyes searched mine, his expression wavering between fury and worry. Mimicking the force of my earlier stranglehold, he abruptly pulled me into his arms. "I want to lock you up. I want to put you in a safe, and only I'll have the key."

I felt his heart hammering against his chest. It was my turn to draw circles on his back, thread my fingers through his hair, and rub his neck.

"Hey, now…everything is fine. Let me just tell you what happened, ok? It's not that bad."

"Elizabeth, you were about to knock me out with a frying pan. I saw the fear in your eyes. Don't tell me it's not that bad."

I waited a beat then said, "It's not that bad."

He released a nervous laugh, and I smiled into his chest and pushed slightly against him so that I could see his eyes. "I'll tell you everything. Just come in and eat something first. Have some wine."

He regarded me warily but finally nodded his assent. He tucked me under his arm and we walked to the dining room table. Rose had very efficiently set out a place for him piled high with ravioli, focaccia, and sautéed sunflower leaves. My mouth started to water even though I was still full from my earlier pig-out.

We sat in silence for a while then I filled the quiet with mundane questions and comments about his day, my day, and Angelica's treatment. He drank three glasses of wine in rapid succession, his eyes growing more liquid with each glass.

I waited until he seemed somewhat relaxed—which was not at all relaxed but no longer on the verge of murdering someone—then told him of today's strangeness.

He listened, fingering the stem of his wineglass, twisting it between his thumb and forefinger. I noted that his jaw flexed and his temple ticked a few times.

When I finished, I met his gaze; his eyes resembled hot coals. I could tell he was trying very hard to keep his temper in check.

"This is so fu—" his voice was lethally low; he caught himself before he could finish the word. "We have to find a way to keep her away from you."

I nodded. "Dan will be following me around the clinic from now on, so I'll have a guard with me at all times."

His jaw ticked again. "I know this woman. She is dangerous."

"Nico…who is she? Is she the one you mentioned before?"

"Yes. I met her at a club that night when she put her hands down my pants, and I—" Nico stood abruptly and walked away from the table.

I followed him. "Why do you think she is dangerous?"

He spun on me. "Because she attacked one of the dancers on my show."

I stepped back. "Oh…."

"Yeah. Oh."

"Why isn't she in jail?"

"She *was* in jail, for two years. She was released last year."

"Why did she attack the dancer?"

"Because I was dating her."

I took another step back as if I'd been slapped. "Oh."

He studied me. An extremely uncomfortable moment passed. I concentrated on breathing.

Nico shifted his weight and placed his hands on his hips. "I don't do that anymore."

"What?"

"Date the dancers. It was only the one time."

I nodded, wanted to tell him it was none of my business, but I couldn't seem to get the words past my throat. I hated that he'd been looking for girl C.

Instead, I turned and said over my shoulder, "Come back to the table and finish your dinner."

Nico followed me back to the table. I poured him another glass of wine and took the seat adjacent to his where I sat and fiddled with the napkin. I could feel his eyes on me, but I didn't return his gaze.

"Hey, what are you thinking about?" Nico placed his hand over mine, drawing me out of my thoughts.

I pulled my hand away and tucked loose strands of hair behind my ears. I really needed to rebraid my hair. In fact, I really needed a makeover. For the first time in a long time I felt like maybe I needed to try a bit harder putting myself together; maybe doing my hair would be a good idea, or wearing makeup, or growing four inches.

"I was just thinking that if we were at your family's restaurant right now, skeevy Frank Sinatra would be playing on the jukebox."

"Skeevy Frank Sinatra? Frank Sinatra isn't skeevy."

"You have to admit, he was kind of a jerk—him and his dumb women." I felt strangely argumentative, hot, and annoyed.

"What do you have against Frank Sinatra?"

"He just seems like the poster boy for chauvinistic men—that is until you came along with your show and picked up the torch."

Nico's eyes flickered over my features; he openly studied me, and his gaze lost most of its warmth in favor of cool annoyance. After a prolonged moment, he wiped his mouth with his napkin and placed it on the table, and then he leaned forward on his elbows so that we were just a few inches apart. "Frank Sinatra once said, 'I like intelligent women. When you go out, it shouldn't be a staring contest'."

I scratched my chin. "I've never heard that quote before."

"That's because you don't know anything about Frank Sinatra, just like you don't know anything about my show."

"I know you have bimbos dancing around in bikinis." I felt better and worse as soon as the words were out of my mouth. The gathering thickness in my throat and my sudden irrationality reminded me of our conversation earlier in the week when we'd discussed his girl B.

"No. I don't." His features darkened. He looked honestly wounded.

"Really?" I folded my arms over my chest and leaned back in my chair. "So those women, they're not wearing bikinis? What—are they robots? Automatons? Fembots?"

"No. They're women, and they're wearing dance costumes. But they're not bimbos."

I snorted. "Right."

He shook his head. "They happen to be very bright, very intelligent women."

"Who all happen to look like the freaks of nature also known as supermodels."

"Not all of them look like supermodels. In fact, maybe only one looks like a supermodel."

"Oh, really?"

"Yes, really, unless you consider yourself a supermodel. Erin, who is a graduate of Columbia with a degree in physics, is shorter than you are. Tamara is about your height and has a master's in Russian literature from Brown."

I squirmed in my seat and fiddled with the hem of my scrubs. "You only hire college graduates?"

"No. Cassandra, our lead choreographer, doesn't have a college degree. But she's a great dancer and a great mom. I'm also her oldest son's godfather. So you can imagine how it upsets me when you refer to her as a bimbo."

I tore my bottom lip between my teeth; my eyes were caught by his disappointed, frustrated scowl.

Before I could respond to this new and interesting information, Nico pushed slightly away from the table and turned his chair so that we were fully facing each other. For a brief moment, I didn't know if he was going to give me a lecture or kick me out of his apartment.

"If you watched the show, or knew anything about it, you would know that each of my dancers plays a key role." I sunk lower in my seat as he launched an impassioned defense of his show. "Three of them are writers on the show. Did you know that? All of them participate in the skits. In fact, Erin has her own segment called 'Are you Smarter than a Bikini Model?' She annihilates her opponents. We had Franklin Orin on—you know, that famous political scientist, always on the cable news programs? Well, she killed it; she wiped the floor with him. He was actually really nice about it.

"Over half of our viewership is women. Our main female demographic is between the ages of twenty-two and forty-eight. When asked why they watch the show, they overwhelmingly respond that it portrays women in a positive light."

I bit the inside of my cheek and huffed. "You have to admit, the commercials do not portray the show to be pro-female."

"Depends on what your definition of pro-female is. If you think pro-female is having a show where various kinds of women—all different ethnicities, with diverse backgrounds and talents, but also all healthy and in great physical shape—work together to make an exemplary product, then, yes, it is pro-female."

I blinked, nonplussed. "Your audience is naked!"

"Not the whole audience; just the group closest to the dancers' stage and it's because they choose to be."

"Come on! All the commercials show you wrestling—half-naked—in tubs of Jell-O. They show your girls doing gymnastics!"

He shrugged, but his grimace betrayed his frustration. "Gymnastics is an Olympic sport but, I admit, some of the commercials don't represent the show in the best light. I don't make the commercials, and I don't have control over the marketing team. They work directly for the network and do what they need to do to bring in viewership."

"But you can't expect me to be ok with what I see on the commercials."

"That's a cop-out, Elizabeth. That's like rating or reviewing a book after reading the first ten pages. Do you really think my sisters or my mother would speak to me if my show marginalized women? More importantly, how can you think so little of me?"

I again squirmed in my chair and stared at the table. I didn't think so little of him. I thought a lot of him; I thought a great deal of him.

But I didn't like that he was right and I was wrong. If I were going to form an opinion about something and offer it freely as fact, then I needed to be knowledgeable on the subject.

Nico shook his head as though exasperated. "Women dance around in bikinis on every beach in the United States, and I don't see you throwing temper tantrums about their behavior."

I was on the precipice of doing something I'd never done with him before. But the urge—the absolute need—to utter those three little words was so overwhelming, I was surprised I didn't shout them as they fumbled from my mouth.

"I am sorry."

Nico blinked at me and was speechless for a moment; he seemed a bit startled. His frown lost some of its severity. "Excuse me? Did you just say...?" Suddenly, he was fighting a smile. "Did Elizabeth Finney just apologize for something—to *me*?"

I firmed my expression and glanced at the ceiling. "I'm sorry I called them bimbos, because I guess they're not bimbos. But, despite your excellent point about bikinis on beaches, I still take issue with the bikini prancing."

He glanced around the room. "Did that just happen? Am I...am I dreaming? No!" He smacked the table with his palm then pointed at me. "A hallucination! I'm hallucinating, right?"

I closed my eyes and completely lost the battle against my laughter.

"Or, the world is coming to an end." I felt his hand close over mine where I held it guarded in the crook of my elbow, and he pulled it toward him and held it in both of his; he waited until I opened my eyes before he continued. "You can level with me. Is the world ending? Is the apocalypse upon us? If so, I propose we forget my no-benefits rule and start humping like rabbits."

"Stop!" Through my chortling and laugh snorts, I attempted to pull my hand from his but he held it hostage.

"No, no, forgive me. Not like rabbits, like Shaw's jird. Did you know they try to copulate two hundred and forty times an hour?"

"What in god's name is a Shaw's jird, and where did you pick up that lovely tidbit?"

Nico tugged my hand until I was upended from my seat. I lost my balance, crashed into him, and landed on his lap. "It's a Middle Eastern rodent, if you must know. If you watched my show, you would know these things. We cover all sorts of educational topics."

"Educational for whom?" I tried to right myself even as he tried to arrange my legs so that I was straddling him. "Educational for rodents?"

"No—educational for students of animal behavior." One of his big hands gripped my hip, pressed me down, held me over his lap; his other arm snaked around my waist. I tried to stand and succeeded only in pressing my boobs against his face.

He nipped at my chest and I pulled back, out of the reach of his mouth, but stopped my halfhearted struggle. "Oh, animal behavior, huh?"

As was our habit, we stared at each other for an extremely tense moment, both breathing perhaps a bit too hard given the briefness of the struggle. His hands relaxed, and he let one rest perilously close to my bottom. I could feel through my thin cotton scrubs that our short wrestling match had left him hot and bothered. His chin and mouth were about two inches from my chest, and he gazed at me with intent——kissing intent.

I gazed deeply into his eyes. My fingers moved to the back of his neck. I licked my lips. His eyes followed the movement.

And then I pulled his hair—hard.

"Ow!" He winced. His hands flew to the back of his head, and I took the opportunity to escape.

I stood and quickly put the table between us. He also stood, stull rubbing the back of his head. "Hey. That hurt."

I lifted my chin and issued my frostiest glare. "I hope so."

"Why? What did I do?"

"Nothing." *Everything.*

"Are you mad about something?"

"Yes. No." I crossed my arms then decided to put them on my hips instead. "I don't know."

"Well, when you figure it out, I'd like to know."

We stood across from each other, the big dining table between us, and I fought to find the source of my fury. Almost immediately, I knew the answer: I was jealous of girl B. I was jealous of his dancers. I was jealous of the one he'd dated, girl C. I was jealous of the obvious respect he shared with the others, of the time they shared with him, of the years, and the friendship.

I was jealous—and I was worried he would guess the truth.

I didn't know where to look. After a long moment, I sighed, shook my head, and glanced over his shoulder.

"Look. I'm not mad at you. I'm just jumpy because of earlier, and I'm low on sleep because *somebody* keeps me up at all hours talking on the phone."

I peeked at him. He was grinning at me with kind, gentle eyes. "Ok then." He clapped his hands. "Off to bed with you. I'll take you home."

"No! I can take myself. I don't need any more friendly kisses." I walked to the door, and heard him follow behind me.

"I can give you an unfriendly kiss if you want."

"No thank you. No kisses, please."

"Suit yourself."

I turned as I exited and found him behind me leaning against the door. His four glasses of wine had rendered him delightfully hazy, smiling softly, and looking at me like I was next on the menu.

I swayed forward then caught myself, fisted my hands at my sides to keep from touching him, and averted my eyes. I stomped to the elevator.

"Sweet dreams, Elizabeth!" he called after me.

I didn't respond. In my jealousy-fueled foul mood, I would probably say something nasty or, worse, something honest.

~*~

My wonderful mood lasted through the day Tuesday. I was suffused with raging jealousy, and the green-eyed monster grew bigger within me every time I thought about those prancing bikini-clad dancers. I tried to ignore Nico in the morning during Angelica's 6:00 am infusion. I did my best to be coolly polite during the 2:00 pm hospital visit.

But he knew and I knew that something was up.

I knew that he knew that I knew that he knew that something was up.

And I hated it. I hated that I felt like I was playing games. I didn't want to play games. I wanted to be honest.

But I couldn't be honest.

If I were honest, I would tell him that I liked him, and that I wanted to be more than friends. I would tell him that I wanted exclusive, full-time, 24-7 benefits in a more-than-friends relationship. I would tell him that I thought about him night and day and that thinking about him had become a second full-time job.

I'd worked myself into an irritation tornado. Therefore, when a pissy Dr. Ken Miles decided to pitch a fit one hour before my shift was over, he was quite lucky I didn't stab him in the neck with a wooden tongue depressor.

"Well?" he said bitchily, hovering at my shoulder.

That's right, *bitchily.*

I was charting in the ER alcove, halfway finished with a discharge summary. I glanced at him, rolled my eyes, and paused the recording.

"What do you want, Dr. Ken Miles?"

He huffed then snorted. "Really? You're irritated with me?"

I set the phone on the desk, mentally preparing myself for a lecture on my childish behavior or some such nonsense. "What? What is it? What did I do now?"

"Our date is in two days!"

"I told you, it's not a date. And, about that, I need to cancel…."

"Whatever—you said we'd be exclusive." He leaned in to whisper. "And then Meg shows me your boyfriend on TV talking all about your 'relationship'." He air-quoted this last part.

Add air quoting to the list of things that annoyed me about Dr. Ken Miles.

I stared at him blankly because his words made no sense. "What are you talking about?"

"Like you don't know."

"I don't. What are you talking about?" I was seconds from finding that wooden tongue depressor.

He blinked, his pretty features marred by a severe frown that morphed into confusion then incredulity. "You don't know." It was a statement.

"No. I don't know. So please stop speaking in riddles. What…are…you…talking…about?"

Dr. Ken Miles pulled out his cell phone and grabbed my hand. I paused a minute to collect my chart, and then I allowed myself to be led away from the alcove to the doctor's lounge. He fiddled with his screen a bit then shoved a video clip in front of my face.

"Here. Watch this."

I stared at the paused YouTube clip for a moment, about to tell

Dr. Ken Miles that I didn't have time for this, but then he hit the Play icon and handed the phone to me. It was a clip from an entertainment news program. A hot, leggy reporter was laughing with Nico.

As I watched it, I felt my temperature rise to near lava levels. When it was over, I shoved Dr. Ken Miles's phone back in his hands and swiftly left the lounge and the hospital.

I decided that the rest of the charting would have to wait. I needed to either go kiss or kill a hot Italian comedian.

CHAPTER 20

I changed my mind maybe one hundred and seventeen times on the ride to my apartment.

String him up or sex him up?

Or both...?

At last, I decided that I would let my knitting group help me decide what to do. I wasn't operating in my right brain anymore. I needed some perspective from an unbiased audience.

However, when I arrived home under the impression that I would find only my friends—my unbiased friends—knitting harmlessly and swapping a few raunchy stories, instead I found Nico sitting among them oozing charm.

Freaking Nico Manganiello.

He was on the couch next to Janie; they were huddled together, their heads a few inches apart as if they were sharing a secret. She was frowning at something in his hands, and he was smiling at her confusion. They looked adorable, and I was boiling over with jealousy.

"What are you doing here?" I didn't try to hide the sharpness of my tone.

Everyone paused and glanced at me, mid-conversation, mid-row, mid-stitch, and they all seemed so and relaxed and casual—unhurried, unworried, and unperturbed. It was maddening.

"Oh, hey, Elizabeth, nice to see you too." Nico flashed me an unbelievably brilliant smile. His eyes weren't twinkling; they were electric.

"What's going on? Why is he here?"

"Nico and I are learning how to crochet." Janie held up a crochet hook; a long chain stitch dangled from one end.

I looked from the chain to Nico to Janie then to the rest of the knitting group. They were all smiling at Nico approvingly.

"Can I speak to you please?" I pointed at him then gestured toward the hallway. "In the other room?"

Nico's smile was slow and deliberate, and full of sensual intention. "Yeah. Sure."

I ignored the rapid pace of my heart while I led the way and held the door open to my room. I waited for him to enter—which he did whistling.

I closed the door and spun to face him, one hand on my hip, the other pointing at him with what I hoped would be perceived as serious business. "What is this? What are you wearing?"

He glanced down at his black suit, white shirt, askew skinny tie. "What's wrong with what I'm wearing?"

I stalked toward him and sniffed. Just as I suspected—cologne. "Suit? Tie? Cologne?"

"Yes. This is a suit," he said as he lifted one of his lapels, "and this is a tie," he pointed to the tie, "and that magical scent filling the air, that is cologne. Men wear these things. It's not a mystery, Nancy Drew, it's clothes and fragrance."

"But why are you wearing them—to knit night? And why are you at knit night?"

"I was invited by your adorable friend Janie." He smiled, and he let his gaze stray to my bed. It was unmade, and a few underthings were scattered about including some of the pink and black lingerie from my last panty dance party. I fought the urge to clean up the disaster.

"Janie is engaged. You've met her fiancé, right? He's the big, scary guy who used to be a criminal, probably still is."

"Hey," he held his hands up, "I'm not interested in Janie. Well...that's not true. I think every heterosexual guy with eyes and a working penis is interested in Janie, but I like Quinn, and I have no intention of stepping on his gorilla-sized toes."

"Then why are you dressed like that? And why were you out

there flirting with Janie?" I sounded jealous. *Grr.*

Nico smoothed his tie and tugged at the wrists of his jacket. "I'm dressed like this because I'm taking your knitting group out to dinner tonight. You're invited too, if you want to come."

"You are?"

"Yes. If you'd looked around the room instead of jumping to, frankly, fascinating conclusions, you would have noticed that everyone is dressed for dinner. And I wasn't flirting with Janie. She and I are learning how to crochet."

"Is that what the kids are calling it?"

"Yes. I understand that there can be some animosity between knitters and crocheters, but I think if we all recognize our shared love for fiber and yarn, then we'll be able to get along just fine."

"Fiona says that all the time. You just quoted Fiona."

"Yes I did. She is very wise."

"Stop changing the subject. I'm upset with you."

"Really?" He did a very good impression of pretending to look surprised. "Why? What did I do?"

"I saw your little interview!"

"Oh? Did you? Did you see that?" He appeared to be unconcerned. In fact, he appeared to be elated.

"Yeah, I saw that…." I waited for him to apologize or explain. When he just stood there looking at me—twinkle, twinkle little star—my temper hit the roof. "What did you think you were doing?"

"What are you talking about? I was giving an interview."

"You insinuated that you and I had a relationship when we were teenagers."

"We did have a relationship."

"No we didn't."

"Yeah, we kinda did."

I glared at him. He glared at me. He had a point. We kinda did.

"Well, I—ok, fine, we kinda did. But then you told the reporter that you and I are 'just friends'." I used air quotes with as much sarcastic flourish as possible.

He glared at me. "We are just friends."

"But you didn't say it like we *are* just friends, you said it like *I'm going to tell you, Ms. Sexy Reporter Lady, that we're just friends, but really there is more going on, and I'm not going to be honest with you about it. I'm just going to sit here and eye twinkle at you and say we're just friends, but we're not.*"

He considered me for a moment, trying to suppress a grin. He bit his top lip, obviously to keep from laughing. "I eye twinkled at the reporter?"

"Yeah. You eye twinkled at the reporter—in fact, you are eye twinkling right now, and I would really appreciate it if you would cease and desist!" He lost the fight against the smile and the laughter, and I couldn't help but join him as I neared the end of my tirade. "I want you to cease and desist with the—the eye twinkling—for the time being.." A reluctant smile split my face. "That would be fantastic."

"All right." He nodded solemnly and placed his hand over his heart. "All right. I'll see what I can do." Nico sighed, suddenly becoming serious. "But, you do know that my eyes are insured by Lloyds of London, right?"

"Wait, what?"

"Yeah." He nodded. "The network insured them for two million dollars."

I studied him. "Really?"

He nodded again, his face a picture of sincerity. "Yes. Well, actually, not the eyes themselves, but the twinkle within them."

My eyes narrowed. Behind his impressive poker face was a Mona Lisa smile. I hit him on the shoulder. "Oh my god, I can't believe I almost fell for that. You are such a jerk!"

Nico burst out laughing again. "You should have seen your

face."

I swatted him again as I echoed his laughter.

Now his eyes were shining, radiant, resplendent, and irresistible.

"Listen, ok, I'll do my best. No more twinkle." He held his hands up. His eyes were still shining as bright as the North Star. He really was making no effort.

"Please." I shook my head in exasperation. "Please do that. So, back to the real issue, which was what did you think you were doing in that interview talking about me at all?"

"Elizabeth, if I don't answer their questions, it will only make things worse. They will continue to badger you. What I was trying to do was alleviate some of the pressure you've been under."

"But you didn't. In fact, it made things worse. And what about you? Did you stop to think how this is going to impact you?"

"No. I didn't. I'm really just concerned about you right now. And they're not going to leave you alone. You stood on a chair and told a room full of people that you and I had a child together."

"Yes. I did that. I was trying to be nice. Obviously, that didn't go according to plan." I bit the inside of my cheek and glanced over his shoulder. Nothing was going according to plan these days.

"Let me do something to make it up to you."

"You don't need to do anything to make it up to me; it's not your fault. It's my fault. In fact, I should be apologizing to you. But—at the very least—could you stop giving interviews in which you tell people that we're 'just friends' in a way that makes it sound like we're really playing hide the salami? Could you do that for me?"

Nico tilted his head to the side, a small smile lighting his expression. "I haven't heard that, hide the salami, since my dad was alive. You got that saying from my dad, didn't you?"

"Yes. I got it from your dad. I think it's hilarious." I gave him a sideways glance. "Your dad was really funny."

"Yeah...yeah he was."

"Just like you." I tapped a finger against his shoulder, and we gave each other mirrored smiles.

A staring contest ensued—the kind that began with smiles and good feelings, and then over a period of several seconds, transitioned into the room becoming too hot and swarming with all sorts of good feelings. He wasn't smiling anymore, and neither was I. In fact, I was pretty sure I was frowning.

Nico studied me and frowned at my frown, and then he turned and glanced around my room. He strolled over to the bed, picked up my discarded black and pink lace bra, and rubbed his thumb over the material.

"So, are you coming with us to dinner?"

I shrugged, though my attention was focused on where his fingers were slipping over the cup of the bra. "I don't know. I'm pretty tired, and I need to be back at ten for Angelica's treatment."

He lifted the bra slightly. "This is the one you were wearing during your panty dance party, right?"

"I don't know. I guess so." That was a lie. I did know. Watching him finger the fabric was doing delicious things to me. He needed to stop. "You can unhand my bra now."

"It is the same one." His eyes narrowed as they studied the slip of material. "Where are the matching panties?"

My stomach tightened. Nico Manganiello should not be allowed to say *panties*. "I don't know. What an absurd question." That was a lie. I did know. They were in the top drawer of my dresser.

"You should wear them, and this, tonight."

"Ha...." My attempt at nonchalance came out more like a breathless choke. "How would you feel if I dictated your undergarments?"

He met my gaze directly, his expression and tone serious. "I wouldn't object."

Another staring match ensued. My heart quickened. I suddenly could not stand the fact that he was holding my bra, his thumb drawing circles over the center of the cup with a reverence that the material didn't deserve. I deserved that touch, and I was jealous of my underwear.

I *needed* him to stop.

"Stop doing that. Put it down." I charged over to where he stood and reached for my brassiere.

He held it above his head and to the side. His eyes watched me with a scorching intensity as I reached for the undergarment again, bumping against him as I clawed at his arm. I didn't realize at first, but he'd turned slightly and was backing me up. By the time I successfully reached and held the bra, he was emphatically filling every molecule of my personal space, and I was trapped, my back against the closet door. I was also breathing heavily. My chest touched his with every rise and fall.

He was looking at my mouth and licking his lips, slowly, drawing the full bottom one—the one I often thought of as juicy—between his teeth and sucking, biting it before releasing it. My eyelids felt heavy. In fact, I felt heavy all over.

And I felt hot. I felt hot and heavy all over.

He was so close I could count the individual eyelashes that fanned against his cheek.

Nico leaned forward and I thought, just for a spare second, that he was going to kiss me. If he kissed me, I was planning to kiss the hell out of him. Instead, his mouth moved to my ear and his knee moved between my legs, his thigh against my center. He tasted the tip of my ear, his hot breath fanning against my neck, and I shuttered.

"Elizabeth…."

I whimpered in response and his leg shifted, causing a delicious friction between my thighs. I automatically gripped his shoulders to steady myself.

He trailed hot, tender kisses from my ear to my neck. I lifted to my tiptoes, my fingers found their way into his hair, and I pressed him closer, arching against him.

I needed to kiss him—like, *needed* to kiss him! I needed his mouth, and I needed to bite his bottom lip, and I needed to feel the wet warmth of his tongue against mine. But, before I could make my need my reality, he pulled away, turned away, and walked away. He left me, back against the door, gasping for breath and with the worst blue bean of my life.

Blue bean being, of course, the female equivalent of blue balls.

My lashes fluttered open, and I was thankful to have the solid weight of the door behind me. If I'd been left adrift in the middle of the room, I might have fallen over or crumpled into an embarrassing puddle of arousal on the floor.

"Nico?" I flinched at how small and unsure my voice sounded. I bit the inside of my cheek to keep from saying anything further; not until I had a plan, and not until that plan involved hot monkey sex.

He didn't turn. He stood in profile, his hands on his hips. He also seemed to be breathing with some difficulty. He swallowed then cleared his throat. "You should...." His voice caught and he cleared his throat again, this time louder. "You should get ready. The reservation is for seven-thirty."

I held my breath and waited for him to say something else. When he said nothing, I felt my eye twitch. "What?"

"I'm sorry about—I'm sorry. I shouldn't have done that. It wasn't very...friendly of me."

I stared at his exasperatingly beautiful face. It took a full ten seconds for his words to sink in. When they did, I felt like I was being torn into several small pieces.

"I don't want to be friends anymore."

He glanced at me over his shoulder, his eyebrow lifting along with a corner of his mouth. "Being friends isn't optional." He stalked back to me, his steps full of swagger, his eyes full of blazing machismo. "We can be friends and something else..." he lifted his hand to my temple and tucked a loosened strand of hair behind my ear, "…but we're always going to be friends."

I smacked his hand away. "No. We're not. We're not friends anymore. I don't want to see you again."

"Why not?"

I lifted my chin. "Because I'm tired of your games."

He had the audacity to look pleased with himself. "Games? What games?"

"That. Right there. What just happened a second ago, and the pornographic shirtless apple fritter scene last Sunday, and the 'friend kiss' and the straddling last night. You're playing with me, and I don't like it."

"I'm not playing with you."

"Yes. You are. You know that I want you…." I swallowed the end of my sentence, suddenly out of breath. His eyes flashed at my words, and he shifted forward. I placed a hand on his chest to keep him from coming any closer, having already admitted too much. "You know how much I want you, and you're trying to use it against me; you're teasing me with it to cloud my judgment."

"If you want me then take me." His words impatient, sounding like an order.

"It's not that simple. I don't want to hurt you."

"You won't." Nico's eyes tangled with mine and ensnared me.

"I will." I wasn't so certain anymore.

"It's too late. You already have me."

I shivered. "I don't."

"You do."

"You're not being fair."

Nico flinched, and pain flickered through his green eyes. He struck the wall next to my head, causing me to jump. "I don't want to be fair! I'm not interested in being nice! You're right. I'm playing games with you, and I'm playing dirty because I want you, I *need* you—I need to be with you, to hear your voice, your laugh, to hold you, to touch you...."

I held back a sob and he pressed closer, making my hand against his chest irrelevant. "I can't love you back."

"That's a lie."

I closed my eyes and shook my head in weary defiance. "It's not. I can't. I won't do it."

We stood like that—my hand separating us, feeling the rise and fall of his chest, the beating of his heart—for an excruciating moment. Then he covered my hand with his. I opened my eyes in time to see him bring it to his lips, kiss it, then step away.

I lifted my eyes, and he caught them at once. Instead of the anger or recrimination I was expecting, I found only steady determination.

Nico tugged at the lapels of his jacked and smoothed his hand down his tie. "Are you coming to dinner?"

I shook my head.

"Ok, then." He winked and said, "Game on."

CHAPTER 21

When cornered, I have a tendency to react much like any other hot-blooded control freak—I do something stupid. In this particular case, I waited two days before doing something stupid. Nevertheless, it was decidedly stupid; so stupid, in fact, that while I was getting ready for the stupid nondate, I kept thinking to myself *Self, this is the stupidest thing that anyone has ever done in the history of forever.*

Regardless, there I was, sitting in front of my mirror, going through the motions of getting ready for my nondate with Dr. Ken Miles. My stomach hurt, I had a headache, my body was revolting, my heart felt sick. And yet, I applied a liberal amount of blue mascara.

I was wearing cotton underwear and a sports bra—basically, the equivalent of a boob chastity belt—and I settled on a pair of black, wide-legged pants. Sandra told me once that they made me look extremely short and suggested I never wear them. But tonight, I wore them. And under the pants I wore leggings…because it was cold outside. My shirt had both buttons and ties and I added two sweaters on top, both with buttons and ties. My shoes were unsexy, laced flats that took forever to take off and put on.

I gave myself a once-over in the mirror. Yep. That was me. And I looked just about ready to go. It would only take me one hour to get out of this outfit when sexy time arrived.

Thinking about sexy time with Dr. Ken Miles made my stomach roll.

This was a mistake.

But in all honesty, I felt driven to it. Since our fight on Tuesday—and it was most definitely a fight—Nico had been relentless. The last two mornings he had paraded around the penthouse in his boxer briefs, brushing against me, teasing me, touching me.

When the appointments were at the hospital, he stared at me with his hot, smoldering Italian eyes. His charisma and magnetism detonated all over everyone and in all directions; he made women on the periphery swoon with his bedroom voice and suggestive smile. I wanted to both choke him to death and kiss him senseless.

He refused to give me a moment's peace.

And I missed our phone calls. I missed *talking* to him. The last five days he was in New York, we talked every day, usually more than once a day. Since he'd returned, we'd barely spoken. When we did speak, he was on a constant seduction offensive; naturally, I was perpetually defensive as I endeavored to deflect his advances.

But he was wearing me down. I felt it in my bones. I was losing the will to do the right thing because I wasn't sure it was the right thing anymore. I wasn't sure who I was protecting. I thought I was protecting him from big, bad Elizabeth Finney and her unreachable heart. But with each passing minute, I wondered if Rose had been right—was I just trying to protect myself?

I mulled over this as I waited for the knock on my door when I would have to face my horrible, horrible mistake.

And yet, when Dr. Ken Miles arrived, I opened, exited, then locked my door. I walked to the elevator. I pressed the button for the elevator.

Then, Dr. Ken Miles spoke. "You look so beautiful, Elizabeth."

I glanced at Dr. Ken Miles from the corner of my eye. He was leering. I sighed. "Thanks. You also look very pretty."

He laughed lightly. "I'm really, really looking forward to tonight."

I might have thrown up a little in my mouth. *What am I doing?*

He leaned close, invading my space. "And I brought some flavored condoms for us, for later...."

That was the moment it happened. That was the moment I knew

with absolute certainty that I couldn't go through with it. I shuddered in revulsion, not at the flavored condoms, because, with Nico, that sounded like fun, but at the idea of seeing Dr. Ken Miles's wang in a condom—his pasty, white wang. Gross.

In fact, penises in general grossed me out in that moment; but one penis in particular still held my interest. And by interest, I meant flaming hot mad lust. I wanted to find Nico. I wanted to find him and maul him and attack his penis. I wanted to kiss him and touch him, but he still terrified me.

I knew what I wanted, but I wasn't certain if wanting Nico was enough. I'd wanted him in the past and had allowed him to invade my heart, and then I'd left him. I hurt him. Neither of us had quite recovered.

Regardless, whatever I ultimately decided, I first needed to extract myself from this horrible situation and send Dr. Ken Miles—and his wang—far, far away.

"Oh god." I drew in a long breath then sighed. "I can't do this, Dr. Ken Miles."

"Uh, what?"

I shook my head and met his confused stare. "I can't do this."

"Is this about dinner?"

The elevator dinged, marking its arrival.

"No, but I can't do that either. The thing is, I don't want to have sex with you."

He blinked at me, and I couldn't help but notice that his pretty, pale blue eyes—vapid in their near colorlessness—didn't heat nor cool, and they certainly did not twinkle. "Uhh...." His mouth fell open, a disbelieving sound rushing forth. He shifted a step closer, and I stood my ground; I lifted my chin to maintain eye contact so that he could read the seriousness of my expression.

However, before Dr. Ken Miles could speak, the elevator doors opened and revealed a man. And that man was Nico Manganiello. And I wanted to die, right there, in my cotton underwear and uniboob bra.

His eyes moved between me and Dr. Ken Miles then back again. His expression morphed from slightly confused to stunned understanding to drawing all the wrong conclusions in the span of three seconds.

The hurt in his glare splintered me into a thousand pieces, and I knew the precise moment that his heart split in two; I felt it because mine did too. I opened my mouth to speak, but then I saw Dr. Ken Miles smirking at Nico, my Nico, with the smuggest expression I'd ever seen on his prissy face. He placed his arm around my shoulders.

I immediately recoiled, but the doors to the elevator were closing, and Nico was still looking at Dr. Ken Miles's smirky face.

"No!" My single word was an involuntary whisper.

Nico's eyes moved to mine and, without really thinking about it, I launched myself into the elevator just as the doors closed. I was in the elevator with Nico, and one of my pant legs was caught in the door.

He moved himself to the corner of the large lift, effectively out of my tethered reach, and gave me his shoulder. His eyes were closed, his head rested against the red velvet wall, and he was laughing. It was a maniacal, unbalanced kind of laugh. I held my hands up and tried to reach him, to touch him.

"Nico, listen. Just listen to me for a minute."

He still wouldn't look at me. "You already told me. At least you tried to, but I wouldn't listen."

"Listen to me now."

"Ah, god, what's the point?" He thumped his head once against the side of the lift, still not meeting my eyes.

"Nico, just—"

"How long have you been with him?"

"It's not like that."

"Never mind, I don't want to know. I don't want to know.

Just—I need to get off this elevator." Nico reached for the buttons on the panel, but I beat him to his goal, pressed the alarm button, and stopped the car.

A shrill ring pierced the small space, and we both covered our ears. As abruptly as the screeching started it stopped, plunging the small car into a fierce kind of silence, made more complete by the absence of the alarm. Nico charged forward again, presumably to start the elevator once more, but I blocked his path with half my body.

He recoiled backward as though dreading any contact with me and disgusted by the thought of it.

"Will you listen to me? Please?" I was yelling, mostly because I was panicked by his inability to meet my gaze.

"How long have you two been together?" His shout matched mine in volume and vehemence.

"We haven't...."

"Then it's a recent thing? You *like* him?"

"It's not like that! Not with him."

"So, explain it to me!" His eyes finally met mine and nearly knocked the wind from my lungs.

"He doesn't...he doesn't care about me. Not like, not like y—"

"Just say it, Elizabeth!"

"Fine. Not like you do."

His eyes were flaming with something between disbelief and outrage, but his voice was eerily quiet. "I don't just care about you. I'm in love with you."

"I know that!" I hollered in response, my hands balling into fists. I didn't know why I was so angry. Nico's anger made sense. Mine did not. But I couldn't help it. I was angry and, dammit, I wanted to yell at him.

"So...?" His eyes widened mockingly.

"So...that's why!"

"So, let me get this straight. That guy..." Nico gestured to the elevator doors behind me, "…doesn't care about you." Then he pointed to his chest with both hands and said, "I'm in love with you." I flinched at his words and the raw intensity in his voice. "He gets to sleep with you and I don't. Did I get all that right?"

I tried unsuccessfully to swallow the building thickness in my throat and shook my head, but said nothing. My warring emotions rendered me mute.

I was an idiot. I was an idiotic nitwit. I'd convinced a small part of myself that the stirrings or feelings or whatever mojo voodoo was going on with Nico would magically become irrelevant if I could just get myself laid. It was a shred, a hope, a flicker of proof that I wasn't, in fact, already in love with Nico.

It was a lie.

I was in love with him.

All attempts at avoiding it were too late.

In retrospect, even though I put the brakes on the nondate early, actually stepping outside my door with Dr. Ken Miles was probably the dumbest thing I'd ever done.

But Nico was making me crazy. He was playing mind games. I couldn't stop thinking about him. It was driving me to distraction. Now, standing in the small elevator, literally and figuratively unable to reach him, engaging in a yelling match, everything felt strangely clear.

"Well?" The single word carried more rage than I thought possible.

I unclenched my fists and flexed my fingers. I was surprised to find that my breathing had become labored and heavy.

He turned away, lifted his hands palms out, and shook his head. "I'm done. Do whatever. I don't care."

"Hey!" I finally found my voice. "You're the one who wanted to be friends! You're the one—turn around!" I pulled my leg from the door and ripped the bottom half of my pants. Finally able to close the distance between us, I pushed at him; it was just with my fingertips, but I immediately regretted it.

He abruptly spun and backed me up against the wall of the lift. I almost tripped over my laced flats.

"You know what I felt at Garrett's funeral? I felt relief." He kept his tone light and conversational despite the weight of the words and his aggressive body language.

"Nico...." His words sliced at me. I gripped the wall at my back. "No you didn't."

He ignored me and continued as though I hadn't spoken. "I felt relief—for Garrett—because he wasn't in pain any more. I saw it every day of that year, but he hid it from you. He thought it would make things easier." Nico chewed on his bottom lip, studying me. "You were in denial the whole time. At his funeral you looked so shocked, like you couldn't believe he was dead."

"You're right."

"About which part?" His gaze belligerent, almost feral.

"I was shocked." I took a deep breath. "I wasn't expecting it."

Nico nodded twice. "I grieved for Garrett the year before he died." He focused his gaze on the red velvet wall behind me. "I said goodbye to him a month before the funeral. And the hardest thing for me afterward...." Nico paused then met my gaze, his voice softening. His eyes lost focus even as they moved over my face; it was as though he was seeing a memory of me rather than the person I was now. It took me back to that moment under the bleachers at the reunion. "The hardest part was watching you trying to deal with it."

I opened my mouth to respond but didn't know what to say.

He was still scrutinizing me, but his expression gave away nothing tangible of his own feelings. "The irony is that I could have saved myself a world of hurt if I'd just walked away from you after the funeral, like you did to me at the end of the summer."

I flinched and my mouth snapped shut.

He took a step back, no longer crowding me, no longer pressing me against the wall. "But I've finally learned my lesson." His eyes fell gradually away, and when he spoke next, he addressed his words to the panel of buttons; he released the emergency stop, and the elevator began to descend.

"Goodbye, Elizabeth."

"Goodbye?" I stared at him and lost my balance a bit when the elevator jostled. "*Goodbye?*"

He didn't respond. His eyes were affixed to the numbers counting down to the lobby.

I rushed for the panel again and pressed the emergency button. The same shrill alarm started, and we both covered our ears. But this time he released a string of expletives that I was fairly certain I could discern based on the movement of his mouth.

"What the hell?" He growled at me when the alarm stopped, and then he tried to reach around me to release the button. I took the opportunity to grab the front of his jacket.

"No—you need to listen to me now. You've had your say. It's my turn." I pushed him against the wall, my hands still fisted in his jacket. "You know what I felt at Garrett's funeral? I felt despair. I felt despair because I loved him, I loved everything about him, and my fifteen-year-old heart couldn't fathom feeling that way about anyone else ever again. And then you started coming through my window."

I shook him when he tried to slide his eyes to the side, and forced him to meet my gaze; "You came to me and held me. You brought me through the numbness; you saved my life. Did you know that?"

His eyes were glassy as they looked into mine. He swallowed, but he said nothing.

"You did. And then four months went by, the summer was coming to an end, my father was taking me away, and my heart started feeling something again, and this time it was for you."

The words hung between us. His expression wavered between

frustration and elation.

"Why didn't you say anything?"

"I couldn't. I was afraid."

"So you let me make love to you, take your virginity? Why did you do that? Why did you come to me that night?"

"Because I wanted my first time to be with someone—someone I had feelings for." I released his jacket. "I used you."

"You didn't."

"I did. I made a decision. I didn't ask you, that night, I just knew what I wanted and I didn't even give you a chance to. . . I'm so sorry."

He rocked backward on his heels as if I'd punched him with the information. "Then why did you leave?"

"Because I didn't think you would ever return my feelings."

Nico's mouth fell open and he blinked, seemingly disoriented. He needed a full minute to recover from my truth. "Why would you think that?" The words were tortured because he already knew the answer. His face twisted with heartbreak, the kind associated with regret.

I sucked in an unsteady breath. "God, Nico." I released his shirt and took a step backward. "I spent my teen years thinking you hated me. Then, when Garrett was sick, you tolerated me. Over that summer, I assumed that you pitied me. You've just always been so untouchable—so beyond me...so beyond my reach.... You make me a coward."

He studied me, his eyes intent. "You're not a coward, Elizabeth."

"Yes I amWith you, I am. When we're together—not all the time, but in flashes—I feel fourteen again, and you're knocking the books out of my hands or pushing me into the boys' bathroom, or...." I closed my eyes, unable to continue.

"I'm so sorry. God, I can't tell you how sorry I am."

"I know." I opened my eyes. I sniffed then shrugged to push the unpleasant memories from my mind. "You were right about Dr. Ken Miles. When you showed up here, in Chicago, I was making plans to have sex with him *because* I don't like him. And tonight, what you saw was me telling him I couldn't go through with it— *because* I don't like him."

Nico considered me for a long minute, and then he stuffed his hands into the pockets of his unzipped jacket. "You haven't slept with him?"

I shook my head. "No. I haven't. I can't do it. Just the thought of it makes me gag."

His mouth hooked to the side and he glanced at his boots. "Me too."

I laughed involuntarily and my body relaxed; I backed up to the panel and let my head fall against it. "I don't know what to do."

I felt his gaze sweep over my ridiculous outfit, and his intentions shifted palpably. I braced myself against a sure onslaught of his charming eye-twinkling brilliance. His voice sent shivers tumbling down my spine.

"You were wrong. I was never out of reach. I'm right here, and I'm completely yours." His hands found and held mine; he pressed them to his chest.

My chin wobbled, and I rushed to blink my eyes against an ambush of stinging moisture. "It's not that simple."

"Yes. It really is." Nico tugged me forward, away from the safety of the wall, and cupped my cheek in his palm. He forced me to meet his stare. "Unless you don't want to be with me."

"I'm in love with you, you idiot!" The words tumbled out of my mouth as fat tears fell from my eyes.

Nico half laughed and released a breath; it sounded as if he'd been holding it for years. Maybe he had. He brought my forehead to his, his big hands slipped around my waist, and he pulled me against him.

"Thank god," he whispered just before he captured my mouth. I moaned, clinging to him, and my nails dug into his jacket then frantically slipped under his shirt. His kiss was hot, demanding, urgent. There was no exploration; only desperate conquering, and the situation escalated quickly.

I wanted to feel him, every inch of his skin. My fingers were greedy, caressing the firm ridges of his stomach, the warm, smooth skin of his back. My body arched against him, craving connection, his heat, his touch. He yanked off his jacket and let it fall to the floor. His shirt followed next.

Large hands gripped my sweater and tugged as his mouth moved desperately over mine. I knew his urgency was fueled by years of restrained desire. I felt my need in him.

His movements became somewhat jerky and frustrated, and he abruptly pulled away from me. I felt the loss of his body acutely.

"What are you wearing? How am I supposed to get you out of this?" He was breathing heavily, half growling, surveying my sweater like it was a Rubik's cube.

I searched his eyes, his words cutting through the dense fog of need, the blood rushing between my ears, the galloping pace of my heart. "What?"

He tugged roughly at my sweater. "This. How does it come off? It's like a straightjacket! Are those ties *and* buttons?"

I groaned, closed my eyes, and pressed my head to the bare skin of his shoulder. "I need to change my clothes."

"You don't need to change them; you just need to take them off." His hands attempted to reach under the three layers I was rocking, but it was no use; there was no way for him to access my skin. Giving up, he tried cupping me over my thick clothes. His face scrunched in an aggravated scowl. "How many layers are you wearing?"

"A lot." I laughed, kissed his chest, and moved my hands to his pants. I enjoyed the way his stomach tightened in response to my light touch. I gripped his waistband and dipped my fingers into the elastic of his boxer briefs. He sucked in a breath.

I couldn't stop feeling him—the hardness, the smooth softness of his olive skin. I wanted to bite every inch of him then lick him from collarbone to co—

"Oh no, not fair. You can't touch me until I can touch you." His hands grabbed mine, and he stilled their downward trajectory.

I tried to reinitiate my assault, but he bowed away and caught my wrists.

"Nico. Let me touch you."

"Elizabeth." He brought my hands behind my back and held me in place. "You take off your shirt first."

"It's actually three shirts…and a sports bra."

"Well…." he looked lost, forlorn. He breathed out, incredulous. Abruptly, as though suddenly struck by genius, he grinned then reached into his back pocket. I only had a moment before I realized his intent when I eyeballed the large pocketknife in his hand.

I stepped back and covered my chest. "What are you doing?"

"I'm cutting your clothes off." He reached for the first tie and batted my hands away. "Hold still."

I opened my mouth to object, but it was too late. Nico, with a force that was as hurried as it was careful, dissected first my sweater, then my other sweater, then my shirt. In all, it took him maybe fifteen seconds. His eyes burned brighter as each layer opened and he wrestled it from my shoulders and dropped it to the floor.

It was hot. I liked it. His hands pawed at me and his mouth captured mine for quick kisses. When I was down to my sports bra, I moved as though to pull it off but he stilled my movements, slipped his finger under the elastic, made a single cut, then tore it in two.

Oh Nico.

CHAPTER 22—Closed-Door Love Scenes

Dear Reader—There are two versions of Chapter 22 included in this book. The first describes a "closed door" love scene where specifics of the scene are minimal. The second version of Chapter 22 describes an "open door" love scene where the specifics of the scene are provided. I've included both so that you, the reader, can choose the chapter that matches your comfort level/preference. I know this is unusual! But I'm not afraid of taking chances and trying new things; obviously, neither are you if you're reading my book. ;-)

—Sincerely, Penny Reid

Nico's hands and mouth were greedy and unrelenting. I purposely overlooked the irrationality of making love in an elevator. In fact, I didn't care where we were. All I knew was that we were finally, finally touching each other the way I'd needed and been starving for.

I was blind to everything other than the fact that I needed him— his touch, his strength and caresses, his sweet words. As ludicrous as it was, my mind couldn't fathom waiting another moment, not even the five minutes or less it would take to get to my apartment.

Nico seemed to feel the same urgency. At first, his movements were frantic, rough, focused, needy. He murmured words of desire and wanting, seemingly lost in us and in the moment; but then gradually, as though sensing his power over me, he became teasing and maddeningly, adorably arrogant.

Freaking Nico!

I couldn't help but try to tease him in return. But his eyes and my name on his lips were my undoing. He looked lost, and in that moment, I was found. I waved my white flag of surrender almost immediately.

I soothed him by reminding him that I loved him. I repeated the words over and over until they became a chant. I loved this man. I wanted all of him, everywhere, surrounding me, always. I wanted to breathe him in and own him, possess him. I wanted to be everything to him as he had become to me.

He drew out my moans and sighs. His hands explored the peaks and valleys of my body with a covetous command. And when we found each other I was overwhelmed by our shared bliss as I gazed into his beautiful green eyes.

I hoped he witnessed the love I saw in him reflected in me. I hoped he knew how momentous and real my feelings were. I hoped he knew that what we did was not lightly done. It was a pledge. It was a gift.

And it was meant only for him.

~*~*~*~

We made our way back to my place shortly after recovering from the dazed euphoria that accompanies great lovemaking. In complete honesty, I don't know if we would have ever left the elevator if given the choice. However, it started to move, and I yelped at the realization that all my clothes but my leggings were shredded—by his knife—and in tatters on the floor of the lift.

In typical Nico fashion, he allowed me to panic for a few seconds before offering me his T-shirt. I pulled it on along with my leggings just in time. When the doors opened to the lobby, Nico pulled me against his chest and improvised a ludicrous story to the waiting mechanic.

The man looked not at all impressed, never cracked a smile, and gave us both a knowing, annoyed once-over. Wordlessly, he sent us on our way.

We stumbled into my apartment, laughing and kissing and—at least I was—embarrassed.

"Unlike you, I'm not used to people seeing me without my clothes on."

Nico shrugged out of his jacket, threw it over his shoulder as if he hated it, and kicked my door closed. He tugged at the T-shirt on my shoulders. "I've never understood why people in the US get so stirred up about nudity."

"Maybe because we value modesty!" I swatted at his hands unsuccessfully; he, somewhat roughly, pulled the shirt off and threw it across the room, again as if he hated it.

"But why hide such...." His gaze devoured me, my bare shoulders, chest, stomach; he gripped the edge of my pants and used his leverage on the material to yank me forward against his chest. "Perché nascondere una cosa così bella[6]?"

And that's when it happened.

In that moment, the world tilted, and I lost complete control of my female organs. Apparently, my vagina, uterus, and ovaries were Italian and, when spoken to in Italian by Nico Manganiello, no longer belonged to me. I had no idea what he'd said. Just the sound, coming from his mouth—no lie—was the sexiest thing ever of all time.

I felt woozy and leaned against him, my lashes fluttering like butterfly wings.

"Elizabeth...? Are you ok?"

When I spoke, I noted that my voice sounded strangely hoarse. "I—I didn't know you could speak Italian."

"Yeah, we all spoke it at home, and I learned formally a few years ago."

"Why...why...would you do that?"

His eyes narrowed as they moved between mine. His big hands stilled on my waistband while his thumb rubbed little circles over my hips. "Does it bother you? O ti piace[7]?"

I shuddered, gripped his shoulders, and let my eyes drift shut.

---

[6]Translation: Why hide such a beautiful thing?
[7]Translation: Or do you like it?

"Oh god...."

He chuckled then *tsked.*

"Mi fai impazzire[8]." He whispered against my ear. Nico licked my neck then blew where he'd made it wet, which immediately made me shiver. "Ho cercato di dimenticarti, ma è impossibile[9]."

"Guh..."

"I tuoi occhi hanno il colore del cielo in estate[10]...." He trailed light kisses down my throat and removed my pants as he moved. "Ti amo da sempre[11]."

"Oh!" I arched against him; my nails dug into his back. I fought another shudder. I failed.

He slid his fingers up my legs, his touch light behind my knees. "Il contatto con la tua pelle. Oh, non ne ho mai abbastanza[12]."

I pressed against him like a cat and reached for his pants, frustrated. His words were seriously making me mindless. I was beyond modesty or shame. I was in an uncharted, murky realm of arousal where I couldn't quite control the sounds I made or the movements of my body.

"Mmm. Il tuo fragranza....[13]" He shifted out of my reach as he bit me. I could only moan my disappointment.

Nico pushed my shoulders and I fell backward. I didn't realize until my back hit the mattress that he'd moved us to the bed. He loomed over me, stood at my knees, his eyes glittering with delicious wickedness.

"Please..." At this point, I was totally cool with begging.

Nico grinned. If I hadn't been in a near coma of arousal, I would have been highly aggravated by the grin. It was colossally

---

[8]Translation: You make me crazy.
[9]Translation: I tried to forget you, but it's impossible.
[10]Translation: Your eyes are the color of the sky in summer.
[11]Translation: I love you always.
[12]Translation: The feel of your skin, I can't get enough.
[13]Translation: Mmm. Your fragrance. . .

confident.

"Anche se a volte sei più testarda di un mulo[14]."

He unbuttoned his pants very, very slowly. He was driving me to madness.

"Mi piace la passione che è in te. La tua lingua tagliente mi eccita da morire[15]."

Nico's movements were tortuously unhurried. With continued languidity, he lowered himself to me. "Non ti lascerò mai andare[16]." His eyes were suddenly sober and serious, and they held mine. I stilled my movements. "Ti amo[17]."

I blinked at him. Even through the sensual cloud, I registered the meaning of his words.

Ti amo. I love you.

I swallowed, brushed my lips against his, and panted breathlessly in return. "Ti amo, Nico."

He nudged my nose with his, his eyes wide, "D'ora in poi in poi non c'è modo di tornare indietro. Sei mia, per sempre[18]." His eyes lit from within with blazing ferocity, scorching satisfaction.

He claimed me with heartbreaking gentleness. When our breath met, I breathed him in. I held him to me, wrapped my arms around his neck, and wanted to be fully saturated and completely crushed by him.

As I returned to earth, I couldn't help but brood over the fact that he could have just read me a restaurant menu and I would have been blissfully ignorant. He had a fatal weapon, and I was rendered stupid and powerless against it.

Italians who speak Italian should be illegal, or at least should come with warning labels—*may make your panties explode.*

---

[14]Translation: Although, sometimes you're more stubborn than a mule.
[15]Translation: I love the passion that is in you. Your sharp tongue excites me.
[16]Translation: I'll never let you go.
[17]Translation: I love you.
[18]Translation: From now on there is no way to go back. You are mine, forever.

CHAPTER 22—Open-Door Love Scenes

He hastily tugged the ruined garment from my shoulders and brushed his knuckles under my breasts. He moaned. I shivered. Nico had barely touched me with anything but his burning, twinkly eyes, and I was panting.

Then he bent, extended his tongue, and licked a circle around my right nipple. It was my turn to moan. I grabbed his shoulders and felt them work under my fingers. He was cutting me out of my pants.

That was also hot.

When my outer layer was peeled away, he cupped me through my leggings and I arched against his hand.

"I can't wait to taste you," he whispered against my stomach, allowing his hot breath to spill over my chest, igniting every inch of my skin. "I've always wondered what you taste like." I could tell he was speaking mostly to himself, but his words drove me insane.

His thumbs curled into my leggings and underwear as he yanked them downward, his breathing uneven, excited, mirroring my own. I fumbled for the front of his pants but he moved beyond my reach. Instead, he roughly trapped me against the plush, velvet wall of the lift and kneeled between my legs. He hooked my legs over his shoulders and supported my bottom with his strength.

I sucked in a sharp breath as his tongue made contact with my center, and I nearly broke into a thousand pieces when he hummed against me. I gripped the wall but could find no purchase. My hands grabbed fruitlessly—his shoulders, my thighs, his hair.

"Nico!"

He ignored my plea as he teased me with his tongue, his fingers, his breath—he was both frantic and languid in his exploration. Every time I felt close, he left me breathless on the cliff by backing away, slowing his strokes to playful caresses; he wound me upward and left me dangling on the edge of reason, teasing me in lovemaking the way he teased me in life.

I tried moving, pressing into him, rubbing against his mouth, but all I could do was groan in frustration. At one point I heard him laugh—a low, happy vibration—and in that moment, I wanted to throttle him. Finally, because he decided it was time, he sent me crashing into oblivion, hooking his finger and rubbing, stroking, licking, sucking.

My body shook, tensed, twisted then exploded. I cried out; I cried his name. My legs gripped the sides of his face like a vice, and nonsensical words were wrung from me that sounded distant, feral, and utterly unrecognizable.

Before I'd completely descended from the clouds, he steadied me with one hand and made quick work of his pants with the other as he stood. I was circling back to earth, and the sight of him, of his body against mine, his wet lips, his hooded eyes, made my insides tighten with an indescribably striking pain.

But then I noticed his smile. The bastard was giving me the boldest, most brazen, self-satisfied grin I'd ever seen. He was obviously proud of himself.

Freaking Nico!

I reached for him and he hissed but then he pressed himself into my palm; his smile wavered. I arched an eyebrow and watched his face. He appeared uncertain, lost—hesitant, even. I touched him, caressed him, teased him by sliding his hardness between my legs. He growled then sucked in a sharp breath as I brought his fingers—which moments ago had been inside me—to my mouth and sucked, swirling my tongue between his index and middle fingers.

My eyes were still half-lidded, hazy. Tremors shook my core, but I wasn't about to give him satisfaction without a little retaliation.

I slid against him; his fingers flexed on my backside. "God, I want you."

"I know I'm good, but I'm not God, Nico."

A tortured chuckle shook his chest, and he pressed me against the wall with his body with intimidating strength. I enjoyed the delicious, sweet torture of his skin against mine, and the friction of our mating. I bit the tip of his finger and scratched my nails down his side.

He hissed. "Be nice."

"Nope." I squeezed him, my hand caught between us, my thumb rubbing circles around his tip.

"Elizabeth...." My name was an appeal, a prayer; he looked like he was in pain. His pleading eyes melted my resolve. I slackened my grip and allowed him to lift me off my feet—which he did seemingly with complete ease—until I straddled him, my legs around his waist, my back against the lush fabric of the wall.

"Elizabeth." He said my name again, his eyes wide, searching. "I love you so much."

"I know, Nico." I nodded once, caressed his cheek with my fingers. His forehead touched mine. I arched as he entered me and we both gasped.

I kissed him, hard. I loved this man. I wanted all of him, everywhere, inside me, surrounding me, always. I wanted to breathe him in, own him, and possess him utterly. I wanted to be everything to him, just as he was to me.

We easily found our rhythm, and my legs gripped his waist. His hands explored the peaks and valleys of my body with a covetous command, his thumbs drawing circles against my tightened nipples. He bit me fiercely when my nails dug into his shoulders then he soothed the abused flesh with his tongue. Our position pushed my breasts forward, and he lavished them with hot, wet kisses.

He drew out my moans and sighs. I knew I was close; I could feel the tightrope strain and pull, and I swore to god that I would beat him to death if he teased me now. My knees began to shake. I pulled his hair, forced his gaze to mine.

I was overwhelmed by both happiness and sadness as I gazed into his beautiful green eyes. I lost myself to another crashing wave of sublime insanity, and in utter bliss, I cried out, "I love you. I love you. I love you."

I felt him come undone at my words; his eyes closed, and his strong body held me against the wall until I could barely draw breath. He moved closer to claim me, and when I was completely his, he shuddered and buried his head in my neck, losing himself in our secret oblivion.

I hoped he witnessed the love I saw in him reflected in me. I hoped he knew how momentous and real my feelings were. I hoped he knew that what we did was not lightly done. It was a pledge. It was a gift.

And it was meant only for him.

~*~*~*~

We made our way back to my place shortly after recovering from the dazed euphoria that accompanies great lovemaking. In complete honesty, I don't know if we would have ever left the elevator if given the choice. However, it started to move, and I yelped at the realization that all my clothes but my leggings were shredded—by his knife—and in tatters on the floor.

In typical Nico fashion, he allowed me to panic for a few seconds before offering me his T-shirt. I pulled it on along with my leggings just in time. When the doors opened to the lobby, Nico pulled me against his chest and improvised a ludicrous story to the waiting mechanic.

The man looked not at all impressed, never cracked a smile, and gave us both a knowing, annoyed once-over. Wordlessly, he sent us on our way.

We stumbled into my apartment, laughing and kissing and—at least I was—embarrassed.

"Unlike you, I'm not used to people seeing me without my clothes on."

Nico shrugged out of his jacket, threw it over his shoulder as if he hated it, and kicked my door closed. He tugged at the T-shirt on my shoulders. "I've never understood why people in the US get so stirred up about nudity."

"Maybe because we value modesty!" I swatted at his hands unsuccessfully; he, somewhat roughly, pulled the shirt off and threw it across the room, again as if he hated it.

"But why hide such...." His gaze devoured me, my bare shoulders, chest, stomach; he gripped the edge of my pants and used his leverage on the material to yank me forward against his chest. "Perché nascondere una cosa così bella[19]?"

And that's when it happened.

In that moment, the world tilted, and I lost complete control of my female organs. Apparently, my vagina, uterus, and ovaries were Italian and, when spoken to in Italian by Nico Manganiello, no longer belonged to me. I had no idea what he'd said. Just the sound, coming from his mouth—no lie—was the sexiest thing ever of all time.

I felt woozy and leaned against him, my lashes fluttering like butterfly wings.

"Elizabeth...? Are you ok?"

When I spoke, I noted that my voice sounded strangely hoarse. "I—I didn't know you could speak Italian."

"Yeah, we all spoke it at home, and I learned formally a few years ago."

"Why...why...would you do that?"

His eyes narrowed, surveyed me; he hesitated. His big hands stilled on my waistband while his thumb rubbed little circles over

---

[19]Translation: Why hide such a beautiful thing?

my hips. "Does it bother you? O ti piace?[20]"

I shuddered, gripped his shoulders, and let my eyes drift shut. "Oh god…."

He chuckled then *tsked.*

"Mi fai impazzire[21]." He whispered against my ear. Nico licked my neck then blew where he'd made it wet, which immediately made me shiver. "Ho cercato di dimenticarti, ma è impossibile[22]."

"Guh…."

"I tuoi occhi hanno il colore del cielo in estate [23]…." He trailed light kisses down my throat and removed my pants as he moved. "Ti amo da sempre[24]."

"Oh!" I arched against him; my nails dug into his back. I fought another shudder. I failed.

He slid his fingers up my legs, his touch light behind my knees then between my thighs. "Il contatto con la tua pelle. Oh, non ne ho mai abbastanza[25]."

I pressed against him like a cat and reached for his pants, frustrated. His words were seriously making me mindless. I was beyond modesty or shame. I was in an uncharted, murky realm of arousal where I couldn't quite control the sounds I made or the movements of my body.

"Mmm. Il tuo fragranza….[26]" He shifted out of my reach as he bit me. I could only moan my disappointment.

Nico pushed my shoulders and I fell backward. I didn't realize until my back hit the mattress that he'd moved us to the bed. He loomed over me, stood at my knees, his eyes glittering with delicious wickedness.

---

[20]Translation: Or do you like?
[21]Translation: You make me crazy.
[22]Translation: I tried to forget you, but it's impossible.
[23]Translation: Your eyes are the color of the sky in summer.
[24]Translation: I love you always.
[25]Translation: The feel of your skin, I can't get enough.
[26]Mmm. Your fragrance. . .

"Please…" At this point, I was totally cool with begging.

Nico grinned. If I hadn't been in a near coma of arousal, I would have been highly aggravated by the grin. It was colossally confident.

"Anche se a volte sei più testarda di un mulo[27]."

He unbuttoned his pants very, very slowly. He was driving me to madness. I pressed my thighs together.

"Mi piace la passione che è in te[28]."

Nico's movements were tortuously slow as he removed his pants and briefs. With continued languidity, he lowered himself to my exposed body, his hot skin kissing mine, forced my legs apart his with a knee. He pressed himself into my center, rocked forward meaningfully.

I gasped.

His voice was a growl, *"La tua lingua tagliente mi eccita da morire[29]."*

I was about to come apart, and he hadn't entered me yet. My skin was flushed, covered in goose bumps, overly sensitized. I shifted beneath him, impatient.

"Non ti lascerò mai andare[30]." His eyes were suddenly sober and serious, and they held mine. I stilled my movements. "Ti amo[31]."

I blinked at him. Even through the sensual cloud, I registered the meaning of his words.

Ti amo. I love you.

I swallowed, brushed my lips against his, and panted breathlessly in return. "Ti amo, Nico."

Slowly, slowly, he filled me and I stretched, arched beneath

---

[27]Translation: Although, sometimes you're more stubborn than a mule.
[28]Translation: I love the passion that is in you.
[29]Translation: Your sharp tongue excites me to death
[30]Translation: I'll never let you go.
[31]Translation: I love you.

him then sighed with relief.

His rhythm purposeful; his hands worshipful; his mouth hungry. Our breath met. I held him to me, wrapped my arms around his neck, wanted to be fully saturated in him, completely crushed.

He nudged my nose with his, his eyes wide, "D'ora in poi in poi non c'è modo di tornare indietro. Sei mia, per sempre[32]." His eyes lit from within with blazing ferocity, scorching satisfaction.

The last sentence, the earnestness with which he spoke, the unfathomable gentleness of his touch, splintered me. When our breath met, I breathed him in. I held him to me, wrapped my arms around his neck, and wanted to be fully saturated and completely crushed by him.

As I returned to earth, I couldn't help but brood over the fact that he could have just read me a restaurant menu and I would have been blissfully ignorant. He had a fatal weapon, and I was rendered stupid and powerless against it.

Italians who speak Italian should be illegal, or at least should come with warning labels—*may make your panties explode.*

---

[32]Translation: From now on there is no way to go back. You're mine, forever.

CHAPTER 23

I'd never made love with anyone but Nico.

This thought occurred to me as we were lying in my bed, touching each other.

Touching is the difference between making love and having sex.

The physical act of making love expresses the desire to touch someone and to be touched in return. A hunger for your partner consumes you. It's an insatiable craving. It's a need for his skin, his hands, his mouth; it's a need to see his eyes. It must be fed every second or else it builds into something unmanageably urgent and ferocious.

I couldn't keep my hands off him, and I couldn't imagine his hands anywhere but on me. As we lay there as one, fitting out hands together and rearranging the furniture in our hearts, I felt fear.

I knew he loved me, and I knew beyond a whisper of a doubt that I loved him.

And I was afraid.

When things are fantastic, it's hard not to expect that the worst is waiting to pounce on you from a dark corner.

One of Nico's arms was wrapped around me possessively as I lay half-sprawled over his chest. He played with my hand, tracing my knuckles and the lines of my palm. I allowed him to explore as he wished, preoccupied with thoughts about his security guards and the knife he carried in his pocket.

I wondered if he carried it for self-defense because he needed to. I wondered if he'd ever used it. I shivered.

"Are you cold?" His voice was raspy, sleepy, satisfied.

"No." I snugged closer.

"What are you thinking about?"

"Do you think Quinn is doing a good job with your security?"

I felt him nod his head. "Yeah, they seem like good guys."

"And they'll keep you safe…do you think?"

He shrugged. "I think so. They're better than the other ones."

"Where were they tonight? Why weren't they with you?"

Nico shifted so that he could see my face; he searched my eyes. "I don't have them with me all the time."

"Why not?"

"What's going on?" he pressed my hand to his bare chest. "Why all the questions about my security team?"

I fought against a chin wobble by biting the inside of my cheek. When I was sure that my voice would be steady, I said, "I just want you to be safe."

His mouth hitched to the side. "I'll be fine."

"You have a stalker."

His smile disappeared.

"And photographers chasing after you and me both," I pressed on. "You need appropriate protection from the loony bins. Your security should be increased; they should live with you and…"

"Hey, whoa! Stop." Nico kissed me and rolled me onto my back; his hand gripped my waist and then traveled upward to caress my stomach, finally resting on my chest.

"Is that why you carry the knife?"

His movements stilled and he lifted his head from where he'd been feasting on my skin. "What?"

"Do you carry the knife for protection?"

"No. I carry the knife because I'm a Boy Scout."

I hit his arm. "I'm serious."

"So am I. You know I was a Boy Scout. The pocketknife is an old habit that never died."

I met his gaze, and I saw the truth to his words. I felt a little flutter of panic in my chest.

"I think you should get a gun."

"Elizabeth!" His head fell to my chest.

"No. Listen. I think you should…."

"No, you listen." He held my face between his two giant palms and forced me to meet his gaze. "I love that you worry about me and want to fire my security guards when they're incompetent, but I'm not getting a gun. Quinn's guys are really good. Really. You have nothing to worry about."

I swallowed unevenly. My voice was strained when I spoke. "I'm going to worry. You should just think about it. If you don't want a gun, then at least think about martial arts or a larger knife."

"Smettila di fare la prepotente[33]."

My body responded with urgent readiness. I plugged my ears with my fingers and fought to stay in control of my lady parts. "No! Not allowed! You are not allowed to speak in Italian when we are having a discussion!"

He laughed, kissed my neck, and pulled my hands from my head. "I wish you wouldn't worry so much."

My eyes shifted to a spot over his shoulder to the smooth white ceiling. "Wish not granted."

~*~*~*~

My phone alarm sounded at 9:40 pm, alerting us that it was time for Angelica's infusion. We'd both been dozing, and my rest was fitful. I hovered between worried and awake and pseudo slumber.

When I left Nico's arms, he groaned in protest. He reached for me, but I'd moved to the edge of the bed out of his reach. I immediately felt bereft of his warmth, his strength, his smell.

His smell.

Something was different. I'd first noticed a change on Monday when he arrived home early; he was free of cigarette smoke.

"Did you stop smoking?" I turned just my head to look at him, found him lounging—naked—in my bed, his arms both extended

---

[33]Translation: Stop being so bossy.

in my direction. The large window overlooking Millennium Park shaded his body in the lights of the city. His skin was smooth. To my eye, his body was perfect. I self-consciously covered my breasts with my hands.

"I did. I stopped two weeks ago." Sleep lent a delicious sandpapery quality to his voice.

"Wait, what about—when I saw you at the hospital, that first time, you left to have a cigarette."

"Seeing you."

I twisted further so I could see him over my shoulder. "Seeing me what?"

He stretched, the sexy beast. "I experienced a brief relapse after seeing you. It lasted about a week."

"Hmm." I grabbed a mostly clean, large T-shirt from the floor and pulled it over my head before I stood.

"*Hmm* what? And what are you doing?"

"Why did you stop smoking?"

"Angelica. She can't be around the smoke. Are you getting dressed?"

"Are you going to start smoking again? After her treatment is over?"

"No. I'm quitting for good. But, you may have noticed, I've been feeling pretty irritable lately, losing my temper faster than usual—you can't wear that."

"Yes. I can wear this." I tugged the hem of the T-shirt lower and walked to my dresser to extract a pair of underwear and yoga pants. At the last minute, I decided to slip on the panty set I wore during my last panty party.

He leaped out of the bed and whipped the T-shirt off my shoulders before I could turn around.

"Nico!" I ineffectually covered my chest with my arms. "Give me back my shirt."

"In my fragile state you should do whatever I want."

"What? What fragile state?"

"Quitting smoking." He threw the T-shirt over his shoulder then gripped my waist with his large hands, his thumbs dancing over the skin on either side of my belly button. "The pants are ok, I suppose, as long as they're temporary. You should wear a different shirt though."

"You quit six months ago and what is wrong with that shirt?"

"Wear something that shows off your great body. Except for the reunion, and that one time I walked in on you dancing around in your underwear, you're always wearing clothes that are too big." He stepped into my space and dipped his lips to my neck then whispered just under my ear, "I want to see you."

"You're such a guy." I wanted the words to sound annoyed, but instead they sounded breathless.

"I know, right?" I could feel his smug smile against my skin. He licked my ear causing my shoulders to bunch reflexively. "Wear something tight that's easy for me to take off."

"Ah, Nico…you need to stop." His light touch trailed just under the band of my pants. I closed my eyes and slipped my arms around his neck then pressed him closer, chest to chest. "I don't want to be late."

He whisper-cussed against my shoulder, his hands grabbed the waist of my pants as if he was going to tear them off, but then he bit me and stepped back. He held his hands out in surrender and walked backward to the bed.

"Ok, yes. Let's go. But then after…" he pointed a finger in my direction, glared at me through his eyebrows, "…you're staying with me tonight." I shrugged my assent, but he continued as though I'd argued. "It makes sense. You'll be up there already for the six am infusion; then you can just come back to bed after. I'll even let you bring some baggy clothes to change into."

I'd already started packing my essentials for work the next day, and then because he'd asked, I pulled on the lace bra and a suitably tight tank top. He trailed after me, to my closet, to my bathroom, arguing with no one, stating his case. I was ready to go in less than five minutes.

I turned and faced him, which caused him to stop short. "Ok. You talked me into it. I'm heading up with my stuff. I'll see you in a minute."

He blinked at me in delighted surprise then drew his features into youthful, boyish lines. "Oh...." He grinned. "Did I just win our first fight?"

I nodded and resisted the urge to pat him on the head, but I couldn't stop the impulse to kiss him on the cheek. "You certainly did. You really showed me—put me in my place and all that."

I left him standing naked in my bedroom.

~*~*~*~

Nico wandered in just as I was finishing Angelica's infusion; Rose was in the kitchen brewing tea.

Our eyes met, tangled, twisted, entwined, and knotted into something that felt unbreakable. He winked at me, mouthed the words *I love you*, and my cheeks—the traitors!—flushed with pleasure. This made him grin wickedly.

He was such a guy.

And I suddenly found myself reacting like such a girl.

I rolled my eyes—at him, at myself—even as my stomach fluttered with giant butterflies. I turned my attention back to my almost slumbering patient and tried through force of will to banish the remainder of my blush.

I found him fifteen minutes later, after Angelica was kissed and tucked safely back in bed. He was in his bedroom and had set out a banquet of fruit, cheese, and crackers on the bed. I noted that he was in a state of near undress, wearing only a pair of black boxer briefs. Apparently he was more comfortable nearly naked than he was clothed.

He looked...edible.

My stomach rumbled quite loudly. I pressed my hand to it.

Either the noise of my stomach rumbling or some sixth sense had him glancing over his shoulder to where I hovered in the doorway. He'd just taken a large bite of food and motioned with his hand for me to enter. I dropped my bag at the entrance to his room and shut the door.

I was nervous.

Why am I nervous?

Nico wiped his mouth with a napkin and crossed to where I hovered.

"Are you already finished?"

"Yes."

"I'm going to go tuck her in."

"I already did. If you go in there you'll just wake her up."

Nico nodded somewhat reluctantly, his eyes dropped to the floor. I studied his eyebrows and noticed that his forehead was wrinkled in consternation. A question meandered into my brain, and before I could examine it for merit, I asked it.

"Are you planning on adopting Angelica?"

Nico's gaze flickered to mine, his expression unreadable. He didn't immediately answer. Instead, he reached for my hand and held it in both of his, and he traced my fingertips.

Finally, he said, "I've thought about it. I want to." His gaze moved from my hand to my eyes. "But she can't live in a city like New York because of air quality. In Iowa she's got the whole family, her cousins, and I visit whenever I can. Also, I can't take her from my mom. She needs a mother."

At his last sentence, my insides—specifically in the area of my ovaries—fluttered a bit. The sensation took me completely by surprise; therefore, when his assessing gaze moved over my features, I'm sure I looked a little thunderstruck.

After a long moment, he sighed. "Let's go eat."

I was tugged toward the bed buffet. He'd already made me a

plate, set out silverware, and poured a bottle of red wine. I sat across from him, careful not to jostle the bed too much.

"This looks really good." My stomach rumbled again, and I gave in to the startling hunger by stuffing grapes and cheese into my mouth.

I was only peripherally aware that he was watching me instead of eating. After a drawn-out moment, he said, "Do you want kids?"

My fork paused just in front of my mouth, and I blinked at him. "I…I uh…."

He was watching me intently, his face and gaze focused. I noted that his chest wasn't moving. He was sitting remarkably still as though he were holding his breath.

Do I want kids?

I placed my fork on the plate then reached for the wine and took a big gulp.

Do I want kids?

The answer was no. I didn't want kids. They were time-consuming and emotion consuming and sticky and required constant maintenance. They were little disease vectors, coughing and picking their nose and wiping it everywhere. They were houseguests that stayed for eighteen years and broke your stuff and put peanut butter and jelly sandwiches in your shoes. They talked too much, and needed too much, and expected too much.

Kids, as a concept, held no allure for me.

Also not helping matters was the fact that I'd spent the last ten years reminding myself of how awful it would be to have kids. I reminded myself frequently because I didn't think a white picket fence was in my future, even if I did want them.

Plus, there's the whole falling in hopeless love with your kids thing; and that kind of love scared the poo out of me.

I realized the answer was more complicated than a *yes* or *no*. The answer was more like *I decided a long time ago that since I'll likely never meet the Mr. Dad to my Dr. Mom, and the since idea of having no control over the intensity of my love for a child doesn't really sit well, I don't want kids. Lucky me.*

I cleared my throat, prepared to speak, but then chickened out and took another gulp of wine.

A small, knowing smile gently curved over Nico's features, and he released the breath he'd been holding. "You don't want kids."

I swallowed the last of the wine.

His smile turned sad. "Why not?"

"Because…." I couldn't look at him. "It's a bit complicated."

"Explain."

"Ok." I moved a piece of apple around the plate with my fork. "I decided a long time ago that I was never going to have children. Once I made the decision, coming up with reasons against having kids became very easy." My eyes flickered to his then back to my plate. "I've been in school for a really long time. The thought of not being in school is…hard to think about."

"What does that mean?"

"It means that my residency ends in August, and it will be the first time since I was five that I won't be in academia. It means I've never thought about answers to these grown-up issues without the assumption that I was going to be alone."

I set my jaw and resolved to meet his gaze. He was studying me through narrowed eyes as though truly considering my words, trying to understand. "You don't want kids because you assumed you were always going to be alone?"

I nodded. "Something like that. And also, they're a pain in the ass."

He grinned. "What about Angelica? Is she a pain in the ass?"

I answered without thinking. "No! She's adorable and smart. She's also a funny kid. When we were making ravioli, she kept putting them on her nose and barking, like she was a dog. Did I tell you she used my shirt as a napkin?" I smiled at the memory. "I think she inherited some of the Mang-nan-genello funny."

He shook his head. "Are you ever going to learn how to say my last name?"

"Nope." I took another bite of the fruit.

Nico sighed. "If your kids were like Angelica would you want kids?"

I nodded automatically, again not really thinking through all the ramifications of my response. "Hell yes."

"Hmm...." He leaned back and peered at me as though assessing a possibility. "Let me ask you this question a different way, but understand that this is purely hypothetical; there is no double meaning here. I'm not proposing anything, ok?"

"Ok."

"If the children were yours and mine, if we had children together, would you want kids?"

My eyebrows lifted then lowered then lifted again; finally, they settled into a deep, knotted V between my eyes.

Kids with Nico would be so....

My gaze instinctively swept over him. I thought about how funny they would be, how sweet, smart, and kind. They might have his eyes and eye twinkle me into submission. I thought about taking little girls to baseball games and little boys to music lessons.

My heart was behaving erratically. It hurt then it felt warm then it twisted then it felt full.

Do I want to have children with Nico?

For some inexplicable reason, adding Nico into the equation changed everything.

Our children....

"I don't know." I answered honestly and sounded as confused as I felt.

This time his smile was huge and split his face. "Ok. Good. No need to decide now."

I frowned at him, lightly huffed. "I'm not dec—"

He waved my words away as though anxious to change the

subject. "I talked to Dan today."

"Dan?" I was still caught in a web of confusion, my brain not quite ready to switch topics.

"Your usual guard? Stocky guy with neck tattoos? From Boston?"

"Ah. Yes. He's nice."

"Yeah, well, he said there haven't been any further sightings of Menayda."

"Menayda?"

"The woman you refer to as 'fancy stalker.'"

"Oh. No. Last time I saw her was Monday. I told you about that."

"I also had a discussion with Detective Long about pursuing a restraining order. I think you should file for one." Nico stacked our plates and moved them to his dresser, effectively clearing the bed.

I nodded absentmindedly, staring unseeingly at his comforter. "Yeah. I can do that."

"Elizabeth?"

I met his gaze. He stood hovering over me at the edge of the bed. He was watching me, his eyes sober.

"Yes?"

"I'm asking you to get a restraining order." His voice and eyes were steel.

I shrugged. "Ok."

"Ok?"

"Yes. Ok. I'll call Detective Long tomorrow."

"Good." He frowned then murmured, "That was easy."

"Hey! You make me sound like I'm difficult! I'm not difficult. I'm just always right."

"Not always." His grin was teasing as he reached for the hem of my shirt.

I couldn't help but say, "Mostly always."

~*~*~*~

That night Nico and I slept together as he held me in his arms.

Let me repeat that: *Nico and I slept together as he held me in his arms.*

In some ways, it felt familiar, like coming home. In other ways, it was frightening and risky. In still other ways, it was just difficult to comprehend.

He spooned me, my back against his chest, my head tucked under his chin. Just before I fell asleep, I thought I heard him whisper, "Finally."

CHAPTER 24

I woke up to Nico lavishing my skin with sloppy, wet kisses. At first, I thought it was a dream, and I didn't want to wake up. Then, when I realized the wet sloppy kisses from Nico's mouth were my reality, I came fully awake. Furthermore, when he leisurely scaled down the length of my body, I almost died. Instead, I reached maximum mindless bliss with embarrassing speed and intensity; I clasped my hands over my mouth to keep from yodeling his praises to the walls and the inhabitants beyond.

I felt boneless. I couldn't seem to move my limbs with any coordination. But before I could form a complete thought, Nico apparently decided that once was not enough, and this time he was going to come along for the rodeo.

Again, I had to turn my head into the pillow to keep from waking up the entire floor of the building.

Afterward, he lay on top of me with unsteady limbs, wrapped his arms around my torso, and held me pinned. He nearly crushed me with his weight. I loved it. I loved him. I loved waking up in his arms.

It was like Christmas and Easter and my birthday and winning the lottery and learning that I could live inside a rainbow without the tradeoff of being a leprechaun. My mind was blown. This was real. He was real.

When our breathing normalized from approximately six minutes of lovemaking, Nico nuzzled my ear and whispered, "Good morning."

I smiled, pressed my cheek against his. "Yes. Good morning indeed."

He shifted to the side, one arm still around me, the other hand petting my skin. "Will you stay with me every night?"

I nodded. "If you wake me up like that every morning."

"Deal. We should shake on it, maybe get some papers drawn up in front of some lawyers, have a notary sign…maybe a priest…."

I laughed lightly. But, then, when I noticed his expression was serious, I immediately sobered. "Nico."

"Elizabeth."

"What…what are you saying?" I was having a hard time concentrating as his big hand was currently meandering over my body in all the right places.

"You should think about it."

"Think about what?"

I watched as he hesitated then swallowed, his Adam's apple bobbing in his throat. "I don't want to rush you."

My eyebrows lifted. I stilled his hand on my chest. "Rush me how?"

"I want us to be together."

"We are together."

"No, I mean…." He sucked in a large breath and released it. He smelled like me and mint toothpaste. "I mean, I want us to make it official. I want us to get married."

Then time stopped or sped up or did something.

One minute I was lying in Nico's arms, having a conversation, and the next minute I was out of the bed locked in the bathroom, alone. I didn't know how long I'd been standing in front of the sink with the water running. All I knew was I hadn't responded to Nico's statement. In fact, I hadn't said anything at all.

My mind couldn't seem to settle on one thought for any length of time; it was like being showered in fortune cookie slips and trying to read them all at once. I shut off the faucet, apparently having brushed my teeth at some point, and turned on the shower. When the shower was over, I must have dried myself off and gotten dressed, because I was suddenly sitting on the edge of Nico's bed in my scrubs, shoes, and socks.

"Elizabeth?"

I started, searched for the owner of the voice. It was Nico. He hovered in the doorway to his room. He wasn't smiling.

"Are you ok?"

I nodded. But I knew my eyes—wide and alarmed—betrayed me.

He watched me for a moment then sighed, slowly crossed to the bed, and sat beside me. "Look. Forget I said anything. Call it temporary insanity."

"Ok."

His eyes narrowed a little as they searched mine; I was struck suddenly that he was looking for something. I didn't know what it was or how to give it to him, so I just met his gaze and allowed him to stare. After a long moment, he gripped my braid at the back of my head and pulled me forward, his lips pressed against my forehead.

"I'm sorry. Can we forget I said anything?"

I nodded again. "Ok." If I was confused before, now I was downright muddled.

His arms slipped around me, and he dipped me back to the bed and held me tightly as he kissed me. It was a nice kiss that quickly turned into a very nice kiss. Then it drove right past extremely nice kiss into the land of smokin' hot kiss.

Before things could escalate, he pressed his lips to the corner of my mouth and pulled away; he held me at arm's length and studied me.

"Are you ok?"

"Yes. I'm just...I'm just feeling a little overwhelmed. Maybe a bit confused."

He grimaced. "I'm sorry."

"Stop apologizing. Please." I moved my palm to cup his face, and he leaned against it, closed his eyes. "Just...give me a minute to find my bearings, ok?"

He swallowed again, his eyes still closed. "I think I can do that."

"I need to play some catch-up."

"I'll wait as long as you need." His voice was gruff. It broke my heart. His eyes were still closed.

I couldn't think of anything to say. There was no way to segue this conversation into something benign without feeling false and fake. Instead, I pulled him to me, hugged him, and held him until I left him.

~*~*~*~

The fact that I'd spent the night wasn't awkward, because Rose pretended as if I hadn't spent the night.

So, in other words, it was extremely awkward.

She smiled at me in a very foxlike way, asked about my plans for the weekend, and generally grinned and gloated into her coffee. No verbal mention of the fact that I'd slept over—just knowing looks and approving smiles.

I was unnerved.

Regardless, Angelica's morning treatment was seamless until she motioned for me to come closer with her little index finger. I bent so that she could whisper something to me.

She said, "Are you my best friend?"

I leaned back, looked into her twinkling green eyes, and choked on my feelings. First Nico, now Angelica. It seemed as if they'd planned it, this emotional attack on the fortress around my heart. Even though I couldn't answer Nico, not yet, I instantly knew how to respond to Angelica.

"Yes. I'm your best friend. We're best friends." I smiled at her, and my chin wobbled.

This family was going to be the death of me. I decided I needed to knit her more sweaters, maybe some matching hats, as well as some dolls. I resolved to buy her a dollhouse...and a real pony. Basically, all my future plans included spoiling her rotten.

Her smile was brilliant, and it wrinkled her nose. The fortress was officially leveled, burned to the ground, incinerated by a four-year-old.

She was also holding up like a champ. A sudden sadness seized my heart. Angelica's fearlessness and lack of concern about needles and infusions and poking and prodding was unacceptable. No four-year-old should be comfortable in an infusion chair.

After the treatment was over, Rose offered me coffee and apple fritters. I declined. My shift officially started at eight, but I wanted to get to the hospital early to finish up charting and have some time with my thoughts. I needed to seriously consider the possibility of Nico's pseudo marriage proposal.

I hadn't dismissed it. I found myself earnestly thinking about it, and I was coming up short on reasons to say no.

I found Nico reading the paper in the dining room, and I wordlessly kissed him goodbye. He smiled at me when I left. His eyes were cloudy but warm with unassuming affection. For a fleeting moment I almost said *Yes, you sweet, sexy man. Yes, I will marry you.*

But then naysaying sense and fear gripped my throat. I couldn't speak. So instead, I tried to return his smile with a bright one of my own.

My ride to work was unremarkable. I fretted in the back seat. Dan, my guard, didn't have any problem finding a door free of paparazzi. It appeared that the attention was finally starting to wane. We made a plan to meet outside the doctor's lounge in the ER. He dropped me off and left to find parking. I walked to my locker, encumbered only by my thoughts.

Marry Nico.

Elizabeth Finney and Nico Manganiello, married.

The entire concept felt surreal. In fact, everything that had occurred over the last half day felt impossible. I still couldn't even pronounce his last name correctly.

We'd just found each other, and it felt like he was slipping away. I wondered if this was *the thing* that would take him away from me. Like the thing that took him away from girl B. He said he had always loved me, but he loved her too.

I knew I was being melodramatic and self-defeating, irritating myself with doomish, obsessive thoughts, but I couldn't help it. I had an ingrained bitterness, a defense against happiness and the eventual hurt that followed.

Maybe my hesitation would cause him to realize that my earlier protestations had been correct—that he'd been in love with an idea of me and not the current, broken, pathetic, real version of me.

I avoided this vein of thought—again avoiding—and cursed at myself for being a feckless, thankless, hopeless, exasperating twit. Mid-curse I opened my locker to grab my lab coat, but then I stopped, gasped, and backed up into the bench running the length of the room. I nearly fell over it in my attempt to escape the contents of my locker.

My lab coat hung from its hanger, just as I'd left it, except someone had taken a knife and sliced it until it shredded. Additionally, my knitting project bag—which contained the baby hat that was in progress—had also been destroyed. I averted my eyes from the tattered white coat and yarn and glanced around the room.

I wasn't alone. I didn't immediately see anyone else, but I knew I wasn't alone.

A chill raced up my spine, and I bolted from the locker room and ran for the ER doctor's lounge. I didn't pause or look over my shoulder to see if anyone followed. My only thoughts were of escape.

Dan was already there, waiting for me. His face creased into a stiff frown of concern when he met my gaze, and he sprinted to intercept me then grabbed my arms.

"What happened? What's wrong?" His eyes darted up and down the length of the hallway.

"My coat...my lab coat...someone...." I pressed my back against the wall and struggled for breath.

"Dr. Finney? Are you ok?"

I nodded. I glanced at Dan's brown eyes then hovered on the swirling tattoos that peaked out from under the neck of his business shirt. He had a scar running from his jaw to the center of his cheek. He wasn't terribly tall, but he was thick, muscular, and imposing in that *I can and will kick your ass* kind of way. He was a scary-looking guy. His presence and scariness made me feel better.

"I'm ok." I finally ceased gulping air and took a long steadying breath. "My lab coat. Someone cut up my lab coat. I was in the locker room and opened my locker. It's hanging up, completely shredded."

Dan absorbed this information then ushered me into the doctors' longue. "Stay here. Call the police. I'll go check it out."

I nodded, happy to find the lounge busy and occupied. I grabbed a cup of coffee with shaking hands, sat in a couch at the far end of the room, and dialed the number for Detective Long. I kept my voice low as I left her a voicemail to tell her about the coat.

As I was finishing my coffee, Dan peeked into the room and motioned for me to come into the hall. He was holding a lab coat with my name embroidered on the pocket. It was completely fine and untouched.

I blinked at it, incredulous. "But...but I...but it was cut up." I gazed at Dan imploringly. "I swear. I was just there, and it was in tatters, like someone had taken a knife and—"

"Shh, I believe you. Your craft bag, the knitting stuff and yarn, was still there, all torn up." He pulled me a little ways down the hall but withheld the coat. "Did you call Detective Long?"

"Yes. I left a message."

"Good. I think whoever did it must have been in the locker room with you. They waited until you saw the shredded coat then replaced it with this one. They were long gone when I arrived."

I chewed on the inside of me cheek as I studied my big guard. Abruptly I blurted, "Nico wants me to get a restraining order."

Dan nodded. "I agree. In fact, I'll let our legal department know so they can start working on it. Maybe we can get it pushed through today."

"Quinn has a legal department?"

Dan eyed me warily. "Yeah."

"What for?"

"Legal stuff."

I frowned at him, confused by his vague response. My hands were shaking so I crossed my arms over my chest.

"Hey…maybe you should go home." He placed a hesitant hand on my back.

"No. I'm fine, really—just a little on edge."

His concerned brown eyes moved over me in plain surveillance, and I tried to give him my best impression of a brave face.

"Ok. Fine. I'll be here the whole time. Hell, I'll even follow you into the bathroom." His words were tinged with a faint Bostonian accent. "But if you need to go home—"

"No. It's ok." I balled my still shaking hands into fists. "I'll be ok."

Dan grimaced, cursed under his breath. "I'm just glad we briefed the hospital security team earlier this week. They sent an updated email out to all staff with her picture, so hopefully someone will see her and call it in."

"Yeah." I said. "Hopefully."

~*~*~*~

I was ok. Well, I was mostly ok.

Admittedly, I was jumpy at first. But as patient after patient filtered through the ER and my attention was yanked from my own concerns to those of helping families deal with sick children or spouses work through a difficult diagnosis, my nerves evened out. Mostly, I felt exhausted.

Detective Long arrived just after noon. I felt foolish, telling the story a second time. She brushed for prints around my locker, questioned me, collected my statement for the restraining order, and took the eerily perfect lab coat and disturbingly shredded knitting bag with her when she left.

By the time Nico and Rose brought Angelica to her afternoon appointment, I did my best to suppress the roller coaster of my emotions. I didn't hug Nico, but I did hold his hand a bit too tightly when he extended it to shake mine; I did stare into his eyes a bit too long.

He frowned, his brow creased with concern. I could read worry in his eyes. We weren't alone, surrounded as we were by our security guards, the clinical research unit staff, and his family. I tried to give him a heartening smile. This only served to increase the hardness of his features.

After I hooked Angelica to the infusion line and stepped away to find her a blanket, he caught me and pulled me slightly to the side in the small space. "Hey. What's wrong? Are you ok?"

I nodded, swallowed, fiddled with the stethoscope around my neck. "Yes. I'm fine." Except my voice was shrill and strained, even to my own ears. I winced then tried again. "Really."

He took an impatient breath. "Is this about earlier—about what I said?"

"No! No, not at all." I hoped he would somehow read my thoughts and guess at the events of the morning. It was a completely ludicrous hope. I noted that we were being watched by the nurses. Fleetingly, I considered pulling him into an encounter room and filling him in on the details, but good judgment prevailed. I didn't need any of the hospital staff recording us, and I certainly didn't need to give any hints or suggestions of inappropriate behavior. Instead, I did my best to reassure him. "Really. I just…listen, we'll talk when I get off."

"What time do you get off?"

"Three."

"You mean in an hour?"

"No. Three in the morning."

"Oh." He stuffed his hands in his pockets. "Can't we talk now?"

My eyes flitted around the room, scanned the hovering nurses. I thought back to the pictures of Nico and me taken after our friends-without-benefits conversation. I didn't want any more pictures. I didn't want to add any more fuel to the fire by separating ourselves for a private conversation.

It could wait.

"We'll talk later. I'll…I'll call you during my next break."

His frown increased in severity, and he glanced at Angelica. "Let me get her a blanket."

I nodded and stepped to the side so that he could find what he needed on the shelf. I only halfway succeeded in arranging a mask of calm over my features.

All through the rest of the visit, I stole glances in his direction. He didn't meet my eyes. Instead, he held Angelica's hand and kept his attention focused on the *My Little Pony* episode playing on her iPad.

When the visit was over, I allowed an obliviously happy Rose to pull me into a brief hug and walked the trio plus their guards to the staff elevator. On the way down, Rose made chitchat about a recent outing to the Natural History Museum and the impressively huge stuffed lions she'd seen in the basement.

Just as the elevator reached our floor, Nico threaded his fingers through mine and squeezed my hand. I met his big green eyes and found them devoid of twinkle. I returned his hand squeeze, but he seemed to grow more agitated the more I tried to reassure him. He held us in place as everyone else exited the elevator, and I didn't realize his intent until it was too late.

I started to exit, but his hand pulled me back, his arm wrapped around my middle, and I—confused, caught, stunned—watched as the doors closed. Rose, Angelica, and all our guards were on one side, and we were on the other, alone in the elevator.

"Nico! What—wait—what are you thinking?"

"I'm thinking you need to tell me what's going on right now. There is something wrong."

I spun and hit his chest; the elevator and my anxiety began their ascent. "That was incredibly stupid! All of our security is on the other floor. We're alone!"

He gripped my wrists. "What is going on? You look petrified. I don't know what I can say about this morning, ok? I was being impulsive; it was stupid. I never should have said it."

"This isn't about that. I had someone…damn it!" I darted to the other side of the elevator and hit the wall, furious. "Don't you care at all about your safety?"

"Yes…wait, what?"

"This. This right here is the problem! There is a crazy person running around this hospital! You have a nutty fancy stalker who is completely unhinged, cutting up lab coats and leaving creepy pictures all over the place, and you're dodging your security!" I had no control over the volume of my voice. I was screeching like a banshee.

"What the hell happened?"

"You push and you push, and you know what? Maybe I wasn't ready for this! I told you over and over again that I didn't want to do this, but you wouldn't listen! You just kept pushing me, and now I'm not going to let you do this to me, do you understand? I'm not going to be left! You are going to start taking your safety seriously. If you get hurt or die, I will kill you!"

Just as I finished my screaming tirade, the elevator dinged, announcing our arrival at the fourth floor. The doors slid open. I could see several people in my peripheral vision hovering at the entrance to the lift. They didn't get on. Something about the way Nico and I were glaring at each other must have warned them away. The doors closed.

He swallowed. I could tell he was trying to school his

expression; he was attempting to build a wall between us. He broke eye contact first and punched the button for the basement, where we'd left our guards, Rose, and Angelica standing there wondering what was going on.

I huffed, blinked against the stinging moisture in my eyes, and took a step toward him. "Nico…I—"

"No." The single word was a sharp reprimand; a line in the sand. "We'll talk when you get off work."

"Something happened this morning."

"I said we'll talk about it later, when I'm not *pushing* you." He wouldn't look at me. Instead, he stood in the opposite corner of the elevator and glared at the doors.

I leaned heavily against the wall. "I didn't mean that."

Silence.

"I mean I did, but I didn't…." After a brief second of indecision on how to continue, I threw my hands into the air. "Why are we always having these conversations in elevators?"

The doors opened once again, revealing two security guards— one of them was Dan—who breathed a visible, audible sigh of relief when they saw us. Without glancing back, Nico left the elevator and followed his guard to a waiting black SUV. Dan stepped into the elevator, his expression stern. It was obvious he was perturbed.

But I didn't care about Dan's silent disapproval. I cared about Nico's silent departure, and I felt crushed by how he'd disappeared into the big vehicle without giving me a backward glance.

CHAPTER 25

As soon as the opportunity presented itself, I sprinted to the doctors' lounge and tried to call Nico. When he didn't answer, I called again. When he didn't answer for the third time, I left him a long, rambling voice mail describing the events of the morning and apologizing for my over reactive outburst. I called him a fourth time and told him I loved him.

My heart plummeted that night when Rose brought Angelica to the evening appointment. Nico was conspicuously absent. I did take heart from the fact that Rose was still giving me knowing smiles. When she reminded me, just before leaving, that I had a key to the penthouse, the sick feeling in my stomach dissolved a little.

If Nico were truly angry with me, surely his mother would know. Surely, she would be prying and pushing me to fix whatever I'd broken. But she appeared to be happy—happy as a crazy fox in a hen house.

I also took comfort from Angelica's happy, albeit sleepy, face when she saw me. We hugged. I indulged myself by sitting next to her the whole time and stroking her hair. When she left, it felt as if she took part of my heart with her.

I counted the hours until my shift was over. When the clock struck 3:00 am I bolted; left my charting for the next day. Dan had been replaced sometime in the evening with a tall, imposing guard named Jackson. Like Dan, he shadowed me throughout my shift, and when we left the hospital and walked to the car, he kept one hand on my upper arm and one hand hovering over his gun.

We arrived back to my building without incident, though Jackson insisted on riding up with me to Nico's penthouse. I bid him goodnight—although he didn't look like he was going anywhere—and tiptoed to Nico's room.

Part of me hoped that he was asleep so that I could strip naked and snuggle against his warmth. Part of me hoped he was awake so that I could apologize then yell at him some more about putting himself in danger.

He was awake. His laptop was the only illumination in the room. I hovered in the doorway briefly, memorizing his face, sending up a silent prayer of thanks that we were both here safe and unharmed.

He looked up from his laptop when I shifted forward and closed the door behind me. His face darkened, and his eyebrows pulled into a deep V of concentration or irritation or concern—or all three.

"How was your double shift?" He didn't sound precisely mad; more like distant.

I closed half the distance to where he sat, and then loitered. I was uncertain if I should cross to him. "Busy. Did you get my messages?"

He nodded. His jaw ticked.

I waited for him to say something. When he didn't, I closed my eyes and rubbed my forehead. "What happened earlier, with the elevator—you can't take chances like that."

"You should have called me right after the police. Why did you stay at work? You should have come home." Now he sounded mad. In fact, he sounded downright furious.

"I stayed because I have a job to do. *My* guard was with me the whole time." I leveled him with a severe glare. "I didn't strand myself alone in an elevator."

"Wait—are you mad at me?" When I didn't answer, his expression went from disbelieving to defiant.

"You separated us from your security team." I flicked on the light by the dresser; he and the room were better illuminated. I was able to discern, but didn't quite register, that he had his small satchel half packed on the edge of his bed.

"I did that because I knew something was wrong. It was a

chance to speak privately. You're working all night, I have to leave, and I'm going to miss you!"

"You were reckless."

He stood and walked to me. "Don't you understand that I can't stand the fact that I've put you in danger? Don't you know that I'm going crazy thinking about what you went through? You couldn't even take a minute to call me? To tell me about it until hours later?"

"I'm not worried about me—"

 "Well I'm worried about you!"

"You're not listening."

"Fine. Why do you think we're fighting?"

"Don't you get it?" I forced myself to lower my voice. "I wasn't thinking about me; I was thinking about you!" Because I couldn't both control the volume of my words and keep from hitting him, I hit him. But once I started, I couldn't stop. I backed him into the wall and gripped his arms as I unloaded my fear. "What if she did come back? What if she was there when the elevator opened on the fourth floor? All I could think was that this was it—that your fancy stalker had a gun or a flamethrower or a bomb strapped to her chest, and that I was going to lose you…that she was going to…."

"Hey, hey." He grabbed my wrists, stilled my flailing hands, and tugged me against his chest. "Not going to happen. You're not going to lose me."

I pulled out of his grip, my hands still shaking, and moved beyond his reach. "You don't know that! Especially when you insist on acting irresponsibly and taking stupid chances with your safety…."

"If you'd told me what had happened—"

"This is one of the reasons why I didn't want to do this, but you kept pushing me and pressuring me, and now you—"

"We rode together in an elevator, alone, one time, which I wouldn't have done if you'd called me and told me what was going on."

"All it takes is one time. I don't…." I shook my head, growled a little, stalked away from him, and whisper-yelled. "I don't want to do this!"

A thick silence followed my outburst.

"Do what?" When Nico spoke, it made me jump. I could tell that his temper was reaching critical mass by the sharp edge to his voice.

"I don't want to worry about you, about losing you, about getting a call from the police one day because you decided to ditch your security team."

We stared at each other for a long moment. Unlike our previous staring contests, which had usually ended in lustful eye sex, this one ended with me closing my eyes in frustration; an errant tear escaping and fleeing down my cheek.

I stood in his room, exhausted, wondering why I didn't just strip naked and invite him to bed instead of arguing about something that could have waited until morning. The answer came to me swiftly: *because you're terrified.*

It was true. I was terrified. I was terrified that he would be hurt or I'd lose him to some nut. Happiness, love, and relationships were impermanent, fleeting. My mother was gone. Garrett was gone. I felt like I was losing Janie in almost every way that mattered.

Therefore, eventually Nico would be gone too. Likely high falutin and experiencing a very satisfying happily ever after with the—suddenly omnipresent in my brain—girl C.

Gah! I was a mess! And I needed more sleep.

The sound of nondescript rustling and zippers pulled me out of my depressing manifesto. I glanced at Nico; his back was to me. He was stuffing a book into the bag on the bed.

The half-packed bag on the bed.

My adrenaline spiked.

I stomped to him and stood at his elbow as he put a folder on top of the book. "What are you doing?" I already knew the answer before he responded.

"My flight leaves at six."

I stared at him in hurt shock. I knew my eyes were about to full-on leak floods of tears any second. "You're leaving? Now? But I thought you didn't have to leave until this afternoon!"

"Now seems like a good time. I think I need to stop pushing you and let you make up your mind on your own."

I glanced between him and the bag. He walked around me, not making eye contact, and retrieved his laptop from where he'd left it on the chair.

"Nico...you're not pushing—I mean, you did, but that's not what this is about."

"Yes. My pushing you is exactly what this is about."

"I feel like you're purposefully misunderstanding everything I'm saying."

"I'm not. I understand you perfectly. You don't know what you want, and I'm trying to give you the space to figure it out. Maybe we both need a little distance to figure this out."

"I don't want distance."

"Well, you're getting it. Whether you want it or not, you're getting it."

He sounded so resolute, so stubborn, pushing again, but in the opposite direction. Like he'd made up his mind hours ago, and discussion was pointless. I watched his back as he walked from one side of the room to the other.

"Please don't leave." My voice sounded so small. I was pleading with him, and I didn't care.

He paused. "I can't stay."

I swiftly moved to his position, forced him to face me, and filled his arms. I kissed his chest, his neck, his face. "Stay, with me; forget I said anything. Just don't leave."

"Elizabeth…" He groaned, nuzzled his nose against my neck. "I have to go. I have to let you go at some point."

I jerked back as if he'd sucker-punched me in the stomach. "What do you mean, *let me go*? We haven't…we just…."

"I have to step back. I've been crowding you, pressuring you. I have to know that you and I want the same thing and you're not just…not just giving in."

I frowned and sad-faced him. I didn't trust myself to speak without begging or saying something spiteful, so I said nothing. He searched my eyes for a long moment, and then he heaved a giant sigh and pulled completely out of my grasp.

"I'll be back next week. We can try each other out for a while—see if it works. We'll take it one day at a time." He shrugged as he spoke.

Try each other out.

See if it works.

Take it one day at a time.

WHAT THE HELL?

I willed myself not to cry.

My head was spinning. Everything was happening too fast. One minute we were tearing each other's clothes off in an elevator, then bringing up marriage, then he was leaving me for a week and basically telling me not to contact him.

I kept thinking that he wasn't being fair. He had pushed me into this relationship, and now he was pushing me out of it. He was leaving, and I had absolutely no say in the matter. I didn't understand how I'd let this happen. How or when had I given him so much power over me?

I sat still and silent, staring at nothing for a long while as he packed his small bag. When he finished, he crossed to me and held out his hand. I didn't take it. I couldn't even look at it.

He sighed. "Listen, I'll…I might be hard to get in touch with this week. We'll catch up when I get back, ok?"

I couldn't talk, and if I met his gaze, I would burst into tears. Therefore, I didn't move. After a long moment, he reached down and pulled me up by the shoulders, lifted my chin, and pressed a devastating kiss on my mouth. He was warm and soft and wet and just delicious. His hands moved down my sides, his thumbs grazed against my breasts, and my body responded to him, to his petting, without the permission of my mind.

Then he broke the kiss and turned away.

I wanted to scream, throw things, threaten, issue ultimatums. I wanted to shake him and ask him why he suddenly felt it necessary to rip out my heart. Instead, I watched him walk out the door and away from me—from us.

Then, like the watering pot that I'd become, I cried.

~*~*~*~

Saturday was a terrible day. I stayed up long enough to administer Angelica's infusion then I went to sleep. And, yes, I slept in Nico's bed because it smelled like him. I woke up in the afternoon just long enough to administer Angelica's next dose then went back to bed.

Rose chased me back into Nico's room and plied me with food. To my utter mystification, she didn't seem curious about why my eyes were puffy or why Nico had left so early. This lack of needling threw me for a loop, and I ended up blurting out, "Nico and I had a fight!"

Rose's mouth hooked to the side. She gazed at me through her black lashes. "L'amore non è bello se non è litigarello[34]."

"Please, Rose, what does that mean?"

"It means you both have passion for each other, and you have love for each other too. You should expect fights; fights are good for the soul and the body."

I studied her, nonplussed. "My training tells me that stress is

---

[34]Translation: Love is not good if there is no fight.

bad for the body; how can fights be good for the body?"

"Because after a fight, there is always the making up."

My eyes popped out of my head, my jaw fell open, and—despite or because of my heartbreak—I laughed. I laughed with the hysteria that accompanies helplessness. It felt good to laugh because it wasn't crying.

When I calmed down, she handed me the plate of food and supervised my consumption of it. She made idle chitchat about different sights that she and Angelica were planning to see and about a recent visit with her daughter Lisa. I half listened. She didn't seem to notice or, if she did, she didn't seem to mind my absence of attention.

After Rose felt that I'd eaten enough, she stood and reached for the plate. She didn't offer a sympathetic smile, which I felt would have been appropriate considering the situation. Instead, she gave me an affectionate, maternal smile; it was heavy with knowing wisdom and patience.

"Ah, Lizzybella, you will be fine. He is not perfect, he will make mistakes and so will you. It's good that you discover this now. But you are perfect for each other." She nodded, and her smile grew as though she were amused.

She was right. He wasn't perfect. He was making a new mistake by pushing me away and I was making an old mistake by letting him go.

"I'm so tired of making mistakes."

Rose patted my hand. "Here is something for you, and I will tell you what it means—okay?"

I nodded. The food felt like a brick in my stomach. I just wanted to go to sleep.

"Amore non si compra né si vende, ma in premio d'amor, amor si rende. It means that love cannot be bought nor sold, but the prize of love is love."

I nodded, again on the verge of tears. She kissed my head then left me.

As soon as the door closed, I flopped on the bed. I lost the final battle and, therefore, the war against my irrationality, and cried myself to sleep on Nico's pillow.

~*~*~*~

I tried to call Nico on Sunday morning. He didn't answer. I tried again Sunday night. He didn't answer. I texted him. He didn't respond.

I hated Nico Manganiello.

I hated that, since he'd left, I walked around like half a person. I hated that I found nothing enjoyable—not knitting, not yoga, not *Star Trek* and Captain Janeway, not FARK.com. Mostly, I hated that I loved him so much.

Work helped a little. I was busy at work. My mind was preoccupied with the problems of others, which put my issues into perspective.

I kept trying to reason with myself that Nico would be back in a week. In one week, I would tell him that I wanted us to be together, and that would be that—I hoped.

I realized, however, that I had absolutely no control over him and his feelings or his decisions. I might spend the next week falling more and more hopelessly in love with him. Meanwhile, he might spend the next week falling more and more out of love with my petty, immature, emotionally stunted self.

Or maybe I was being too hard on myself. And maybe I needed to stop. Perhaps I deserved better. Perhaps I should demand better.

I needed to do something, stop making the same mistakes.I felt frustration.

I felt fear.

Therefore, Sunday night I resorted to asking Rose if she would call him to see if he answered. She happily agreed and dialed his number. Again, he didn't answer. However, he immediately texted her back.

"What does it say? What did he say?" I bounced from one foot to the other, impatient to see the screen.

Her brows lifted but her face was calm and passive. "Here, you can read it yourself."

She held the phone out to me, and I took it from her hands and greedily read the screen: *Tell Elizabeth to stop calling.*

I read and reread it a few times. My heart sank. I handed her the phone and buried my face in my hands. I felt the despair of being left.

~*~*~*~

Work officially began at 5:00 pm on Monday, but I arrived early. I left my building right after Angelica's 2:00 pm infusion. I didn't want to be alone with my thoughts. I arrived shortly after 3:00 pm and immediately started seeing patients.

I noted that both Meg and Dr. Ken Miles were also working in the ER.

Dr. Ken Miles, unfortunately, noticed me, despite my efforts to slip stealthily into clinic rooms under the radar. At one point, while I was charting between patients, he seemed to be speaking especially loudly in the next alcove about something—a girl, a conquest. I heard the word 'tits'. I rolled my eyes. For as much as he liked to point his finger at me, as much as he liked to say that I was immature because of my harmless, lighthearted pranks, he was one hundred times worse.

As evidence, I reasoned, he used the same finger to pick his nose that he used to point out my immaturity.

I skipped my dinner break, preferring instead the distraction of people with real problems, and redoubled my efforts to ignore him. This was easy to do at first. But then, just as I was making my way up to the fourth floor to meet Rose and Angelica for the evening visit, Dr. Ken Miles stepped out of a clinic room and bisected my elevator trajectory.

My guard, Dan, hastened forward and walked at my elbow,

apparently planning to usher me past Dr. Ken Miles, who stood in the center of the hall and glared at us, his pale blue eyes focused on mine.

"Hey. We need to talk." He lifted his chin toward me; his face was marred with an unhappy frown that didn't diminish his prettiness. Instead of looking severe, he looked like a pouty little girl.

"Not now. I have a patient in the CRU," I mumbled as Dan and I passed.

"We still need to talk," Ken called after me. "I'll find you later."

I shrugged and didn't turn around. I noted that Dan was sending shifty-eyed glances in my direction. I ignored him.

Angelica's visit, apart from her being sleepy, was uneventful. She was nearing her fourth and final week on therapy, and some of her lab values had improved. I shared the news with Rose and was gratified to be on the receiving end of one of her strangling, full-body hugs.

I wished that Nico were there. The results were early but promising. I wanted to tell him in person, celebrate with him, with Rose and Angelica, with this family that I loved. Instead, the profound moment felt bittersweet.

Rose, Angelica, and their guards left shortly after the visit was over. Dan and I saw them off then walked the corridor back to the ER. I was fighting against losing myself in my thoughts. I was looking for a distraction, any distraction that would keep me safe from any prolonged pity staycation.

Just as I thought *I'll take anything, any distraction whatsoever, anything but more morose meanderings*, Megalomaniac Meg appeared out of nowhere and stepped into our path.

Before we could alter course, Meg darted forward toward Dan. Her eyes were wide and fearful; I registered the strangeness of her expression before I registered her words. "Oh my god, that woman. I saw that woman in the hospital. You have to come with me!"

Dan stiffened. "What woman? What did you see?"

Meg's eyes bounced from me to Dan. "That woman who stalks Nico Moretti. She is here, in the hospital. I saw her."

Automatically I shifted closer to Dan and he moved closer to me. "We need to get you out of here."

"No." I shook my head. "We should call the police first."

"This freaking hospital only has cell coverage in the doctor's lounge." Dan ran a hand over his forehead and scanned the hallway.

"I know where she is." Meg tossed a thumb over her shoulder. "You could go get her now."

Dan glanced from me to Meg. "No, my first priority is to keep Dr. Finney safe."

"But the safest thing to do is to remove her as a threat. If you go with Meg, I can go to the doctor's lounge and call the police. You could restrain her until they arrive. Didn't you say that Quinn's legal team was working on getting the restraining order in place on Friday?"

Dan nodded then grimaced at his phone and its zero reception. He cursed again. "The restraining order went into effect today so, yes, if she is here, then she'll be arrested." He searched my eyes then glanced down the hall once more. "Fine. This is what we'll do: I'll walk you to the lounge—"

"But she might get away by then!" Meg sounded frantic, her arms moved wildly toward the hall.

He held his hands up, fending off Meg's frenetic arm waving, and addressed me. "I will walk you there and you will stay put. This doctor," he pointed at Meg, "will then take me to where she saw the woman. Meanwhile, you will call the police and Quinn, ok?"

I nodded, my hands sweating. I wiped them on my teal scrubs. Dan gripped my elbow and steered me to the break room. He released a steady string of expletives the entire way there.

When we arrived, he physically placed me in the room and glowered at me with what I assumed was his most serious I-mean-business face. "You will stay here until I get back."

I swallowed, nodded, and pulled my phone out of my pocket. I pressed 9-1-1. "Fine. Yes. Just go get the loony toon so we can all rest easier."

"We have to hurry!" Meg tugged on Dan's hand.

He pulled it out of her grasp and swung his glower in her direction. Under the weight of it, she stumbled backward a few paces.

"After you." He motioned to the hallway.

Meg, perhaps still a little wary after Dan's impressively menacing scowl, fumbled for her footing and direction. Finally, after a delayed moment, they were off.

I walked farther into the empty room and crossed to the couch, and had just sat down when the 9-1-1 operator asked, "What is your emergency?"

I was poised to answer, but before I could, a voice that sent shivers of fear racing down my spine sounded from behind the entrance of the break room. "Put the phone down."

My eyes shot up and I was looking directly at the Fancy Stalker, who must've been neatly tucked behind the door, and now she was shutting it. I was alone with the Fancy Stalker.

And she was holding a gun.

CHAPTER 26

She was dressed in scrubs and a lab coat. Gone were the fancy boots and clothes. However, she still looked impeccable; her long brown hair fell in a sleek waterfall over her shoulders, and her eye makeup was wicked impressive, the elusive smoky eye.

I wondered why I was noticing her talent for eye makeup while she was holding me at gunpoint.

"That was too easy." She cocked her head to the side. Maybe it was my imagination, but her movements appeared to be jerky, sudden, and somehow reminded me of horror movies and machines. "For a doctor you sure are dumb."

I licked my lips since they'd become inexplicably dry. I didn't like sitting while she was standing, so I stood very slowly.

"Oh. Hi, there," I croaked.

"Stupid." She sneered at me in derision and screeched, "You are nothing! I am going to show him you are nothing!"

From the phone I heard, "Hello? What is the nature of your emergency?"

I moved my hand to cover the receiver, hoping that she didn't hear the dispatcher or notice the movement, but I was disappointed.

"I said to put the phone down or I swear to god I will shoot it out of your hand."

I flinched and, on complete autopilot, I dropped the phone.

Her lip curled in a snarl as she abruptly crossed the room and stomped on the cell with the heel of her shoe. Again and again she smashed the black rectangle into the linoleum, and with each stomp of her foot she emitted grunting screams, either from effort or just from being a crazy person. She didn't stop until it was a million pieces of unrecognizable glass and electronic bits.

Then she screamed again, her features feral, spit raining in all directions. "I HATE YOU! I HATE YOU!"

I tensed but kept my hands at my sides. I fought the urge to cower into a small ball under the disturbing weight of her wild gray eyes and the black revolver.

She wiped the back of her hand across her mouth, her eyes trained on me, and a weird laugh tumbled from her lips. I shivered. It was worse than the screaming. I didn't dare look anywhere but directly at her even though every fiber of my being was urging me to run.

"You know, it was so easy. It was so easy. I know you...." She lifted and pointed the gun at me. I tried not to think about the fact that at any moment a bullet was going to tear through my skin. "But you're not the type Nico likes. *I'm* his type, he should want to be with me! Why doesn't he want to be with me?"

I didn't move or make any sound in response. Her next words made me jump.

"We went out, did you know that? I thought he liked me, but he used me." Her voice became smaller, whisper quiet.

"You and Nico?" I couldn't help my automatic surprise to her statement.

"Yes, me and Nico! Don't you say his name!" She shook the gun at me, "I've been watching you. You only saw me when I wanted you to. I've been here." She laughed again then whispered, "I've even watched you undress."

Nausea rose in my throat, and I forced myself to swallow it back. I forced myself to start thinking of a way to leave this room alive.

"Everyone hates you." She nodded, her face pinched with bitter superiority. "Meg *hates* you."

I choked and my question slipped through my lips before I could stop it. "You know Meg?"

She clicked her tongue, obviously pleased that I was surprised by this revelation. "Oh yes. How do you think I've been able to move around here so easily? Who do you think cut up your lab coat? How do you think I got those pictures of you and Nico?"

"How…how do you know her?"

"I thought she was you. I followed her to the train. When I approached her, she was disgusted that I'd have confused the two of you. Isn't that funny?" She waited as if she expected me to laugh. When I didn't, her features hardened. "I'm the one who showed her that disgusting video, where you made a fool of yourself by screaming lies at your high school reunion. Pathetic."

I couldn't breathe. The room tilted a little, and I fought to stay upright.

"Oh, she thinks I'm harmless. She likes that I frighten you, but she doesn't think I'd actually *hurt* you. But you and I…we know better."

"She…why would she do this?"

"Because she hates you! You're nothing special. You're small, unremarkable, plain. You have nothing, *nothing* that he wants. I don't know why you're deluding yourself. Why are you doing that? Huh? Why are you lying to yourself that he wants you? Do you know how *sick* you are?" She emphasized certain words by jabbing the gun in my direction, and her eyes had lost focus, like she wasn't talking to me—she was talking to herself.

In my peripheral vision, I noted my distance from the coffeepot—filled with hot coffee—and the drawer with the knives. I thought about picking up a chair that was about three feet from where I stood, and throwing it at her, or jumping behind the couch and using it as a shield.

"ANSWER ME!"

I jumped at her abrupt command. Luckily, I jumped closer to the coffeepot.

"Ok. Ok…look. Maybe we, you and I, maybe we can just talk." I lifted my hands in faux surrender and tried to keep my voice level and calm instead of panicked and hysterical.

"I don't want to talk to you." Again she jerked her head to the side. Two fat tears pooled in her eyes and ran down her cheeks. She rubbed one of her eyes with the back of her hand and ruined her smoky eye makeup.

I stiffened. At that moment, I saw in her eyes that she was seconds away from shooting me. If something was going to happen, it needed to happen now.

And, luckily for me, Dr. Ken Miles happened.

"I know you're in here, Elizabeth. You can't hide from me all night—"

I heard him before I saw him. He was speaking loudly, as usual, but this time I didn't mind. In fact, I could have kissed him at that moment. It likely would have been a peck on the cheek, but still a kiss nonetheless.

She spun toward his voice, and I didn't hesitate to act. Dr. Ken Miles—Ken—stopped abruptly at the entrance and stumbled back a step when he saw the gun. His hands flew up to cover his face and he screamed in a way that reminded me of a little girl.

I felt lightning in my veins, and I used her temporary state of distraction to grab the coffeepot. With strength, speed, and agility I didn't know I possessed, I bounded to her in three steps and bashed the side of her face with the pot. It made contact with her temple and shattered, hot coffee and glass shards raining down on her like justice.

She screamed. This time it was with pain. Her arms came up in an automatic response to fend off any additional attack and swipe at the wound.

I was surprised that the force of the impact against her temple didn't immediately knock her out but wasted no time dwelling on it. Instead, I tackled her, and the gun dropped to the ground—fired off one round—then skidded across the floor toward Ken.

"Oh my god!" I faintly registered Ken's shrieked exclamation as I struggled to keep the crazy woman from throwing me off.

"Get the gun, Ken!" I ordered him as her fist swung around and nearly collided with my jaw, missing by millimeters.

I couldn't waste time or attention on Ken. I was battling a rage-fueled crazy woman who had mostly recovered in the few seconds that passed since my assault with the coffeepot, and she was swinging like a champion cage fighter. I dodged a right hook but then collapsed as her knee connected with my stomach. Her fist pounded my kidney, and suddenly I couldn't draw breath.

"Stop!" As though from a great distance I heard Ken's voice, but I couldn't focus on it. I was in crazy pain. I couldn't think. I could only roll to the side and hope the next blow she landed didn't hurt as much as the first two.

The gun went off again, and I winced at the thunderclap then ringing between my ears.

"I said stop!"

But she didn't stop. She lifted her fist as though to disfigure my face, her gray eyes beyond insanity and firmly in the realm of animalistic. I braced myself for her knuckles, but they never came.

Instead, the gun went off a third time, and her left side whipped around as though she'd been struck. Awed, I watched her stumble backward then fall to her knees. Her eyes were no longer on me. Her head was tipped downward, and her hand was covering a spot on her abdomen where blood was seeping through her fingertips.

I blinked at her and time did that thing again, where it both slowed down and sped up. Once minute I was watching her movements in slow motion almost to the point of stillness. Then, suddenly, I was on my knees next to her fallen body. I'd taken off my lab coat and bunched it up to stem the flow of blood from her side.

There were other people present as well—Dan, Meg, Ken, and several ER triage nurses and other faceless colleagues of mine. The nurses immediately reacted, issued orders, pulled me away from her, and placed me into the strong embrace of somebody.

It didn't occur to me to find out who that somebody was until several moments later after the stalker had been loaded onto a stretcher and carried to the operating room. I glanced up at the owner of the arms and found Dan looking at me with plain concern and visible regret.

His brown eyes, usually so guarded, were soft and sincere, and he didn't seem to mind that I was getting blood all over his nice suit as he held me.

"Dr. Finney…Elizabeth, I'm so sorry. I never should have left."

"Shh. No, no, it was my idea. I—I shouldn't have…." I shook my head, unable to finish the sentence, my brain no longer capable of forming words.

Instead I leaned into him and wrapped my arms around him, thankful for the comfort, but all the while wishing he were someone else.

~*~*~*~

The police came. In fact, a lot of police came. I gave a statement. Ken gave his statement. And, when it was time for Meg to give her statement, I punched her in the face.

It took both Ken and Dan holding me back to keep me from giving her a second black eye.

Ken pulled me aside and Dan hovered at my shoulder. "Elizabeth…are you ok?"

I nodded as I flexed my hand. I noted that none of the police officers seemed at all concerned that I'd just assaulted someone.

Ken pulled his hand through his curly blond hair. "I…I just wanted to say…I wanted to tell you…." His eyes moved between mine, and he frowned as though he had just decided something. "But none of that's important now. We should just…let's just agree to be friends again—normal friends."

He stuck out his hand, and after a brief pause, I accepted it in mine. We shook.

"Good." He said, still frowning. "Good."

I nodded. "Yeah. Good. And thanks, by the way, for…." I

glanced around the break room and gestured toward the blood and coffee on the floor. "Thanks for shooting her."

Ken grimaced and sighed. "I was actually aiming for her knee."

I didn't respond, but I wanted to tell him that I wouldn't have cared where he shot her; I was just thankful that he did. I was thankful to be alive.

I was sent home shortly thereafter with instructions to take off my afternoon Tuesday shift. However, I was asked to return for the evening shift at 11:00 pm Dan argued against this as we left. He expressed his opinion quite loudly that I needed time off to recover and, at the very least, I needed to see a therapist or a trauma counselor. In fact, during the entire drive back to my building, he ranted that I was a ridiculous and unreasonable person and, therefore, when I collapsed from exhaustion, it would serve me right.

I could only shake my head—which hurt like the devil—and try to pacify him in small ways.

What he didn't understand and what most laypeople don't get is that you can't call in sick when you're an emergency room physician, especially not in an inner-city Chicago trauma center. There are no mental health days off. If you don't show up, people suffer; people die. Sure, sometimes the hospital can find a replacement in a true emergency. But my situation wasn't an emergency.

I could walk, talk, and think. I could see patients.

In the end, I made a few concessions. I agreed to make every attempt to reduce my shifts over the next two weeks; I further agreed to ask Dr. Botstein to allow me a few extra days off. By the time I arrived at the penthouse door, it was close to three in the morning, and I likely would have agreed to hosting a panty dance party for all of Quinn's security guards.

I wondered what it was about life and death situations that bonded people in such an indescribable, intangible way. I now felt that Dan and I would be friends for the rest of our lives. We had no choice in the matter. We had an understanding because we had shared an urgent situation and come through it together. There was no escape.

We stared at each other in the hall for a full half minute then abruptly he pulled me into a hug. "You're an idiot." He whispered in my ear, his Townie accent suddenly thick and unmistakable.

I laughed. "Thanks."

Dan pulled away and physically set me inside the penthouse, much like he'd physically set me inside the doctors' lounge earlier. "For god's sake, please talk to someone. If you wait too long, you'll be wrong in the head."

"I'm already wrong in the head."

"Yeah, but you're funny wrong in the head. I don't want you to be basket-case wrong in the head."

My mouth hooked to the side. "Because you like me?"

"No. Because basket cases are the worst people to guard. I don't need that shit."

I laughed lightly as he reached for the doorknob, essentially pushing me into the apartment, and then he closed the door.

I stood in the entranceway for several long minutes, dazed, and then I tiptoed to Nico's bedroom, careful not to wake up Rose or Angelica. The first thing I did was strip off my clothes and take the longest shower in the history of forever. The second thing I did was brush my teeth. The third thing I did was burrow in Nico's bed and surround myself with his pillows.

And, predictably, I couldn't sleep.

~*~*~*~

I didn't mention the stalker episode to Rose during Angelica's infusion that morning. But I did ask her the favor of borrowing her cell phone. She happily agreed, obviously feeling guilt-free about ignoring Nico's text request from Sunday.

I called Nico's cell and it went straight to voicemail, which I expected. When the beep sounded, I took a deep breath and said, "Nico, it's me. I'm using your mom's cell phone because mine was…broken last night. I'm not sure if you already heard from Dan or Quinn about what happened, but I want to talk to you about it, so if you could call me back, that would be great. I'm on your mom's phone…bye." I glanced at the phone but didn't hang up. After a short moment, I brought it back to my ear. "I love you."

Then, I hung up. I tossed the phone to the bed and sat on the edge, my elbows on my knees, my face in my hands. I breathed out then in, strangely aware of the sensation of breathing.

While I listened to myself breathe, my brain and heart abruptly reached an accord: I was going to fight for Nico and that was that. I was going to push, play games, and fight dirty. And if he ultimately left me, if he didn't want me in the end, I would be devastated and heartbroken and want to drink scotch alone while listening to Radiohead. But I would live.

And, after just living for a bit, I would start eating alphabet soup.

Even if Nico and I didn't end up together I would always be grateful to him for helping me realize love was a choice that I was capable of making just as much as it was a risk I was capable of taking. I was older and wiser and wouldn't enter into it lightly because I knew now how precious it was.

I was yanked out of my odd meditation by a buzzing on the bed next to me. Rose's cell was ringing. I grabbed for it, swiped my thumb across the screen, and brought it to my ear.

"Hello?"

"Oh, thank god, Elizabeth!"

My heart jumped, my eyes immediately stung with tears of happy relief. "Nico." His name was a prayer of thanksgiving. I fell backward on the bed, surrounded again by his pillows and the smell of his cologne; all of it merged with this voice, and it was the next closest thing to having him there.

He cursed for a while. He ranted for a while after that about Quinn and incompetence and guard dogs and machine guns. I just let the sound of his voice wash over me, a miraculous soothing balm for the largest wound—missing him.

After a bit, he quieted. I heard him sigh on the other end. "I don't know what I would've done if…." He sighed again, his voice thick with emotion. "I can't even say it."

I nodded. "I know. I know how you feel. Nico, I can't stand this. I can't stand being away from you, and you not taking my calls. Can we just forget about the last few days? Please? Can we forget about me losing my temper on Friday and the stupid, awful things I said?"

My entreaty was met with silence. I worried my lip and waited.

"Nico?"

I glanced at the phone screen to make sure the call hadn't been dropped. Sure enough, the call was still live.

"Nico? Are you there?"

"I'm here."

My heart plummeted and crashed to the earth with each protracted second of silence. I closed my eyes because I knew what his silence meant.

"I can't believe it. I can't…I can't believe you're still going to make me wait, after what happened. You're going to make me wait until you come back next week, aren't you?"

"Elizabeth, listen to me. You just went through a terrible trauma because of me—because of who I am and what I do—"

"No! I just went through a terrible trauma because a crazy person decided to hold me at gunpoint. You aren't responsible for putting that weapon in her hand."

"There's something I haven't told you. She and I, we, I dated her."

"I know. She told me when she had me trapped. If she hadn't been holding a gun I might have scratched her eyes out."

He ignored my attempt at brevity. "It was just once, just one time. She wouldn't leave me alone after that."

"Is that why you wanted to be with me? Girl A? Because girl C might be cray-cray? Are you settling for me because you know I don't—"

"No! I want to be with you because I—I can't. . ." He man-sighed, I heard a loud whack then crash as though he'd hit something and it broke. "I don't want to push you. I've already done that and now you almost—you could have died."

"Nico, we're going around in circles. You're not responsible for what she did."

"But I am responsible for wanting to be with you, for introducing all this craziness into your life. The paparazzi, the media, the stalker—those are because of me."

I sniffled, determined not to cry. These tears would be tears of frustration and anger. I couldn't lose it, not yet, not when I had him on the phone, not when we were talking for the first time in days.

"Being with you is my decision."

"You said yourself that I pushed you into this."

"I was out of my mind with worry! I was reacting without thinking!"

"You need time."

"I need you!" I growled at him, at the phone. I was suddenly angry at the phone because it felt like a barrier between us.

Again, I was met with silence.

I dug my nails into my palm as a reminder to stay calm. "Nico...listen to me." My voice wavered, shook dangerously. I had to take three calming breaths before I could continue. "Yes, I did just go through something terrible; there was a minute, a moment when I thought that I might die."

Nico cursed again. It was a whispered curse, both impressive in creativity and vehemence.

I continued. "And when you go through something like that,

you realize what is really important, what matters, right?" I hoped he would fill in the blank before I said it. When he remained silent, I supplied the answer. "You. You matter. We matter. We belong together. You've known it for eleven years, and I've known it for five days. You can't take this away from us."

"I'm not." He didn't sound at all convinced of his own words. My heart constricted painfully. "I'm giving you the space and time to be sure, to be certain. I'm sorry for not returning your calls, I wanted to—you can't know how much—but I'm trying to do the right thing."

"You're pushing me away."

"I'm not pushing you away!" His voice rose. I could sense his frustration through the phone. "Do you think I like this? Do you think this is easy for me? It's not! It's fucking hell!"

"Then why?"

"Because, regardless of why you said it, you were right. You were right about everything, especially when you said that you never wanted this, never wanted me." It hurt to hear him repeat the words back to me. I hated myself for saying them. I hated my short temper.

"I even admitted it to you last week at your knitting group. I told you I was playing this as a game to win. I don't want you to be with me and then leave me when you realize what life will be like with the paparazzi and all the crazies. I want you to be certain. And we can't build something on a shaky foundation. We can't be together because I pushed you into it."

"Why?" My voice cracked. "Why don't you believe me?"

"Elizabeth…." He paused. For a second I thought he was going to hang up but then he continued. "I'm not walking away. I'm not pushing you away. I'll be back next week, and we'll talk about what comes next."

I bit the inside of my cheek to keep from saying anything else because I could feel my mounting anger, the next words out of my mouth would likely be ill-advised, reckless, and hateful. I needed to calm down.

"I love you." His voice was soft like a lovely caress. I knew he meant it.

My tears burst free with a suddenness that surprised me. I closed my eyes again at the onslaught and managed to respond in an extremely watery voice. "If you love me then stop hurting me."

We were both quiet for a long time. I listened to his silence, and he listened to my silent sobs.

Finally, because I knew that I needed sleep, and because I needed to rip off the band-aid if I had any hope of recovery, I said, "Goodbye, Nico."

And I hung up the phone.

CHAPTER 27

It was Tuesday, and I was not knitting.

I woke up to administer Angelica's afternoon infusion and spend some time with her and Rose. Just being around Angelica did wonders for my spirit. She was bravery and joy defined.

When the time came to depart, I was surprised, upon walking out the door of the penthouse, that I now had four bodyguards assigned to me.

My entourage and I meandered down to my apartment. It felt lonely, so I invited them all in. Only two took me up on my offer. Luckily, the girls came soon after, and when they arrived, the guards left to take their posts by the door.

I'd already filled my ladies in on as much detail as I could manage.

I told them about the faux date with Dr. Ken Miles and some of the elevator discussion that ensued; glossed over the more explicit details of Thursday night with Nico; told them about the Friday morning kinda sorta marriage proposal; the lab coat incident; my freak-out in the elevator; our fight early Saturday morning resulting in his speedy departure; then finally all about the shootout in the doctor's longue.

Sandra promptly pulled me into my bedroom for a private chat, and we left everyone in the living room reeling from my story.

"Let me tell you how it's going to be." Sandra glared at me; her face was severe and rigid. "You *are* going to make an appointment with this person." She pressed a card into my hand. "You are going to talk through what happened yesterday. Additionally, you are going see them for no less than six months to work through all the other pain and loss you've suffered. Do you understand?"

The card she handed me was for a trauma counselor, and I had every intention of making an appointment.

I didn't object.

I nodded dutifully.

I slipped the card into my pocket.

She studied my passive response, and her face morphed from stern to pensive concern. "Now I know something's wrong." Sandra reached for my shoulders and pulled me into a tight hug. "Oh, peanut…."

After another squeeze, Sandra pulled far enough away to watch my face. "Are you ok to go back out there?"

I nodded. "Yeah. I feel…horrible." We both smirked at each other.

"Yes. I imagine you do. You went through a lot last night."

"Honestly, I haven't even started processing last night." I rubbed my forehead with my index and middle finger. "The time, apart from Nico, has been really difficult."

She nodded then threaded her fingers through my hand and tugged me toward the living room. "Come on. This subject should be discussed with an audience and alcohol. If I don't let Fiona have her say on the matter, she might frog my work in progress."

Sandra tucked me under her arm and led me back into the living room. At first, they didn't stop knitting; the needles clicked furiously as they all just looked between Sandra and me as we entered.

"Are you going?" Fiona narrowed her eyes at me as I took the seat next to her.

I nodded. "Yes."

"If you don't call, then I will call for you, tie you up, and drag you there." Her tone was very motherly and matter-of-fact.

I gave her a small smile that didn't reach my eyes, though usually it would have. "I know. I promise."

I glanced around the room and found that everyone was watching me with sympathetic eyes. I wanted to crawl under the table. I didn't want sympathy. I wanted help. I wanted them to help me figure out how to talk some sense into Nico.

Abruptly Sandra shouted, "I call shenanigans! No one in their right mind would fight against falling for that hunka hunka burning love!" Sandra waved a thick wooden knitting needle through the air as though it were a wand. "He's smart, he's crazy sexy, he's in love with you, and he's got those Johnny Depp eyes—except they're green."

I said nothing because I was momentarily stunned by her shift in tone and mood.

Sandra poked me with her needle and winked. "I don't understand why he left in the first place."

Then I realized what she was doing. She was trying to turn the topic away from the events of the previous evening; she was trying to give me some space. She was a great co-pilot.

"You should have called us earlier. We could have come over on Saturday night. Why did you wait until today to tell us all of this?" Marie's expression was a cross between concern and exasperation.

I shrugged. "I don't know."

"At least you should have called us immediately about the stalker and all that craziness yesterday." Ashley's face was shadowed with concern. "That's a scary meatball right there."

"For the record, I don't think you necessarily overreacted in the elevator on Friday, especially given the situation and what you'd just been through. And also, in hindsight, she did turn out to be dangerous." Kat gave me a supportive smile.

"I wish I'd said nothing at all on Friday." I mumbled, "Maybe he was right to leave." Now I was just being morose and purposefully obtuse.

Sandra clucked with abject horror. "Those are damn lies! Just stop fighting it, Elizabeth. Give yourself over to happiness, and stop being such a wanker!"

"I'm not fighting it, ok? I just—I mean, maybe he's right. Maybe I do need time. Aren't I allowed time?"

"No!" The room answered in unison, even Janie.

I scowled at her.

She scowled back. "Don't look at me like that. You're in love with him, and you're miserable about it. Time isn't going to help. I would be a bad friend if I told you to continue with your crazy mental arm wrestling over something you've already decided."

"The problem with Elizabeth is that she knows she's hot. Plus she makes the money. She's a hot doctor—no one wants to deal with that. She might as well be wearing a sign that reads, *Only Nobel Prize winners and professional athletes need apply.*" Ashley's attention didn't stray from her knitting as she made this declaration. She held the lace weight work in progress directly in front of her face and squinted as she attempted to knit the difficult pattern.

"Or raunchy standup comedians who she is already in love with." Marie sipped her wine and smiled at me over her glass. It was a knowing, teasing smile that she employed whenever she was trying to get a rise out of its intended target.

"I'm...." I struggled, squeaked, then managed a sigh. "I don't know what I am. Everything is just impossible."

"Why impossible?" Kat's quiet question forced me to meet her gaze. Her expression was compassionate but threaded with challenge and disbelief.

"Because—because I can't be laissez faire about this! I don't want to *try things out*. I want everything to be settled and decided. I want him to stop pushing me away for my own benefit. I have a brain! I am capable of making my own decisions! I can and do use it with frequency!" I buried my face in my hands.

"Well it can't get any more decided than marriage." Fiona studied me. "Why didn't you just say yes?"

"Because I was afraid, ok? It was so sudden and...I don't know what I would do if something happened to him. I don't want to lose him. I can't go through that again."

"Sorry if this comes across as depressing, especially in light of what you've just been through, but, hon, he could die tomorrow in a car accident. For that matter, so could you; so could any of us." Fiona's voice was gentle and kind. "Why are you fretting about something you have no control over? Don't you know you have to take happiness and love when and where you find it? If you love him and you know that he truly, deeply, madly loves you—and deserves you—then give yourself to him without condition."

"I do. I know all of that!" If I hadn't been out of tears, Fiona's compassionate tone would have prompted a complete deluge of waterworks.

Janie's voice cut through the prolonged silence. "Elizabeth thinks..." I glanced at her through my fingers. She waited for me to pull my hands from my face before she continued. "Elizabeth *used to* think, and I'm not so sure whether she still does, that people only have one great love...that you can only fall in love once."

This proclamation was met with silence and furrowed brows of confusion and incredulity.

"What are you, a Disney princess?" Ashley's annoyed outburst surprised the room. She dropped her knitting to her lap and glared at me, apparently sincerely perturbed by Janie's revelation. "Get over yourself! We all have to fall in love more than once—even if it's with the same person."

"It's true." Fiona nodded. "Greg and I fall in and out of love constantly, depending on what time of the month it is, how much sleep I've gotten, and whether he's done the dishes within the last three days."

Ashley snapped her fingers and pointed at Fiona. "Right! That! See? It doesn't matter how much you avoid it; love finds you. Love will hunt you down, throw you over its shoulder, pull you kicking and screaming caveman style by the hair, and bludgeon you with its love club until you submit. It's the most relentless force in the universe. There is nowhere you can run—"

"Ok, Dirty Harry." Fiona lifted her voice over Ashley's impassioned monologue. "I think we can all agree that you've made your thoughts on the subject very clear."

"So what am I supposed to do? I'm just supposed to wait around until we've spent enough time trying each other out? I can't stand the thought of him being hurt. I can't stand the way he's hurting me. I can't go through this again." My heart already felt shredded.

"Too damn bad, blondie." Ashley cocked a single eyebrow and pinned me with her blue eyes. "The love beast has reared its ugly head, and your flesh is lunch, dinner, and dessert."

"Love beast?" Marie and Sandra both said at the same time.

Ashley *tsked* then picked up her knitting again. "You know what I mean—and damn it all, I've dropped another stitch!"

"Elizabeth, what is it that you want?" Fiona's eyes searched mine. "It sounds like you've admitted to falling in love with him."

"I have. I do. I love him. I insanely love him." I studied my fingers.

"Then what is the problem?" I glanced up to find Marie, and everyone else, watching me with plain confusion.

"I don't want to lose him, and I don't want him to leave me." There. I admitted it.

"Why do you think that's going to happen?" Kat said.

I fixed my attention back on my twisting fingers. "Well, when he says things like 'let's just take it one day at a time', and 'we'll try each other out for a while and see if it works', and 'maybe we need a little distance to figure this out', then yes. Maybe he's being reasonable and I can't see reason, but I suddenly feel like I'm a pair of shoes, and he hasn't made up his mind whether or not he wants to buy me. Meanwhile I'm at the bottom of the ocean, drowning in it, over my head in love with him."

The room was silent for a long moment. When I briefly looked up from my hands, my gaze snagged Fiona's. She was smiling at me softly, gently.

"But didn't you just say you needed time?"

"No! I mean...yes, I needed, like, ten seconds of time to figure out if I'm ok with him taking some time! ...and I don't think I'm ok with it. I don't want him to have any time that isn't me and him time. I'm tired of alone time. I want us, all the time!"

"Elizabeth, have you told Nico this is how you feel?"

I shook my head. "I tried! I really, really tried. But he...he wouldn't listen. Especially after what happened yesterday, now he's saying cracked things like I'm in danger because of him. He's making me crazy! I don't even know how I feel other than miserable. What am I supposed to do? Ask *him* to marry me?"

She nodded. "Yes."

I blinked, flinched, and wrinkled my nose. "That's preposterous."

"It sounds like he's trying to give you space. It sounds to me like he's wanted you all along, and he's been waiting for you to play catch-up."

I gazed into her elfish eyes, considering her words. "I feel like I'm losing him."

"Then go find him."

"How?"

"Tell him how you feel."

"Except for this morning, after the fancy stalker episode, he won't take my calls. I've tried calling him nonstop for the last four days and he doesn't pick up. And today he told me that I shouldn't call him again this week!"

Every day without talking to him had been torture, and now that I had talked to him, the idea of going another four days made me feel sick. What made it worse was that I didn't know what to expect at the end of those four days. Obviously because I loved punishing myself, I slept in his bed. It still smelled like him. I was pathetic.

"Have you tried asking his mother to help?"

"Yes, I'm ashamed to say, I asked for her help on Sunday. But he won't listen to her; he only responds with texts."

"Then go to him."

I *tsked* nonchalantly, but new tears of frustration ebbed near the surface. "I can't. I can't fly out to New York, ask him to marry me, live through his rejection, and make it back here in time for my next shift."

"Yes you can, and he won't reject you," Janie said.

Fiona and I turned our attention to her hazel eyes. She was making progress on her crochet washcloth. "Really? How?"

"Take Quinn's jet." She shrugged. "He can have it ready to go in an hour."

"He wouldn't do that for me."

"But he'd do it for me." Janie glanced up, her golden eyes sparkling.

"I can't—"

"Yes. Yes you can." Sandra abruptly stood and pointed at everyone in the room with a sweeping motion. "From the sound of it, you were miserable before the fancy stalker episode. I know you've been through a lot, Elizabeth, but if you don't do this, you're just going to continue being miserable with regret. And to make sure that you do, because I've learned how you like to chicken-shit out of stuff, we're all going with you!"

"Yes! I love it!" Ashley smiled for the first time that night. "Call Quinn, Janie. Let's go now!"

"Wait!" *What?* I felt like I was being slapped awake from a trance.

"I'll text him to meet us at the airport." Janie pulled out her cell phone, which she was still getting used to, and began to tap the screen.

"This is madness." I shook my head. "He's probably taping his show. How am I ever going to get past security?" I shook my head.

After four days of moping and waiting, I couldn't quite follow the conversation. I was stunned at the swiftness with which my knitting group had decided my future.

"We'll worry about that later," Marie said, and along with everyone else, she had already started packing up her knitting bag.

Fiona reached for my hand and squeezed it. "Go to him, Elizabeth. Go to him and tell him you want to marry him. Tell him that you can't live without him."

"Right now, I feel like I can't even breathe without him."

"Good." She winked at me. "Men love that kind of stuff."

~*~*~*~

The next hour was a blur.

I had to hand it to Quinn, though. The man had mad skills and was, honestly, a bit of a badass. The plane was ready and waiting to depart by the time we all arrived. Quinn gave us an overview of the plan—his plan—as soon as we were buckled up.

There would be a limo waiting for us at the airport. It would drive us directly to where Nico filmed his show. I would have one hour to find, talk to, and resolve things with Nico before I had to be back in the car on the way to the airport to make it back for Angelica's infusion and my 11:00 pm shift at the hospital.

At one point Sandra asked, "What about security? Nico's security? How do we get past them?"

Quinn's mouth hooked to the side, he raised a single eyebrow, and he pinned her with his steady icicle gaze. "I am security."

I think everyone but me swooned a little, even Fiona. I rolled my eyes and scoff-snorted.

Typical Quinn.

Everything was going according to plan except me. I was freezing up with anxiety. I played the words I would say to him over and over in my head, working through the moves like a chess game, continually changing them. In my mind, the conversation ended in disaster each time, with him wanting space or telling me I was too late.

I realized there were a million ways he could reject me, and only one way to accept me. The odds were not in my favor.

I was also feeling a little ridiculous. I could just wait until he returned from New York in a week and have this conversation with him then. But part of me felt like that would be too late. If I waited 'til then, he might not believe me; he might force us into relationship limbo because he was afraid of pushing me.

Waiting would be rational and reasonable and completely suffocating.

We pulled up to the giant skyscraper that held Nico's studio. My fingers were talons, gripping the leather bench. I glanced around the car at my good friends who always had my back: Janie, Quinn, Kat, Marie, Sandra, Ashley, and Fiona. They were all watching me, waiting for me to move.

"Go get him." Fiona whispered on my left.

"We'll run interference!" Sandra smiled; it was a big goofy grin followed by two thumbs up.

I almost choked.

"Let's go." Quinn exited the car first then pointed to me. "You. Out. Now."

I released an unsteady breath and allowed my friends to push me from the car. They filed out soon after. Quinn was already walking and I jogged to keep up with him. I shook my hands, opening and closing my fingers. My heart was racing. There was no turning back now.

He led us past a pair of armed guards then through a back door then down a series of hallways. We sounded like a disorganized army clomping through the sterile passageway. Quinn stopped at an elevator, which we all crammed into and took to the fortieth floor.

I was lost in my own head and allowed myself to be guided through the maze. We stopped while Quinn engaged in a discussion with a tall, intimidating looking man wearing a black suit. Another man wearing a flannel shirt walked up; he had a large headset—the double headphone kind—strapped to his ears. He was shaking his head.

Quinn pointed to me. The man glanced at me, frowned, then shook his head. I stepped forward so that I could hear the conversation.

"...I can't let you on the set; it's a live taping, and the audience is full."

"When my people called they said Mr. Moretti would be free until eight." Quinn's voice was deadpan.

"The schedule had to change. One of our guests had a conflict. I'm sorry but we can't let anyone out or in for the next ninety minutes. I'll be able to take you backstage where you can wait until the show is over."

My heart dropped to my feet and I wanted to scream *Oh the humanity!* But I restrained myself when I remembered what had happened the last time I had screamed on impulse in the middle of a crowd.

I could feel Quinn gathering his scariness around him like a weapon. He stood a little taller, his eyes grew a little colder—if that were possible—and his air became a bit more menacing. I held out hope that he would be able to bully us into the studio and I'd find a way to talk to Nico alone.

Meanwhile, Mr. Headphones glanced at me again, did a double take and a once-over—obviously absorbing my scrubs, braid, lack of makeup, and the smudges under my eyes—and said, "Wait a minute, are you...?" He crossed his arms. "Aren't you Elizabeth Finney, Nico's doctor lady?"

I nodded, unable to stem the verbal geyser that spewed forth. "Listen, I just need five minutes. Five minutes. I need to talk to him now—right now. But it's ok if you can't make that happen. And it can't wait; it's an emergency. Well, not a real emergency;

just an emergency to me. I know I'm acting like a crazy person, but I've flown in from Chicago, and I can't believe I'm asking you to interrupt his show, and it's very selfish of me and unprofessional, so I completely understand if you have to say no— no pressure or worries—but I have to see him or else…or else…or else I might die, not actually die, just die a little, every day, on the inside, knowing that I could have done something but didn't. Which will likely make me die sooner—but it won't be your fault, but in a way I guess it would be."

I wondered if he followed my path of mixed messages because I didn't. During my nonsensical tirade, the ladies huddled around us, and I felt all their eyes behind me, watching the man with the headphones, waiting for his verdict. He surveyed me for a long moment, his face a scrunched-up mess of amusement and confusion.

He crossed his arms over his chest. "What do you want to talk to Nico about?"

"I want to ask him to marry me."

He nodded thoughtfully. He stroked his chin. If he was surprised, he didn't show it. "You'll have to do it in front of everyone."

I thought about this for a split second then nodded my head. "Ok. I can do that."

"And you'll have to get his attention as part of the show. I have no way of letting him know you're out there."

I twisted my fingers. "What can I do?"

"Have you watched the show?"

I shook my head.

"You have to get naked." The answer came from Sandra on my right. Everyone looked at her, their expressions serious. "Remember, I'm a fan of the show. First of all, you have to be wearing your underwear just to be in the front-most audience section. If you want to make it on stage then you have to get naked, or at least mostly naked, or be a crazy good dancer. The dancers pick out members of the audience to come up and dance with them.

The man spoke up again. "But even then, you're still in a crowd of people about thirty feet or so from Nico."

I clenched my teeth, inhaled and exhaled through my nose, then started to undress.

"Oh my god." Ashley and Sandra held hands. Everyone else watched me with stunned disbelief.

Janie tugged on my arm. "It's like our panty parties. Do you want me to go with you?"

"No!" Quinn shook his head. "Absolutely not."

"She has a point, actually." Marie gave Quinn then me a practical smile. "If we all go in there, we'll have a better chance of getting his attention."

Quinn looked at the ceiling as though appealing to a higher power. "This is ridiculous."

"That's true." The man nodded at Marie. "Most people are just trying to get attention for themselves, but if all of you went in there and tried to help Elizabeth, Dr. Finney, get on stage, she'd have a higher chance of success."

"That means you too, Quinn." Fiona lifted her eyebrows at him even as she pulled off her shoes. "If I have to go out there and dance in my underwear after having two kids, then you better start stripping."

Quinn released a breath through his nose that reminded me of a horse, but I knew he would be undone by one pleading look from Janie. Some of my frayed nerves were calmed by the realization that my girls would be going with me. I would not be alone, and at the very least, I would be able to tease Quinn Sullivan about this moment for the rest of my life.

I was down to my lacy black bra and matching, thankfully modest, boy shorts first.

Ashley was next. "Thank god I shaved yesterday!"

Sandra was stripped to her underwear soon after. "I didn't, but I need to. No one look at my downtown."

"I need to take you all to get waxed." Marie sashayed out of her jeans.

"No, thank you, waxing is medieval. Do my stretch marks look terrible?" Fiona pointed to a nonexistent mark on her side.

"You look beautiful." Kat folded her clothes and handed them to the headphone guy.

"Can I leave my shoes on? Or do I have to go barefoot?" Janie's red shoes matched her fire engine red panty and bra set.

"Does it make a difference?" Quinn, we all tried not to notice, filled out his grey boxer briefs exceptionally well.

She nodded. "With my shoes on I'm almost as tall as you. Between the two of us I'm sure we can draw some attention."

"Lady, you're going to draw attention, but it will have very little to do with your height." Mr. Headphones regretted his words almost as soon as he said them when he found himself face to neck with Quinn.

"Watch your mouth and keep your eyes to yourself."

"Ok." Fiona pulled Quinn back a little. "Ok. We'll measure testosterone levels later. Let's just get in there before the hour is up."

CHAPTER 28

Sandra explained the typical order of the show: opening monologue, sketches, celebrity guests, live musical performance or comedy bit, celebrity guest, dancing, then Jell-O wrestling.

We snuck in during the live musical performance to cover the sound of our entry. The audience relegated to the front was absolutely crazy, but fun crazy. They weren't pushing or shoving. It was more of a club atmosphere than a show or a concert. Two other sections of audience were farther back—in seats and fully dressed. If I hadn't been so keyed up, I might have enjoyed myself. As it was, I had only one goal: to get noticed by one of the dancers and get on the stage.

The group of girls surrounded me, and Quinn helped us push to the front. The stage where the dancers were located was closer to the audience. Nico and his celebrity guests were farther back. There was no way for me to get close enough for him to see me.

The dancers, however, walked back and forth during the live performance, pointing to people in the audience and motioning for them to come up on stage. People who were chosen were few and far between. I noted that only seven or so audience members had made it thus far, and all but two of them were completely naked.

I was about to unclip my bra, but Fiona stilled my hands. "Not yet! I have an idea!" Fiona pulled me to Quinn then hollered something in his ear. His eyebrows jumped, but then he looked at me and shrugged.

Before I was quite aware of what was happening, Quinn had picked me up. "Climb on my shoulders," he bellowed over the music.

I nodded and climbed up his hard torso and bicep with the help of Janie and Sandra. I sat on his shoulders, dually balancing and trying to get the attention of the nearest dancer.

I placed my thumb and forefinger to my lips and made a loud

whistle, perfected after years of hailing cabs in Chicago, then waved my hands in the air as one of the girls approached.

She was a short, curvaceous brunette, and at first she laughed at my antics, but then I saw recognition flicker across her face. She stilled, squinted at me, then pointed.

She mouthed the words *Elizabeth Finney?*

I swallowed, nodded. She smiled. She waved me up, and even over the loud live performance, I could hear my group of girls squee. Ashley gave Quinn a high-five as he deposited me back to the floor. I wobbled up to the stage and was immediately permitted entrance. The brunette crossed to me and offered her hand.

"I'm Erin. What are you doing in the audience? Why aren't you backstage?"

I held Erin's hand like it was a lifeline. "I only have an hour, and I need to talk to Nico."

"What? In front of everyone?"

"Yes. I don't know. I don't care. I just need to tell him…"

Her brown gaze moved over me, a question on her face. "I won't be able to get you to the other stage because the two don't connect. But I can get you a microphone."

The live music ended and the crowd thundered with applause. I glanced up briefly and noticed that I was standing on stage in my underwear in front of a live studio audience of about a thousand people—if not more—and a viewership of millions.

I nodded and squeezed her hand as the applause receded. "Do you think it will be ok for me to interrupt the show?"

She smiled. "Yes!" her voice quieted to a whisper. "Nico loves surprises! Just wait 'til the part where we're supposed to dance, after the next interview. It'll only be another five minutes or so. Let me get the microphone."

She winked at me and left me in a crowd of maybe fifteen naked people and ten dancers in bikinis. But I didn't notice any of them because Nico was speaking, and I wasn't the only one.

The entire studio hushed. He commanded their attention with his twinkly eyes and easy smiles. But, I noted, he didn't look like my Nico. He looked like *the Face*. He even sounded a little different. He introduced his next guest. Everyone was enraptured. I craned my neck, tried to find my girls, and found them watching the show.

They laughed at his jokes, magnetized and transfixed by his charisma, and I wondered why this man—this talented, amazing, generous, smart, funny, kind, sweet man—was at all interested in me. Self-doubt churned in my stomach, but then I reminded myself that the self-doubt, my questioning the veracity of his feelings, was why he'd left me two days ago.

I steeled my resolve. By the time Erin returned with the microphone, I was ready. I was ready to lay it all out there. I was ready to believe in him and us.

The music started, which signified the end of the last celebrity interview, and Nico stood to shake the hand of his guest. I watched on the big screen as he turned to the camera and the audience and wagged his eyebrows.

His voice resounded over the speakers. "I don't know about you, but I think I could go for some Jell-O."

High-pitched female screams and catcalls filled the studio, and I couldn't help but laugh at this caricature of Nico. He looked like a naughty little boy who was asking for dessert, and the audience was eating it up.

The main camera switched to the stage where I stood, and it focused on all the dancers while Nico turned his back to the audience and started to take off his suit. Those audience members who were previously naked had been given some underthings for minimal coverage, most likely so the show would make it past the censors.

Erin and the other dancers did a little routine, and I wondered when I should interrupt. I kept looking to her for a sign. I didn't have to wait very long. Before I knew what was happening they surrounded me and said—in unison, into their headsets—

"Cut the music!"

The audience *woooooed* and clapped, obviously thinking this was all planned. Abruptly, not three seconds later, the music stopped. Erin met my gaze, a big grin on her face, and she whispered, "Go for it!"

I stole glances at the rest of the dancers and found them issuing me equally reassuring smiles. I gulped, breathed out, stepped to the front of the stage, and switched on the microphone. The audience was still applauding.

I endeavored to speak over them, knew it was now or never. "Can I—" I winced at how my voice sounded over the microphone. The crowd quieted down, and their attention shifted to me. I felt the full force of two thousand or more eyes upon me. I gathered another steadying breath and planted my feet on the stage. "Can I have a moment of your time, Nico?"

The studio fell into a hush, and I watched as he turned around, completely perplexed.

"I'm over here, on the other stage." I lifted my hand and waved. A few stragglers moved to the side so that he could have a clear line of sight.

From thirty feet away I saw the crack in his façade. I detected his confusion, my Nico. He leveled me with stunned green eyes. I pushed down my doubt and gained a step toward him as far as I could manage without jumping off the stage.

"I promise this won't take very long. I just wanted to ask you something, and it couldn't wait. But first…" I tried to swallow and failed. "I need you to know that I love you. I love you so much that being without you hurts like…getting tasered or punched in the stomach. I know this because recently I was punched in the stomach." This sentiment elicited a good amount of laughter from the audience, but his mouth didn't move and his expression didn't change.

I gave him a nervous smile and continued. "I can't stop thinking about your smile. I want to keep it in my pocket, keep it just for me, and take it out and look at it a hundred times a day." A few women *aaawwwwed,* and one or two guys yelled out something less than polite but were quickly hushed by a nearby neighbor.

I could discern the heavy rise and fall of his chest, even from my position and the distance between us. His eyes were tangled with mine, beautiful thorny vines. I couldn't read them, but I could see that he was as singularly focused on me as I was on him. The crowd, now silent, completely faded away. It was just him and me, Nico and Elizabeth, and I was cutting myself completely open.

I hoped it would be enough.

"But the thing is, Nico…I can't do this unless I know it's going to be forever. I'm not going to do this half-assed. I can't try this out or try this on like it's a pair of shoes I might want to buy. If we're going to do this, you have to be all in, because I'm not willing to settle for anything less than all of you for as long as we can, for as long as we have. You, us—we're worth the risk."

I tried in vain to wipe the sweaty hand not holding the microphone on my bare thigh. "Therefore and in summary…" my voice was shaking as I got down on one knee, thankful I'd chosen boy shorts as my underwear selection for the day. I was vaguely aware that people around me gasped. "…Nico Mang-gan-aniello," I winced a little as I butchered his last name, "will you do me the honor of becoming my hus—"

"Yes!" He yelled his response before I could finish, and his microphone carried the answer like a gunshot. "Yes, Elizabeth Finney, I will marry you."

I exhaled and immediately closed my eyes, overwhelmed by relief, ready to collapse with it. A smile I was powerless against and tears of joy—the traitors!—brutally ransacked my face. My hands were shaking and so were my knees. At first, I was only dimly aware of the deafening cheer that erupted from the audience, but soon it crashed over me like a wave and engulfed me in its undertow.

I was lifted off my feet by hands, and my eyes opened to find that Nico had jumped off his stage, run through the seated audience, jumped the railing into the crowd then climbed onto my stage. He wrapped me in his arms and held me tight, so tight I thought I might break. But I didn't care.

I didn't care if I broke because I had a forever with Nico to mend, and forever started now.

CHAPTER 29

The first thing Nico did after our embrace was cover me with his suit shirt. The second thing he did was pick me up and carry me off the stage.

The crowd continued to applaud, hoot, and holler like moonshine drunk corn farmers. He ignored the thunder of their approval and, instead, kissed me as he carried me. I didn't notice much; all I wanted to see was him. I was still crying a bit, but the tears were good tears caused by laughter and relief.

Less than a minute later, we were in his dressing room, and he kicked the door shut with his foot. He turned, set me down, and pressed me against the door. His hands lifted to my face and the pads of his thumbs wiped away the watery tracks.

"Where did you come from? How did you get up on the stage?"

I opened my mouth to respond, but before I could, he kissed me. Then he yanked me against him, and his large hands moved into the suit shirt and gripped my bare waist. Abruptly, he retreated, his eyes flashing like fireworks. "Why? Why did you do that?"

Then, once more leaving me no time to respond, he kissed me again. His tongue swept into my mouth, urgent and demanding. Nico greedily pressed his hard lines against my soft curves, pushed me against the door. His roughness was inexorably overpowering; my limbs and brain became useless against the ravenous assault.

Thankfully, he held me in place with his body, his knee between my legs; otherwise I might have dissolved into a puddle of wanton woman on the floor.

"Why didn't you just…" *kiss* "…have them…" *kiss* "…tell me…" *kiss* "…that you were here?" *kiss*.

With Nico interrogating me and kissing me in intervals, I had difficulty comprehending or following his questions. His hands were everywhere, as though checking to confirm I was real. My hands were also everywhere because, dammit, he felt good.

"The guy..." *kiss* "...with the headphones..." *kiss* "...said that he had no way..." *kiss* "...to let you know..." *kiss* "...that we were here."

Nico lifted his head, his eyes hazy even as they searched mine. His hand was under the shirt, absentmindedly caressing me through the lace of my bra. I moaned.

"What guy with headphones?"

My response was breathless. "We saw him outside the studio. Long brown hair, in his forties maybe—"

"Was he wearing a flannel shirt?"

"Yeah. That's him." I arched against him, pressed myself into his palm.

"That son of a bitch." Nico paired his language choice with an acrid smile.

"What?"

"That's my producer, Larry. I-" He hesitated, stole another kiss. "First of all, we moved up the taping schedule today because I was going to fly back to Chicago tonight." Nico paused, his eyes examining my face. "I had to see you. You need to know, you must know, as long as you'll have me I'm yours. God, Elizabeth-" he grimaced as though in pain and his hands tightened on my body, "- I've been going crazy, every day, you're all I think about. When I close my eyes you're all I see. I need you." he brushed a soft, lingering kiss against my mouth, "I love you."

"Oh." My face crumpled a little and my heart expanded until my chest felt full. "Nico...."

"I'm so sorry I wasn't there."

"And I'm sorry I was so awful to you. I'm sorry for everything."

His eyes were twinkling and dreamy. I lost myself for a moment in their depths before I realized that he was speaking again.

"Wait, what?"

His eyes narrowed teasingly. "I said, Larry could've easily told me you were here. I wear an earpiece while onstage. He must've…he must've seen an opportunity for a ratings stunt."

"He also said you wouldn't be offstage for another ninety minutes but it's only been thirty or so."

"I'm going to kill him. What a bastard."

"Let's plot his death later. I have to leave in seven minutes if I'm going to make it back to Chicago in time."

Nico blinked at me. My words had an immediate sobering effect. "You have to go back? Tonight?"

I nodded. "I have to get back for the infusion, and I have a late-night shift."

"No…." He shook his head. "No, no, no—why are you going to work? Shouldn't you be taking time off?"

I stroked his back, loved that I could touch him. I never wanted to take that for granted. "It's ok. I'm really fine."

"You're not fine." His brow pulled into a deep V. "Don't tell me you're fine."

"I have a plan."

His frown intensified. "Well, let's hear it."

"I'm going to…." I cleared my throat, firmed my voice. "I'm going to see someone, a psychiatrist, a friend of Sandra's. And I'm going to cut back on double shifts."

"For how long?"

"The next two weeks."

Nico considered me as he mulled over this information. "I'm glad you're going to see someone. That's really good. But you just went through something extremely stressful. Don't you think you need some time off?" He didn't look convinced.

"Well," I continued, as I brought the back of my hand to his stomach and brushed my knuckles against his bare skin. "I'm going to ask for a few days off."

Finally, his eyes brightened. "Ok. Good. That's good."

"I'm glad you approve." I cupped his cheeks and brought his face to mine to place a gentle kiss on his lips. "I have three minutes left."

"I can't leave till after the next taping." His eyes moved between mine. After a moment, his forehead fell to my shoulder. "Damn. This sucks."

"Yes…I agree."

"I thought . . ." His voice was muffled by my neck. He placed a wet kiss just under my ear, making me shiver. "I wanted to explain, about Friday. I thought I'd scared you, Friday morning, when I told you what I wanted—when I told you I wanted to marry you. I pushed you into this, I know that, but I shouldn't have left angry. I should have waited until we had time to talk, come to an agreement."."

"You overreacted."

He nodded. "I did."

"It's okay." I waited until he met my gaze before continuing, "In case you haven't noticed, I am an expert on overreacting. You're forgiven as long as you forgive me."

"For what?"

"For the multitude of mistakes I've made as well as the ones I haven't made yet. There will be many. It's my talent, making mistakes. My expertise is overreacting and my talent is making mistakes."

"Well, then, we have that in common." His mouth tilted in a sheepish smirk.

I glanced at the ceiling; our nookie window was closed. But, that was ok. There were nights and nights and days and nights of nookie ahead of us. I threaded my fingers into the hair at the back of his neck.

"Do you—" I cleared my throat. "Do you still want to marry me?"

"Oh god, yes." He kissed me again, unhurried, measured, for a full minute. Upon separating, we both sighed.

"You need to know, about that morning when you asked me to marry you, I wasn't scared so much as surprised. I…." I held him tighter and spoke to his lips. "I haven't thought about getting married and spending my life with someone…not since I was fifteen."

He nuzzled my neck. "Like having kids?"

"Like having kids."

Slowly he pulled away—but not completely. Nico wrapped a possessive arm around my waist and led me to the couch. He sat first then pulled me to his lap; my knees were on either side of him, my arms draped over his shoulders. A twinkly, content gaze caressed my face.

He looked happy, and I realized that I was also happy. I smiled. It was a stupid, blissful smile. I was in goofy-love.

"So…what now?" I nipped his juicy bottom lip.

"Now?" Nico tugged me closer until our chests were flush. He brushed his lips against mine and said, "Now we have a lot to discuss."

"Discuss?"

"Yes. Lots of discussions."

"And touching? Lots of touching too?"

"Yes. Lots of that. Discussions and touching."

"And stroking?"

He grinned, his eyes now smoldering lethally. "Rest assured, there will be touching of all kinds…a virtual cornucopia of touching…a touching feast."

"Good. Then what?"

"Then we get married, then a lot more touching and maybe fewer discussions for a while."

"I have one and a half minutes left before I have to leave. Do you want to start now?"

"Yes. First, you need to learn how to pronounce my last name—
"

"Ok. That seems fair."

"—since it'll be your last name soon, too."

"What? No. I'm not changing my last name. Not going to happen."

"Ne parleremo più tardi[35]."

A-a-a-a-and my honorary Italian lady parts stand at attention.

"Ah! Nico!" I sucked in a sharp breath, "You're not allowed!"

"Ok, ok. No more Italian." He petted me, his hands caressing me under the suit shirt. His movements were deliberate, a fondling stroke from my back to my bottom; then he squeezed. "For now."

I glowered at him in an attempt to restrain all my lady minions. "So what's the next item on the list?"

"We need to discuss our arrangement."

"Uh…we have an arrangement?"

"Yes. We have an arrangement. Our friends without benefits arrangement."

"O-k-a-y. I thought that we were—I thought—I mean we've—"

"We haven't officially ended the arrangement."

"But we *are* getting married."

"Yes. We are. Therefore, I think we should officially end our friends without benefits arrangement and replace it with a new friends with benefits arrangement."

"A friends *with* benefits arrangement?"

"Yes."

"Hmm…" I eyeballed him. "What kind of benefits?"

"All benefits. A full benefits arrangement from A to Z, in sickness and in health, nothing held back." As though to emphasize his point, he kissed my chest.

"So…you'll let me borrow your T-shirts?"

---

[35]Translation: We'll talk later.

"Yeah, sure."

"And you'll make me more mix-tapes about us?"

He lifted a single brow, putting me on eye-twinkle-twinkle-little-star alert. "You finally caught on to that, did you? You wicked creature...."

I couldn't suppress my grin but continued as though he hadn't spoken. "And I'll knit you scarves."

"Ok. I like scarves. Can you make me one with Space Invaders?"

"Pashaw! Yeah! I'm a really good knitter."

"I know."

"And you'll learn how to crochet?"

He nodded once. "I'm already learning."

"And how to knit?"

"Don't push it."

"Apple fritters?"

He wagged his eyebrows, his eyes dancing beneath. "Definitely."

"And we'll take trips together, and visit your family—"

"We'll visit your family."

I rolled my lips between my teeth then paused. Before I could answer, I had to gather a deep breath. "Yeah...."

"We'll visit your dad and go to his wedding."

I nodded. I had to clear my throat before answering. "Yes. We'll go to his wedding and we'll be happy for him, for them." And I meant it.

"And we'll be happy."

I tightened my arms around his neck. "Always."

"Well..." he said, and then he lifted his chin, his mouth curved into a devastating, charismatic, sex-on-an-Italian-stick smile. "Almost always."

Epilogue

Part 1: Meet seventeen year-old Nico

Soft skin. Shaking hands. Hot breath.

She swallowed. I felt the movement of her throat under my mouth. She was nervous. So was I. My hands were also shaking. *Shit.* This was crazy.

But, just because it was crazy didn't mean I was going to stop. Stopping hadn't even crossed my mind. What did cross my mind? *More.*

My insanity was fueled by fifteen years of wanting to touch her and six years of watching someone else do it. I was seventeen, but jealousy and envy burned long and cut deep.

I knew I wanted to be with her since before I knew how to eat with a fork. The wanting to touch her part started when I was four and she was three. Obviously it wasn't sexual, that came later accompanied by the resentment of rejection. It was about being close to her, kissing her big cheeks, petting her soft skin, sharing her warmth. My earliest memory was thinking that I wanted her to stay with me always. My mother liked to remind me that I used to ask if we could keep her.

My present reality—her naked, yielding breast beneath my hand, her hips straddling mine, her underwear and my jeans separating us—was its own kind of torture. She didn't respond like the other girls. She wasn't waiting for me to undress her.

She was tearing at my clothes, pressing her breast into my palm, and rocking against me. I wasn't waiting for her. She was waiting for me.

This was crazy.

I should have questioned it. I should have stopped her. But when the girl of your dreams climbs in your bedroom window and starts taking off her clothes, thinking has very little to do with what happens next.

I only knew I wanted her. I wanted her loyalty, I wanted her acceptance, I wanted her admiration; I wanted all the things she gave to others without thought, but had withheld from me for years.

She reached between us and beneath my pants, lifting on her knees and slipping her hand inside my boxers. The sheets rustled. She stroked. I shuddered. I was already painfully hard and I wondered if she knew the difference. Probably not. Her blue eyes, naïve and unsure, were assessing. She stroked again.

"Stop—don't." I grabbed her wrist to still her exploration, gritted my teeth. "What are you doing?"

"Am I doing it wrong?" She whispered; her eyes were narrowed, as though she were calculating a solution to a problem.

"No." I breathed out. Definitely not.

"Good." She licked her lips and I was mute.

I didn't respond. I didn't have a chance. Her mouth crashed to mine—all slippery lips, teeth, and tongue. It was untutored, sloppy, insistent. I withdrew her fingers from my pants and placed them on my shoulder. My hands lifted to the hot, tortuously silken skin of her back and brought her completely against me, her naked chest meeting mine. I groaned.

I was aching.

I was in pain.

She rocked her hips against me again—a jerky, instinctual, unpracticed movement—and I couldn't breathe. She broke the kiss, roughly tugged off my pants and shorts, discarded the last of her clothes, then pulled me on top of her. The bed squeaked.

I came to her willingly. Her legs were open. I wanted to feel her everywhere. My hands were greedy as they stroked, touched, grabbed every inch I'd been denied. Her eyes were fixed on mine.

"Let's do this." She nodded, her nails dug into my back as though anchoring me to her.

"What are we doing?" I didn't know who I was asking—me or

her.

When I hesitated she lifted her hips to mine. "Nico. . ." Elizabeth placed a tiny kiss on the corner of my mouth. "Please. Please do this for me." She was looking at me with trust, like she needed me; that look annihilated any remaining capacity for thought.

If I'd been thinking I would have done something to prepare her. But I wasn't. I wasn't thinking about anything except her softness, the wet warmth between her legs, and the painful stiffness between mine.

She gasped as I entered her. Her gaze moved to a place over my shoulder and tears gathered in her eyes. She gritted her teeth. She was tense everywhere.

She was holding her breath and the only sound in the room was my labored breathing. I told myself to go slow. Her leg brushed against mine, the inside of her thigh against my hip. I wanted to touch her so I did. I skimmed my fingertips up the back of her leg, from her bottom to her knee, as I moved inside her.

She closed her eyes, released a breath, but was still frozen beneath me.

I'd been with virgins before. But—virgin or not—this was the first time that I'd cared so much about whether the girl enjoyed it. I made myself stop while still buried inside her and bit her neck. I tasted the skin beneath her jaw then dipped my tongue in her earlobe. I slid my hand from her leg, along her side, and pinched the puckered skin of her breast.

Please.

I needed her to relax. She moaned. I moved.

Please.

I needed her to enjoy this. Her breath hitched.

Please.

I *needed* her to let me touch her again when this was over.

Part 2: Meet thirty-two year-old Nico

When I walk on a stage or in front of a camera it's easy to become *The Face*. People make it easy. They want arrogance and dirty jokes and I love acting conceited and telling dirty jokes.

Win-win.

In fact, when I fly first class, when I walk down the street, when I stop by a drug store to buy detergent and gum—it's effortless. I am who people expect me to be. I know so many punch lines, I don't even bother with the jokes anymore.

When I'm interviewed about the show—or, more recently, my movies—it's usually by some spray tan female with fake tits. She always asks about objectification. It makes me laugh. Now *there* is a joke.

Some bimbo, three chromosomes away from a blowup doll, is asking me about objectifying women. Meanwhile she's slipping me her number, her hand is rubbing *do me* circles on my thigh, and she's shoving her silicon sweater puppets in my face.

Don't misunderstand, I'm not complaining, not even a little. I love my job most of the time. I love what I do. Making people laugh gets me high every time. Every. Single. Time. My life is filled with moments of pure ecstasy; moments when I can get a crowd laughing so hard, every individual audience member has their eyes closed and they're fighting to breathe.

Nothing matters; everything that came before and all worries about the future cease to have relevance. They fade away.

A perfect moment. . . and then it's over.

It's a feeling almost impossible to duplicate or eclipse.

I've only felt something that surpassed it three times in my life. All three times were with the same girl and, during all three of those times, the moment crested over days and weeks, if not months. Obviously, I'm in love with her. But, she's not just the girl

I love. She's the girl I've hungered for, the girl I've worshipped for the majority of my life.

This is *the* girl.

The first time was almost exactly sixteen years ago, after our best friend died. I climbed in her window, found her staring at the ceiling. She'd just showered and her hair was so wet it soaked through the feathers of her pillow.

She looked at me as I approached; I saw that she wasn't crying, not anymore, but she had been crying recently. She was devastated, near despair; sorrow that's impossible to escape. She was drowning in it.

And I remember thinking that she was beautiful. Even in her grief she was beyond lovely to me.

I didn't pause to consider my actions; I just lay next to her, gathered her small body in my arms, and held her to my chest. That's how I discovered her hair and pillow were wet.

I don't know how long we lay like that, but it couldn't have been more than an hour. I shifted because my arm was asleep and she reached out for me.

She grabbed my shirt in both of her fists, like a person does when they're startled or afraid.

She said, "Stay with me." When I didn't immediately respond she added, "I need you to stay with me."

It knocked the wind from my lungs. It was like I was flying and falling at the same time. I'm sure she had no idea. But, for me, it was a perfect moment. I felt ten feet tall.

For years afterward I would think about it and the days that followed; about how, during those weeks, she needed me. For a long time it was the best and the worst period of my life. I used it as fuel for my early standup routines and learned quickly that bitterness in comedy is rarely funny—and funny only if it's also sincerely self-deprecating.

The second time occurred just before we got married. She

surprised me while I was taping my show in front of a studio audience of hundreds in New York City. I was undressing—as I always do—at the end, preparing to Jell-O wrestle with two closet lesbians who got a huge kick out of elbowing me in the face and other essential body parts.

I heard her. Of course, at first, I thought it was feedback from my earpiece or my mind playing tricks on me. But it wasn't. It was her.

I didn't comprehend everything she said, but I did comprehend that she was in a black bra and underwear. Well, at least everything below my waist comprehended her lack of clothing because it immediately reacted to her, to her body. I loved her body. Thoughts of it kept me up at night; what I wanted to do to it, how I wanted to touch and taste it.

She was standing on the dancer's stage, looking at me. Despite the distance between us, she was really looking at me. One of her hands was holding a microphone, the other was palm out and toward me, beseeching.

Then I heard her say, "But the thing is, Nico. . . I need you."

It didn't really matter what she said next, what she asked. I would have said yes to anything. I would have given her anything. Not to get too Italian and melodramatic about it, but if she'd asked me to cut out my heart I would have. But she wouldn't want that.

I trust her. I know she wants my heart in one piece and she always has.

I am of the opinion that women don't really understand men. Most men, real men would do anything for the woman they love. When a man loves a woman enough to marry her, he loves her to the point of obsession. It's the devotion of a male for his mate.

He watches her sleep. He smells her clothes searching for her scent. He craves her admiration like a drug. He lives for her smile, for her laugh, and especially for her touch.

Being needed—by his woman—is ecstasy for a man.

Which leads me to the third time Elizabeth surprised me. It happened just recently and made me think that maybe I have many more of these moments in my future. Maybe I'm one of those blessed bastards whose life will be a series of perfect moments.

We're at a really good point in our relationship and still live in the Windy City. I'd moved the show once we were married and most of the cast moved with me. Over the summers I was filming movies and Elizabeth would come along. She never had any trouble finding a visiting clinician program.

Publicity died down fairly soon after the wedding. The asshole photographers basically disappeared or, when they did pop up, kept their distance.

I guess people are less interesting once they get married.

Regardless, the citizens of Chicago never seemed to make a big deal about us. I was hardly ever approached. And, when I was, it was usually by a tourist.

On this particular day we were in the park, specifically the concrete benches next to Crown Fountain; although, most of the locals just call it The Faces. I was sitting and she was lying on her side, her head was in my lap, watching people as they watched the interactive artwork.

My hand wound around her long braid and I moved my thumb over the silk of her hair. I loved it when she wore her hair like this. Call me sick and twisted, but I loved tugging on her braid or ponytail to get her attention. Maybe it was a holdover from when we were kids, but I didn't think so because—in retaliation, but only rarely—she'd grab a handful of my hair and pull a lot harder than necessary.

This always made me want to rip her clothes off.

Elizabeth seemed to expect and accept that teasing was going to be a constant in our relationship. Getting a rise out of her wasn't as easy as it used to be, with her love came patience. But I didn't mind, because truly flustering her was a lot easier now that I was allowed to touch her whenever I wanted.

And I wanted. I wanted a lot.

Elizabeth shifted on my lap. "I spoke to Angelica this morning."

"Really? Is something wrong? I just talked to her two days ago."

"No, she's great. She's doing really great. We talked about her friends. The homeschool group your mom has her in seems to really be working out well and she's started ballet class."

I nodded though I felt uneasy about the dance classes. "I knew about the homeschool group; I didn't know that mom had decided on the ballet."

"It's a small class and I talked to the teacher about arranging a special cleaning of the studio. I think it'll be really good for her."

"You talked to the teacher?"

She shrugged, her eyes focused on something in the distance. "Yes. I thought we could drive down there next weekend and visit."

"Definitely. I want to meet the teacher, make sure she understands the situation."

"Nico, the exercise will be good for improving her lung function."

I grunted my response.

"See that lady over there?" Elizabeth, perhaps trying to change the subject, indicated with her chin toward a woman about thirty or so feet from where we were.

I glanced at a woman, maybe in her mid-fifties, hard to tell. "Yeah."

"Every time one of the faces smiles she also smiles."

I returned my attention to Elizabeth. "How long have you been watching her?"

"About five minutes. Wait—just watch—she's about to do it." I didn't watch the woman. Instead, I watched Elizabeth, full of expectation. I knew the moment the other woman smiled because

Elizabeth's grin was immense.

"See? Did you see that?" She sighed, looked happy. "She has a great smile."

I responded without thinking about it, "You have a great smile."

Elizabeth turned her head, still on my lap; her blue eyes met mine then flickered over my face. "I'm going to start calling you Romeo."

"Why is that?"

"Because you're Mr. Romantic. It's taken me a while to become accustomed to it, and it used to make me crazy, but I think I'm finally ready to accept the compliments."

"Should I call you my Juliet?"

"No. Juliet is universally acknowledged to be an idiot. If you're going to call me a Shakespearian something, Beatrice from Much Ado About Nothing fits best."

I barked a laugh. "Yeah. *My lady tongue.*"

She wrinkled her nose. "You like my tongue."

"Yes. I do." I nodded, tugged her braid so that her chin and mouth jutted upward, "I like everything about it."

"I accept that compliment, Romeo," She sounded breathless, "and I raise you a compliment about your hands."

I felt my body involuntarily stiffen. Judging by the wicked glint in her eye, she felt it too.

"Elizabeth. . ."

"Romeo. . ."

I ground my teeth. Her smart mouth made coherent thought difficult at times. This frustrated me because she was an excellent thinker. Usually, when this happened, I'd speak in Italian. However, at present, we were in a very public place; and I'd promised early on in our marriage never to speak Italian in public again.

Sometimes I even kept that promise.

She lifted her fingers and placed them over mine where I held her braid captive; she then stroked from my arm to my shoulder. "You need to learn how to take a compliment, Romeo."

"Forgive me, Beatrice," I bent closer and released her braid, instead moved my hand to cradle the back of her head. "But I'm still not used to *your* compliments."

She *tsked*. "That's a shame." Our noses touched; her nails gently scratched my neck. "I should give them more often."

"Yes, you should." I nodded my agreement because I did agree, and nipped her pouty bottom lip. I freely admit: I liked to be stroked everywhere, including my ego.

"Here's one," She leaned back; her eyes—so lovely, so brilliant—searched mine and I experienced a moment of perfection, of bliss when she said, "My Nico, you're going to make an excellent father."

The End

About the Author

This is the second full length novel published by Penny Reid. Her days are spent writing federal grant proposals for biomedical research; her evenings are either spent playing dress-up and mad-scientist with her two people-children (boy-6, girl-4) or knitting with her knitting group at her local yarn store (Silver Linings in Tampa, Florida). Please feel free to drop her a line. She'd be happy to hijack your thoughts!

Come find me-

Email: pennreid@gmail.com (sign up for the mailing list to receive exclusive excerpts from my next book)
Blog: reidromance.blogspot.com/
Twitter: twitter.com/ReidRomance
Ravelry: ravelry.com/people/ReidRomance (if you crochet or knit…!)
Goodreads: goodreads.com/ReidRomance
"The Facebook": facebook.com/PennyReidWriter

Please, write a review!

If you liked this book (and, more importantly perhaps, if you didn't like it) please take a moment to post a review someplace (Amazon, Goodreads, your blog, on a bathroom stall wall, in a letter to your mother, etc.). It helps society more than you know when you make your voice heard; reviews force us to move towards a true meritocracy.

-Book List/Plan, Knitting in the City Series-

Book 1: Neanderthal Seeks Human: A Smart Romance, March 2013 (Janie and Quinn)

Book 1.5: Neanderthal Marries Human: A Smarter Romance, June 2014 (Janie and Quinn)

Book 2: Friends Without Benefits: Another Smart Romance, October 2013 (Elizabeth and Nico)

Book 3: Love Hacked, March 2014 (Sandra)

Book 4: Beauty and the Mustache, September 2014 (Ashley)

Book 5: (Fiona)

Book 6: (Marie)

Book 7: (Kat)

Acknowledgements

If you know me then you know I like to acknowledge people. I mourn the lost decades of hats that can be tipped.

First and foremost, I want to thank my husband. He had to live through my disbelief and rampant weirded-outness when *Neanderthal Seeks Human* was well received by strangers. Because of this, I feel sorry for him and will purchase him ice cream where ever we go from now on (contingent on the availability of ice cream). And, for whatever reason, he believes in me. I still don't know why but I'm very thankful.

I want to thank all the people who had a hand in editing this book (content edits, development edits, typos, line edits, copy edits, edit edits). This list is long, so bear with me.

To my primary BETAs, Karen and Penny, who read the book as it is written and offer feedback and encouragement. Thank God for you both!

To my secondary BETAs (aka beta BETAs) Jexa, Angie, Silvia, Laura, Cat; your brutal honesty and detailed notes took this book from mediocre to magnificent (yes, I just called my own book magnificent). Thank you so, so, much for disliking the first draft. It was crap.

To Heather (my BFF) for reading the final content draft and giving me the thumbs up.

To my professional editors, Kristin and Janet, thank you for your thoughtful reviews and edits.

And to Michelle, Kimberly, and Carey, friends and authors who provided the essential last read-through/proofread. Michelle, I love your face. Kimberly, you are a ninja. Carey, you are a gorgeous goofball. I love you all.

Lastly, I want to thank the amazing community of independent authors and review bloggers on Facebook, Twitter, Goodreads, and elsewhere on the interwebs; especially the bloggers/reviewers who read and review indie books. I am proud to be part of this community of creative and supportive badasses.

I tip my hat to you all.

Sneak Peek of *Love Hacked: A reluctant romance;* book #3 in the Knitting in the City Series, coming March 2014.

CHAPTER 1

He was bald in a way that made me think of both melons and sex. Tan suit, green tie, white shirt—Chuck was a honeydew.

I met Chuck standing in the concession line at a Cubs game. I saw him and just knew, this was the guy. He was *the one* mentioned in my Sunday horoscope. As all very important and highly intelligent females do, I read my horoscope every morning—right after finishing the obituaries and just before I peruse the comics.

That morning my horoscope had read: *Be watchful, today you will meet the catalyst of your future life.*

At the time, when I'd accosted him in line and forced him to talk to me, he'd been wearing a baseball hat. I'd liked his face and his friendly smile. Though I sensed he'd been bewildered and a bit overwhelmed by my attention, he'd readily agreed to the date.

But now, without his hat and illuminated mostly by a single candle on the table, his jaw seemed to mirror the top of his head; it had become a rounded, shiny, nondescript curve of yellowed melon colored flesh.

"The Bella Costa is an excellent vintage. Light on the nose, but a spicy pallet with notes of blackberry and cracked pepper." He smiled at me. He was looking for approval.

My left eyebrow arched all on its own. "Cracked pepper? In wine?"

"Yes." He chuckled. "Forgive me. I'm a bit of a connoisseur, really a student of the grape. Last summer I spent a week at the Louis Martini sommelier workshop in Napa."

"Is that so, Chuck?"

He chuckled again, shook his head.

Chuck the chuckling honeydew.

"You're very funny, Sandra."

"Am I? I wasn't aware that I'd said anything humorous." I laughed with him, scrunched my nose, but didn't know why we were laughing. This happened to me often, people finding me funny for no reason I could discern. Therefore, I'd learned long ago to just smile and nod, yet continue to speak with sincerity. This usually made them laugh even more.

Most people strike me as disappointingly predictable in their normalcy.

However, I wasn't about to let Chuck's normalness derail my optimism. I'd bought a new dress for the date—crime scene red, strapless, indecently tight, lifting my modest bust up and out and *well, hello there, how are ya?*—and dolled myself up in expectation. Perhaps the zebra print stilettos I'd borrowed from my friend Janie were a bit much, but I had high hopes for Chuck.

The horoscope had said he would be a catalyst for my future life and I was beyond ready for my future life to begin.

I tried not to daydream about it, but I couldn't help myself. Even as I was getting ready for the date my mind provided Instagram-style status updates of our future together: Cubs season tickets, screaming profanities at Red Socks fans, sharing a hot dog at Portillo's , watching horror movies every Friday night while naked on the couch, reading the paper together on Sunday mornings, and a cornucopia of impressive bedroom acrobatics.

But first I had to get past the fact that, so far, he appeared to be very, very normal.

His laughter tapered but his smile remained as he said, "No one calls me Chuck anymore. I usually prefer Charles."

"Oh." I stopped laughing. "I'm sorry, Charles. I didn't-"

"No, no. It's okay." He placed his hand on the table between us. "Somehow, with you, I don't mind at all."

Oh. Well. Crap.

His words made my stomach tighten with a flare of despair.

I returned his warm, melony smile with as much effort as I could muster; my spirits deflated, but I refused to take it to frown town. I wasn't ready to give up yet. "Well, you don't know me very well. I could be a complete freak show."

He chuckled. "You're adorable."

I perked up a bit at the compliment. "Is that why you agreed to meet me so late? My adorableness? Sorry about that, by the way. My shift ended at nine. It's not every guy who will agree to a ten P.M. first date."

He waved his hand through the air as though it were nothing. "It's not a problem. It's not every day that I meet a gorgeous redhead with green eyes that's so easy to talk to."

So easy to talk to.

I smiled in return, endeavored to mask my impending forlornness, then turned my attention to the menu in my lap. I tried not to sigh.

Our first date had just started, and I was trying to rally against the fact that it might as well already be over.

Unless Chuck said something astonishing in the next five minutes, he was most certainly *not* a catalyst for anything; except perhaps another evening of me abandoned in this restaurant.

I could see the events of the evening as though they'd already occurred, because they had. This was just like every single one of my first dates.

It always started the same: the guy tells me he feels comfortable with me even though we don't know each other. He'll search his brain for the reason why then tell me that I remind him of someone else—a first girlfriend, the girl next door, or the girl who got away. I'll probe deeper and he'll admit it was an older woman, a kind teacher or an aunt or, worse, his mother. He'll tell me how much that relationship meant to him then he'll unload—about his life, his dreams, his expectations, how he failed his parents or siblings or friends or how they failed him.

In the end, he cries. If I'm lucky it won't be in the restaurant.

Eventually, he thanks me. He tells me how lovely I am and then shakes my hand. He asks if he can call me again to talk. I give him my friend Thomas's card, a board certified psychiatrist with a focus on family counseling. We part as friends and I have another guy in my friend arsenal; another guy to hang pictures in my apartment or help me move.

And he has a female *just friend* to introduce to the girl he eventually marries.

Trying not to be resigned to my fate, I perused the menu without reading it. I already knew what I was going to order. It's one of the reasons I always pick Taj's Indian Restaurant for my plethora of first dates. Their butter chicken is amazageddon (amazing + Armageddon) good. If I had one final meal on the face of the earth it would be Taj's butter chicken.

The other reason, I noted with somewhat buoyed spirits, would arrive at my doomed table any minute.

"You know, you remind me of someone." Chuck's words meet my ears right on schedule. I almost mouthed along as he continued, chuckling; "You look a lot like this girl I used to know."

I didn't meet his gaze, wasn't listening to him anymore. Instead braced myself for what came next.

Or, rather, who came next.

Like clockwork, I sensed my waiter approach. I didn't need to look up to know he was carrying two water glasses. Mine had no ice and no lemon.

"Good evening." He said, his velvety voice sent ripples of delicious awareness from my nose to my toes. "I'm Alex and I'll be serving you tonight."

Be cool. Be cool and act cool. Be chill, act chill, be ice. You're an ice cube. Just be cool.

Heat suffused my neck and cheeks; but, as I was expecting him, I was able to temper the warmth before it became a telling stain. I paused a moment, gathered a deep breath, then lifted my chin and eyes to meet his gaze.

Ahh, Alex the waiter.

Alex the waiter was on my Spank Naughty list in third place, right after Henry Cavill the actor, then Henry Cavill as Superman. He was proof that God existed and that God loved straight women.

As usual, he was looking at me with thoughtful, deep set indigo eyes behind black horned-rimmed glasses. As usual, his mouth was curved in a small fleeting smile. As usual, he stood at the edge of the booth, a six foot three hovering, angular, lissome behemoth.

His strong jaw was dusted with black stubble and was marred by a deep, irregular scar that ran from the center of his bottom lip as a jagged slant to one side of his chin; slightly crooked nose, likely broken on more than one occasion; close cut black hair, a little longer on the top as though it had mohawk aspirations; and a mouth just a bit too wide and soft for the rest of his rugged face.

As usual, he was dressed in all black.

If you went for rough edges, chip on the shoulder, effortlessly sensual, young and dangerous with the build of an Olympic swimmer, which I usually did not, he fit the bill and caught the fish—hook, line, sinker, sexy.

I usually gravitated toward nice men—meaning, men who looked like they were nice men. Men who smiled a lot, liked to golf, paid their parking tickets, owned sensible suits and shoes, considered sweater vests appropriate Sunday attire. Men who knew a Mallard from a Muscovy and had all their ducks in a row. Men who would and should theoretically make good husbands and fathers.

Men with no outward sign of emotional baggage.

But with Alex, despite the flashing, Las Vegas strip style neon warnings marquee of emotional baggage, I couldn't help it. The first time I heard him speak I was sunk; it was his voice that made my stomach do a sky dive to my toes without a parachute. His voice reminded me of jazz and the bedroom and a strip tease: melodic, deep, soothing, slightly sandpapery, but with an irreverent, careless quality.

I daydreamed about him reading me a book, the newspaper, a greeting card, an eviction notice—anything. As much as it was possible, I was infatuated with his voice; I often asked him questions about the menu— even though I already knew what I was going to order—just so I could hear him speak. When he spoke, life was good.

It did things to me.

Alex the waiter and his bedroom voice almost made all my failed first dates worth the bother because Alex saying, *I'll be serving you tonight* was typically the highlight of the evening. It was all downhill from there.

I gave him a polite nod and, as usual, Alex's smile flatted into a straight line.

Alex the waiter, it seemed, didn't like me much.

"Hi. Can you tell me about-"

"Let me order for you." Chuck startled me by reaching across the table and tugging on my menu.

My gaze turned from Alex to melon face. "Oh no, I know what I-"

"I insist. Then I can pair the wine seamlessly." Chuck winked at me then turned to Alex; "We'll start with a bottle of your Parducci, chilled at forty degrees for ten minutes then aerated. I'll have the chicken tandoori and the lady will have saag paneer."

Chuck handed Alex our menus then grinned at me, so pleased with himself. I didn't grin back. I don't believe in rewarding poor behavior.

Other than accepting the menus, Alex didn't move.

"So, Sandra—I was about to tell you about this—well, this girl you remind me of." Chuck leaned forward and pushed his knife a few millimeters closer to his spoon.

"A girl?" I cleared my throat, keenly aware that Alex still hadn't left.

"Yes. You remind me of her." He glanced at his silverware, muttered mostly to himself. "It's really uncanny."

I stared at Chuck, horrified. Alex cleared his throat, drawing my attention back to him. He must've liked my horrified expression because, uncharacteristically, he was smiling again and wider this time.

"Butter chicken?" Alex asked.

I nodded once then released a sigh. "Yeah. This won't take long."

Alex returned my single nod, his black eyebrows ticking upward a half centimeter. "Then, shall I cancel the other?"

"Yes please, thank you."

Alex's smile was wry, his nebulous eyes moved over my face. I was surprised to see his gaze linger on my mouth for a short second before he turned and sauntered back to the kitchen. I watched his backside and broad shoulders as he walked away. He had an irreverent, careless walk—not quite a swagger; it was a bedroom walk, just like his voice.

I sighed again, thinking how nice it was watching Alex walk away, and found myself wondering about Alex's age.

I guessed twenty-two or twenty-three, a late bloomer. His body didn't seem to be quite fully grown; his hands were just a bit too big and he had that gait of a careless teenager, not a grownup

But his eyes were unfathomable and steeled. When I looked in his eyes the rest of his physicality seemed to age; he had the eyes of man.

A wicked, wicked man.

"Sandra?"

I yanked my gaze away from Alex's backside, found the honeydew watching me, his expression muddled confusion.

"What was all that about?" Chuck indicated with his head in the direction of Alex's departing form; apparently, he wanted an explanation for our strange conversation.

"Oh, nothing. Why don't you tell me more about your mother?" I rested my hands on my lap and prepared myself to listen to whatever Chuck was ready to tell me.

"Uh, I didn't—I mean, wasn't talking about my mother."

"Your father raised you, right?" I kept my voice gentle, my face carefully blank of expression.

He nodded, appearing both mystified and awestruck. "Yes, how did you know...?"

"But he didn't raise you, did he? Did he travel a lot or did he work a lot?"

Chuck leaned forward, his elbows hit the table in front of him, and his story gushed forth like blood from an untended arterial wound. "He didn't travel. My parents divorced when I was only seven and my mom took my sister, I stayed with my dad. He worked, he worked all the time."

And so, it began.

I listened to Chuck's tale of upper middle class childhood abandonment and neglect. I felt for him, I did, just like I felt for all the others. It seemed our society was raising a generation of fractured children, more an accessory to their parents than living, breathing, feeling beings. They plugged him into the wall via television and video games; then took him out when convenient, mostly around the holidays.

When Alex came back with the bottle of wine, Chuck didn't seem to notice as he was knee deep in relating a story about his father's new wife—I noted that Chuck still called the woman 'dad's new wife' even though they'd now been married over fifteen years. Therefore, I completed the cursory wine tasting and nodded once at Alex that I was pleased with the bottle.

When Alex came back with the garlic naan, Chuck was banging on the table with his fist. He was elbow deep in a story about winning a cross-country race in high school; it was a success about which—even to this day—his father had no idea.

When Alex came back with my butter chicken, Chuck held his face in his hands and was crying; he was struggling to stand from our booth. I stood and gave Chuck my support, helped him to his feet and pressed Thomas' card into his hand.

"God, Sandra, I can't thank you enough. I—I just feel—"Chuck choked, a small sob escaped his lips.

I rubbed his arm with an open palm. "It gets better. Talking about it will make a difference."

He nodded, either unable or unwilling to speak, and wiped his eyes with the back of his hands.

"You're not alone, Charles."

Chuck reached out and grabbed my hand as Alex walked around us both and placed the butter chicken on the table in front of my seat.

"Oh, God. Dinner. I am so sorry." Chuck's lost eyes scanned the table and I gave his hand a calming squeeze. He seemed completely blind to the patrons at the only other table occupied in the restaurant; they were casting curious glances our way.

"Don't worry about it. Just go home and take care of you." I gently pulled on Chuck's hand, led him to the door. "Go get some sleep, and call Thomas's office in the morning." Chuck's shell shocked eyes found mine, new tears threatened to spill so I gave him a small smile. "Tell him that Dr. Fielding sent you and you'll get a discount on your first two sessions."

He nodded, abruptly pulled me into a hug then, just as abruptly, withdrew and dashed out the door.

I watched his retreating form for a short moment and considered the fact that I was going to have to finish that bottle of wine by myself. This wasn't necessarily a bad thing. I had Saturdays off and could afford to sleep in. I waited until Chuck disappeared around the corner at the end of the block before turning to my booth and my waiting plate of butter chicken.

On the way back I stepped to the side to allow the last customers to exit; their departure meant I was the only paying customer left in the restaurant. Therefore, as I strolled back to my table, I decided to ask Alex to pack up the chicken and re-cork the wine—no need to make him stay late on my account.

However, as I neared my table I realized that it was now occupied; well, Chuck's seat was occupied—by Alex. My seat was empty. My steps faltered as our eyes met.

He was looking at me. Looking *at* me, like I was something to be observed, studied; and his plainly untrusting gaze seemed to grow more guarded as I approached.

I paused as I drew even with my abandoned seat and stood, stalled. It struck me as a very odd moment. I was standing at the edge of a table where Alex was sitting. We'd, in essence, switched places.

"Hello." I said.

"Hello." He said.

My attention flickered to the table. In front of him was a plate of saag goat or lamb—impossible to tell which—a side of mango chutney, and he'd already raided the previously untouched basket of garlic naan.

Also, he'd poured himself a glass of my wine.

I met his gaze again. The circumspection in his eyes was disconcerting. He licked his lips.

"Please have a seat." He motioned to my untouched plate of butter chicken.

I looked at him. I looked at the wine. I looked at my plate of butter chicken. I shrugged.

"Sure. Why not?"

I sat, placed the napkin on my lap, and took a generous bite of the chicken and jasmine rice. It was, as usual, a delicious replacement for physical contact, my comfort food.

I glanced at Alex again. He, also, was delicious. Delicious and watching me as though I were not delicious. In fact, his expression made me feel rather fetid. My heart rate increased inexplicably. I felt like a skittish rabbit. This was noteworthy as I usually felt like an optimistic octopus.

"How is your butter chicken, Sandra?"

I started, my fork suspended in the air for a beat, but quickly recovered. "How do you know my name, Alex?"

"Your credit card, Sandra. I make an impression of it every Friday night."

"Oh." I frowned at him. Something was just *off* about him. He seemed to dislike me, but was having dinner with me, uninvited. I wasn't used to people disliking me. Hmm… curious, that. "I'm not here every Friday night."

"Fine then, you're here every *other* Friday night."

I ignored his last comment. "The butter chicken is quite good, thank you. How is your saag goat?"

"It's saag lamb and it's divine."

I almost choked on my chicken when he said *divine*. His voice made everything sound divine.

"That's excellent news, Alex. So, Alex, why don't you tell me about yourself?"

He smiled. But the smile did nothing to settle my apprehension. If anything, my heart rate increased from skittish rabbit to frightened rabbit having a minor coronary artery.

Curiouser and curiouser!

"What do you wish to know, Sandra?"

"First of all, stop saying my name. It's creeping me out."

"Why is that?"

"Because I never told you my name."

"And?"

I ignored his question. "Secondly, why don't we start with your parents."

"My parents." His tone was flat.

"Yes, tell me about your parents."

"Certainly." He wiped his hands on his napkin and leaned back in the booth; apparently he was relaxed. "My parents were Romanian circus performers. I grew up in the circus as part of the act."

I stared at him. He stared at me. I knew at once he was lying. The omnipresent caution in his eyes was now somehow altered by a flicker of emotion; I thought it resembled amusement, but he was difficult to read.

I shook my head once. Placed my fork on the plate and leaned back in my seat. I surveyed him. The side of his mouth hitched slightly; it did nothing to thaw his features.

"That's not true." I said matter-of-factly.

His smile grew, was plainly sincere, yet lacked warmth. "You're right. It's not true."

I studied him for a long moment before I asked the obvious question.

"Why did you say it then?"

"Because you make men cry."

I believe my eyes bulged. He'd surprised me. *Score one point for Alex.*

"Ah. That." I nodded, reached for my glass of wine. "You found me out. I'm a man-eater." I took a healthy gulp.

"Well, that's good news."

I choked, coughed, but managed by sheer luck to keep from spewing my red wine all over the table. My eyes bulged further. Did Alex the waiter just turn my 'man-eater' comment into a double entendre? Did that actually occur?

How very scandalous!

"Drink some water." He lifted his chin and indicated to my neglected water even as he poured more wine into my glass.

After two large swallows of water I felt capable of speaking, though my voice was raspier than usual. "Alex, that was quite a naughty thing to say."

The carefulness in his gaze wavered and as a slow, decidedly salacious grin spread from his mouth to eyes. I held my breath. When he smiled, actually smiled, he looked a bit more innocent and devious at the same time, boyish and rakish. It was devastating and made me feel like a teenager with a crush on the bad boy in high school.

I suddenly wanted to kiss him.

I reached for my wine glass instead and finished half of it while I watched him over the rim.

At last he broke the silence and sounded truly pleased with himself. "It was naughty, wasn't it?"

I nodded, set the glass down. "Was that your goal?"

His eyes narrowed at my question. "Why do you make men cry?"

I picked my wine glass up again, took another swallow. "Do I make men cry?"

"Would you care to hear my theories?"

"You have more than one theory?"

"Do you ever respond to a question without asking another question?"

"Does it bother you?"

"No. But it does confirm my hypothesis."

"What hypothesis?"

He sighed, all the residual warmth from our earlier flirty banter evaporated. "That you're a shrink." He might as well have accused me of being a traitor or a murderer or a Kardashian.

I finished my glass of wine and he—reaching over the table—swiftly refilled it. Peripherally I noticed that he hadn't yet touched his wine. "Why do you think I'm a shrink?"

He frowned again, his eyes guarded. "In the beginning, I thought you must be bringing these men in here to break up with them. But then, these encounters became too frequent. Naturally, I considered the possibility that these men worked for you and you brought them here to fire them. I thought that perhaps you were their boss and you'd chosen this restaurant as the place to let them go, deliver the bad news."

"But you ruled that out." I sipped my wine then gulped it, held the glass in both hands as though it might protect me. I didn't know why I did this.

He nodded once. "From time to time, I overheard pieces of your conversations, realized you didn't know these men. Then, briefly, I considered the possibility that you were delivering another kind of bad news—like they had cancer or had lost a loved one."

"But you ruled that out too." I finished another glass. He motioned for me to set it on the table; I did as he silently instructed. He refilled it without looking at me, his attention was transfixed on the wine bottle and my glass.

"You didn't seem to know them, the men, at least not very well. It became clear that this was your initial—or almost initial—meeting, like meeting a new client."

"Ah." My assenting head bob may have been over exaggerated as, after two rapid glasses of wine I was feeling my skipped lunch and yogurt breakfast.

"Why do you do it?" His tone was sharp, as were his eyes as they moved from the bottle to me; he looked not at all amused. In fact, he looked increasingly dangerous, angry.

Sad, that. He had such a handsome face when he allowed himself to smile. But then—I tipsily admitted—dangerous, angry waiter Alex was also mighty fine.

Mighty fine indubitably.

"I don't do it on purpose."

"Really?" He didn't believe me.

"No. I don't." I held his granite gaze. "I don't like it when they cry. It's why I schedule these first dates for so late in the evening."

His hostile façade cracked, his eyebrows tugged low over his eyes like thick, shadowy unhappiness umbrellas. "Wait, what? Dates? These are dates?"

I nodded, my movements perhaps a little dramatic in my despondency. Copious amounts of red wine on an empty stomach will do that to a girl who hasn't been kissed in over two years. "Yes. Dates. First dates. Did you think these men were my patients?"

His stare was piercing, as though he were attempting to reach into my head and read the truth from the grey matter of my brain. After a prolonged moment he expelled a heavy breath. "But… but you are a psychiatrist?"

I nodded into my half empty glass of wine, my third glass. "I am a psychiatrist."

"And you make your dates cry."

I frowned at him, "Wait a minute, do you think I do it on purpose? Do you think I like ending each date with a goodbye cry instead of a goodbye kiss?" I may have slurred the word 'kiss'. I couldn't be sure.

Regardless, my questions were met with flinty silence; but he looked interested so I continued.

"Do you know when the last time I was kissed was? Guess!" I flicked my hand in his direction then slapped it on the table. He didn't flinch. "Two years."

I may have slurred the word 'years'. I couldn't be sure.

"Two. Years. Actually, it's been over two years. It's been two years and quite a few months, like maybe ten months, which makes it almost three years. And, you know what? The last kiss…" I frowned and shook my head in such a way that was certain to illustrate my dissatisfaction with the last kiss. I leaned forward and whispered my next words, letting him in on the secret of my non-existent sex life, "It wasn't a good kiss."

His lips stiffened, tugged ever so slightly to the right. I was tipsy, but

I didn't miss the way his eyes moved to my mouth during my tirade. He was probably looking for lip fungus or some other physical manifestation to explain my kiss-dearth.

"And I'm a good kisser, Damnit!" I gripped my wine glass and finished it with two large swallows, relishing in the delightful vertigo settling behind my eyes and making my gums tingle. I set the empty goblet on the table and attempted to level him with a penetrating gaze, instead I found myself struggling to keep my eyes from crossing. "And I don't have a lip fungus, if that's what you're wondering."

His attention abruptly moved from my mouth to my eyes. "I wasn't wondering whether you had a lip fungus, but thank you for getting that awkward conversation out of the way."

"You're welcome!" I scooted to the end of the booth. Everything looked a little blurry and the room rocked as I stood and proclaimed, "I have to go pee!"

"Bathrooms are behind-"

"I know where the bathrooms are, Alex." I squinted at him, my feet stumbled and I inadvertently did a jazz square as I tried to remain upright. "I *do* take all my first dates here, you know. Granted, they usually leave before the entrée. Now, if you'll excuse me."

I half bowed for no reason in particular and walked to the ladies room. I felt satisfied in my admonishment of the pretentious upstart. How dare he… How *dare* he accuse me of making my dates cry on purpose. How dare he be so masculine and strong and sexily somber. How dare he stare at my lips and warm my internal organs up to figuratively inferno levels of hotness. How dare his magma voice melt ice and steel and my femme innards. How dare he…

Wait.

I blinked. Halted. Backed up two steps and peered into the kitchen. It was dark. I thought about that for a minute and came to the conclusion that the kitchen was closed and the cook and the manager and the dishwasher had gone home. I shrugged for no one's benefit then continued on my way to the bathroom.

I flipped on the light, closed and locked the door, did my business, all the while attempting to reignite my train of thought. I failed at finding indignation. Instead I settled on the words: masculine, strong, and sexily somber. Then recalled the word kiss.

Mmm… kiss.

I washed my hands inattentively and scanned my appearance. The awesome strapless red dress I wore still looked fantastic, hugged my body in all the places girls are told men like to look.

I winked at myself in the mirror, as I was prone to do. "Hey, sexy lady, I'm not drunk, I'm just intoxicated by you."

My mirror theater provoked a half laugh, half moan and I covered my face with my hands.

The dress paired with a padded push up bra should have guaranteed me a night filled with torrid passion. It was why I'd purchased it. Alas, and to my inner orgasm enthusiast's infinite sexual frustration, the hottest thing that happened so far was a hand squeeze from Chuck the chuckling—then sobbing—honeydew.

Glancing up, I also noted that my teeth were now slightly green due to the consumption of red wine. For no discernible reason, I took a paper towel and scrubbed at my teeth until they appeared whiter. I often did this, especially when intoxicated.

Satisfied, I nodded once at my reflection, and stumbled out of the single stall bathroom, into the small square space at the back of the restaurant. I managed three steps before I realized that the path leading to the front of the restaurant was blocked by Alex.

And I discovered this fact by bodily colliding into Alex's chest.

END PREVIEW

Love Hacked: A Reluctant Romance
Coming March 11, 2014

CPSIA information can be obtained
at www.ICGtesting.com
Printed in the USA
LVOW04s1713281015

460129LV00028B/1470/P